MISSED
OPPORTUNITIES

MISSED OPPORTUNITIES

A novel by

LaTonya Y. Williams

Q-Boro Books
WWW.QBOROBOOKS.COM
An Urban Entertainment Company

Published by Q-Boro Books
Copyright © 2007 by LaTonya Y. Williams

ISBN-13: 978-1-933967-01-1
ISBN-10: 1-933967-01-3
LCCN: 2006935249

First Printing March 2007
Printed in the United States of America

10 9 8 7 6 5 4 3 2 1

Cover Copyright © 2006 by Q-BORO BOOKS all rights reserved
Cover Layout & Design—Candace K. Cottrell
Cover Photo by Jose Guerra; Cover Model: Tiffany Harris
Editors—Stacey Seay, Candace K. Cottrell, Tiffany Davis

Q-BORO BOOKS
Jamaica, Queens NY 11434
WWW.QBOROBOOKS.COM

Dedication

This book is dedicated to my Aunt Caroline. Your life is an example of how women can triumph despite the toughest circumstances.

Monica

CHAPTER ONE

Why do I keep doing this?

Monica was a big woman, but fierce as hell. She would dare you to find one man to disagree. Shit. You wouldn't find one. As far as Monica was concerned, she could have any man she wanted. And she dared any bitch to try her!

He's not even worth it. I need a man, not a mama's boy.

Staring at her shapely figure in the mirror, Monica found it hard to take her eyes off herself. Caressing her thick thighs, she thought about the way her man would be doing the exact same thing in a few short hours. Getting all stirred up, her hands worked their way under her dress up to Ms. Dolly. She was tingling and starting to feel a little warm.

Whoa! Slow down, Mama. It's not time yet. She took a long sigh.

Embarrassed like a teenaged girl, she smoothed down her dress once more. She took a chance on picking out a lavender dress because it complimented her complexion.

When she first laid eyes on that hot number, she was sure Kendall would be trying to dip his stick in her as soon as his parents' anniversary dinner was over.

You really need to end this relationship.

She sprayed another layer of perfume on her neck. As a big girl, it was important for her to smell delicious and sweet at the same time; the kind of sweetness that left a scent long after she left the room. Anything to give the skinny bitches something to talk about.

With her natural hair in an Afro, she had her mother to thank for blessing her with "good hair" as each curl dangled perfectly around her ears. Monica's favorite MAC make-up complemented her deep, dark-hued complexion. Oprah's compliment of Beyonce's skin being like butter stuck with Monica. She tried every single beauty product known to man until she got the same result.

Monica was ready to receive the "but you have such a pretty face" insult. This saying really meant, "You are so gorgeous, but I can't get past the fact that your ass is twice the size of mine."

None of that seemed to bother her, because when it was all said and done, Monica fished for any and every single compliment. Like Mo'Nique from *The Parkers*, she embraced fat to mean "fabulous and thick." She grabbed the brush and applied a little more color to her full cheekbones, exactly the way the girl at the make-up counter demonstrated on her face just two hours before. The technique worked a lot better when she puckered her lips like a fish.

Only one more glance in the mirror. She slow-danced and bent over to make sure her butt cheeks didn't show. The dress passed the last test; everything was perfect.

If everything was so perfect, then why did she feel so nervous? Kendall. Lately, he'd been getting on her last nerve. Trying to tell her how to dress, talk, and act. She never appreciated the way he talked down to her. Monica believed she was one classy lady, evidenced by the way she dressed: impeccably. She spoke with absolutely perfect diction. Her education had paid off and she was rising up the ranks at her job.

No matter how many times she analyzed it in her head, she couldn't figure out why he was now so critical of her. Hell, they'd been together for close to three years, and he never had a problem with her style or attitude before. She hoped he wasn't thinking about marriage, because that was the furthest thing from her mind. But he seemed to be trying to mold her into the image of his mother all of a sudden.

Being a manager at Macy's, Monica got a huge discount on her clothing, jewelry, perfume, hell everything. And she deserved to have the finer things in life. She'd been working extra hard to move up in the company, trying to break through the glass ceiling to become Assistant Store Manager and then Store Manager. That's when she would earn the big bucks, and nobody would be able to tell her anything. Monica kept her eye on a convertible Mercedes SL 600, in black with the tan leather interior. In a few years, she'd be pulling that sweet ride up in front of her fabulous crib, where her personal maid and chef would handle all the cleaning and cooking.

Her husband would . . . she needed to stop right there, because she hadn't worked her fantasy out that far yet. But she wanted to get married and have some kids. Concentrating on her career was all she could handle right now. Knowing she was blessed to have a man at all, Monica wasn't so sure Kendall was the marrying type. He only had a two-year degree; therefore, his income potential was very limited. He worked as a tech assistant when what he really needed to do was go back to school, earn a bachelor's degree, and become an engineer.

Don't even get yourself worked up, girl.

Kendall didn't want to hear that. He loved his job, and one thing she'd learned was, it's not easy to persuade a black man to leave a job he loved. All the talking in the world wouldn't convince him that high-paying jobs weren't that hard to come by anymore. To make matters even worse, her man still lived at home with his parents. Sure, he was saving money to purchase a home, but, in her mind, that didn't make it right.

This brought Monica to the question of why she continued to stay with him. Well, Kendall was a hardworking, loving man. He was the type of guy your mama would tell you to hold on to, especially if you're a big woman like Monica. This was why she'd held on this long. However, her patience was wearing thin.

Monica was holding out for someone with a larger bank account and "put it down" bedroom skills to come along; once she found a man like that, she would be kissing Kendall's ass good-bye.

She sang along with the CD, swinging her hips and breaking it down so hard to Jamie Foxx's melodic voice, she barely heard her man knocking at the door. She licked her finger and patted Ms. Dolly.

Ooooh, I'm so hot!

"Hey, baby." Monica cheesed from ear to ear. She knew one look at her in the sexy dress and they may not make it to dinner. Glancing at Kendall dressed in his white suit and his hair braided back, Ms. Dolly was warming up. In a matter of minutes, she allowed herself to get all worked up.

Monica was definitely attracted to her man. Since she

was a big woman, she loved herself some big men. She didn't need no skinny man she could break in two. Not as much she liked to ride that dick till the sun came up.

Kendall stared her down from head to toe. He shook his head as he came inside. "No. I know you're not wearing that."

"Yes, I am." Monica tossed up her arm. "What's wrong with my dress?" She modeled for him by sashaying down the middle of the living room floor.

Kendall wrapped his dark chocolate arms around her. "Nothing. You're beautiful and you smell nice, baby."

She closed her eyes and inhaled his cologne. "Right."

"This would be great if it were just the two of us. But, baby, you're going around my folks, and this isn't appropriate for all the old people that are going to be there."

Monica pulled away. "Like hell it ain't!" She straightened her dress. "Kendall, I'm not changing. Do you know how long it took me to pick out this dress?" She snatched up her shoes in one hand. "And these stilettos to match? No, you couldn't. 'Cause if you did, I would say you're out of your damn mind."

Kendall scratched the back of his neck. "I'm not trying to start a fight with you. I was just saying that—"

"I know what you're trying to say, but it's not going to happen." She leaned over to fasten the buckle on her shoe. With all the pressure on her stomach, she damn near lost her breath. "Now, let's go."

When they pulled up in front of the Windermere Country Club, Monica was infuriated to see all of the guests standing outside. "Why is everybody out here?" she asked as she quickly applied a final coat of espresso-colored lipstick.

Kendall shrugged. "I'm not sure."

"What do you mean? Didn't you let the manager know that all the guests needed to be seated immediately?"

"I thought I did, but—"

Monica sighed. "You're hopeless." She stormed inside and tapped the blonde-haired girl behind the podium on the shoulder. "Miss. Miss."

She held up one finger and turned her head slightly. "I'll be with you in one second."

Frustrated, Monica took a deep breath. "Excuse me. Where is the manager?"

"I said, I'll be with you in a second," she snapped.

No, this little hoochie didn't!

"Darling, you obviously have me mixed up with someone else."

She turned to face Monica. "I beg your pardon?"

"No, I'm the one that should be pardoned. My family is waiting to be seated, and I don't appreciate that one bit." Monica gritted her teeth as she smiled. "We've paid over two thousand dollars to make sure this dinner is perfect and you're pissing me off already." She looked down at her nametag. "Nancy, you need to pick up that phone and get Melvin's ass down here right away."

Nancy cleared her throat. "Just wait right here." She disappeared down the hall.

Monica glared at Kendall. "You should've taken care of this. And why are you standing way over there?"

"I'm letting you handle your business." Kendall crossed his arms.

She rubbed her forehead. Damn. Now her make-up was all messed up. She would have to go fix it. "That's the problem. Why do I have to do everything? This is not my family, it's yours."

"I know that. But, you're good at what you do, Ms. Manager." He winked.

Kendall was dressed very well in his suit. All of Ms. Ruthie's boys were wearing white in her honor. To see his mother would explain why Monica and Kendall were a couple. Ms. Ruthie was an exact replica of Monica in thirty years or so, give or take a few years.

Monica didn't look anything like her own mama, who had a fairer complexion and a much slimmer shape. Monica took after her father's side of the family. All of her aunts were big-boned.

"Are you Mrs. Porter?" a voice behind her asked.

Monica turned around. "Yes, who wants to know?"

"Allow me to introduce myself." He extended his hand. "I'm Jake, the assistant manager. Melvin left town this morning for a family emergency, and I'm in charge. The luncheon scheduled at noon today went over, and we're getting everything set up to your liking. I do apologize for the inconvenience."

Monica put her hands on her wide hips. "How much longer do we have to wait?"

"Only a few more minutes. Nancy, be sure to discount these folks twenty percent off the final bill."

She tightened her full lips. "Twenty?"

"Fifty."

She smiled. "That's more like it."

Never happier because she got what she wanted.

"Who do you think you are?" Monica shut her eyes tightly. Her head felt like it wanted boil. "You got some nerve to criticize me!"

"Woman, are you crazy?" Kendall asked. "No man would approve of his woman dressed like that."

"Dressed like what?" She tugged on her dress once more. It *was* a little short. She'd been pulling on it the whole time during service. One time, the damn thing clung to one of her sweaty thighs, and no matter how much twisting she did, it wouldn't work its way back down. Completely embarrassed, Monica pretended like she didn't hear the teenaged boys snickering in the adjacent row.

Those little bastards.

"I wouldn't have had this problem, Kendall, if you hadn't shown up early. All I could do was pull it out of the shopping bag, touch up my make-up, and then I was out the door," she said.

Now, there was one thing Monica didn't believe in being late for, and that was church. If she could rush to work, run all the yellow and some red traffic lights, then she could show the same amount of respect for the Lord.

"Why can't you wear those nice suits you wear to work?" Kendall asked. "Why you gotta buy a new dress every week, anyway?"

"Because I like to look good. I work hard, and I should be able to do something for myself." She folded her arms. "Hell, I make enough money."

Kendall gripped the steering wheel tighter. "This don't have nothing to do with how much money you make."

"Are you sure?" She turned to face him. "It always seems to come back to that."

"That's because you're always bringing it up!" Kendall responded as he clutched the wheel even tighter.

Seeing the sweat roll down his face let Monica know he was angry. However, she was not about to back down. She was sick and tired of his constant nagging.

Under her breath, she mumbled the words, "You're just jealous."

Now why did she have to say that?

"What!" Kendall stopped the car in the middle of the street.

"What are you doing?" Monica shrieked. The driver behind them blew his horn madly. "Drive the car."

"What the fuck did you say to me?" Kendall snatched his keys from the ignition.

"Drive the car!"

Another car slammed on brakes, almost hitting them.

"Oh, Lord," Monica whispered as she sank down further in her seat.

As the driver passed by, he yelled out, "Crazy muthafuckas!"

"You shut the fuck up!" Kendall got out of the car. The white guy in the silver Mercedes sped off. He scurried over to the passenger side. "Say it to my face, while I'm not driving or my back isn't turned. I'm not walking out the door. Say it to my face, Monica."

"You are crazy!"

"No, not that." He patted his hands against his chest. "Tell me how you make more money than me. How I'm a broke muthafucka! Oh, and I still live at home with my mama!"

This was getting ridiculous. Kendall managed to create a traffic jam on Lee Road, as if the traffic on that street wasn't already bad enough. "You're a broke, sorry excuse of a man! Go back to school and get a real degree. Make some real money, then you can criticize me about how I dress and how much money I spend."

"Finally." Kendall looked up and pointed his hands up at the sky. "Did you hear that, God? She makes more money than me! I'm a sorry excuse of a man. How did I end up with this perfect woman when I'm such a deadbeat?"

Monica closed her eyes and wished she were somewhere else. She couldn't believe this nigga was showing his natural black behind. Now, he could forget about slithering up to Ms. Dolly tonight. He might not get close enough to even sniff for a week. Or even two, for that matter.

After he ranted and raved on for another minute, he finally got back in the car.

"Now, do you feel better?" Monica waved her hands in the air. "Do you feel like a man? Or less than a man? Which is it!" It was her turn to show out now.

"Just shut the fuck up." Kendall said, still trying to catch his breath. He had really worked up a sweat. His blue dress shirt was soaking wet.

"No, you want to act like a fool. I want to act like a fool, too." Monica bounced in her seat. "What you did was insane. I can't believe you made a spectacle over a little comment. It only means you're insecure. You're an insecure little man. Oops. Big man!"

"You really don't know when to stop, do you?"

"Excuse me. Did I say anything when you were on the street making yourself out to be a complete jerk? Not to mention, some of the Light Center members saw you. We're going to be the talk of the town. You do know that, don't you?"

"You really don't know. You know, you could drive a nigga to kill your black ass." He laughed as he parked his 10-year-old Lexus next to her new one. Even that seemed to bother him.

"Bye, Kendall." Monica grabbed her purse and Bible.

Once Monica got inside, she went to the bathroom to run the shower. As the sweat dripped down her legs, she frowned when she caught a sniff of the odor down there. Everybody had pet peeves, and hers was BO. Her obsession was so extreme that she did her best to clean every crease and crevice with shower gel at least twice to her satisfaction.

The sudden pounding at the door startled her.

"It's about time he came to his senses."

Monica grabbed a towel and ran toward the door. Peering through the peephole only confirmed her suspicion.

I knew he would come back. Damn fool.

"Kendall, go home."

"Let me in," he pleaded. "We're not through talking." His voice sounded sincere. She knew he wanted to apologize, but she didn't care. He would pay for the way he humiliated her.

"Not today. Call me in the morning."

"You see how you do me?"

Monica leaned against the door. She could sense the frustration in his voice. Still, she'd already made up her mind that she would make him pay.

"It's not right."

Monica held her breath. "Go home, Kendall."

"I'm a good man. And you treat me like shit."

He sounded like he was crying. She peeked out again. Poor baby was slobbering.

Monica fought to suppress her laugh.

"It's not right."

After twenty minutes of begging, he reluctantly went away.

Monica couldn't wait to get on the phone and tell her best friend all about it. Lorenzo had been Monica's best friend since they were small. As she shared all the details with him, he laughed his behind off.

"Girl, you are a trip!" Lorenzo yelled through the receiver.

"I couldn't believe it myself."

"Honey, I wouldn't have done that to my man. See, I'm all about building my man up, not tearing him down."

"And that's why you always get your feelings hurt,"

Monica added. "You can't make the man think he's better than you. No, I ain't having that shit."

"Oooohh." Lorenzo cackled. It sounded so hard, Monica thought he was about to have a heart attack. "Oooohh. You need to quit!"

"I'm just telling it as it I-S, is." Monica puffed out her espresso-glossed lips. "Let me break it down for you, darling. I know I'm a big woman, but I can still have any man I want. And once you get some of Ms. Dolly, you can't walk away from this. But, I likes to make a brotha beg for it."

"I hear ya," Lorenzo said. "Sounds like you know it all."

"Yes, I do."

"Well, then. While you snuggle up to your pillow tonight, I'll be snuggling up next to Michael."

"Now, see, you know you wrong." Monica snapped. "You're hooking up with Deacon Sanders again? You need to leave Sister Betty's husband alone."

"Sister Betty better serve her man better."

"You're wrong for that."

Sometimes, it was hard to be Lorenzo's friend because she didn't agree with him all the time. Monica had other gay friends, but they were in serious, committed relationships. One couple even adopted three children before moving to Florida. As far as Lorenzo was concerned, he didn't have time to settle down. Monica thought he was playing a very dangerous game with his life and the lives of others. Engaging with married men had major repercussions, considering the wife and children who could be affected.

"I'm just calling it as it I-S, is," Lorenzo mocked.

Monica grinned. "You're a mess!" She glanced at the clock and realized it was getting late. "Hey, I'm going to bed. Alone."

"You do that."

They said their good-byes, and Monica placed the cordless back on the base. As she sank her mouth into the last spoonful of strawberry cheesecake ice cream from the box, she frowned. She couldn't believe she'd eaten the entire thing.

Oh, well.

She yawned and stretched out her arms. No sense in crying over spilled milk. She promised herself she'd get up thirty minutes earlier and walk the ice cream off on the treadmill. Things didn't go as planned because the next morning, she overslept and barely made it to work on time.

CHAPTER TWO

Monica joined Lorenzo for dinner at the Jinja Asia Cafe. The food was so delicious, Monica had to make sure she placed a take-out order to eat later. She wasn't sure what secret ingredient the cook added to the dishes, but she figured it must be crack, because she was addicted in the worst way. It was the kind of addiction that woke her up in the middle of the night to eat chow mein.

"Baby, how long are you going to stay mad? I told you I was sorry. What else do you want me to do?"

Monica deleted the final message. She was disappointed to see she'd missed fifteen messages. The day before, Kendall had left twenty-one. Making her man suffer evened the score as far as she was concerned. Not wanting to face the sisters at church, she avoided Sunday service altogether.

Monica didn't want to answer questions about what happened the Sunday before. She recognized many faces as their cars passed by while she and Kendall argued in the middle of the street. What really pissed her off was the fact that no one even bothered to stop.

Not even Mother Green had stopped, and she was known to make every member's business her business too. Once Monica asked Pastor McKissick, Jr. to go by the hospital to check on Ms. Ruthie, and within hours of their conversation, Mother Green called to share her sympathies. She possessed a gift; she could show a great deal of concern, but her real motive was to find out everything she could to spread to the rest of her friends.

Dear Old Mother Green meant well, but Monica had a problem with letting people in on her business. Now, she considered whether she should find another church to attend. If her relationship with Kendall ended, then she would be forced to, because most of his family attended there. The Darden Family was regarded as lifetime members of the church, since Kendall's great-grandparents were among the founding members over a hundred years ago.

Monica only joined the church so she could keep the single women off her man. However, she'd grown spiritually since joining, and she enjoyed attending service on Sunday and Bible Study on Wednesday night. Loyally serving in the Women's Ministry, Monica cooked and delivered meals to the elderly shut-in members.

"Why you got that fake smile on your face?" Lorenzo asked.

"Oh." Monica snapped back into reality. "I was checking my messages."

Lorenzo clutched his hands together. "Let me guess. It was Kendall begging you to forgive him for all his wrongdoings."

Monica chuckled. "Yeah."

She crossed her arms and leaned back in her seat. After

inhaling the large plate of Mandarin chicken, noodles, and dumplings, she needed a few moments to catch her breath. No matter how many meals she ate, she never felt full. It frightened her, because it was getting harder to stop, and her weight was at an all-time high.

"Everybody ain't able. I would've gave in before the night was over." Lorenzo stuffed in a mouthful of noodles.

"It's been a week, so he's starting to wear me down."

"Why do you play games?" Lorenzo raised his penciled eyebrows. "I mean, it's a little childish, don't you think?"

"No, it's not." Monica responded. "Keeping my man in check isn't childish at all. And why are we talking about me, anyway? What about the deacon? How are you two lovebirds doing?"

"We're not." Lorenzo's face scrunched up as if the mere thought would bring him to tears. "He broke up with me. Said he couldn't keep seeing me."

Monica tossed up her hand. "It's not like he hasn't said that before."

Lorenzo shook his head. "No. I think he really meant it." He started to hyperventilate.

Damn. Is the dick that good?

The deacon had to be at least fifty years old. With all the young bucks Lorenzo messed around with, it was hard to believe he was so hung up on that old man.

Monica moved to a closer seat and rubbed her best friend's back. "I'm sorry, baby. It's going to be all right."

"I . . . I . . . know." Lorenzo hollered so loud, the couple in the nearby booth looked over.

"I can see we need to change the subject. On a lighter note, I wanted to show you something." Monica pulled out a small black box and opened it. "Look at what I bought today."

She held up the diamond bracelet.

Lorenzo reached out his hand daintily. "Oh, my God. Is this the real thing?" He grabbed it and wrapped it around his tiny wrist. He only weighed a little over 150 pounds.

Monica cocked her head to one side. "Of course, it's real."

"Hhhmmm. How much this set you back?"

"Only two grand." Monica grinned.

"Good goooogly-dee." Lorenzo pretended to faint. "Only two grand? Honey, you gots it going on!"

"It's an early birthday present," Monica added. "Plus, with a broke man, I have to buy stuff like this for myself. I work hard, and I deserve the finer things in life."

Monica knew she needed to stop perpetrating. As department manager, she was not pulling in that kind of money. What she was doing was maxing the hell out of her credit cards. Just when one card filled to the limit, Monica applied for another or a credit increase. Right now, she was looking at a debt total of close to $100,000. With her salary, there was no way she could pay more than the minimum payments each month. She hoped her promotion would come in soon, so she could start paying the balances down. Monica wanted to double or triple the payments and pay them all off. If only it could happen in the next month or two.

"That's right," Lorenzo joked. "You go ahead. Shop, shop, shop till you drop."

Leaving the restaurant with five take-out boxes in tow, Monica kissed Lorenzo good-bye and headed home. When her cell phone rang, she glanced down at the caller ID before answering.

"Hellooooo," Monica sang.

Silence.

"Yes," she said.

"I guess you're not mad anymore." Kendall replied.

"No, I was never mad." Monica checked her rearview mirror before driving onto the I-4 ramp. "I've been busy, that's all."

"If you expect me to believe that, then you must really play me for stupid."

"Kendall, don't be so dramatic. I'm not lying to you." He sighed. "Are you in the car?"

"Yeah. Me and Lorenzo just had dinner together."

"How is that queen doing?" Kendall said in a girly tone.

"Hey, don't play," Monica said sharply. "You know that's my best friend. I'm not going to let you make fun of him."

"Sorry. I better not saying anything else, or you'll put me on punishment me for another week."

Monica smirked. "I don't know what you're talking about."

"Play dumb. You know."

"So, did you want something? Or do you just want to go back and forth on the phone? I'm not even using my evening minutes yet."

"Excuse me. Since you're speaking to me, I better be gracious and make it quick. What are you doing tonight?"

"Nothing. Why you ask?"

Ms. Dolly could use a little company.

"I want to stop by. Do you mind?" Kendall asked in that sexy voice she loved.

"No, I don't mind." Monica bit her bottom lip. "When you coming?"

"I'm sitting in your parking lot now."

"If I didn't know any better I would think you were stalking me, Kendall Darden."

"And you would be right." He chuckled.

"I'm about five minutes away," she said. "See you in a few."

Adjusting the volume on her CD player, Monica rocked from side to side to "Oh" by Ciara. She made a left turn in the Windward Apartments parking lot. She saw Kendall's car parked in the back under a large tree.

When he got out of his car and jogged towards her, she took a deep breath. Even though she wanted to have sex with him, she knew it was crazy to make it easy for him after the way he disrespected her. Monica tried to think of a logical excuse to get out of giving her man a taste of Ms. Dolly while he followed her upstairs. If he tried to have sex, she would tell him her period was on. That always worked. When she entered her apartment, Monica went straight to her bedroom and kicked her wedged heels off.

"You're straight to the point."

"What do you mean?" Monica asked.

"First, you finally answered my phone call, when you know I've been calling you like I'm some kind of punk or something. Now, I've been here for less than five minutes and we're already in the bedroom."

"And what are you trying to say? That I want to do the nasty with you? Negro please!" She rested her hands on her hips. "You followed me in here!"

Kendall pinched her shoulders. "Don't get so testy. I was only kidding with you."

"I don't believe you," Monica said.

"You don't have to." Kendall disappeared down the hallway.

Monica scratched the back of her head. She thought he was going to at least beg for it. Not once had Kendall ever let an opportunity for sex pass him by. In fact, sometimes she thought he had a sex addiction. She used it to keep him in check, but for the first time, it didn't work. Ms. Dolly obviously wasn't putting it down like she used to.

Suddenly, Monica felt insecure. She wondered if this had anything to do with her weight gain. Sure, she put on another five pounds, but who would notice?

That's it!

Monica had put her dieting off long enough. Starting first thing in the morning, she was getting rid of all her favorite foods; they were making her gain all this weight. She was going to start back with her salads. She promised herself to renew her membership at Gold's Gym.

"Did I do something to bother you?" Monica asked. She slid beside Kendall on the couch.

Kendall switched the channel on the remote. He seemed fixated on the Miami Heat game. "No. Not tonight, anyway."

Monica folded her arms. "What's that supposed to mean?"

"You haven't returned my phone calls. Now, when you want some, then you answer."

"When I want some? You know that's the furthest thing from the truth."

"Is that so?" Kendall turned down the volume of the television. "Then answer this question . . ."

Monica looked him straight in the eye. "OK."

Kendall shook his head. "Forget it."

"No. Ask the question."

"Forget it," Kendall said. "You're just going to lie anyway."

Monica stood up from the couch. "I don't appreciate you calling me a liar. I don't have a reason to lie to you. You ain't shit to me."

Kendall laughed. "Now see? Look at how you're acting!"

"How I'm acting?" Monica pointed at her chest. "I don't fucking believe you have the audacity to call me a liar in my own apartment, then get upset that I'm offended. Get the hell out!"

"Calm down."

"Get out."

"No, I'm not going anywhere."

Monica grabbed Kendall's shoes and tossed them out the door.

"Woman, are you crazy!" Kendall shouted. "Those are my brand new Jordans."

"Don't you mean your dirty-ass Jordans?" She smirked.

Kendall tightened his jaw. "You got some nerve." He stared her down as he walked past her to the door.

"Bye!" Monica slammed the door shut. Leaning her back against it, she slid down to the floor. She took three deep breaths, as her therapist instructed her to do when she felt angry. Closing her eyes, she replayed the events that took place in her living room.

Deep regret settled heavily on her shoulders. She knew she shouldn't have treated her man that way.

What is wrong with you?

It was as if she enjoyed making him miserable.

Another deep breath.

With all this anxiety, she needed to calm her nerves. Before she realized it, she tore into a box of Edy's and shoved spoonful after spoonful of butter pecan ice cream into her mouth.

This would go great with brownies.

Opening the refrigerator, she pulled out the plate of triple fudge brownies. Snatching off the plastic wrap, she dropped the largest brownies inside the box of ice cream. Turning off the lights in the kitchen, she headed toward her bedroom.

Chapter Three

"This is a great performance review," Theresa stated. "I see no reason why you shouldn't be promoted."

Monica grinned. "You really think so?"

Theresa pointed. "In a few weeks, you will be the next Assistant."

Monica leaned back in her chair. "I'll be so happy when it finally happens." Her thoughts drifted to the negative balance in her checking account. Somehow, she'd miscalculated her bills and how much she spent over the weekend, and although the bank paid the checks, the additional charges left her with an eight hundred dollar deficit.

"Being an ASM is a high stress position," Theresa added. "Are you sure you're ready for that?"

Monica raised her thinly arched eyebrows. "Yes, I am."

"Well, you and Kendall have been a couple for a long time now. I just thought you were ready for marriage and a family. With all the extra hours you'll be expected to put in, I don't see how you'll have the time."

"You're doing it," Monica chimed in.

"It's not easy. Harvey works an eighty-hour a week job, so we barely see each other. I'm not sure how our marriage has survived. And I feel so guilty leaving Lola every morning." Theresa drummed her fingers along the desktop. "Maria seems more like her mother than I do. I'm so jealous of their relationship."

Monica laughed. "At two years old, I doubt Lola even notices how much you're gone."

"You'd be surprised." Theresa stood up. "But then, you're not even a mother, so what do you know?"

"Damn. Where did that come from?" Monica snapped.

Theresa waved her arms in a frenzy. "Just forget it. Scratch that last comment. I didn't mean it the way it came out."

Monica rubbed Theresa's back. "Sit back down. Let's keep talking. I can tell you need to get it out."

Theresa hung her head low. "It's nothing." She took a deep breath. "Whew! OK, OK. Maybe later." She straightened her jacket. "I'm fine."

"Are you sure?" Monica searched her eyes for an honest response.

"Not really." Theresa cleared her throat. "But I will be."

Monica was stunned. She'd never seen Theresa this vulnerable before. She always believed her manager had the ideal professional and personal life, and it was hard to see her unravel like that. It just went to show, nobody had it all. That's why Monica truly wanted to drop Kendall's behind and focus more on her promotion. She wouldn't have a problem putting in all the hours if he was out of the picture. She was tired of his complaining and felt he acted too much like a little bitch. There could only be one bitch in a relationship.

Once more, she studied the review carefully. The only

area identified as a weakness was her interaction with her subordinates. The associates were now asked to rate their managers on the company survey. Monica received the lowest rating in the store. Being black and female, she felt those two strikes worked against her. As far as she was concerned, they were jealous of her holding any kind of supervisory position, and being tough was the only way to earn respect.

So what if they didn't like her? At least they knew she meant business, and their asses would be fired if they didn't comply. No one complained, since her sales team rated the highest in the district, and she rewarded them with parties, luncheons, and sometimes even cash. Whatever it took to make her monthly goal, Monica did it. There were many times she rang on the register, placed merchandise on the floor, and stocked shelves to get the job done. She expected the same level of commitment from her staff.

All that said, Monica was labeled as "hard to get along with." In her early years with the company, Monica tried to be well-liked, but it seemed like people wouldn't take her seriously.

The situation that changed it all was during her second year as a manager of the children's department. An associate she hired based on her mother's recommendation gave away thousands of dollars' worth of merchandise to family and friends. When questioned by security, she admitted to stealing and blamed Monica for being so mean.

"I can't stand that bitch," she told Ray, the Loss Prevention Manager. "Monica thinks she's better than us, just because she's a manager. She's always bragging about all the money she makes."

This was a bold-faced lie. Monica wanted to motivate the blacks in the store to pursue a higher education, and she used her own success as an example. Yeah, earning eight dollars per hour was OK, but she couldn't understand why they didn't want to better themselves.

That was the last black person she hired to work for her. She got sick of trying to help a sista out and getting burned in the end. After that, Monica decided she had to be who she was and to hell with anyone who had a problem with it. She'd worked too hard to get where she was. And she still had the student loans to prove it.

Monica drove her car along the Beachline headed to Merritt Island, the small town in Florida where she grew up. Her stomach rumbled, as she knew her mother was going to get on her last nerve, but it was time to see her again. Or else, Caroline would curse her out, real ghetto-style, for staying away so long.

The drive along the road helped clear her mind, but she still dreaded the trip once a month. Tapping her fingers on the steering wheel, she caught a glimpse of a mini-van in her rear view mirror.

Monica laughed at the sight of a white soccer mom taking a swing at one of her children in the back row. The lady used so much force behind her blow, her van veered into the right hand lane. For a brief moment, Monica pictured herself doing the same thing. There was no way in hell she would purchase a mini-van, though. A Cadillac Escalade was more like it.

If only I could get that promotion.

Her life would be ten times better if she got the raise. With less stress about how to pay the bills, she could gain more control over her life. Having a sense of balance meant cutting out bad habits like overeating and overspending. Then she would be attractive enough to find a new man. That was incentive! For now, she had no choice but to stay with Kendall, because he was the only one who wanted her.

Monica laid her head on the headrest. Why was she doing this to herself? Beating herself up before her own mother got the chance. Caroline was very opinionated and rarely kept her thoughts to herself. To everyone on the outside, Caroline was as beautiful inside as she was outside. With her terra cotta colored skin, there was no denying there was some Indian in Caroline's family. What begrudged Monica most, however, was that her mother had a shape that wouldn't quit.

What most people didn't see was the nasty attitude her mother showed only to a chosen few, meaning the men she loved and her daughter. In today's terms, the way her mother treated her as a child would be considered abuse. Back then, it was good old child rearing. Monica definitely grew up with a healthy fear of her mother, and tried her best to stay out of trouble. If she didn't, Caroline was liable to use any means (or tools) necessary to spank her, whether it be a shoe, belt, extension cord, or a switch.

Be positive! You are a beautiful black queen. Any man would be blessed to have you.

That was her affirmation for today.

Turning up the volume on her Anthony Hamilton CD, she rocked her head to the music to relax. She hadn't taken a day off in over two weeks, so she needed to make the best of it. As she drove closer to the thick cloud of smoke, it resembled the pictures she had witnessed on the news. The cones and flashing lights on the police cars warned her in advance that she would have to detour off 528 and take 520 the rest of the way, adding another twenty minutes to her drive.

Monica prayed the fires would only last a few more

days and be over. No way did she want to relive the Great Fires of '98 when I-4 and I-95 were both shut down. She couldn't have left town if she wanted to. Walking outside to ash flying to the ground and covering her car was no pretty sight either.

She coughed as her nose caught a whiff of burning smoke. There was no way anyone could convince her secondhand smoke was safe.

Her cell phone rang.

"Hello."

"Hey, slut," Lorenzo said. "Are you coming to my opening tonight?"

"You know I'll be there." Monica responded. "And the only slut is the one I'm talking to. Ha. Ha."

"Yeah . . . right . . . bitch!" Lorenzo shouted.

Monica adjusted the phone on her shoulder as she quickly turned onto the Merritt Island Causeway. "What's with you?"

"Excuse the swearing, darling." Lorenzo said. "You know how I get before these things."

"I know, but damn." Monica squinted as she pulled down the sunshade. "Everything is going to be wonderful as usual, and you're going to make a whole lotta money before this is over."

"I hope so. Girlfriend has bills and very few sponsors these days."

"I find that hard to believe."

"Well, believe it, honey."

"I'm about to have lunch with Ma, then we'll be on our way."

"Oh, my goodness!" Lorenzo screamed. "You did not tell me Ms. Caroline was coming. Tell your mama that there will be no layaway this time. It took her almost six years to pay off the last painting I sold her."

Monica laughed. "Now, you know you need to stop. It wasn't no six years."

"Close as hell to it," Lorenzo snapped. "Make sure y'all black asses is early. Toodles!"

"Bye." Monica shook her head as she closed her flip phone.

Monica pulled her Lexus next to the burgundy Chevy Malibu in the carport. She examined the street and found that besides some of the colors of a few homes, not much had changed since she moved away ten years ago. Chain fences divided up the yards, a sight you would never see in the exclusive subdivisions her co-workers lived in now. Children riding on bikes and scooters up along the narrow street reminded Monica of when she and her mother first moved into the working class neighborhood of Winter Cove. At the time, it seemed more like they were rich, especially compared to their life in the Dainey Projects.

Caroline didn't know a thing about decorating and hired an interior decorator to fix up the place. Monica thought it was a beautiful mansion and was grateful every day, for she knew how many overtime hours her mother had to put in every week to keep a roof over their head and food on the table. That's exactly where she'd adopted her own work ethic and never strayed from it. At fifteen, Monica got her first job at Wendy's and stayed there until she graduated from college. Sure, she could've taken on a supervisor or management position, but she wanted to do what she was doing now: managing at Macy's, a big department store, and soon she would be Store Manager calling all the shots. She quickly pushed the thought out of her head. She'd dreamed about the ASM promotion so long she was starting to get sick over it.

"Who is that?" Caroline asked.

"Me," Monica yelled as she followed her mother's voice to the backyard. Rusty ran up and greeted her. She patted the old Shih Tzu on the head. "Hey, girl."

"Hey, Ma," Monica said. "How long you been sitting out here?" she asked once she sat down beside her mother.

"About twenty minutes or so." Caroline smacked a mosquito on her arm. Dressed in black jeans and a yellow shirt, Caroline's slender frame was always the source of envy for Monica. If only she had taken after her mother, she wouldn't have to constantly deal with the stress of losing weight.

"I was sitting here wondering why I haven't seen Kendall over here in so long. You still together, ain't you?"

Monica jangled her clunky key chain. "Yes. But I don't know for how much longer. I'm sick of him."

"Kendall is a good man. You better hold on to him." Caroline waved her pointy finger. "It's not like you're getting any younger, or smaller. How much you weigh now?"

Monica rolled her eyes. "I don't know. I haven't been on the scale lately. I've been working."

"Uh-huh." Caroline frowned. "You better stop working so much and start paying more attention to your man. Where are we going today? 'Cause I'm already hungry."

It wasn't fair that Caroline could eat whatever she so desired, and Monica would gain five pounds just watching her eat.

Monica smiled. "It's up to you. I didn't want to drive all this way and not have seafood. But, it's your pick this time."

"Don't forget I still need to get something to wear to Lorenzo's show." Caroline adjusted her ponytail. "So, somewhere close to Merritt Square."

"Well, Ruby Tuesday is at the mall. You always like their chicken with penne pasta." Monica jangled her keys again. "You want to just go there?"

"All right. Go get my purse," she ordered.

"OK."

Monica navigated her way through the dark house to the bathroom. Her mother never bothered to open the blinds or curtains. Monica couldn't stand to live all penned up in the house the way her mother did. Passing the pictures on the sofa table, she admired a picture of her and Kendall. They shot the photo while they were vacationing in Jamaica.

Monica realized she hadn't spoken to him in a week. She pulled out her cell and dialed his number. As the voicemail came on, she left a quick message and grabbed her mom's fake Dooney on the way out of the house.

Caroline slid in on the passenger side. "Every time I get in this car, it's dirty. What you driving in a Lexus for if you can't keep it clean?" She scowled.

Monica sighed. "Ma, I'm working all the time."

"Shoot. Pay somebody to do it. You make enough money." Caroline added. "This is ridiculous. You're lazy! That's what you are."

"Ma, please don't start." Monica waved her hand. "We're supposed to have a good time. It's my first day off in two weeks."

Caroline looked at her daughter. "Next time, we'll take my car. This is one thing I can't stand."

Monica took a long breath. She knew this was only the beginning of the constant criticism that was more like verbal abuse. The mere thought that she had to endure it for the next ten hours made her cringe. As usual, she would find a way to make the most of it.

As predicted, Caroline enjoyed a glass of wine, a pasta dish, and dessert. Monica pretended to savor her cold pasta salad from the buffet. As they caroused through JC Penney, she prayed her mother didn't hear her stomach growling.

"Are you coming with me?" Caroline asked, holding a few dresses and a pants suit in her hand. "I might need your help zipping this one up." She pointed at the midnight blue dress.

"I really wanted to search the men's department for a suit for Kendall," Monica said. "You know he always shows up to these events dressed down. I think he does it on purpose, so the men won't try to hit on him."

"Let that man be," Caroline snapped. "Now come on in here, so you can help me. Plus, I need your honest opinion on how these look. You know I wants to be sexy, now!" She laughed.

Monica shook her head in embarrassment. She hoped her mother wouldn't humiliate herself the way she did last year. All the men she flirted with were either gay or married, but still she managed to pique the interest of one young, twenty-something man. They dated briefly, but it ended badly when the young buck didn't know the stint was over. It wasn't until Uncle Henry threatened to kill him, that young buck stopped all the calls, surprise visits, and emails.

"What do you think about this?" Caroline paraded around in the waiting area. She stopped in front of the mirror and smiled. "This one looks better than the first, and I love the way the material feels."

"Real nice, Ma," Monica said wryly. Now, she felt more insecure about the candy apple red dress she

planned to wear to Lorenzo's showing. She knew the
dress was a little tight when she tried it on, but she
planned to lose at least ten pounds before the event, so it
would slide on easily. It's not like she wasn't a true size
twenty-eight; Nia dress sizes always ran small.

"I look good, if I must say so myself." Caroline grace-
fully sashayed once more. "There, I said it." She glanced
in Monica's direction. "And take that smirk off your
face. Ain't nobody told you to stuff your mouth full of
junk and gain a hundred pounds."

"What are you talking about?" Monica asked. "I
haven't gained that much weight." She was shocked her
mother even noticed her envious stare.

"Hmph!" Caroline put her hands on her hips. "Don't
hate, appreciate!"

Monica waved her hand. "Oh, please. Is that the one
you're getting? I need to get a few things for myself."

Caroline glanced down at her watch. "No, you don't
either. We're not going to be late to see Lorenzo. You
should've gotten whatever you needed before you
came." She pulled up her dress and went back inside her
dressing room.

Monica sucked her teeth.

"I heard that!" Caroline yelled. "You better check that
attitude before I get out there."

Who does she think she is?

Monica hated the way her mother still treated her like
a child. She forced her head up toward the ceiling.

Lord, give me the strength to get through this day.

On the drive over to Anthony LaPaglia's house, they
rode in complete silence. Monica complained of a mi-
graine and her mother backed off. They arrived two
hours early.

"This is some house," Caroline said. They walked uphill toward the circular driveway. Two white limousines and a catering van were parked in front. The peach colored home resembled a Jewish synagogue, and had four long stained glass windows on each side. "How does Lorenzo know this guy?"

"Lorenzo and Anthony are friends. With benefits. If you know what I mean." Monica struggled to catch her breath.

"Well, I can't wait to see what it looks like on the inside."

"Ma, it's gorgeous."

The double doors were wide open because service workers were coming in and out. When they entered the tiled entrance, Caroline's eyes became fixated on the ceiling.

"This artwork is so beautiful."

"I know. Stunning," Monica said as she tugged on her red dress. Her eyes searched around for her best friend.

"Hey, bitch!" Lorenzo yelled. "I'm upstairs."

"My mom is with me, so can you refrain from your use of profanity?" Monica gritted her teeth.

Lorenzo leaned over the rail from the second floor. His ponytail dangled on his shoulder. "Hey, Ms. Caroline. How are you?"

Caroline grinned from ear to ear. "I'm good, baby. Don't pay any attention to Monica." She waved her hand. "She's just in a bad mood."

Lorenzo studied Monica from head to toe. "I can see why." He held both hands up while he elegantly walked down the stairs. He pointed at his chest. "I almost didn't recognize you, girlfriend. Oh, no!"

Monica put her hands on her hips. "Don't start with me, Lorenzo. You know I will whip you."

"Let me get a closer look here." Lorenzo grabbed

Monica's hand and twirled her around. "I'm going to have call my girl, Jenny, 'cause you are getting way too big."

Monica snatched her arm away. "I said, don't start with me. Ma, you got nerve to talk. With your high cholesterol, you shouldn't eat the way you do, either. And Lorenzo, I can't decide if you're on crack or got AIDS."

"Now the real Monica is here." Lorenzo clapped his hands twice. "Let's party!"

Caroline burst out in laughter. "Hush your mouth."

Monica smiled. "Just tell me what you need me to do, so, *we* can get started."

"Uh-huh. I have to pick out my painting first, before anyone puts their greasy hands on it," Caroline said as she followed one of the young men carrying a painting covered in gray cloth.

"Ma, behave yourself. Remember what happened the last time."

"I'm just checking out the art work. I have to help myself to a Lorenzo Rawlins original." She grabbed a glass of champagne from the table and entered the room.

"Ms. Caroline is a hot mess."

"I know," Monica said as she dialed Kendall's number on her cell phone.

"What are you doing?" Lorenzo asked. "I thought you were here to help."

Monica tried to shush him. "I am. Hello. Kendall, where have you been? I've been trying to reach you all day."

Lorenzo sucked his teeth. "Come on."

"Hold on." Monica put her hand over the receiver. "I'm coming. Give me one minute."

"Well, when you're ready, I'll be in here." Lorenzo pointed to the dining room.

Monica put her hand up to her ear. "Hello." She

moved to the other side of the entryway until she could see three bars on her cell phone. "Can you hear me?"

"I hear you just fine," Kendall responded.

"I guess it's my phone acting up," Monica said. "Kendall, are you on your way?"

"No. I left you a message. I got called in."

Monica's jaw dropped. "Are you serious? And I thought I worked too much. Kendall, that's why you need to go back to school."

"You're tripping. Look, I'm sorry I can't make it to Lorenzo's big night. Give him my regards."

Monica didn't want to be at this event without a man on her arm.

"Kendall, you need to call your boss and tell him you have other plans. You promised me you would be here with me."

"I need the overtime. I'm trying to save to get out of my parents' house."

"You can afford your own place. You just like living up under your mother and having her cater to your every need."

"You don't know what the hell you're talking about."

Lorenzo poked his head out.

Monica held up her index finger. "One minute."

"What?" Kendall asked.

"I'm talking to Lorenzo."

"Well, get back to your friend, and, I'll get back to work."

"Kendall."

Monica saw the disconnected message on her cell phone. She wiped her hand across her forehead.

Shit.

She smeared her make-up.

Once Monica started helping Lorenzo with last minute details, she forgot all about being pissed at

Kendall. With only one hour left, she would be amazed if the showing would even take place, never mind begin as scheduled.

Lorenzo disappeared to finish getting ready while Monica dished out last-minute orders to the waiters, servers, and the florist who placed a large arrangement in the front entryway, blocking the view of one of Lorenzo's show pieces, appropriately titled *Sisters Dancing*. She knew how much it meant to Lorenzo for this oil painting framed in dark cherry wood to make a grand statement.

Monica barely had a second to change into her pumps, spray perfume all over to mask the perspiration, and run downstairs to greet the guests as they arrived. In her head, she calculated she must have burned at least six or seven hundred calories, so she gave herself permission to indulge on the cheesecake platter.

Wealthy black women dressed in evening gowns and men dressed in tuxedos made the event seem so formal, as a result, Monica truly felt more like hired help than a guest. There were even a few white people scattered about in the room.

Why didn't I shop for another dress?

She pinched herself on the arm. As she tried to calm herself from hyperventilating, a gray-haired woman walked by and scoffed at her.

Wanting to give the woman a piece of her mind, she reminded herself why she was really there: to be a support system for Lorenzo, so this thing was so much bigger than her. If this exhibit was a success, Lorenzo's career would be launched, which was also bittersweet. She would lose her best friend, as his plans to move to New York City would happen sooner.

Monica caught a glimpse of Lorenzo laughing with

Pierre, his manager. Funny, he didn't seem so nervous anymore. Quite confident and austere, she noted as she admired him. No one was more deserving.

Almost close to tears, she realized not one of his family members was present. Ever since he stopped lying to everyone and admitted he was gay, his father denounced him from the family and banned him from the family home. It wasn't long after that his mother refused to speak to her own son. Monica remembered how at five years old, they played with Barbie dolls, and Lorenzo's dolls always wore the most glamorous clothing. He would take some fabric and use his mother's sewing machine to create some spectacular dresses.

Lorenzo's "coming out of the closet" moment shouldn't have come as a surprise to anyone who spent more than ten minutes with him, but the Rawlins said they never knew. Darryll and Claire Rawlins proudly visited their oldest son, Darryll, Jr. at the Tomoka Correctional Facility every Saturday morning; he was serving thirty years to life for cocaine possession with the intent to sell. But they refused to have anything to do with Lorenzo, who was one of the most revered artists in Central Florida, and well on his way to becoming an international success. Lorenzo never got into trouble a day in his life, never used drugs, never harmed anyone, or even got a traffic ticket.

When he was alone, she stood beside Lorenzo, whom she admired from afar in his black velvet tuxedo, the two top buttons of his shirt open, revealing his hairy chest.

"I'm so glad you took off that damn bowtie," Monica said. "You're so debonair."

"Thank you, darling. I didn't like it either," Lorenzo added. "Francesca doesn't know a thing about fashion, even though I pay her to."

Monica laughed. "You need to pay me that money." Her eyes wondered around the room. "I know this is a bit premature, but congratulations."

Lorenzo clapped. "Isn't this fabulous?" He grabbed her head and turned it to the left. "See that man over there with the bleached blonde hair?"

"Uh-huh."

"He wrote a check for two of my highest priced paintings."

Monica's mouth fell open. "Are you serious? Come here." She hugged him tightly as a tear fell.

"So, is that what you and Pierre were talking about?"

"Yes. I'm leaving in six weeks."

Monica poked out her espresso-glossed lips. "I'm so sad for me, but happy for you."

"Thank you, darling," Lorenzo said as he was pulled away by Pierre and introduced to a distinguished couple.

Monica caught a glimpse of her mother making out with one of the waiters.

She smiled. *Maybe he'll give her a ride home.*

CHAPTER FOUR

"I need to get drunk tonight," Monica said as she waved the bartender over.

"Monique, right?" Kevin asked with a dimpled smile. The speakers at Roxy's were blasting LL Cool J's latest hit.

"Monica," she corrected.

"Oh yeah." He leaned in closer within ear distance. Still shouting, he said, "You know I love me some big, black women."

Monica grinned and breathed hot air in his ear. "And I already told you, I would break you in two."

Kevin chewed on his gum. Then lifted his shirt and revealed a very muscular abdomen. A bona fide six-pack and a serious hard-on was a definite turn-on. "I'd like to see you try!" he yelled back. Two white girls on the opposite end stood up from their chairs and screamed. Kevin performed a strip dancer number before mixing Monica's favorite drink: a Very Bloody Mary.

He placed the glass in front of her. "For the beautiful lady."

Monica winked. "Thank you, baby."

"You slut!" Lorenzo shouted from behind.

Monica turned around and laughed. "Hey, girlfriend."

They embraced. Monica stepped back to check out her best friend's club attire. "What, you going to a rodeo later?" she snickered.

Lorenzo swung his arm in the air. His black leather pants and matching jacket and boots made him look more like a skinny male stripper than sexy. "I just might be looking for me a cowboy to buck me."

"Now, you're just being plain nasty."

"Whatever, darling!" Lorenzo snapped. "Don't get me started on you. I saw you flirting with white boy Kevin. You know he goes both ways."

"I know. But, I can see why the women and men want him. He's fine as hell!" Monica poured a little drink on her breast. Then she lifted her large breast and licked it while eyeing Kevin at the same time. He stuck out his tongue and flickered it back and forth.

"See, good for eating coochie and sucking dick," Lorenzo commented.

Monica burst out laughing. "Hell yeah!"

"What's so funny?" Tiffani asked as she walked up behind Lorenzo.

"We're tripping off of Kevin, that's all," Lorenzo responded in a flat tone.

Tiffani folded her arms. "Oh. Well . . . hello . . . Monica."

Monica rolled her eyes. "Hey, Tiffani. What are you doing out? Thought your man held you on a tight leash."

Lorenzo spit up his drink. "Fuck!"

Tiffani slung her full head of hair weave over her shoulder. "Well, you thought wrong."

"Hmmph." Monica finished her drink, then signaled Kevin to bring her another one.

Tiffani leaned over to Lorenzo. "You didn't tell me *she* was going to be here."

"Wait a minute. I know you didn't call me a bitch while I'm standing right here." Monica pushed Lorenzo past her, so she could get closer. "I will drag your bony ass all up and down this club.

"No, I didn't call you a bitch."

Monica knew she didn't, but she wanted to fuck with her anyway.

Tiffani looked away from Monica and slapped Lorenzo on the back of the neck. "I don't appreciate you begging me to hang out with you when you already asked her to come too."

Lorenzo kept this dumbfounded look on his face. His voice went up an octave. "I didn't know she was going to be here."

Monica glared at Tiffani, waiting for the opportunity to kick some behind.

Tiffani flung her purse strap on her shoulder. "Well, I'm outta here."

She stormed off and Lorenzo trailed behind her like a lost puppy.

"Bye!" Monica waved.

A few minutes later, Lorenzo came back and sat down.

"Well, that was a quaint reunion, wasn't it?" Lorenzo asked.

"Don't mess with me." Monica's speech slurred. She cleared her throat. "Especially after the day I had at work."

"Well, what happened to Ms. Thang to get you all worked up?" Lorenzo sat down on the nearby stool.

Monica sat back down too. "Melanie is working my last nerve. I put her on the schedule to work two straight weekends in a row, and she got all mad. Had the nerve to call me a fat bitch when she got down the hall away from my office."

"Ooohhh. No, she didn't!" Lorenzo snapped his fingers. "I know you told her off."

"I'm going to write her up first thing Monday morning." Monica leaned on the counter. "What really made me mad, was she complained to Mr. Langston. I need this promotion, and another associate complaint may have ruined my chances." She thought about the car note she was three months behind on and the embarrassment she would feel if the repo man showed up on her job to take the car back.

"I hate to hear that . . . look, I'll be back." Lorenzo eased out of his seat and over to a guy who was checking him out.

Monica watched them talk with jealous envy. He was muscular with the most gorgeous face. Obviously, DL.

Lorenzo waved good-bye to her as he followed Sexual Chocolate out of the club.

"Shit!" Monica knew she was way too inebriated to drive her car home. She pulled her cell phone out of her purse and dialed Lorenzo's number.

No answer. His voice mail picked up.

Resting her face on her elbow, her vision was starting to go. Staggering out the front entrance, the security guy helped her up.

"Where's your ride?" he asked.

Monica looked to her right and saw a red Corvette pulling up at the stop sign. "Over there." She pointed.

"OK." He released her from his grip.

Monica got inside her car and locked the doors. She called Kendall.

"Hello. Where have you been?" he asked.

"I'm at Roxy's. Lorenzo left, but I need you to come pick me up." Monica wiped a tear away.

"Sure, baby."

Monica leaned back in the seat and dozed off to sleep. A loud bang instantly woke her up.

"Get your black ass out!" A young boy who couldn't be a day over fourteen was pointing a gun at her.

Monica's eyes grew wide as she attempted to start the car.

"Bitch, don't make me kill you." He tapped on the window with the gun. "Get the fuck out!"

Monica quickly put the car in reverse and backed out, hitting a car behind her. Then she pulled off. Running the red light, she drove full speed down Colonial Road, not sure what direction she was headed. Her vision blacked out. A second later, she could see her car jump over the median. She saw it happening, but couldn't do anything to stop it. Was she dreaming?

Not able to handle the steering wheel, her Lexus skidded and hit a pole. Grabbing her face, she saw blood dripping from her hands and lost all consciousness.

"Wake up."

"She's breathing," a male voice said.

"I saw the whole thing," another male voice added. "Is she all right?"

Monica opened her eyes.

"You were in an accident. You're going to be fine. What's your name?"

"Mooo . . ." Her lips felt numb.

"She's drunk."

"Baby."

Monica opened her eyes when she heard Kendall's voice. By this time, the paramedics were loading her on the stretcher to put her in the ambulance.

"I'm right here." He gripped her hand. "I love you."

Monica's eyes welled up with tears.

* * *

"Let me help you with that," Kendall said as he placed his arm beneath Monica's arm wrapped in a cast.

"Thank you, baby." Monica eased in the doorway of her apartment. Slowly, she walked to her bedroom with Kendall's assistance. Once she lay comfortably on the bed, she kicked off her shoes and closed her eyes.

"You want anything to drink or eat?" he asked.

"A glass of apple juice and some chips," Monica responded. "No, bring me the strawberry cheesecake."

"You're going to eat cheesecake for breakfast?" He scratched his head.

"Didn't you ask me what I wanted? Kendall, don't play with me."

"I'm sorry." Kendall sighed. "One slice or two?"

"Just bring me the whole thing, and a knife to cut it myself." Monica ordered. She didn't have time for his diet talk right now. Tomorrow, she had a meeting with the Mr. Langston scheduled. She prayed it wouldn't be her last day. Having been arrested for DUI, Monica spent one night in the county jail. It was the absolute worst night of her life.

Just thinking back to the night of the accident made her stomach turn. The hospital staff treated her like a criminal, and as soon as the doctor signed her release papers, the police escorted her to the car. From there, she was taken to Orange County Jailhouse, processed, and put in a holding cell with three other women. Monica was surprised to see one woman in a business suit, and the other two women were dressed in clothing similar to hers.

This was nothing at all like what she'd seen on television shows or the movies. After talking to the women, Monica realized they were normal. With nothing but time to kill, she listened to each person share a brief life story and how they ended up there. It felt more like some kind of AA meeting than a jail stay. Once she stood before the judge, her bail was set, and Kendall posted it a few hours later.

She was relieved that she didn't have to tell her mother about this, and was grateful to Kendall for being there for her.

Monica savored the last bit of cheesecake before drifting off to sleep. Her bed never felt softer or more heavenly. In retail, missing a day's work caused her to fall seriously behind in paperwork, and she'd missed five days. With a major floor move in the women's department, Monica knew she wouldn't see the light of the day for a while. Not to mention she was afraid to show up at work, because Mr. Langston requested a meeting first thing the next morning.

This was so messed up. She could just kill someone if she was going to lose her job over this. Not to mention her bills were stacking up, and she really had no earthly idea how she was going to get out of this hole she dug for herself.

No one made her buy a new outfit every time she went somewhere; just her selfish need to impress. The more she thought about it, it was mainly people she didn't know or didn't even care for that she was trying to impress. A knot formed in her stomach when she thought of all the clothes sitting in her closet, shoes on the floor, expensive furniture, and window treatments.

It wasn't easy being a big woman, even though she worked like hell to make it appear that way. To receive the looks of disgusts from strangers, she knew they were calling her fat bitch, lazy ass, dumb nigga, or even worse. That's why she had to take everything she did to the max; her make-up, hair, clothing, shoes, everything had to be flawless. And even her job. She knew she was fabulous and thick, and she was determined to make everybody else know it too.

A knock at the door interrupted her slumber a few hours later. Kendall stuck his head in.

"Hey, baby." He smiled. "You want some lunch?"

Monica sat up in the bed. "Did you make it?" she inquired.

"No, I was going to run out and pick some up from Denny's."

"Oh." Monica frowned. Now, she would have to wait at least an hour to eat. "Can you order the Deluxe Scrambler? And I want the eggs scrambled with cheese. My pancakes I want with fresh blueberries. And, do I have whipped cream in the fridge?" She paused as she recalled the inventory. "No, you'll have to stop and get it from Albertson's."

Kendall scratched his head. "Anything else?"

Monica cocked her head to one side. "Why did you say it like that?"

"I'm asking a question," he said as he gestured with his hands. "Do you need anything else? Because I don't want to run out later. I have to go to work in three hours, and I want you to make sure you have everything you need."

"Kendall, I can't believe you're going to work today," Monica complained. "Why can't you just call in? See, that's why you need to find a real job where you don't have to clock in or out. I mean, this is just ridiculous. I need you here with me, and you can't be because of your lousy job."

Kendall threw his hands up. "Here we go again. I don't have time for this." He turned around and left.

Monica heard the door shut, and she sat there with a stunned look on her face. "What is his problem?" Her stomach growling changed her attention to a more important matter. Slowly easing herself down the hall, she stopped to catch her breath.

This walk wouldn't be so hard if you'd lost those fifty pounds already. You're so damn lazy.

She instantly felt guilty and thought of turning around and going back to bed. She calculated the time it would take Kendall to drive: fifteen minutes to Denny's, wait another twenty minutes for the food, stop by the grocery store. Give or take another thirty minutes, depending on traffic. Oh no, that was way too long. She wouldn't make it.

It's not like she had to eat the entire meal. At her Weight Watchers meetings, she learned she didn't have to clean the plate just to feel like she got her money's worth. With that in mind, she tore into a honey bun. Rubbing her stomach, she realized she hadn't enjoyed anything so sweet in a really long time. The hospital food was just plain disgusting. And she didn't even want to remember the poison they served in jail disguised as dinner.

When she heard Kendall using his key to come inside, Monica quickly hid the honey bun wrappers underneath her mattress. This time she wouldn't forget to throw them away. It took her a good week to get rid of the ants that invaded her bedroom when she forgot the last time.

"I'm back," Kendall announced.

Monica heard him opening packages in the kitchen. Her stomach felt funny, but she ignored it. She couldn't wait to tear into that Scrambler.

"Here you go," Kendall said as he placed the tray with the Styrofoam box on her lap. "Breakfast . . . I mean lunch in bed."

Monica rubbed her hands together as she inhaled the aroma of bacon. "I can't believe it's still hot."

"Well, that's because I didn't make it to Albertson's."

"Ugh," Monica pursed her lips tightly. "So, I don't have any whipped cream to put on my pancakes?"

"Hold on, now. I just ordered it at Denny's. That's all." Kendall laughed. "Damn, girl. You act like you want to hurt somebody."

Monica held up a fist. "I will. There's two things not to play with me about: my money and my food."

Kendall shook his head. He took a bite out of his sandwich.

Monica chewed on a piece of bacon. Then she put her hand on Kendall's. "Baby, I appreciate the way you've been here for me. I don't know if I could've done this without you." A tear rolled down her cheek.

Kendall put his arm around her shoulder. "You're my woman, and I love you. I'll be there for you, no matter what."

Monica tried to hold back her emotions, but she decided to release them. "I've been going through so much lately with my job and my bills are stacking up. And, I know you're not going to say anything, but I've put on so much weight. I don't even feel attractive anymore. And that's not like me at all."

"Shhh." Kendall kissed her sweetly. "You're so beautiful."

Monica grinned as Kendall worked his lips southward. His tongue circled around her breasts.

She loved this man so much. She couldn't believe the way she'd treated him lately. It didn't matter anymore that he earned less money than her. And that he lived at home with his parents.

"Oooohhh." Monica sang as Kendall's tongue entered her vagina. She turned on her side and spread her legs wider.

"Your pussy tastes like honey," he said.

Monica cooed. She loved his ass.

She realized that what did matter was he went to work every single day. He took care of his responsibilities. He had more money in the bank than she did. He loved her. He proved it by being with her at the hospital and promising never to leave her side. Not for one moment.

As he gently glided in and out of her, Monica ignored her back pain and gyrated with his thrusts. Creating a rhythmic harmony, she lost herself in the pleasure of her sweet orgasm.

"Damn, baby." Kendall arched his back as he rocked harder to release his juices inside of her. He lay on top of her, their sweaty bodies stuck together. "That was good."

"Baby, I'm so sorry about the way things have been lately—"

Kendall put his hand on her lips. "Stop it. We've both made our share of mistakes."

"But, I know I was so wrong to treat you the way I did." Monica started to cry.

"It's all right. I forgive you." Kendall smiled.

"And, I'm never going to take another drink again. Never . . . ver . . . ever." Monica prayed she wouldn't lose her job or worse: serve more jail time.

CHAPTER FIVE

As Monica stepped out of Mr. Langston's office, she thanked God she still had a job. He knew nothing about Monica's arrest, and she wanted to keep it that way. The meeting was about Melanie's complaint of having to work two straight weekends in a row. After Monica gave her side of the story, Mr. Langston pretty much took her word for it.

Before setting foot on the sales floor, Monica went to her office and wrote up Melanie's corrective. Theresa stopped by to check on her.

"Hey, how did the meeting go?" Theresa asked.

Monica threw up her hands. "Oh, I was so relieved. It was about Melanie."

Theresa sat down. "Wonderful," she replied.

Monica rested her elbows on her desk. "I appreciate you not saying anything about this. For a minute, I questioned whether I could trust you to keep my arrest under wraps."

Theresa folded her arms. "You can trust me. I consider you my friend as well as a colleague."

"That's good to know." Monica picked up the written corrective. "I have to go over this with Melanie. Can you sit in on it?"

"Oh, yes. Of course."

"Theresa," a voice spoke through her radio.

Theresa held it up to her mouth. "Yes."

"The fitting rooms in the children's department are trashed. No one cleaned them last night."

"Shit." Theresa shook her head and picked up the radio once more. "Where's Pablo?"

"He's on his way."

Theresa scratched her head with her perfectly manicured nail. Monica looked at her own mucked-up nails. She needed to get them fixed during her lunch break.

"OK, I'm coming down." Theresa responded. She stood up. "Are you sure you want my job?"

"Yes, I'm ready."

"What time is Melanie scheduled today?"

Monica glanced at the schedule on her bulletin board. "She's coming in at 1:00."

"I'll see you at 1:30 then."

Monica smiled. "Perfect."

Later that evening, Monica and Theresa went to dinner. Theresa chose the Melting Pot, because it was her favorite spot. Monica didn't really care for the food, but she needed to eat less anyway.

The hostess showed them to their table. They followed her through the dimly lit hallway. A handsome man wearing all black welcomed them.

"Here's your table, ladies," the hostess said. "The man who greeted you is Alex. He is your server this evening."

"Oooohhh," Theresa said. "He can serve me any time." She glanced down at her ring finger. "I need to take this off."

Monica held an astonished look. "Theresa. I can't believe you." This comment caught her completely off guard. She always thought Theresa was happily married.

"What?" Theresa plopped down in her seat. "There's nothing wrong with a little flirting."

Monica cocked her head to one side. "If you say so. I need to go to the restroom."

Alex walked up to their table. "Welcome, ladies. My name is Alex, and I'll be waiting on you this evening."

As he continued his spiel about the menu, Monica was disgusted at how Theresa hung on his every word. His grin was so wide and he had the most perfect set of teeth. With a perfectly tanned complexion and black curly hair, he resembled a Greek god.

"Yes, we know." Theresa batted her eyelashes. "Can you bring us apple martinis?"

Alex raised one eyebrow. "Sure thing. I'll make them sweet just for you."

When he turned around, Monica and Theresa both checked out his behind, and it was evident he did a lot of squats to have those buns of steel.

Theresa licked her lips. "Oh my goodness." She fanned herself. "He's so hot!"

The family sitting in the booth across from them, laughed in unison.

Monica shook her head in embarrassment. "I need to go to the restroom. I can't hold it any longer."

When Alex placed their drinks on the table, Monica asked, "Can you show me where the bathroom is?"

"Oh, sure." He held out his arm.

Monica wrapped her arm around his muscular bicep. "Don't get jealous," she said to Theresa.

Theresa dropped her jaw.

Alex escorted Monica to the ladies room and she thanked him. After she relieved her bladder, she touched up her make-up. Adjusting her black wrap dress, Monica examined herself carefully. The new body shaper she purchased did just the trick.

Confidently, she strutted back to her booth, where Theresa handed Alex a business card.

"Was that your phone number?" Monica asked.

"Uh-huh," Theresa replied.

"I can't believe you did that."

"What?" Theresa's voice went up an octave. She leaned in closer. "You're making a much bigger deal of this than it is."

Monica picked up the menu. "You're probably right. Let's just order." She ran her fingers along the couples' selections. The Lobster Indulgence sounded delicious, but it was Theresa's night, so she kept her opinion to herself.

"Well, I think you liked the lobster last time. Do you want to go with that?" Theresa asked.

"It's your night. So order what you want."

Theresa frowned. "Are you all right?"

"Yes. Never better."

Alex approached the table once more. After Theresa ordered the lobster dinner, she leaned forward. "Is this about Alex? Were you interested in him?"

Monica thought Theresa was tripping. But she decided to go along with it. "And what if I was? Do you think a big woman like myself couldn't have him?"

Theresa scoffed. "Monica, are you crazy? Kendall is so handsome. I've never dated a black guy, but I would so date him. I know you can have any man you want."

Monica twisted her lips. "Well, the answer to your question is yes."

Theresa's eyes grew wide. "You dirty whore!"

Monica chuckled. "Calm down. I'm just playing with you. I don't want him."

"Are you sure?"

"Positive," Monica responded as she took her first sip from her apple martini.

Theresa took a deep breath. "Good, because I'm meeting him for drinks later."

Monica almost spit up her drink. "Tell me you're kidding."

Theresa scratched the back of her neck. "No, I'm not." She smiled nervously.

"You slut!" Monica snapped her fingers. "Tell me about it tomorrow." She took another sip.

"Maybe." Theresa stuck out her tongue. "It depends on how naughty I am."

"Whoa!" Monica rubbed her forehead. "This is unreal."

"Everything OK, ladies?" Alex asked.

Monica jumped. "Oh, you scared the shit out of me."

Alex laughed. "I'm sorry."

"No, it's quite all right."

The two enjoyed their dinner and talked incessantly about work. Although, the portions were small, Monica tore it up. In her mind, she already planned to make a stop on Mills Avenue and pick up a Big Mac value meal from McDonald's on the way home.

"There's a reason why I invited you to dinner tonight," Theresa said as she chewed on her cheesecake dipped in chocolate.

Monica's mouth fell open. "Mr. Langston found out! He knows."

Theresa slapped Monica's hand. "No. It's good news, silly. You've got the promotion. First thing in the morning, Mr. Langston is going to make you an offer."

"Oh my God!"

"I know." Theresa clasped her hands together. "This is great, isn't it?"

"Wow!" Monica threw both arms in the air victori-
ously, like she just won an Olympic gold medal. "Yes!"

"Congratulations!" Theresa rose from her seat and
hugged Monica.

Monica shook her head. "Thank you so much." Tears
flowed down her cheeks. "I can't believe this."

"Well, believe it. You've earned it." Theresa sat back
down. "You're now a part of the work-your-ass-to-
death club."

Monica laughed. "Yeah. I'm ready." This couldn't
have come at a better time. The calls from the bank about
her car loan were getting out of hand. They were even
calling her at work. She was almost to the point of asking
Kendall for the money.

The next day, Monica showed up at work two hours
early, dressed in her black suit. She wanted to look her
best and even spent extra time applying her make-up.
Appearance meant everything, and it truly gave her the
confidence she needed to keep her nerves under wraps.

Her hands were damn near trembling when Mr.
Langston stepped into her office. She wanted to seem
surprised, but she immediately inquired on the pay.
When he told her he would get back to her on that, Monica broke out in a cold sweat. In her mind, she knew she
needed at least another thirty thousand dollars to dig
herself out of the hole, and another ten thousand to stay
out of it.

Disappointed didn't scratch the surface of how she felt
when she found out her raise was only seven percent,
taking her to a measly seventy thousand. How was she
going to survive on that?

Monica ran her fingers through her hair as she attempted to sort it all out. Well, she would have to remain
in her apartment for another two years. After she paid

off her Lexus, she could pay more on her credit cards, and eventually become totally debt-free. Only then she would be in a position to save for a house. Maybe by then, Kendall would've proposed and they could buy a house together. With his income, even as pathetic as it was, they would earn more than enough to purchase a gorgeous home. With her Macy's discount, she could decorate the house beautifully.

Yeah, it looked liked this marriage thing wasn't such a bad idea after all. Monica would have her own spending money, and afford all the nice things she'd dreamed of having.

On her way home from work, she dialed Kendall's cell.

"Hey," Kendall said.

"Baby, I've got good news!" Monica exclaimed.

"Oh yeah?"

"Yes, I'm the new ASM at Altamonte Mall," Monica said proudly.

"That's good. Look, I'm a have to call you back." Kendall sounded distant.

Monica frowned. "OK."

He hung up.

Before Monica had a chance to think about the strange interaction, her cell phone rang. She was surprised Kendall called her back so quickly, but she saw it was Lorenzo.

"Hello, girlfriend!"

"Hey, slut!" Lorenzo yelled. "Why are you burning up my cell phone?"

"Because I wanted to share my good news," Monica replied. "I got the promotion!"

Lorenzo screamed. "Go 'head, girl! We're rich now. We needs to go celebrate."

Monica smiled. "True. True." She nodded. "As long as

it doesn't involve drinking, because you know I'm a re-
tired alcoholic."

"Are you for real, for real?"

"Yes." Monica replied as she parked and disconnected
the car charger from her cell phone. Then she remembered how she and Theresa enjoyed those apple martinis
the other night.

She walked to the mailboxes. "I don't even know how
this thing is going to play out in the courts. Kendall
seems to think I'll get community service."

"Oooohhh, I'm praying for you on that one. And you
already volunteer with the Light Center, so that would
be fabulous."

"I know. God, please make this work." Monica
breathed heavily into the phone. Talking and walking
seemed to exhaust her now more than ever. If only she
could get her lazy behind on that treadmill tonight. Ten
minutes a day would do her a world of good.

"It's going to happen," Lorenzo said. "We can still do
VIP at Roxy's, and order virgin piña coladas all night."

"It doesn't make sense for you not to drink because of
my irresponsible behavior," Monica said as she unlocked
the door to her apartment. The awful stench reminded
her to take out the garbage. Quickly, she rushed over to
open a window.

Lorenzo snorted. "Oh, please. I don't need it anyway.
Remember, my daddy is suffering with his bad liver after
all his years of drinking hard liquor."

"That's right." Monica bagged up the garbage and
tossed it outside her front door. She would take it down
on her way to work in the morning. "How's he doing
anyway?"

"When I talked to my cousin, Gwen, she told me he's
not going to be here much longer. But, he's still not answering my phone calls." He sniffled.

"That's a damn shame." Monica felt anger toward Mr. Rawlins every time she thought of how this hurt Lorenzo. No matter what, a parent was supposed to love their child unconditionally.

Sure, she didn't have the best relationship with her mother, but she was grateful. Even though her mother got on her last nerve at times, Monica appreciated spending time with her. As she knew, there were many women whose mothers weren't alive. Thinking that Lorenzo's father might die, she knew as his best friend, she should do something. That night, she typed up a letter to send to Daryll, Jr., requesting to be put on his visiting list. Just to make sure he would, she put an old photo of herself, fifty-five pounds ago, inside the envelope too.

For months, Monica thought of writing to Lorenzo's brother, but she kept it on the "to do" list of things that never got finished. Time was of the essence, and she had to follow through, no matter what. Then she accomplished another goal she hadn't done in a long time; she exercised on the treadmill for twenty minutes. Huffing and puffing, and feeling like her chest was close to combustion, she stopped to catch her breath.

Still, Monica patted herself on the back for doing what she could. And she promised herself she would do at least twenty-one minutes on Thursday.

A week later, Monica entered the private dining room at Gina's on the Lakeside. The staff at Macy's was throwing a celebration dinner in her honor, and she worked a half-day to get ready for the occasion. Monica's appointments for a manicure, pedicure, and hairdo were scheduled tight, so that she only had thirty minutes to get to each one. Successfully making it on time to her hair appointment, she thanked Robin for fixing up her curly tresses.

Since Kendall claimed he had to work late, Monica didn't have a date. Lorenzo planned to meet her there. She could always depend on him, and she hoped to resolve this issue he had with his father soon.

Nervously, Monica adjusted the jacket of her suit. Even though she knew she was probably packing on more pounds, she hadn't weighed herself to verify it. The proof was in the fact that she was no longer able to wear most of the clothing in her closet, and found herself shopping online to locate plus-size formal wear she could fit. To her surprise, there were only a handful of name brands to choose from. Her favorites were Anne Klein and Nine West. With her experience in retail and Lorenzo's artistic skills, Monica was thinking she should go into business for herself and really take advantage of this untapped market. She made a note to herself to explore it further.

Tonight her navy pin-striped suit with the white collared shirt slimmed down her blossoming figure and boosted her confidence to the point to where she could smile in front of all those white folks and pretend her life was damn near perfect. Even though it seemed her relationship with Kendall was falling apart.

How did this happen?

For the most part she'd been really good to him since her accident, and not once had they had the smallest disagreement. That could have a lot more to do with the fact they saw less of each other, since Kendall was working just as hard as she was. She wondered if there was another woman in the picture.

Oh, please!

Monica almost laughed out loud at the mere thought of Kendall being able to afford two women on his small paycheck.

"She's here!" Theresa announced to the modest num-

ber of guests standing around inside the Promenade
Room. Only one couple was seated.

Monica tried her best to put on a fake grin to mask her
disappointment over the small turnout.

"Hi, everyone." She waved her hand.

The guests came closer and formed a crowd. Monica
recognized many faces from her store, some from out of
town, and new faces of managers she would work with at
the Altamonte store.

As they clapped for her, Monica took a bow. "Thanks
so much!"

Mr. Langston stepped out from among the crowd and
rested his hand on her shoulder. "Helen, you're taking
one of the hardest working managers from my store. I
hope you know what kind of jewel you're getting."

Monica gasped. "Oh my God," she said in a bashful
tone. "You're going to make me cry."

"No. We're here to party," Theresa replied. "So, let's
take our seats. Our scrumptious dinner is ready to be
served by this awesome staff here at Gina's."

Everyone nodded in agreement, as Gina's was a popular restaurant for formal occasions, especially with the
breathtaking view of the lakeside.

"Let me escort you." Theresa wrapped her arm
around Monica.

"Thanks." Monica timidly sat down at her rightful
place at a table with top executives at her company.

Talk about being uncomfortable, but Monica would
use this opportunity to her advantage by impressing the
"white shirts" with her stunning vernacular and knowledge of the company, so she'd be that much closer to becoming Store Manager and getting the salary, benefits,
and bonuses she needed to get herself out debt.

Nervously, she talked with her new boss, Helen Daveen. She was an older, slightly overweight woman, with

graying hair. Her pale white face showed her age; she had some wrinkles and thin lips that stayed fixed with a smile, resembling the Joker. Monica's first impression of her new boss was that Helen wasn't going to be as easy to please as all the other store managers in the past.

Theresa sat down beside her. A few minutes later, Lorenzo arrived. He looked so handsome in his burgundy silk shirt and dress slacks. Monica was eager to see which guest he would be taking home with him tonight. She was always curious about Ken in the Jewelry Department, with his pretty self.

"You can thank me later," Theresa whispered.

"For what, pray tell?" Monica asked under her breath.

"Not sitting you at the table with all the skinny bitches." She giggled.

Monica rolled her eyes. "Right. I owe you for that one." She was proud to have stuck with her exercise routine thus far. And she managed to lose two pounds in the process.

The next obstacle was to curtail her eating habits. Monica definitely needed support, so she signed up for Curves. A co-worker lost close to seventy pounds going to the fitness center and no longer needed to take her blood pressure medicine. After a quick tour and practice session, Monica observed the equipment was simple and easy to use, and provided the cardio she needed to burn calories. It helped that most of the women exercising for the twenty-minute workout were big, some bigger than her. She could be comfortable and not concerned about skinny women or men gawking at her.

Exactly one year before, Monica purchased an annual membership at Gold's Gym. When she went for the tour, it seemed like a pretty decent place. Monica scoped out the place, looking for other full-figured women, which she was delighted to find. The gym offered free exercise classes and personal trainers at an extra cost. Monica took advantage of the two free training sessions with Todd, one of the trainers at the gym, and learned how to properly use the equipment. Todd put her on a schedule for arms on Monday, legs on Wednesday, and abdominals on Friday. She also added Yogalates on Tuesdays.

With a full workout schedule and a fifteen-hundred calories-a-day diet, Monica shed seventeen pounds in one week! Todd was so nice to her, encouraging her to push herself and cheering for her whenever she gave him a weekly report of her weight loss. It was comforting to have someone in her corner, believing she could do it.

Even though it was mostly water weight, she considered it a major accomplishment. By week two, she had lost another ten pounds, and by the end of the month a total of close to forty pounds. As she made real strides to achieving her goal, she put the same amount of renewed confidence into her career and relationship with Kendall. When Kendall joined the gym, they began to spend a lot more time together.

Monica was enjoying her life, and she believed it was only going to get better. On most Sundays, when she wasn't scheduled to work, they attended church together. At that point in her life, Monica was interested in going out on dates with her man, doing things instead of simply going out to eat.

They would do things like ride on roller coasters at the theme parks, play putt-putt golf, and play volleyball at the beach. Since she was able to fit into a size twenty again, and she didn't worry about whether her butt would fit in the small roller coaster seats or feel insecure about the way she looked in a bathing suit. Monica hadn't been that small since college. The best compliments were the stares and whistles from men. Nobody could tell Monica she didn't have it going on.

One early morning, Monica was at the gym riding on the bicycle before she went to shower and dress for work. When she got up to leave, she heard a guy on the elliptical machine behind her say "Her big ass needs to ride for another hour," followed by laughter that seemed to come from every person in the gym.

Feeling good about her new figure, she was ready to dish out an ugly insult to the ignorant hard bodied jerk. As she was about to turn around to curse him out, she realized it was Todd. She was completely stunned that it was her personal fitness coach, and she said nothing. Humiliated, Monica never bothered to pick up her bag from her locker. She jumped in her car and sped home. Taking the day off from work, she cried and ate to ease the pain of reliving the incident many times in her head.

Monica nearly ate all the healthy food in her refrigerator and cabinets to quench her appetite. The next day, on the way home from work, she stopped by Albertsons to replace all of the groceries she demolished with all of her favorites: bags of chips, boxes of ice cream, bagels and cream cheese, sausage, and frozen pizzas. Not one fruit or vegetable went into her shopping cart. Each night, she binged in front of the television. Her routine of going to the gym was quickly substituted with trips to the grocery store to purchase more food.

This continued for another month, then Monica gathered the courage to get on the scale. Convinced she'd only put on ten pounds or so, she was surprised to see her weight had ballooned to two hundred seventy-five pounds. She'd gained all the weight she lost and picked up another fifteen pounds.

Ashamed and embarrassed, Monica threw herself into her work, ate herself into oblivion, and began to make expensive purchases. Shopping for clothing, handbags, shoes, and jewelry made her feel important. Monica made up her mind that if she was going to be fabulous and thick, the least she could do was dress the part.

She was annoyed that Kendall kept his membership at Gold's Gym; his body became more toned, and hers became flabbier. She was too hurt and disappointed to tell Kendall about her humiliating day at the gym; she blamed her absence on work. Every time they went out, Monica looked more like his mother than his date. She kept her distance whenever he hung out with his friends from the gym. The last people she wanted to go out to dinner with were Todd and his skinny girlfriend, Barbara, whom Monica secretly nicknamed "Barbie."

Just thinking about the whole ordeal brought Monica to tears as she drove home from the party. A beautiful night at Gina's was ruined, as she had truly enjoyed herself at the party. She wanted to reclaim her life again. As her career was taking off, Monica wanted the same satisfaction in her personal life as well. And that meant working on her relationship with Kendall.

Monica dialed his cell number as she was approaching her apartment building on Michigan Avenue. When his voicemail picked up, she decided to leave a message. "Hey there, Sexy Man," she said with a Jamaican accent. "I was thinking about you, and wanted to know if you could stop by later. I'm in the mood to eat something sweet. Your cum." She licked her lips and made a smacking sound into the receiver. "Ah. Ah. Ah. I can taste it, and it's honey dripping from my lips."

Monica laughed once she hung up. Once inside her apartment, she changed into some lingerie she bought weeks ago, but had never worn. She randomly placed vanilla-scented candles all around the room. Settling on her bed, listening to the Quiet Storm on 94.5 FM, she waited for Kendall to call or surprise her at the door.

CHAPTER SIX

Monica reported to her new store promptly at 7 AM for her first day. After speaking with Helen Daveen's assistant, Lolita, Monica learned her schedule was completely booked for the entire day. Working with Helen would be different, since she was the first woman store manager Monica had ever worked for. Monica was a perfectionist and took her work seriously; she was up to the challenge, as she aimed to please. Lolita showed Monica to her new office, which was tinier than her last one.

Monica chuckled because she thought it was a joke. She found it difficult to mask her emotions once she was told it wasn't. Her facial expression, which showed pure anger, let Lolita know she wasn't happy. Less than an hour later, Lolita returned to explain there had been a mistake, and Monica was supposed to be in Jim's office, the children's manager, instead. Monica knew Jim wasn't aware until this morning that he would be moving, and now this would cause some issues with a man she didn't even know.

As Ciara so beautifully sang in the song, "So What?"

As far as Monica was concerned, Jim was her subordinate and she deserved the larger office. She happily moved her boxes, which she never bothered to unpack, down to Jim's office. It was nothing like the one she had before, but she would take it. He promised her he would be out by the end of the day. Since she had meetings with every manager and a walk-through of their departments scheduled each hour, she was fine with that.

She began her tour with Tabitha in the men's department.

"Well, as you can see, Ms. Porter, I run a very tight ship," Tabitha said. "I'm very proud that the men's department is number one in the district for profit and sales gains." Her voice showed lots of enthusiasm.

"Actually, it was second to the Fashion Square, as my department was first in sales gains as of last week," Monica corrected. She should've let her slide with that comment, but she jumped at the chance to show Tabitha who was boss. She needed to make sure her staff gave updated stats. "However, I expect that to change, now that I'm no longer there."

"Right." Tabitha forced a fake smile, and her eyes grew larger, as if they would pop right off her face. "Continuing on with the tour, each morning I'm on the sales floor to make absolutely sure . . ."

Monica tuned her out as her eyes wandered to two associates laughing behind the checkout counter. "A tight ship, huh?"

"Excuse me?"

Monica pointed. "Over there. No customers around, but two associates are carrying on, as if they have nothing else to do."

"Well—"

"I think you need to handle this." Monica turned around. "I've seen enough." She walked away as she heard Tabitha reprimand the associates and explain that Monica was the new ASM. Once more, Monica gazed over in their direction.

Monica couldn't help but take another look at the guy. Dressed in a tan, single-button business suit, he didn't seem like any of the other associates. She walked back in Tabitha's direction, trying to avoid eye contact.

"What were their names?" Monica asked, trying not to make it obvious that she was interested. "You formally introduced me to the rest of your team, but I didn't get their names."

"You're right." Tabitha folded her arms. "Michelle and Barron."

"Thanks," Monica responded. She saw Lorenzo approaching her. Always prompt, he planned to take her to lunch on her first day.

"How's your day, darling?" he asked as he kissed her on the cheek.

"Interesting, but I think it's going to be OK," Monica replied.

"Oh, really?" Lorenzo asked as his eyes searched the sales floor. "Where is he, Ms. Thang?"

"What?" Monica looked puzzled.

"Whoever has you blushing?"

"You need to stop." Monica tossed up her hand.

"Oh, you little slut. You're not going to tell me." Lorenzo grabbed Monica's hand and pulled her closer. "Come on."

Monica tried to snatch her hand back, but realized Lorenzo actually had a grip. "Will you stop? I am at work."

"Tell me who it is, and I'll let your hand go," Lorenzo teased.

"You better let go—"

"Tell me who it is."

"It's nothing."

Lorenzo's voice went up. "What is?"

"Will you be quiet?" Monica frowned. "Customers are looking at us."

"I don't give a damn about these people." Lorenzo sucked his teeth at a woman with her young son.

"Now we need to go."

"I'm sorry." Lorenzo smiled. "Let's go. We'll discuss this . . ." Lorenzo's voice trailed off and his eyes became fixated on something else. "He is staring at me," he said. "And he is gorgeous."

Monica saw it was Barron, who made eye contact with her the moment she looked up. "No, he's straight."

Monica started to walk away.

"And how do you know that? Uh-huh. I knew it." Lorenzo hit her in the back as they exited the store.

Monica rolled her eyes. "Now, I'm about to break your little bony ass."

"I knew it. You slut!"

"Back off!" Monica pretended to swing on Lorenzo. He ducked out of the direction of her fist.

He cackled. "Oooohhhh! Getting all testy about her new boy toy!"

"I have a man. Thank you very much."

Lorenzo twisted his lips. "Yeah, right. How come he stood you up at my party the other night?" he sang.

"Kendall has been working a lot," Monica quickly responded.

They walked up to the counter at Nature's Table in the food court. She ordered the vegetarian chili with wheat crackers and a water. Lorenzo picked up a deli sandwich and smoothie.

"Just like me." Monica swallowed a spoonful of hot chili and burned her tongue. She sipped on her water. "I'm busy too."

"Oh, yeah," Lorenzo said in disgust. "You mean to tell me, hard-up Kendall Darden turned down a night of sex to work. Tell that lie to one of your other friends, because I'm not buying it. Oops. You don't have any."

Monica tossed a napkin at him. "Shut up. That's because you run them all off."

Lorenzo held his hand to his chest. "Oh, please. If anything, you've managed to scare off all my female friends. Poor Tiffani was shaking at the club that time we saw you."

"Good. She deserved it." Monica snapped. "And you shouldn't be friends with my enemies anyway. She stole my man, remember?"

"I know you ain't hurt over losing Curtis. He's kicking her ass enough for the both of you."

Monica laughed. "Dang, it's that bad?"

"Girl, let me tell you. I saw her at Chaka Zulu's party two weekends ago, and she wouldn't even take off them damn sunglasses. Trying to work it like J-Lo, but more like Scary-Ho!" He snapped his fingers.

"Well, when you put it that way . . ." Monica chewed on a cracker.

"So, let's get back to you." Lorenzo flashed a toothy white smile. "Are you in love?"

"All I know is his name."

"Well, the way he was eyeing you, I think that's going to change real soon, sweetheart."

"No. He works under me. I can't do that."

Lorenzo moved in closer. "That brotha don't look like he'll be there much longer. You better jump on it, if you know what I mean." Lorenzo started dancing freak-style at the table.

Monica laughed. "You're so crazy."

That's why Monica loved Lorenzo; he was so animated, exactly what she needed to relieve herself of the anxiety from her first day. When she returned to Macy's, she continued on with her meetings, then moved her belongings into her new office. Later that evening, she headed for home, carrying an armful of manuals to review.

"I'm sorry about today, Mrs. Porter."

Monica turned around. She saw it was Barron. "It's Ms. Porter."

Barron smiled. "Oh, I assumed you were married. Sorry, again."

Monica tried her best to look annoyed, but she was able to fully see just how gorgeous he really was. Lord, have mercy. She could've fainted.

"Tabitha is a good manager, and she expects nothing but the best from us. Usually, we take our work very seriously." He licked his lips.

Monica wanted to wrap her lips around them. She took a deep breath.

"Michelle, the other associate you saw me joking around with. Well, she announced she was getting married, and I was only congratulating her."

"I understand."

"Well, it won't happen again. I promise." He licked his lips again.

Damn.

For the first time, in a very long time, Monica felt Ms. Dolly tingle.

"Let me get those for you." Barron extended his hand.

Monica pulled back. "No, that's quite all right. I got it."

"Are you sure?" Barron chuckled. "You looked like you were struggling there a minute ago."

Monica smiled. "OK, I give."

Barron followed her to the car, where he placed her things on the back seat. "Nice car."

"Thank you."

"Well, I have the ES 430. Only it's blue." He showed her his Lexus key chain.

"How are you able to afford it on your salary?" Monica asked, but quickly realized her question was offensive. "Sorry, that is none of my business."

"Now we're even." Barron's smile revealed his dimples. "Well, I have my own business. I work here for the health benefits."

"That makes sense. What kind of business?"

"Real estate." Barron handed her a card that read Michaels Development. "I purchase and renovate properties. Then I resell them for a profit."

Monica nodded. "I'm impressed."

"See? And you was about to write a brotha off."

Monica tossed up her hand. "No, I wasn't."

"It's OK." Barron's eyes remained fixed on her. "It was nice meeting you. It's nice to see some color in the store. If you know what I mean." He winked.

Monica slid into her car, and then turned to watch him speed off in his Lexus ES 430. Careful not to smear her make-up, she used a napkin to pat the perspiration beads off her face. While driving home, she tried to call Kendall, but when his voicemail picked up, she hung up without leaving a message.

Monica sprinted on the treadmill for ten minutes and walked for another forty minutes. Eating a light salad and skinless baked chicken, she retreated to her bedroom to prepare for the next day. No matter how hard she tried to study the policy manuals and make revisions, her first assigned project, she continued to think about Barron. Finally, she couldn't take it anymore. Reaching at the tip of her closet, she pulled out Mandingo. Fully undressing, she lay back in her bed and worked him in a circular motion, then north and south. When she concentrated on Barron licking his lips, she imagined him sucking on her breasts.

"Yeah," she hummed. "Do it, baby."

Monica squeezed her butt cheeks, as she felt herself about to climax. She moved Mandingo in and out faster. Harder, as if Barron's penis was the twelve inches she forced inside.

"Huh." She grunted louder. "Oooohhh." She felt it coming. Closer.

Concentrate. Big dick. Big dick.

Then, she felt her warm wetness.

That was good.

If she couldn't experience the real thing, imagining it would have to do.

Now relaxed, she cleaned herself up and went back to her revisions.

"Thanks for picking me up," Monica said.

"Anytime. Well, at least for another month."

Monica frowned. "Don't remind me. I don't know what I'm going to do without my best friend."

"I don't know either, but you better make some more friends." Lorenzo pulled his Volvo from Macy's and made a right on Palm Springs Drive.

"I don't know what it is about me, but I can't get along with other women." Monica gestured with her hands. "Take today for instance. I dealt with this rude customer who wanted her money back for jeans that she'd obviously had for a year. Talking about they shrunk when she washed them."

"How do you know she's had them for a year?" Lorenzo asked.

"Because, that's when we last sold them. It's been about ten months since they were on clearance at forty percent off."

Lorenzo wrenched his nose. "Oh, no she didn't!"

"I know." Monica shook her head. "So, I told her I

wouldn't give her a refund, but I would allow her to exchange them just this once. And she had the nerve to say, 'No, thank you, Fat Bitch, I wanna talk to your manager.' Now, at this point I am livid. But, I kept my cool." Monica took a deep breath. "I told her I was the manager in charge, and that was the final decision. Take it or leave it."

"You go, Ms. Thang," Lorenzo cackled. "And then what did she do?"

"She smiled, showing her buck-ass teeth, and exchanged them worn out jeans for a new pair of DKNY." Monica twisted her lips. "Crackers think they can get away with everything. There's no way you would see a successful black woman try to pull off a stunt like that."

"Only a crackhead," Lorenzo added.

"Exactly." Monica ran her fingers through her hair. "I really need to call Robin for a deep conditioning. This looks like wire."

"Not to me. It's pretty, darling."

"Thank you. Seeing how your hair has been jacked up, I'm going to call Robin anyway."

"Oooohhh, no she didn't!" Lorenzo responded.

Monica laughed.

"Oh, shit!" Lorenzo screamed as he slammed into the bumper of the car in front of them. "Oh, my God!"

Monica reached over to check him out. "Are you OK?" She searched his face for a bump or bruise.

"Yes, I'm fine." He pointed, but his voice was shaking.

Monica observed a man on the passenger's side of the other car helping a young woman out.

Monica jumped out in a panic. "Is she hurt? I'm dialing 9-1-1 right now," she said as she waited for an operator to answer. She couldn't get over the stupid expression on Lorenzo's face. "Would you get out of the car? What is wrong with you?" She tried to summon him out of the car with her hands.

"Oh, yes. I need to report an emergency. We were in an accident on State Road 436." Monica ran up to the couple, where the woman was lying on the ground.

When the man turned around, Monica's hands went numb and she dropped her cell phone.

"Kendall, what is going on?" Monica asked.

The woman must be a cousin or co-worker.

In her mind, she tried to make sense out of what was happening. Then, she glanced down at the engagement ring on the woman's finger.

Kendall held up his hands. "Monica. I can explain."

"Explain!" Monica shouted as she slapped his face. Lorenzo came up from behind her and grabbed her arms. "Let go of me."

Monica wrestled Lorenzo's skinny behind to the ground and pushed Kendall. "You're going to explain! What the fuck!" Monica said as she cried. Her voice went hoarse, and she couldn't say anything.

Kendall went back to the girl, who couldn't have been of legal drinking age. She lay lifeless, but was now responding.

Lorenzo put his arms around Monica. "I have to go. Right now or I'm going to kill somebody." Monica walked back in the direction of the mall, and then she started running.

"Awww, hell no!" She picked up a stick she saw lying in a pile of dirt and charged toward Kendall. When she hit him in the back with the stick, it broke in half. Kendall hollered and fell to the ground.

Monica went to stomp his eyes out with the heel of her shoe, but she heard the police siren nearing them.

"Go get in the car!" Kendall instructed.

Not wanting to go back to jail for assault, Monica did as she was told. She straightened her hair and clothing as best she could and leaned on Lorenzo's car. Standing on her own seemed impossible at this point. As Kendall and Lorenzo explained the situation to the police officer, an ambulance, followed by a fire truck, pulled up to the scene. By now, Monica learned the injured woman's name was Charlene.

The paramedics rushed to the girl's aid and put her on a stretcher. Kendall never looked in Monica's direction, and hopped inside the ambulance. She wished she'd been able to kick him to sleep. There should two bodies on stretchers. Kendall should've had a sheet over his face and been pronounced DOA (Dead on Arrival).

Monica shook her head in disbelief. She wanted to wake up from this nightmare. Feeling like her heart was stabbed with a knife, she couldn't believe Kendall actually could do this to her. Sure, there were times when Monica thought another woman was in the picture, but she always dismissed those ideas. Kendall was a good man, and she never believed him to be a liar.

Monica closed her eyes and tried to picture all the times her phone calls had gone unanswered; Kendall had been lying in the arms of another woman.

"Since my car has only a little bit of damage, I can drive it home." Lorenzo put his arm around Monica.

Her emotions got the best of her and she started to cry.

Lorenzo took a step back. "No, I'm not going to let you cry in front of that sorry-ass fucker. You're leaving here with your dignity."

Monica did her best to straighten her face. She had seen the loving way Kendall tended to Charlene, and had wanted to run over there and remind him that she was his woman. What happened to the three years he'd spent confessing his undying love for her?

Lorenzo helped her into the car.

They drove away, leaving behind what was left of her relationship. Not a damn thing.

CHAPTER SEVEN

Although a month had come and gone, Monica replayed the car accident over in her head like it was yesterday. She thought about the way Kendall rescued his fiancée, the same way he'd helped her when she was in an accident. She thought of the horrid look on her face when the man she loved for three years turned around to face her. That part of her life was over. All that time was wasted.

Was she to blame for this? Of course, she was. She should've appreciated Kendall. Her mother's voice rang in her head, *Kendall is a good man, and your big ass is lucky to have him.* In hindsight, she saw it coming and did nothing to stop it. Her constant criticism about his job and living with his parents, knowing full well Kendall's pay was decent and he was saving his money for a home, just made matters worse. Now, there was another woman in the picture who would be moving in the house he was saving for; she would be the one enjoying romantic nights, and having his babies.

Why did she always have to find a way to ruin her life?

Monica's thoughts were interrupted when she saw Kendall exiting from Gold's Gym with Todd. She wanted to speak to him, but couldn't force herself to get out of the car. Since he was no longer answering any of her phone calls, she only called his cell phone twenty times a day. Every day, she would make a promise not to call him, but as every hour passed, she dialed his number and listened to his voice mail message. At least she was strong enough to leave only one message per day.

When Ms. Ruthie asked Monica not to come to her house anymore, she felt betrayed by his family. The night of the car accident, Ms. Ruthie listened to her pour out her soul and even cried with her. She seemed honest when she reassured Monica that this relationship with Charlene was only a fling, and if she was patient, Kendall would come back to her. That was Monica's prayer each night.

Monica's breaking point was the desperate act of showing up on his job at RIP Communications and facing the embarrassment of being escorted out of the building by security. Monica couldn't believe Kendall would allow her to be treated that way. Her hurt eventually changed to anger, and she truly wanted him dead. She decided to give him one last chance to come to his senses.

Monica opened the car door when Kendall and Todd parted ways in the parking lot. This was her chance! She stooped down and eased her way around the side of a Mercedes-Benz parked next to his car. When Kendall neared his car, Monica approached him.

Kendall stopped in his tracks. "Monica, you need to go home."

Monica grabbed his arm. "Why won't you talk to me? You never even gave me a chance."

"I gave you so many chances. Monica, you never appreciated me. I'm through." He wiped his sweaty forehead.

Monica tried to show sincerity with her swollen red eyes. "No, you didn't. You didn't tell me. I thought we were lovers and friends."

"I'm sorry I hurt you," Kendall replied. "But I couldn't pretend everything was fine when it wasn't. I'm tired of lying to my family."

"I was good to you for three long years, and you know it!" Monica shouted as she pointed toward her chest. "Who was there for you when your mama was in the hospital? Who supported you when you lost your job, paid your tuition when you was too broke to do it?"

"And you never let me forget it!" Kendall screamed as spit from his mouth landed on Monica's face. "Always putting me down in front of your faggot-ass friend. I know I'm a good man, and you didn't appreciate it. So, I found someone who did!"

"No. I love you, Kendall." Monica cried as she wiped the tears from her face. "Don't leave me like this. I'm sorry!"

Kendall reached in his pocket and threw a wad of cash in front of her feet. "This is every cent you ever gave me. Now, pick it up like a dog. Same way you did me."

Kendall pushed past Monica, who was clinging to his sweat pants.

"Don't leave me! Please don't leave me!" Monica shook her head from side to side.

"It's too late!"

"No. No. I'll do better."

"Go home, Monica."

Kendall pulled Monica off his pants and sped off in his car. All she heard was the bass bumping from his speakers. Totally devastated, she continued to sit on the pavement, crying until she felt her insides cave in. Having not eaten in days, she hurled up clear fluids. Monica wiped her face with the sleeve of her blouse and willed her life-less body back to her car.

Monica leaned back in the seat and rested her eyes for a minute. With the lack of sleep, her eyes were heavy and refused to open. When she opened them again, the clock on her dashboard read 12:30 AM. Knowing she needed to wake up early for work, she drove home.

The next day, instead of finishing her notes for the manager's meeting, Monica was online checking out the Orlando Sentinel website, reading the wedding an-nouncement for Charlene and Kendall. She jotted down the place and time of the blessed event. She wanted to stop by the pawnshop on her way to Curves, so she wrote a note to leave early.

As she sat in the food court twirling her fork in the salad that she'd only taken a few bites of, Barron Michaels approached her table.

"I saw you were alone." He pointed at the empty chair. "Need some company?"

Monica's eyes drifted down at her barely eaten salad. "I'm done. Maybe next time."

"OK."

"No, wait." Monica smiled. "Go ahead."

Barron sat down. "Good, because there aren't any other tables left."

Monica laughed.

"Now, that's the first time I've seen you smile."

"I'm busy. I don't have time to smile."

"Too busy to have a little fun?" Barron asked. "Come on, now. Let me tell you something." He moved in closer. "Life is too short. And you can't let these white folks rush you out of here."

Monica nodded. "You're right."

Barron took bite of his Big Mac. "I noticed you're going through a rough time, and I don't think it's all about this new job."

Monica twisted her lips. "I'm sure you've heard the gossip."

"Yes." Barron touched her chin. "But, what you won't hear is anyone saying that you're falling apart. Ms. Porter, you're one classy lady. I mean, you coming in here making these women look bad. Not a hair strand out of place, clothes are banging, and your face. Awwww, I need to stop while I'm ahead."

"No you don't, either," Monica responded. "Go ahead."

Barron took his time, shook his head. Then he stared into her eyes. "Well, you're absolutely stunning. I've never met a woman more beautiful."

Barron went back to eating his food. With three bites, he finished his burger and fries. He stood from the table, holding his tray. "Keep smiling."

Monica turned around to watch him as he headed back to the store.

"Wow!" She buried her head in her hands to hide the expression on her face. She beamed with joy.

That night, while she sat in the bed of her dark apartment, she thought back to her encounter with Barron. She loved the way he undressed her with his eyes. And when he licked those sexy lips like LL Cool J, her heart fluttered.

"Ms. Dolly, I hear ya talking, girlfriend," Monica said as she took out the business card with Barron's information on it.

She quickly dialed the number, as she had done all day, but this time she actually let it ring.

"Hello."

"Hello, Barron. It's Monica." Monica's voice trembled.

"I know. I have Caller ID." He laughed. "I also know this is the sixth time you've called me tonight."

Monica gritted her teeth. "Oh. Sorry about that."

"There's no need to apologize," Barron replied. "Seriously, so what's so important that you needed to talk to me?"

Monica cleared her throat. "I was curious about your plans for the rest of the evening."

"Can you hold on for a minute? I have somebody on the other line."

"Sure."

It took all but ten seconds for Barron to return.

"That was quick."

"You will never say that about me again." He chuckled.

"I hear ya, but I'll be the judge of that." Monica bit her bottom lip. "One thing I can't stand is a minute man."

"You don't have to worry about that," Barron bragged. "Yeah . . . well, I don't have any plans."

"Oh, so you told your girlfriend you had to go?"

Barron laughed. "She can't do nothing for me anyway."

"So you do admit, you have a girlfriend?" Monica asked. She wasn't so sure she wanted to go along with this anymore."

"Yeah, I got somebody." Barron breathed into the phone. "But that don't have nothing to do with what I want to do with you."

Monica raised her eyebrows. "And what is that?"

"Eat your pussy for the next three hours. Is that all right with you?"

Ms. Dolly released a flow so·strong, Monica crossed her legs to control it.

"Do you have objections to what I just said?"

"None at all," Monica responded. She held her hand to her chest as she gripped her cordless phone tighter with the other hand. "I was thinking, maybe we should get together. Tonight. If you want to."

"Now, Ms. Porter," Barron chuckled. Even his laugh sounded sexy. "Are you calling me for a booty call?"

"What if I am?" Monica flirted. She felt Ms. Dolly release more warm juices.

"Well, if you are, then I'm available."

Monica gave Barron directions to her place. Then she hurried up and showered, lathered her body with her ginger body scrub, and quickly applied lotion to every crevice of her body. Slipping into a gold-toned teddy, she slipped on her matching robe and lit scented candles in random spots in her apartment. Turning on her sound system, she quickly clicked the remote to the Jamie Foxx CD.

It was the next morning, and Monica was listening to Lorenzo rant on for what seemed like a lifetime about his plans to move to New York City.

"I can't wait for you to come up to visit me," Lorenzo said. "My place is so tiny, it's half the space of my place now, but I'm throwing in my designing ideas to hook it up, girlfriend."

"I know it will be gorgeous," Monica added. She zoned out for a minute while she kept thinking about her night with Barron. She couldn't get over the way he licked and sucked every part of her body. He even sucked her toes like they were candy. No man had ever tended to her sexual needs the way he did. It was as if she had a sign on her forehead that read "All You Can Eat Buffet," because Barron truly got his money's worth when he was finished with her.

"And what do you have to say for yourself?" Lorenzo asked.

"Huh?" Monica snapped back into reality. "What did you say?"

"Obviously, you weren't listening to a thing I was saying, Ms. Thang. So, come on with it!"

Monica scratched her head. "Come on with what?"

"Listen here, slut!" Lorenzo shouted through the phone. "Don't get all proper on me. Now, tell me about Barron. And don't leave out nothing. Hold on for one second. I need to visualize."

"Are you ready?" Monica asked.

"Yes. Come on with it!"

"Well, it was good." Monica grinned as her eyes lit up. "Better than anything I've ever experienced before in my entire life."

"Ooooohhh! Damn!" Lorenzo screamed. "It's like that!"

"All that and a bag of chips. The sundae with the chocolate drippings, nuts, whipped cream, and a juicy red cherry on top." Monica scribbled on her note pad, pretending to be hard at work when two managers peered inside her office as they walked by. She recognized one of them as Tabitha, and decided to stop her.

"Hey, let me call you back. I have to take care of something." Monica said.

"Well you better—" Monica heard as she quickly hung up.

She knew it was wrong for her to treat her best friend like that, but it was so hard to get off the phone with him. As fast as he spoke, he hardly ever took the time to swallow or even catch his breath. Every sentence just rolled off his tongue, and into the next one. No pause or anything.

"Excuse me, Tabitha!" Monica yelled down the hall from her doorway.

Tabitha turned around. "Yes?"

"Can I see you for a moment?"

"Well, I was on my way to lunch," Tabitha replied.

Monica rolled her eyes. "It will only take a second."

Tabitha spoke a few words to Jerry, the children's manager, probably telling him how much she hated her. Then she slowly approached Monica. Now, Monica knew that heifer moved faster than that.

"What is it?" Tabitha asked as her eyes grew wide.

"I wanted to review your schedule, but I realized I don't have a copy of it on my desk."

"I wonder why you don't have this week's schedule. I turned it in before all the other managers. Maybe it's lost in that pile of papers on your desk." Tabitha smiled innocently.

"That's probably it." Monica held up her hand, really wanting to choke the shit out of her. "I'll check my desk once more."

"You do that." Tabitha shook her head. "If you don't find it, I'll be sure to email it once more."

Monica forced a smile, as she straightened her suit jacket. "I'll find it."

Once Monica was back in her office, she discovered the document under a pile of folders. She highlighted the times Barron was scheduled to work. It would be way too awkward to see him on the sales floor. Although he promised to keep their rendezvous a secret, Monica couldn't risk anyone finding out. She worked way too hard for this position, for an issue like this to ruin her life. Without this job, she would have to file bankruptcy for sure.

For a brief moment, she felt dirty about the way she allowed herself to have a sex with a man she knew nothing about. Nothing about his sexual history, which would've been important, considering the kinky sex they engaged in. It was straight from a sex scene from the show *Nip/Tuck*, where she watched Christian Troy use those women like sex slaves so many times before.

Monica rubbed her fingers over the red marks around her wrists. They were still sore, so she pulled out a tube of antibiotic ointment to help heal them. Then she took her checkbook from her purse. She counted the large wad of cash and filled out a deposit slip. If she left before two o'clock, the money would be available today. Finally, she could make her car payment.

CHAPTER EIGHT

Monica sat in her car outside of the Light Center. She watched intently as the members of the bridal party, wearing sage green dresses, lined up on the stairs in front of the church.

Wiping tears from her face, she took in a deep breath. Patiently, Monica waited to enact her plan. She drummed her shaking fingers along her steering wheel.

By this time, the groomsmen exited the church in ivory tuxedos. Monica's heart beat rapidly, and she gripped her chest to keep from hyperventilating. Glancing down the street, Monica caught sight of the limousine pulling up. As the rest of the family members made their way along the entrance, Monica knew it was time. She grabbed her pistol and looked around for security or police.

With the gun behind her back, Monica, wearing a black dress like she was ready to attend a funeral, crossed the street. Loud screams warned her of the happy couple's arrival and she aimed the gun at the door. Running up the stairs with the gun pointed, as if in a *Matrix* movie, Monica fired several shots until her gun was removed from her grip and she was tackled down to the ground by Kendall's brothers.

She didn't care that she was going to spend the rest of her life in prison. All she wanted was to make him pay.

As her face hit the ground, she looked up and witnessed the bride and groom stagger into the crowd. Charlene held her chest and cried out, as Kendall struggled to breath with blood running from his mouth onto his tuxedo.

A tap at the window interrupted her thoughts.

Monica gasped as she came back to reality and saw Lorenzo standing beside her car. He tapped once more. "Let me in."

Monica hoped he wasn't here to ruin this for her. Reluctantly, she unlocked the doors. She knew he would cause a scene if she didn't.

Lorenzo climbed in the back seat. "Let me follow you home, before you do something stupid."

Monica shook her head. "I'm not going home. And you need to get your ass out this car, if you're not here to support me."

"What are you talking about?" Lorenzo asked. "Why don't you hand me that gun? You're making me nervous with that damn thing in the car. You know I hate them things."

Monica smirked. "Is that why you sat in the back?"

"Hell yeah!" Lorenzo snapped his fingers. "I'm not trying to die."

"I don't know if I can do that." Monica leaned forward and ran her fingers along the gun resting on her lap. Nervously, she tapped her foot as the wedding party came out front. The limousine drove up, just like she'd pictured a thousand times in her head.

Monica put her hands behind her head. She took another deep breath.

"Monica, he's not worth it."

"I know. But, he hurt me." Monica shut her eyes tightly. "And I want him dead."

"Monica, I know you do." Lorenzo added. "And he will pay for what he did to you. God will be your avenger."

Monica balled up her fists. "No, fuck that."

Lorenzo grabbed her arms, and reached over to unlock the door. Her mother stepped inside of the car.

"Mama, get out of the car!" Monica hollered as she fought to free her hands.

Caroline wrapped her arms around her daughter. "Shhh. Everything's going to be all right."

Monica felt her mother's hand remove the gun from her lap.

Lorenzo hands tightened around her wrists. "If I let go, tell me—"

"Lorenzo, I ain't telling you shit. Mama, this is none of your business. Give me back my gun!"

"We're not going to let you do something you're going to regret for the rest of your life." Caroline reasoned. She opened the passenger door and got out with the gun in her purse.

"No." Monica cried out.

Lorenzo released her arms, and Monica stared helpless as the limousine drove off with Kendall and his new bride.

"Happily ever after," Monica sadly stated. "It's not fair. It's just not right."

"I know it's not. But, he'll get his."

Tamara

CHAPTER ONE

Tamara sat in the living room surrounded by the three boxes she'd stayed up all night packing. Humming along with the theme song to *The Tyra Banks Show*, she felt empowered by the lyrics. With her nerves on edge, Tamara wondered why he was taking so long to pick her up.

Having graduated from high school a month ago, Tamara was ready to begin her new life in Orlando with her boyfriend. When they first started dating, she was a freshman, and he was a senior. She couldn't believe the quarterback of the football team took an interest in her, since none of the boys in her own class even seemed to notice her. She dreamed of becoming a model one day. Tamara grew up in Ocala, a small town outside Gainesville, where there was a slim chance of her being discovered by a modeling agency.

Tamara concentrated on her academics, managed to graduate with a 3.8 GPA, and was accepted into all the state universities. Without hesitation, she quickly mailed her acceptance letter back to the University of Central Florida.

Barron held a job at Macy's while building a successful business as a real estate developer. Tamara couldn't be more proud of him for accomplishing so much at such a young age, and she expected with their smarts and talents, they would be a true power couple, like Will Smith and Jada Pinkett-Smith, or Jay-Z and Beyonce. Not to mention the brilliant children they would produce.

Glancing up at the clock, she made a mental note that he was now seven hours late.

"Maybe he's not coming," Aveena said as she walked past her into the kitchen. "You want something to drink?"

"Is there some orange Kool-Aid left?"

"Yes, Tamara Dearest," Aveena replied. She poured a glass of the remaining Kool-Aid.

Tamara sat down on the bar stool at the breakfast counter. "Thank you, Mama."

Aveena rested her hands on the counter. "You know you can still change your mind and attend school up there in Tallahassee with your friends. Just say the word, and I'll load those boxes in my car."

"No, I want to live in Orlando." Tamara took another gulp from her glass. She hoped her mother wouldn't go on about how she was against her moving in with Barron. She'd heard everyone in the family's comments about their disapproval with her "shacking up with that boy."

"What you mean is, you want to live with Barron and be his live-in girlfriend." Aveena frowned. "What do you young people call it now? Well, we called it shacking up, and no matter what you young people call it, it's still not right. It's a sin in God's eyes, and you really should reconsider."

Tamara rolled her eyes. She was sick of hearing this.

Why didn't her mother just understand that she and Barron had real love for each other; love that had surpassed their age difference and distance? Already, their relationship had lasted longer than most marriages.

"Now if this boy had any real respect for you, he would at least take you down to the courthouse and marry you," Aveena said as she continued washing the dishes in the sink.

"Mama, you know his name. You never had a problem with me dating Barron in the past."

Aveena splashed a handful of water on her daughter.

"Mama!"

"The hell I didn't. I thought you were way too young to be taking company. But, your father convinced me it would be all right. Now, look at you. Ready to serve as the boy's wife, cook his food, clean his dirty draws, without so much as an engagement ring on your finger."

Ashamed, Tamara placed her hands on her lap. "I told you, we're going to get married."

Aveena twisted her lips. "Uh-huh."

Tamara heard a car door slam outside, and she jumped up and ran out the door to greet her boyfriend.

She gave him a big hug. "Where have you been? I've been waiting for almost eight hours."

Barron smiled. "I told you I had a few details to straighten out. Are you packed?" He fidgeted with his hands.

Tamara playfully punched him in the chest. "Of course, silly." She grabbed his hand and headed toward the door. "Oh, Mama's on the marriage talk again. I thought I should warn you."

"I knew it." Barron squeezed her hand. "Don't worry, I can handle your mama."

Once inside the house, Barron kissed Aveena on the cheek. "How are you doing, Mrs. Young?"

"Well, I was doing fine, until you showed up to take my daughter away from me." Aveena wiped a tear from her eye.

"Mama, you're not losing me. I'm going to visit you all the time."

"That's what you say," Aveena responded. "I know how it is when you first leave home. You want to spend all your time with him and forget about everybody else."

"Mama, that's not going to happen." Tamara squeezed her mother tightly around her waist.

Aveena used a tissue to wipe her nose. "Well, go tell your Daddy you're leaving."

Tamara went down the hall and knocked on her parents' bedroom door. "Daddy, I'm leaving now."

A few minutes later, William came out. He helped Barron load the boxes into the Lexus.

Tamara hugged her mother once more.

"Your sister's going to be mad she didn't get to see you off."

"We talked this morning."

"All right, young lady," William said as he gave his daughter a big bear hug, just like she was still his little girl. "Call us when you get there. Let your Mama know you made it there safely."

"Yes, Daddy."

"Now, son, you take care of my baby. And make sure she don't come back here with no babies, you hear?"

"Yes, sir." Barron shook his hand.

Tamara climbed into the passenger side, while Barron closed the trunk. Finally free from her mother's tight grip, she relished her new found freedom. Aveena could boss her stepfather and Techon around some more, but Tamara didn't have to take it anymore.

She couldn't wait to see what Barron's new apartment looked like. She imagined it to be a two-story townhouse with a spiral staircase, a big kitchen to cook in, a large living room, and a bedroom upstairs. On the way there, Tamara tried her best to stay awake. The excitement of beginning her new life wore off, and now her lack of sleep the night before got the best of her.

Barron tapped her on the shoulder. "We're driving through downtown Orlando."

Tamara opened her eyes, staring in amazement at the tall buildings lit in the night sky. "It's so beautiful."

"I thought you would like it," Barron said as he massaged her shoulder.

Tamara snuggled up against his arm. "I love you, and I can't wait for us to spend the rest of our lives together."

"It's all I've thought about," Barron replied.

When they drove through Landtree Apartments, Tamara immediately liked the complex. She was glad they weren't run down like some they had passed on the way. With the racquetball and tennis courts and a large swimming pool, Tamara knew they had lots of activities to do. She thought about the pink bikini in her suitcase.

"It's in the back, near the laundromat on the second floor." Barron pointed. "Let's get your stuff out."

Tamara picked up her purse and suitcase, while Barron toted a box in his arms. She followed him upstairs, and allowed her eyes to wander around the lushly landscaped grounds with tall oak and palm trees.

"Here we go," Barron said after fumbling with the keys.

"Why do you have all those keys?" Tamara inquired.

"Those are old keys to my parents' house I never gave back." He winked.

Tamara dropped her purse and suitcase in the entryway and inspected his place, which was quite large for a one bedroom, but nothing like she expected.

"This is definitely a bachelor pad," she noted as she

observed the lack of brightness, as black was his color of choice. The leather couch, tables, and entertainment center were all black. The dining room table was black with a glass top, and the bedroom set was a dark cherry wood with a black comforter. "I need to add some color here; make it feminine."

Barron held up his hands. "Awww. Not too much like a woman, now."

Tamara giggled. "No, I'm thinking marigold, sage green, and hint of tangerine for contrast."

"Somebody's been checking out the magazines," Barron smiled, revealing his dimples.

"More like watching HGTV and TLC, especially *Trading Spaces,* where they decorate on a budget." Tamara slid beside him and propped her bare feet on the coffee table. Her toes were painted candy apple red.

"I catch that show from time to time. Unlike the thousand dollars they spend on *Trading Spaces,* you have less than a hundred," Barron said as he turned to a pre-season football game. "Check this out, I can still catch the rest of the game. And Miami's kicking ass, too."

"Who cares about football!" Tamara wrestled him for the remote. She snatched it and jumped up from the couch. "I got it! I got it!"

"Come here." Barron tackled her down to the floor.

Nose to nose, Tamara's eyes were locked with his and she felt a sharp pulsation through her body. She pulled his face to hers and landed a wet kiss on his lips. As his tongue entered, Tamara closed her eyes to savor it. She stripped off her clothes faster than him, down to her red thong.

"Oh, I see." Barron smiled. "You got this red thing going on with the underwear, toes, and fingernails. I like, I like."

Tamara blushed. "I did it this morning. I'm glad you

noticed." She tongued him harder as she rubbed her hands across his muscular abdomen. It was rock hard and so was his dick. She slid his black briefs down past his ankles and tossed them to the side.

Barron massaged his penis as he put on a condom.

On top, she rode him fast.

"Slow down, baby."

Tamara obliged, even though she was eager for him to finish. It hurt so bad.

"Slow down." Barron gripped her hips to steady her. This time he forced himself deeper inside her pussy.

"Ouch!" Tamara jumped up.

Barron grabbed his bouncing penis. "Why did you do that?"

Tamara picked up her clothes and ran in the bathroom. Completely embarrassed, she plopped down on the toilet and buried her face in her hands.

Barron knocked on the door. "What are you doing?"

"It hurts. I can't do it!" She yelled while she used tissue to dry herself.

"Yes, you can." Barron pleaded. "You're the one that initiated it. Now, come out and finish what you started," Barron snapped.

Tamara didn't like the tone Barron used with her. He sounded so angry.

"No. No. No," Tamara chanted like a schoolgirl.

"You don't have to get on top. And I'll do it slow."

Tamara thought it over. She scratched her head. Her friends told her that it always hurt the first couple of times, but the more she did it, the better it would feel. And pretty soon, it would be good.

"And, I'll use KY jelly. Then it won't hurt so much."

And pretty soon, it would be real good. Even though she wanted to believe it to be true, the now part was excruciating.

Sex just didn't seem natural to her, even though Pastor Johnson said it was ordained by God. Well, not fornicating, but sex within a marriage. Even though she wanted to be Barron's wife, she knew that she wouldn't get the privilege if she didn't know how to please her man.

Mustering up the courage, Tamara came out of the bathroom to find Barron fast asleep in bed. Obviously, he decided not to wait. She knew he relieved himself, as he'd done so many times in the past.

Feeling like a failure, Tamara showered and slipped in the bed beside him. She had a busy day ahead of her, as she would need to find a job to help with the bills. Barron made it clear that she wouldn't live there for free.

Switching the channels, she finally settled on watching *The Young and the Restless* on Soap Net. She was eager to find out how Phyllis was handling the pregnancy, while hoping her favorite character would end up with Nick. With Sharon missing, Tamara grew more addicted to the storyline each day. When the show ended, she kissed Barron on the cheek, and lay wide awake for another hour. It seemed strange to sleep in a bed other than her own.

The next day, Tamara drove Barron to work and used his navigation system to locate the address to the temp agency he wrote down for her. For three hours, she completed paperwork, took a typing test, and waited to speak with the job coordinator. Dressed in black slacks and a red silk top, Tamara was sure she'd made a positive impression. The other jobseekers wore jeans and T-shirts, which she thought was just downright tacky. Her mother always told her to dress for success, even if you worked as a janitor cleaning the building. Always look as if you're running it.

Tamara was delighted to receive her first job assignment as a data entry clerk at Info-Tech. She couldn't wait to call her mother and share the good news.

"Mama, I got a job!" Tamara cheered.

"Oh, that's good." Aveena's voice lacked any emotion. "What are you going to do?"

"I'm working for this computer firm called Info-Tech," Tamara said as she read the name off the card.

"That sounds like a high paying position. And you expect me to believe you showed up at this company and they gave you a job?"

Tamara kicked her feet on the coffee table. "I went to this temp agency, and they were so impressed—"

"So, this is temporary?" Aveena interrupted. "I think you should've went down to Burger King or someplace like that, where you won't have to worry about searching for new job every week."

"No, that's the way they do it down here," Tamara explained. "If you want to get hired at a big company, they put you on as temporary, and when you show them you can handle it, they make you permanent. The best part is, I'm going to make seven dollars per hour." Tamara beamed with joy. She knew her mom would be impressed now.

"Well, they're certainly paying a lot of money. What are you going to do?"

"I'm a data entry clerk."

"What is that?"

"I don't know," Tamara said. "I guess I'll find out tomorrow."

"Let me get this right . . ."

Tamara sighed. Now, she wished she'd never called.

"You call me excited about a job, that you don't even know how to do, or what it is. All you know is you're going there tomorrow." Aveena raised her voice, and Tamara knew she was only doing it because her stepfather must have been within earshot. "I think that's foolish, and how are you going to get there?"

"I'll be riding the bus."

"You better not be driving without no driver's license."

"I'm not. Don't worry."

"Because Orlando is a big city, and you don't want to get in no accident. Just wait till you learn your way around there. Then, I'm sure Barron will teach you how to drive."

Tamara rolled her eyes. Her mother didn't learn how to drive a car until she was thirty years old, and didn't think Tamara was old enough to learn either. Walter never agreed, so he taught Tamara the basics and she passed the written portion of the test. She was too embarrassed to tell Barron she didn't have her actual driver's permit, only the restricted. She knew Barron thought of her as a young girl, but she was more than willing to convince him that she was a woman; in more ways than one.

"Mama, I have to go. I don't want to run up this phone bill," Tamara lied, knowing Barron's phone had unlimited long distance. "Tell everyone I said hello, and I'll call you in a few days."

"You're not going to speak with your sister?"

"Mama, I have to go."

"All right. All right. If you say so. I'll call you tomorrow then."

Tamara frowned. "Fine. Bye. I love you."

"I love you, too."

Tamara hung up before her mother thought of anymore to say. Plus, she planned to cook dinner for Barron, before she had to pick him up. Changing the radio from some jazz station Barron liked, she found 102 JAMZ and blasted "I'm Bossy" by Kelis.

She searched on the Internet and located the address of the closest driver's license office. Making an appointment for Friday, she would take Barron to work and hopefully pass the driving test on the first try. She prayed a policeman didn't stop her before then.

Then she got started on dinner. In the freezer, Tamara found frozen mixed vegetables and fish sticks. She boiled the vegetables and put the fish sticks in the oven. Then, she cooked up a pot of mashed potatoes with garlic and butter.

"You did good, girl." Proud of all she'd accomplished in one day, including unpacking all the boxes, Tamara patted herself on the back.

Tamara went in the bedroom and pulled out her black lingerie. She planned to wear it tonight and go all the way with her man. After showering, Tamara rubbed apple-scented lotion on her body. She put on a pair of dark hip huggers and a red tank top. Staring at herself in the mirror, she decided on the brown sandals and headed out the door.

Confident she knew how to drive to the Altamonte Mall, Tamara didn't bother to use the navigation system. Unable to recognize any of the buildings she was passing, she grew more anxious by the minute. She knew the drive was no more than forty minutes away from their apartment, and by now an hour had passed. She figured she must be lost.

I can do this.

After trying to drive and operate the navigation system at the same time, she finally pulled into the Wal-Mart parking lot. She pulled up Macy's, got the address, and followed the voice instructions to get there.

"Did you get lost?" Barron asked. He kissed her on the cheek.

"Yes." Tamara laughed nervously.

"I knew it was either that, or your forgot to pick me up."

"I would never forget you," Tamara said as she noticed a group of women looking in their direction. "Are those women your co-workers?"

"Oh yeah. When you're in retail, you work around a lot of women." Barron waved at them.

They waved back.

Tamara caught a glimpse of them laughing in the rearview mirror. "I can't believe you. They were talking about me, and you waved at them like they're your friends."

Barron burst out in laughter. "You're not serious, are you"?"

Tamara smacked him in his side. "What's so funny?"

"Ohhhh." He doubled over, laughing even harder.

"I'm glad you're amused at my expense," Tamara whispered. She tried to mask her emotions, but her feelings were hurt. "I don't know them, but they obviously want you. And they hate me."

"Hold on for a sec. You are serious." Barron turned to face her. "Wait. Turn over here, I need to stop at the ATM."

Tamara wiped her face as she drove up to Bank of America. She moved over to the passenger side, because she no longer wanted to drive.

Barron withdrew money from his account and returned to the car. Once he placed his wallet in his pocket, he picked up Tamara's small hand. "First of all, you don't ever have to worry about any of those chickenheads on my job. I'm your man, you're my woman, and that's never going to change." He grabbed her hand and kissed it. Then he planted small kisses up her arm all the way up to her face. Last, he kissed her softly on her lips.

When the song "Touch" by Omarion came on, Barron started popping and locking.

"Just back into it and let it touch . . ."

He stopped his hand just an inch short of her face. She pushed it away. He laughed and went back to bopping his head to the music.

That was the Barron she fell in love with, not the serious and business-minded professional he'd become this past year. There were times when Tamara wondered if she would fit in his new world; she felt insecure about her young age, and many of his new friends were so much older than him. Since she was only starting college, she had nothing in common with them.

At moments like this, she was completely comfortable around him. No matter the challenge, Tamara would figure out a way to blend into his life.

"This must be it," Tamara said as she stared at the assignment card once more. She noticed a few people waiting outside the front entrance.

"They must be employees," Barron commented. "Are you ready?"

Tamara felt a slight tingling in her stomach. Now she was hungry! During breakfast, her nerves were so bad she couldn't touch her toast.

"As ready as I'll ever be." Tamara fidgeted with a long strand of hair. "How do I look?" She sat up straight.

"As good as when I checked you out five minutes ago." Barron laughed. "Now, will you get out of here? You're going to make me late for my appointment."

Tamara smacked him a wet one on the lips. "I'll see you tonight."

With her purse and lunch bag in tow, Tamara went around to the side entrance, where she was to report for training. Seated in the room were two other black women.

"You new?" the girl with blonde stacked hair and blue highlights asked. Her black skirt was so short, her panties were visible, and her stomach stuck out from beneath her super-tight, zebra-striped shirt. Her friend didn't look quite as bad, since she wore stretch pants, and her shirt flowed down past her behind. She would've looked decent if she wasn't wearing a pair of clear high heels.

Tamara cleared her throat. "Yeah."

"Well, the lady told us to wait in here," she said as she examined Tamara from head to toe. She felt like she was being inspected by her mother. She knew her pink shirt and khaki slacks made her stand out. She was told the dress code was business casual. Not wear what-you-wore-to-the-club-last-night gear.

Tamara quickly slid into a seat in the far corner and put on her matching pink sweater to try to warm herself.

"Mary Poppins." They both laughed.

"Anywayz . . . back to the story. Girl, I told that bitch if she had one more thing to say I was going to bop her dead in her fucking mouth."

"No, you didn't!"

Tamara sat patiently, trying to block out their conversation, waiting for the woman in the office to rescue her from another episode of Tom Joyner's "It's Your World."

"OK, are you Tamara?" the lady asked.

"Yes, ma'am."

"Oh, please, just call me Marilyn." She glanced down at her clipboard. "Well, we're waiting on one more person to show up."

Tamara silently prayed Marilyn would get started. She was only a few minutes away from walking out the door and catching the bus home, if she had to sit out there a second longer. Not to mention, her stomach was growling nonstop.

"But, it's already seven-thirty, so let's begin."

Tamara breathed a sigh of relief.

Two hours into the training session, they had watched two videos, which the ghetto girls talked and laughed through the entire time. Tamara wished Marilyn would reprimand their outrageous behavior, but she continued to put their new hire packets together.

After the last video ended, they were assigned to a computer to learn how to process invoices from trucking companies. Surprised she'd learned anything from the videos, she picked up the training very quickly.

"Why, you're finished already?" Marilyn asked.

Sheila, the girl with the clear heels, popped her chewing gum. "Damn goody-goody."

They snickered.

Marilyn picked up her headset. "Kimberly, I have just the girl for you. Yes, her score is near perfect." She leaned over Tamara's shoulder. "Only one error. And that's the one we need to change."

Tamara was so proud she'd made a good impression. She hoped she'd go to a nice area and maybe earn more money, too. She could barely contain her excitement.

Marilyn jotted down some notes and then handed them to Tamara. "You're going to work on the second floor of this building. You'll be handling special accounts here at Info-Tech, which usually requires two years experience. But, I'm sure you can handle it." She smiled.

"Thank you," Tamara said with enthusiasm.

"This is where you'll report." She pointed to the room number on the small piece of paper. "I'll be up later to see how you're adjusting and drop off your badge. You'll need it to enter the building and clock in or out."

Tamara nodded. "OK."

Tamara took the elevator to the second floor and a skinny brunette greeted her at the door. "Are you Tamara?"

"Yes."

"I'm your supervisor, Kimberly." Without so much as a handshake, she turned around and quickly strutted down the narrow aisle with rows of gray cubicles. Tamara struggled to keep up with her fast pace. The constant sound of fingers typing on keyboards seemed to echo throughout the floor. Five rows down, Kimberly showed her to her station. "This is where you'll be working. Darla?"

A pimply-faced young woman popped up from another cubicle.

"Yes, Kimberly."

"This is Tamyra."

"No, it's Tamara," Tamara corrected.

Kimberly looked irritated. "Whatever," she said. She eyed Darla. "You're training her."

Darla fidgeted for a few moments.

"Now!" Kimberly shouted.

"All right. I'm going."

"Just get your butt over there!" she shouted from her office down the hall.

Darla stared in Tamara's direction. She nervously giggled. "I'm sorry."

Tamara held up her hands. "It's fine. Really."

When Darla came all the way out from her cubicle, Tamara was shocked. Darla must've weighed well over four hundred pounds. No wonder it took her so long to get up.

"It would be easier if you came over here."

"You're right," Tamara replied as she rolled her chair over.

"So, where are you from?" Darla inquired.

"I'm from Ocala."

"I knew you weren't from around here." Her smile revealed a large gap between her front teeth. "That's near Leesburg, right?"

"It's actually closer to Gainesville."

"I've never been there before, just passed the signs on the Turnpike. Hey, Brandy, you ever been to Ocala?"

"No," Brandy peered from the next cubicle. She was a pretty girl, with long micro-braids. "Hello, Tamara."

Tamara smiled. "Hey. You actually resemble her."

"Who?" she asked.

"The singer, Brandy."

Darla laughed. "She gets that all the time."

"Well, I'm glad another young girl is over here. Everybody else is old and married with children. Do you have any kids?"

"No, and I'm not married, either. I just moved in with my boyfriend, and we plan to get married soon." Tamara glanced at their ring fingers. "Are either one of you married?"

"No," Brandy responded. "But, I have a little girl. Her name is Chyna." She handed Tamara a small picture of her daughter.

"Oh, she's a mini you."

"I know. That's my heart."

"Darla, what about you?" Tamara asked.

Darla waved a ring with a small diamond in front of her. "I'm getting married. My sweetie, Robert, proposed to me last Christmas." She removed a picture hanging on the wall of her cubicle. "Here he is. Isn't he handsome?"

Tamara raised her eyebrows. "Yes, he is." She wondered why this fine, dark-haired man would be engaged to Darla. "How long have you known him?"

"For a year," Darla replied all dreamy eyed. "We met

in a chat room and fell in love. He came down to meet me in person, and then asked me to marry him."

"Where does he live?" Tamara asked as she handed the picture back to Darla.

"He lives in Toronto. After we get married, he's moving here. We're getting a house together." Her chair squeaked as she reached up to put the photo back.

Tamara felt sorry for her, because she knew the only reason that man was marrying her was to get a green card. Although she hadn't known Darla longer than twenty minutes, she knew she was a sweetheart. She hoped this man, Robert, wouldn't break her heart and divorce her as soon as he earned his citizenship.

With all the media frenzy around Terry McMillan and her husband claiming to be gay once he became a citizen, Tamara thought any woman would be suspicious. But Tamara assumed that with the way Darla's behind spread as wide as an elephant, she would be happy for any man to notice her.

Brandy stood up, changing into a pair of strappy gold heels. "It's time for lunch. Tamara, do you want to eat with us?"

"Of course." Tamara grabbed her purse and lunch bag.

"Where are you going with that?" Brandy inquired.

Tamara held up her bag. "To the cafeteria."

Darla laughed. "We're going out to eat. What do you have in there?"

"I have a ham sandwich, and some mashed potatoes that I cooked yesterday."

"Well, we can snack on that later," Brandy said. "As for now, we're going to Wendy's. My treat, since you don't have a paycheck yet."

"Awww, thank you." Tamara hugged her.

"You're welcome."

They rode in Brandy's almost broke-down green Saturn to Wendy's. She was amazed they made it there and back. With no air in the car, it was so hot Tamara could barely stand to sit there. Still, she was happy to have made friends at work. It would make the days more interesting. Darla spent the remainder of the day training Tamara. The work was somewhat different from what she learned that morning. Since she would be handling special accounts at IT, the paperwork was more detailed and took more time to complete. Darla showed patience when Tamara made a mistake and walked her through the steps once more. She reassured Tamara that in a few days, it would be a lot easier.

When her shift ended, Tamara caught two buses before she was dropped off in front of Landtree Place. Once Tamara was settled in from her first day at work, she called her mother. She rattled on about her mean supervisor, how ghetto some of the women were dressed, and how she'd been promoted when she mastered the training demo on the computer.

"Well, that's good," Aveena said in a flat tone. "Are they going to pay you more money?"

"No, but Marilyn said the job I had usually required two years experience. They might make me permanent sooner."

"I guess they would. And you being so naïve went right along with them. You let them give you a higher position with the same pay. You should've stayed down there with the other new hires."

Tamara rolled her eyes. "Mama, this is a good thing. Just wait and see. But the girl, Darla, I'm worried about her. She's in love with this guy who is clearly using her for a green card."

"At least, he's marrying her," Aveena responded. "Which is more than I can say for you."

Trying not to seem bothered by the comment, Tamara

pretended she received another call. "Mama, I'll have to call you back. It's Barron beeping in."

Tamara wished Barron was calling her. He didn't even check to make sure she got home safely.

"Just call me later this week."

Tamara sighed. "That's fine. I'm busy anyway."

Disappointed that she allowed her mother's negative attitude to get to her, Tamara retreated to the bedroom. She wondered when Barron would be coming home. Changing into one of Barron's shirts, she snuggled up under the comforter and fell asleep.

CHAPTER TWO

Tamara woke up early to prepare a big breakfast and enjoy a little time with Barron before he headed out to Macy's. With his business and full-time job, she hardly ever saw him. When she opened the refrigerator, Tamara searched for the groceries she asked him to pick up last night.

Barron kissed her on the back of her neck. "Good morning."

Tamara moved her hair away from her eye. "Where is the stuff I asked you to get?"

"Oh." Barron poured the remaining contents from the orange juice carton. "I was so tired. Man, I forgot."

Tamara slammed the refrigerator door shut.

Barron rubbed her arm. "What's wrong with you?"

Tamara poked out her bottom lip. "Nothing."

"It must be something. You 'round here slamming doors and shit."

Tamara tossed up her hands. "This isn't how I thought it would be."

"Awwww." Barron opened his arms wide. "Come here, baby. Are you feeling neglected?"

Tamara rested her hands on his muscular arms. "Just a little. I'm working until three, then I'm at school until eight o'clock three times a week. I look forward to spending time with you, and then you're not even here."

Barron kissed her softly on the lips. "Now, I told you it would be this way. I'm trying to get my business off the ground. If I'm going to garner any kind of success, I have to commit myself fully to this."

"I know. I didn't realize how much time you would be away from me, that's all." Tamara took a sip from his glass. "I mean, there are times I've heard you coming in early the next morning. I wonder what kind of business you're conducting in the wee hours of the morning."

"Well, you don't have to wonder. Just know that your man is breaking his back to make a beautiful future for us." He licked his full lips.

"Speaking of the future, when am I getting my ring? I keep telling everybody we're engaged, but no one will believe it if I don't have anything on this finger." She waved her empty ring finger in his face.

"Yeah, well, you know how busy I am."

Tamara's head jerked. "No, I don't."

Barron took a deep breath. "We can pick out one this weekend if you want. I'll put a deposit down on the ring you choose."

"Yeah!" Tamara cheered. She played with the hairs on his chest. "I want some."

"You sure?" Barron pulled her in closer. He embraced her tightly and kissed her again. He glanced at the time on the microwave. "Yeah, I can be late if you can."

"A few minutes won't hurt anyone."

Barron lifted up her slender body in his arms and

placed her on the counter top. He slid her pink panties down past her ankles and tossed them on the floor.

Spreading her legs wider, he ravaged his tongue inside her pussy. Tamara held her feet together, as she squeezed tightly. Never, in all her eighteen years, had she experienced anything like this.

"Ooowww!" Feeling as though her vagina would explode, Tamara released her warm juices all over Barron's face. He licked his lips, then inserted his penis inside her.

"Uhhh." He groaned as he wrapped her legs around his neck.

Tamara closed her eyes and tried her best to take it all in.

"Oh no!" she screamed.

"Please, don't stop me." Barron said.

Tamara cleared her throat. "Oh, my God . . . keep going."

Barron plunged deeper. "Are you sure?" His butt muscles tightened each time.

Tamara took a deep breath. "Yes."

Barron lifted her up higher. "I'm a fuck you like you're my woman. But, you have to be able to take it."

"I can take it." Her hair wildly flopped in the air as he pumped her up and down, as if she was riding a horse.

Just when she knew she couldn't take it any longer, Barron grabbed her shoulders and thrust upward so hard, her vaginal lips split.

Tamara screamed, and pushed Barron off of her. Limping in the bathroom, she sat on the toilet and wiped the blood away.

Barron knocked on the door. "Are you OK?"

"Uh-huh." Tamara took a deep breath.

When she went to work, she told Brandy and Darla about the embarrassing moment.

Brandy stuck out her tongue. "Oooh, girl. Your man must have a big dick, because he burst your cherry."

Brandy and Darla laughed and gave each other high-fives.

"What are you talking about?" Tamara asked emphatically.

"It's kind of like . . ." Darla tried to explain, while Brandy continued to crack up. "When you lose your virginity, but you really lose it."

"No." Tamara raised her eyebrows. "We've done it like four times already, but this never happened."

"Well, did you go all the way?" Darla patted Tamara on the leg. "I mean . . . did you let him cum inside you?"

Tamara shrugged. "I'm not sure."

"Nope." Brandy replied. "Girl, there's nothing to be ashamed of. Once your cherry is popped, you can get to pleasing your man like you're supposed to." Brandy stood up and starting dancing real freak-style.

"Will you sit your hot behind down?" Darla pulled on Brandy's arm.

Brandy laughed. "What? I'm just ready to get my dance on. Are you going with us to the Ocean Club tonight?" Brandy asked as she gathered her things to leave. "It's Ladies' Night."

"Free drinks until ten," Darla chimed in.

"No, I can't get in. Remember, I'm only eighteen," Tamara said as she rested her back on her chair. "Plus, I'm going to take advantage of the overtime hours. Barron's birthday is next week, and I want to buy him something nice."

Brandy tossed her hand up. "They can have that overtime. I barely make it to work as is."

"Which explains why your paycheck will be a measly fifty dollars." Darla snickered. "And don't ask for me a loan, either. I have to pay for my wedding gown this week. Which reminds me, have you ladies put your deposit on your bridesmaid's dresses yet?"

"I was going to do that today," Brandy replied.

Darla shook her head. "Yeah, sure you were."

Brandy smiled and wrapped her arm around Darla. "I was. You can ask Tamara. Didn't I tell you at lunch that I was going over to David's Bridal this afternoon?"

"I don't recall," Tamara responded. "But I went Monday. So, you don't have to worry about me." She playfully poked out her tongue in Brandy's direction.

Darla popped Brandy on the arm. "Liar."

"Ouch!"

"Excuse me," Kimberly interrupted. "Either you're working overtime, or you're clocking out for the day. I don't care, but you're disrupting the rest of us who are actually here to work." She looked in Brandy's direction.

Brandy's head jerked. "Why you gotta look at me?"

"Because . . ." Kimberly smiled coyly. "You've used up all of your personal days. The next time you call out, I'm writing you up."

"I can't help it if my baby is sick," Brandy snapped.

Kimberly tightly clutched her clipboard as if it were Brandy's neck. "You've used that excuse long enough, almost as much as your car wouldn't start."

As she went inside her office, Brandy punched her fist into the wall. "I can't stand her!"

"You know she's only trying to upset you," Darla said as she put her hand on Brandy's shoulder. "So, don't let her."

Tamara sat motionless as their interaction played out. To her, it was like watching a scene from the stories. That's what her mother called the soap operas. Ever since the age of seven, Tamara watched *General Hospital* religiously at three o'clock. She would rush home from the bus stop to catch it. Since her mother taped every episode of *Young and the Restless*, followed by *the Bold and the Beautiful*, and lastly *Guiding Light*, Tamara watched them with her mother every night.

Kimberly stuck her head out the door. "Oh, and you may be sneaking out of here early today, but just know that if those piles on your desks aren't gone by Friday, you will be here Saturday."

"I'm going for my second fitting for my dress Saturday. You can't do this." Darla picked up her purse. "You can't make us work overtime, you know."

"I can enforce mandatory overtime if we're close to deadline, and I will get Steven involved if I have to. And as for you, Brandy, you need to work over forty hours in order to get paid time and a half."

Brandy sucked her teeth. "This is between you and Darla. So, keep my name out of it."

"Nevertheless." Kimberly's voice went up an octave. "Plan to be here."

Darla took a deep breath. Then she put her things back on her desk and sat down.

"What are you doing?" Brandy asked.

"I'm staying." Darla logged back onto the computer. "I can't miss my appointment Saturday."

"Are you serious?" Brandy leaned forward. "You know Kimberly's just trying to mess with you. Come on, girl, so we can get to Ladies' Night."

"I guess you're going by yourself tonight," Tamara said as she spun around in her chair.

"Oh, shut up!" Brandy shouted.

"Be quiet!" Kimberly yelled from inside her office. "If I have to come out of my office again, I'm firing someone on the spot."

"And I'm a kick your lily white ass if you do," Brandy mumbled under her breath.

"That is enough. Did you just threaten me?" Kim-

berly asked. "Brandy, I want you to leave, right now."
She pointed toward the elevator.

Brandy held up her hands in surrender. "And I'm not
coming back, either. You don't pay me enough to put up
with this shit!"

"Good. Save me from having to do the paperwork."
Kimberly's eyes scanned the entire second floor. By now
a small crowd had gathered. "Get back to work!"

As if on cue, everyone went back to their cubicles, and
the loud sound of typing resumed.

Darla shook her head. "With Brandy's financial problems, she doesn't need to lose this job."

"What problems?" Tamara turned around to face
Darla. She crossed her arms.

"She's three months behind on her rent and on the
verge of eviction." Darla scratched her head.

"What?" Tamara's eyes grew wide. "How come she's
always coming in here with a brand new outfit or a gold
chain, if she can't pay her rent?"

Darla shrugged. "Beats me. I know she's working
part-time at the jewelry store."

"I can't believe this. And she has a daughter. She does-
n't care that Chyna won't have a place to stay?"

"I guess not," Darla replied. "I'm tired of loaning her
money. And she hasn't paid me back one cent."

"That's a shame."

"I know." Darla opened her file of invoices and started
entering the data on the computer.

Tamara spun around and went back to work. Besides
the fact that Kimberly was a real pain in the neck, Tamara
loved her job. She earned more money than she ever had,
and her friends made it fun. Brandy was so crazy, and
Darla was so sweet. Knowing she didn't have any other
friends or family, the two of them looked out for her, always making sure she had a ride.

If it wasn't for Brandy and Darla, Tamara would die from loneliness and boredom, since Barron was gone all the time. She did her best not to complain. It wasn't easy, and at times she even wondered if she'd made the right decision to move to Orlando. Perhaps her mother was right all along.

Tamara and Darla walked out together. She searched the dimly lit parking lot for Barron's Lexus.

"I thought Barron knew you were getting off late."

Tamara shrugged. "I did too. He should be here by now."

"Well, do you want me to wait?" Darla asked as she hung her purse on her shoulder.

"No, you go ahead. Barron will be pulling up any minute." Tamara tried her best to sound confident, but deep down inside she wasn't.

"Are you sure?"

"Yes, I'm sure." Tamara smiled.

Darla said reluctantly. "Now, you call me if you need me to come back."

"I will."

Tamara waved to Darla, as she sped by in her silver-toned Toyota Matrix.

Leaning along the column for nearly an hour, Tamara checked the time on her watch for the hundredth time. As each minute passed, she became angrier. Finally, she couldn't wait another minute, so she ran to catch the bus.

"Where the hell have you been?" Tamara asked when Barron traipsed into the house. "It is six in the morning, in case you forgot to look at a clock."

"I know what time it is," Barron responded.

Tamara followed him into the bathroom as he ran the shower. "Are you going to answer my question?" She folded her arms.

"I was with Stephan. We spent the night preparing for

our presentation to Dell Construction. This development deal is a million-dollar contract, and we can't mess this up."

Barron stepped into the shower.

"Are we going to talk about this?" Tamara asked.

"Talk about what?"

"I sat on my job waiting for you to pick me up." Tamara's eyes teared up. "I just want you to be honest with me and tell me where you were."

"Look, I told you where I was. Now, if you don't believe me, that's your fucking problem."

"Excuse me!" Tamara snatched the shower curtain away.

"You heard me!" Barron closed the curtain again. "Now, take your little ass back to bed!"

Fuming mad, Tamara climbed back in the bed. She needed to get at least another hour of sleep before going to Info-Tech. She stayed up late waiting for Barron to come home, but she also studied for her first algebra test. With all her worrying, she doubted she remembered any formulas at all. Since she took Algebra I and II in high school, she hoped to earn an "A" in the class.

I know what he's up to.

Tamara didn't believe for one second that Barron spent the whole night with some guy. She might be young, but not stupid. No, he was dipping his stick somewhere else. The idea of that disgusted her all together.

How can he make love to me, and then turn around and do it with somebody else?

Tamara closed her eyes, pretending to be sound asleep when Barron entered the bedroom. Quickly, he dressed in a dark blue suit and ran out. A few seconds later, she heard the front door slam shut.

Tears spilled onto her pillow, as the pain of her

boyfriend cheating on her pierced through her chest. It's not like she should be surprised; she'd heard the rumors as soon as Barron left for college.

Barron's sister, Erika, would blab his business all over school, so it could get back to Tamara. She knew Erika was jealous of their relationship, so she pretended the gossip didn't bother her. She made the grown-up decision not to obsess over what Barron did in Orlando, as long as he treated her like his woman when he was home with her.

Tamara thought she could continue with this charade, until she moved in with him. But, Barron was just too damn bold with his shit; staying out all night and the constant calls on his cell phone. Barron thought he was so slick, keeping the phone on vibrate, and trying to shut it off quicker than the speed of lightning whenever he got a call from someone he didn't want to talk to in her presence.

Not able to sleep, Tamara dragged herself around the apartment until she was dressed in pair of white pants and a pink top. She polished her fingernails and toenails pink, too.

Tamara grabbed her purse and backpack, and then headed for the door. She wished she were back in high school and living with her parents. Her life was so simple then. Now it seemed like it was unraveling, and she wanted to kill herself; swallow a bottle of pills and sleep for all of eternity. But she knew suicide was a sin, and no matter how much she wanted to die, she wanted to at least go to heaven. Each day, she asked God to forgive her for "shacking up" with Barron. That's why she really wanted to get married and stop living in sin.

As Tamara approached the bus stop, she frowned when she noticed the same old dirty men from her apartment complex sitting on the bench. She really needed to save up money to buy a car. Public transportation was a real bitch.

"Hey, pretty thang. You want this seat?" the one with gray hair asked. His smile showed his piano grill.

"No, thank you," Tamara responded with a slight smile. She couldn't stand their smelly asses.

"Well, I was gonna say, if you want this seat, then you gots to give up them goods."

Tamara thought of something smart to say, but before she got a chance—

"Your dried-up dick wouldn't even know what to do with it," a woman's voice from behind commented.

"Jackie, mind your own business."

"Arnold, you better leave this girl alone, before I tell Norma Jean on you."

Tamara turned around to face the older, light-skinned woman with a green scarf on her head. "He's married?" She pointed at the ugliest one.

Jackie shook her head and laughed. "Yeah." She rolled her eyes in their direction. "And if I hear tell they bothering you again, I won't hesitate to tell it."

"I didn't say a thing to her," the other one chimed in.

"Awwww. Shut the hell up, Curtis." Jackie tossed up her hand, causing her key chain to jingle.

Tamara stared down at the ground as she fought to control her laughter. It was good to hear a woman putting a man in his place. She could learn a few things from Ms. Jackie.

CHAPTER THREE

"I can't believe you just showed up at IT today, like nothing happened," Tamara remarked. After witnessing the fight between Brandy and Kimberly, she was stunned to see her sitting in her station the very next day. Apparently, they fought like that all the time, and there was some type of understanding between the two of them.

Brandy hissed. "Kimberly knows she ain't going to let one of her best employees go."

Tamara knew Kimberly was in a desperate situation, and Brandy was taking full advantage by showing up hours late, or sometimes not at all. Since Brandy had her second job, she complained of being tired and often slept in.

With all the piles of invoices surrounding Kimberly's desks, there was no way she would release a trained employee until they were caught up. Each day, at least five more boxes of trucking invoices were delivered. Tamara knew Kimberly was just itching for the day when she could fire Brandy for good. Tamara hoped she would straighten up her act before that happened.

Nevertheless, she was happy to see her friend return and have someone to talk with. It helped the days go by so much faster. With her classes in the evening, her schedule seemed so mundane. The time she spent with Brandy and Darla made her feel she had a real support system; they would really be there for her if she needed them. She thought she'd have that with Barron, but she was wrong.

"You know it's not safe for a young woman to catch the bus around here," Brandy said. "I need to talk to Barron."

"No, you don't either," Tamara replied. "We're barely speaking to each other. Plus, I'm saving my money to buy a car."

"Then, why are you buying him a birthday gift?" she asked as she popped a left turn into the Fashion Square Mall entrance. She drove inside the parking garage and found a space on the second floor.

Tamara opened the car door. She grabbed her purse and backpack. "I'm trying to make a peace offering. I don't like things the way they are right now. I love my man."

If only she could last until her first semester ended. Then she could transfer to Central Florida Community College and move back home. Once she earned her two-year degree, transferring to a state university would be easy.

"I thought Barron was going to buy you a car."

Tamara tossed up her hand. "Please. I'm saving my money to get my own car. I can't rely on him. He's not the same guy I dated when I was in high school."

"And who is?" Brandy twirled her braids between her

fingers. "Seeing as how my baby daddy be tripping all the time, I had to learn it's best to have a Plan B."

"Oh yeah. What's yours?" Tamara inquired.

"I gots me another nigga on the side!" Brandy joked. "That's what."

Tamara shook her head. "No, I'm not trying to go out like that."

"That's because you don't love dick the way I do," Brandy responded as she pointed to the left. "Here's Zales right here. They have some good sales and with my employee discount, I'm a hook you up."

The manager immediately recognized Brandy when they entered. "Hello, Brandy. I have that Figaro in the back for you."

"Thanks, Walter. This is my friend, Tamara. She's interested in a watch for her boyfriend." Brandy grabbed Tamara by both shoulders and pushed her toward the counter.

"That's too bad," Walter said.

"What?" Tamara asked nervously. She hoped with all the overtime hours she put in, she had enough money to afford something.

"That you have a boyfriend." Walter raised his full eyebrows.

Brandy cleared her throat. "Will you get my stuff? Ain't nobody got time for you to be up in here flirting with my friend."

Walter grinned. "Oh, my bad."

Tamara blushed. If she wasn't with Barron, she would at least talk to the man. He was so fine, but a little short; only a few inches taller than her. His butt fit nicely inside his tan dress pants. His clean-shaven face complemented his dark skin. Walter definitely took pride in how he dressed, and he gave the impression he had money.

Walter reappeared with a large white box. "Here you go."

Brandy's eyes lit up as she opened the box. "Hello, baby. Momma missed you." She held the diamond encrusted piece up to her neck and stared in the mirror. "Yes, all eyes will be on me at Grown Folks Night." She hummed a song as she took a few dance steps. "You see anything, Tamara?"

Tamara pointed at two watches inside the glass case. Walter unlocked the case and handed them to her. She held one in each hand, and although she liked them both, she knew she couldn't afford either one. She only brought two hundred dollars with her, but the cheaper of the two cost six hundred.

"And they're both on sale?" Tamara asked.

"The platinum one is twenty-five percent off." Walter took out a watch with a black leather band. "Here is one that's a little cheaper."

Tamara turned up her nose. "No, I'm sure he would like one of these. Barron owns his own business, and he likes to impress his clients."

"Oh, I see." Walter smiled. "Well, did Brandy tell you that I might be able to help you out?"

"No, she didn't."

"Tamara wouldn't be interested in a second job," Brandy said quickly. "She goes to college. Just ring me up."

Walter smiled. "Oh, so you're a college girl? Well, I could definitely use you."

Tamara moved in closer. "What are you talking about? Yes, I'm interested in a hook-up."

Brandy waved her manicured hand. "Not this kind. How much do I owe you?"

"Sixty-five."

Tamara was stunned. The price tag read well over a thousand dollars.

While Brandy paid for her necklace, Tamara placed the watches back on the glass counter. She really wanted to give Barron a nice gift, but settled on treating him to dinner at Houston's instead.

When they left the mall, Tamara turned to face her friend. "Now, how is it you were able to buy that necklace for about ninety percent off? Barron works at Macy's, and I know for a fact employee discounts aren't that much."

"Will you just drop it? You wouldn't do it anyway. So, leave me to my business."

Tamara folded her arms. "No, because I really want to get that watch for Barron, and if you can help me, then you need to do that."

"No." Brandy started the car and backed out.

"Would you please just tell me?" Tamara pleaded. "I already know it's something illegal, but I'll do anything at this point."

"Damn!" Brandy took a deep breath. "I'm a tell you, but this stays between you and me. And you better not share this information with anyone."

"I promise."

"Well, he hooks me up and I hook him up."

"With what?" Tamara asked.

"You know."

Tamara racked her brain for an answer. "No, I don't."

"What do women have to work with?" she hinted.

Tamara shrugged. "Are you going to tell me?"

"Pussy."

Tamara frowned. "You're having sex with that man in there for a discount?"

"You don't have to put it like that. But, yeah."

Tamara leaned back in her seat. "Drive the car."

"See, I knew you couldn't handle it!" Brandy shouted.

"That's just nasty," Tamara said. "How could you sell yourself short like that? And for a gold chain. I had more respect for you."

Brandy slammed on her brakes. "Get the fuck out of my car!"

Tamara's eyes grew wide. "What?"

Brandy pushed her in the arm. "You heard me, bitch. Get out!"

"What are you doing?" Tamara asked. She couldn't believe her own friend turned on her all of a sudden.

"You have no muthafucking right to judge me. Now, get your country bumpkin ass out of my car."

Tamara grabbed her stuff and got out. She stood there in complete shock as Brandy sped off. Close to tears, Tamara's eyes scanned the parking lot to get a hold of her surroundings. She'd never been to this mall before, so she had no idea where she was or how to get home.

As she headed in the direction of the bus stop, she heard a car horn.

It was the green Saturn.

Without any hesitation, Tamara got in.

"I'm sorry." Brandy said. "I just don't need anyone passing judgment on me."

"I understand."

"Anyway, if you want the watch, I'll get it for you."

"Do you mind?" she asked. "I'm trying to get some sleep." Tamara pulled the covers over her eyes as the light from the room tried to invade her sleep.

"I'm trying to get dressed for work," Barron responded as he turned the light back off. "And you need to ask me nicely. I paid for that bed you're sleeping on."

"Whatever!" Tamara mumbled and shifted her thoughts back on the man from her dream. Although she was at-

tracted to him, she never got to see his face. All she remembered was he was fine like P. Diddy.

Tamara cringed when she heard the shower come on
and thought of how wet the floor would be, since he refused to pull the shower liner inside the tub. Having
stayed up half the night cleaning the apartment from top
to bottom, she hoped her efforts weren't a waste of time.
Knowing her mother was a neat freak, the sight of dust
would make her sick.

When she heard his cell phone vibrating on the
dresser, she decided to see who was calling. The letters
M.P. showed up, but before she could answer it, the call
went to voice mail.

Damn.

Scrolling through his numbers, she located the phone
number and wrote it down. She would call back at a later
time and see if it was one of his women. Why else would
he have the initials, instead of the first name? He thought
he was so damn slick.

When the shower cut off, Tamara dove back in the bed
and pulled the covers over her head.

"I see you cleaned up the place," Barron said as he
walked in with a towel wrapped around his waist.

It wasn't hard to notice, since Tamara rarely cleaned or
dusted. Balancing her work, school, and study schedule
hardly left any time to keep the apartment tidy.

"Yep," Tamara said dryly. She slid her arm underneath
her pillow for more support.

Barron was so sloppy, leaving his dirty clothes all over
the place. One more piece of evidence that he no longer
had any respect for her.

"I'll be pulling in an all-nighter at Stephan's again."
Barron kissed her on the lips. "I love you."

Tamara sucked her teeth. "Sure you do."

Barron rose from the bed and rapped the words:

"I'm trying to be sweet,
but you act so cold.
I know I'm a good man,
and this shit is getting old."

Not wanting to cause trouble for herself, Tamara forced a fake smile. "I'm sorry, baby. Have a good day."

"Now, that's more like it." Barron sucked on her neck.

Tamara pretended she was turned on. "You better stop before you start something you can't finish."

Barron stood up to reveal a hard on. "Never, baby." He licked his lips.

To keep her man satisfied, Tamara obliged to a quickie. But in her mind, she wondered who M.P. was. Every time Barron came home in the middle of the night, or early the next morning, Tamara wanted to hide behind the door and hit him in the head with a frying pan. It was to the point where she couldn't even stand to look at his lying ass; he wasn't even cute to her anymore. In all her life, Tamara never imagined she would possess these kinds of negative emotions toward the man she professed to love so much.

Tamara waited until Barron was gone before she jumped out of bed.

"I'm calling to confirm our lunch date," Tamara said. She tossed his boxer briefs and T-shirt in the hamper.

"Look at you." Darla laughed. "You're so formal, calling to confirm."

Tamara giggled. "I know. I can't wait for you to meet my mom." Having Darla around would certainly help her mother's visit go smoother, since Aveena was usually nice to Tamara around other people. Tamara really wasn't in the mood for her mother's constant criticism.

"I called Brandy last night, and she promised me she would try her best to make it."

"And did you ask her to be on time?" Darla asked.

"Oh, please!" Tamara took out a frying pan to scramble some eggs. "I know better than to ask for miracles."

"Yeah, I know." Darla replied. "Hey, did you get the watch for Barron?"

"That's right, I didn't get to tell you about our little jewelry shopping excursion." Tamara dumped the eggs on a plate and sprinkled cheese on top. "We were so busy at work yesterday."

"I'm just glad we got all those invoices finished. I didn't want to go in for the third Saturday in a row."

"Tell me about it. Even though I could use the overtime pay, since I'm saving up to buy my own car."

"Oh really, so Barron's not buying you one after all?" Darla teased.

"Why do you and Brandy keep giving me a hard time about that?" Tamara snapped. "I admit I was stupid to believe everything my man told me in the beginning." She gathered her dishes and plunged her hands in the warm, soapy water. Then, she inspected a plate to make sure it was clean.

"We've all done it." Darla tried to sound supportive.

"Back to the subject." Tamara cleared her throat. "You're not going to believe the discount Brandy's getting at that jewelry store."

"How much?"

"She's practically getting that shit for free in exchange for sexual favors." Tamara knew she was wrong for sharing this with Darla after she promised Brandy she wouldn't tell anyone, but she couldn't keep it to herself. She knew Darla wouldn't say anything.

"Are you serious?" Darla took a deep breath. "I knew she couldn't afford all that stuff, but I can't believe she would sink so low to get it."

"I know. That's the same thing I said to her."

"You did?" Darla asked. "What did she say?"

Tamara sucked her teeth. "She kicked me out of her car. Cursed me out, and told me to get the fuck out."

"No!"

"Yes, she did." Tamara turned off the kitchen light and headed toward her bedroom. She picked up a bottle of red polish from her dresser.

"I can't believe it!"

"I was so mad at her. But she came back." Tamara sat on the bed and applied polish to her nails.

"How long did she take to come back?"

"About five minutes." Tamara responded. "So, you know I won't be accepting any rides from her any-more?"

Darla laughed, and then snorted. "I don't blame you."

"Well, you better not say anything," Tamara threatened.

"Of course not. I won't repeat it. I'm just like blown away by all of this."

"Yeah, I know." Tamara hopped on the floor. With cotton between her toes, she waddled her way to the bathroom to wash her hands. "And, she's always bragging about her diamond bracelet this and platinum chain that. And to think I was actually jealous of her."

"Not me."

Tamara silently laughed. As big as Darla's behind was, Tamara knew Darla was jealous of everybody at IT. There was only one other lady that fat, but now even Julie was on a diet. Tamara overheard her when she stopped by Darla's cubicle to tell her how she was losing all the weight. Julie handed her a pamphlet on Nutri-System, and explained how she ordered the meals she wanted and they shipped them directly to her home at the beginning of the week.

Darla sounded like she was interested, but after lunch Tamara passed by her cubicle and spotted the pamphlet in the garbage. Tamara fished it out and put it in Darla's desk.

"Anyway, I better get out of this bed if I'm going to make it on time for lunch."

"You better!" Tamara shouted as she said good-bye and hung up.

She tossed the cell phone on the counter as she continued to wash the sink full of dishes. She was anxious about her mother's arrival, but Tamara looked forward to her mother meeting her best friends. She hoped her mother would realize Tamara was all grown-up and responsibly handling her business.

With a newly furnished apartment, a good job, decent grades in all her classes, and close friends, Tamara felt she'd accomplished a lot in two months. Now her relationship with Barron was a different matter, and she hoped he'd stay gone all day. That way, she didn't have to worry about her mother being able to sense the rift between them. It wouldn't take a rocket scientist to figure out they weren't getting along.

Tamara still loved Barron, and she wished they loved each other the way they used to when Barron would come home to visit and they spent every second together. Those were the good old days, but now, he barely looked her way.

As Tamara slipped her red Tommy Hilfiger shirt over her head, she caught a glimpse of herself in the mirror. She'd finally gained some weight. She slid her denim mini-skirt up to her waist, and admired her full calves. Growing up, she was teased for being so skinny. The next time she went home, she couldn't wait to see how Randy and them would respond when they saw her shapely figure. Yep, she was definitely looking like a real woman now.

The ringing phone interrupted her thoughts.

"Hello."

"I don't know where I'm going!" Aveena shouted. Tamara moved the phone away from her ear. She never understood why people always shouted into the receivers of their cell phones.

"These directions you gave me are no good."

"Yes, they are, Mama," Tamara said. "Where are you?"

"I'm sitting at this light at Curry Ford Road."

Tamara took a deep breath. "Just come down two more lights to Michigan. Then you're going to make a right, then drive past two more lights, until you reach—"

"I can't remember all of that!" Aveena yelled. "Now, you're just going to have to stay on the phone with me until I get there."

"Yes, Mama." Tamara rolled her eyes. She inspected every room in her apartment to make sure they were perfect to her mother's standard. While she directed her mother to her apartment, she straightened the pillows on the couch and plopped down.

Fifteen minutes later, Tamara ran downstairs to greet her mother and sister.

Techon was the first to get out of the car. Dressed in gaucho pants and a sleeveless brown top, Techon's figure was far more shapely than Tamara's. Having different fathers, Techon took more after Walter's side of the family.

"Hey, Tee." Tamara welcomed her with her a huge embrace. "I've missed you."

"Ditto!" Techon leaned closer toward Tamara's ear. "Mama been tripping the whole way here. So, just ignore her."

"Oh, God." Tamara nodded as she tried to control her nervousness.

"Are you going to help me with these care packages or what?" Aveena asked as she leaned on the car door. She looked exhausted.

"Hey, Mama." Tamara hugged her mother around the neck and kissed her softly on the cheek. "Thanks for coming."

Aveena wiped her forehead. "It sure is hot down here." She pointed at the back seat. "I got you some things. I know you probably done ran out of most of the stuff you brought with you. I also picked up bras and panties. And then they had a sale on all the toiletries at the Dollar General."

"For real?" Tamara blushed. She grabbed one box while Techon grabbed the other.

As they entered the apartment, Tamara placed the box on the living room floor and instructed her sister to do the same.

"Let me show you around first," Tamara said with enthusiasm. She couldn't believe her mother was actually in her apartment. It only took a minute to show the living room, kitchen, bathroom, and bedroom.

"Good Lord." Aveena shook her head. "I can't believe Barron is paying eight hundred dollars a month to live in this tiny place. We only pay four hundred dollars for a whole house."

"The cost of living is expensive in Orlando," Tamara responded.

"It seems outrageous to me." Aveena frowned. "Now, I know that boy could've found a cheaper place than this. And probably nicer!"

"Mama, stop!" Techon yelled. She grabbed her mother's hands. Even though she was the youngest, she always acted like she was Aveena's sister, rather than her daughter. "Remember, we are here to support Tamara. Aren't you glad to see her?"

"I'm here, ain't I?" Aveena asked. "And don't be raising your voice at me. If I didn't know any better, I would have back-handed you for talking to me like that."

"Yes, Mama." Techon sat down on the couch and picked up an old copy of *Essence* on the end table. "Oh, I've been meaning to read this one with Monique on the cover. I heard she was in an open marriage."

Her mother followed her lead and sat on the adjacent love seat. "You young people. Now, what kind of nonsense is an open marriage?"

"I don't know." Techon flipped through the pages until she found the cover story. "But I'm about to find out."

"And speaking of marriage, where is the ring you supposed to have on your finger?" Aveena stared at Tamara's ring finger.

"I don't have it yet," Tamara replied as she clasped both hands together. "Mama, you want some Kool-Aid? I made your favorite, orange."

"Uh-huh." Aveena leaned back on the love seat. "Don't be trying to change the subject. Me and your daddy said we would give you six months, and if that don't boy don't put no ring on your finger, then you coming home."

"I remember." Tamara handed her mother a glass. Then she sat down beside her. "Barron's just busy, that's all."

Aveena quickly emptied the glass and handed it to Tamara. "It sure is hot out there."

Tamara held a blank stare; she couldn't believe her mother drank the Kool-Aid down that fast. Techon hid her head behind the magazine and giggled softly.

Tamara went to refill the glass. "Well, I already called my friends. Brandy and Darla are going to meet us at the Cheesecake Factory. Wait until you see this place, it is so gorgeous. And the food is absolutely delicious."

"Uh-huh." Aveena fumbled through her purse. "It sounds expensive."

"Mama, I'm paying. So, you don't have to worry about that."

Aveena smiled. "Let's go."

Upon their return from lunch and sightseeing, Tamara caught a glimpse of Barron's Lexus in the parking lot. She had prayed he wouldn't be there when they returned. That's why she never bothered to tell him her mother was coming to town.

"Well, look a there. Isn't that Barron's car?" Aveena asked.

"Yes, Mama," Tamara responded as she sank lower in her seat. Barron told her he was going to be out all night. Just her luck! She hoped she wouldn't get caught in all the lies she told her mother.

When they entered, Barron was propped up on the couch watching television. He stood up and scratched his chin. "Hello, Mrs. Young." He gave her a hug and kiss on the cheek.

"Hello, Darren," Aveena said.

"Mama, it's Barron!" Techon yelled.

Aveena shot her daughter a mean glare. "I know the boy's name."

Barron chuckled. "Hey, little sister. How you doing?"

"I'm fine." Techon playfully punched Barron in the stomach.

"Hey, baby. How are you?" Barron kissed Tamara on the lips.

"I'm good." Tamara showed a slight grin.

Barron smiled. "Looks like somebody brought me back something from my favorite restaurant."

"It was Mama's idea," Tamara said. She handed him the take-home bag.

"Well, good looking out, Mrs. Young." Barron placed

the box on the table. "I'm hungry, too." He dug his plastic fork in and ate a mouthful of pasta. "Thanks, baby."

Tamara rested her hand on his shoulder. "No problem."

"We're not going to hold you." Aveena put her purse on the couch. "I'm going to use your bathroom, and then we're getting back on the road."

"Oh, no." Tamara tried to sound disappointed. She wasn't sure how much longer she could keep up this charade. "I thought you would stay longer."

"Now, you know I got to get home to get William's dinner on the table." Aveena closed the bathroom door.

Tamara gave Techon one last hug. "I'll call you tonight."

"You know I'll have a lot to tell you."

"Don't remind me." Tamara laughed.

Aveena came out of the bathroom. "See, your daddy is a hard working *husband*." She cut her eyes in Barron's direction and gritted her teeth. "And husbands deserve a home-cooked meal every single night."

Barron held up his fork. "I couldn't agree with you more."

Aveena straightened her ruffled silk blouse. "Techon, let's be on our way."

Tamara went outside to see her family off.

"Well, Mama, I'll see you later," Tamara said as she followed her mother down the steps.

Once they were to the car, Aveena grabbed her daughter's hand. "Tamara, I don't like this situation one bit. I'm praying you're going to see the light and come on home."

Tamara shook her head. "I'm staying here with Barron. I love him."

"Something tells me you're going to regret this."

"Mama, I can't believe you." Tamara pointed at her

chest. "You've been telling me ever since I been with Barron that I was acting grown and needed to get out of your house when I graduate."

Aveena's voice went up. "That's because you didn't have no business having sexual relations."

"Well, I'm a grown woman now," Tamara cried. "And now you want to tell me to come home."

"Mama, let Tamara be happy with the man she loves," Techon chimed in. "The same way you love Daddy."

Aveena put her hand on her hip. Her hair blew with the wind. "I don't condone this. Something ain't right about that boy. Just like you said, you're grown. I'll just have to leave it in God's hands." Aveena turned around. "Techon, let's go."

Tamara stood there and watched her mother's car drive away. It seemed as if no matter how much she tried, her mother would never accept her relationship with Barron. She wished she could change the way she felt about him, but it wasn't that easy for her. She'd been with Barron for four years, he was her first, and she wanted him to be her last. How was Barron any different than any other man? No matter who she was with, there would be problems. She might as well be with a man she loved more than life itself.

As the wind picked up, Tamara dried the tears from her face, and went back inside. She barely closed the door before she felt herself being pushed into the wall.

"What the hell was that about?" Barron asked as he balled up his fists as if he was ready to do more damage.

"Barron!" Tamara leaned on the wall to support herself. "What are you doing?"

Barron put his hands around Tamara's neck and threw her to the floor. "If you ever disrespect me in my home again, I'll whoop your ass."

"OK." Tamara's voice was barely above a whisper.

Barron grunted. Then, he released his tight grip from around her neck.

Tamara turned to her side to catch her breath. She knew if she made a sound, he would come back and finish what he started.

"Silly-ass bitch!" Barron spit on her face, and then stormed out the front door.

Tamara lay on the floor balled up in the fetal position. First the argument with her mother, and now this had to happen.

Once she was sure Barron wasn't coming back, Tamara swallowed four Aleve pills and climbed into the bed. Her back ached so badly, she stacked up three pillows in a random order and leaned on them. Unable to calm her nerves, Tamara turned on the television. Finding today's episode of *Young and the Restless*, she slid down to get comfortable.

Tamara's thoughts drifted back to the first time Barron physically attacked her. It was a month before her graduation, and she had stayed out all night with her friends. Barron had told her he wouldn't make it to her graduation, due to prior commitments. Tamara was so angry that she decided to make the most of her big night. She hit all the parties, which was something she'd never done before.

All of her weekends were spent with Barron, and when he stayed in Orlando he ordered her to stay home. Being extremely jealous, Barron worried she would cheat on him. Tamara knew there wasn't another man for her, so she obeyed his wishes. Her parents expressed their concern about her commitment to Barron, but she always shrugged it off. She blamed her time spent home on her commitment to academics.

Tamara remembered that night like it had just happened. She was driving her mother's car down Main

Street when she saw a set of headlights flash behind her. Tamara recognized Barron's car and turned right, as soon as she crossed the railroad tracks.

Barron walked up and opened the car door. "Where you been?" He furrowed his eyebrows close together.

"I was out with—"

"With that nigga?" he asked.

In an instant, Tamara felt a blow to her jaw. Before she fully realized Barron hit her, he slammed her face into the steering wheel.

Tamara wiped the blood from her nose. She touched her teeth to make sure they were all there.

"I'm sorry." Tamara stumbled over her words. "Please . . . I'm sorry . . . I'm—"

"Are you sorry for disobeying me!" he shouted in her ear so loudly, she felt her inner eardrum rattle.

Her voice was shaky. "Yeeesss."

"Now, take your silly ass home!" Barron ordered.

"OK!" Tamara cried out. "I really am sorry."

Tamara called her parents to tell them she was staying at her friend Fatima's house. She knew if William saw her come home with her face messed up, he would try to kill Barron. Her mother never liked Barron, so she would use this incident as a reason to forbid her from seeing him. Tamara couldn't let that happen. After all, if she had stayed home, this wouldn't have happened anyway.

When Tamara arrived at Fatima's house, her friend helped her clean up her face. In the morning, the ice pack had reduced most of the swelling. Tamara applied two layers of foundation, which Fatima swiped from her mother's make-up case, to hide the bruising on her forehead and her left cheek.

Barron called the next day and apologized for his angry outburst. He blamed it all on stress. Having her heart set on marrying the man, she believed all of his lies.

She couldn't see past the fact that Barron was every bit of his abusive and cheating father.

It was known all over town that Cheryl Michaels was an abused woman. Many had publicly witnessed Thomas beat his wife. Even though her children, Barron and Erika, were always well behaved, Tamara's mother never believed for a second that Barron wasn't capable of inflicting the same type of abuse toward a woman. From day one, Aveena opposed the idea of her daughter dating an older boy, and then when she learned it was Barron, she outright objected. On the other hand, Tamara's stepfather wasn't as quick to judge her boyfriend the way her mom did. That was the only reason why the relationship continued, because her stepfather persuaded Aveena to give Barron a chance.

Tamara was fast asleep when Barron snuggled up next to her in bed. He ran his fingers along her arm.

"Are you up?" Barron asked in a low whisper.

Tamara squinted, trying not to let the light shine in. "I was sleeping."

"Oh." Barron kissed her on the back of the neck. "I'm sorry about what happened earlier. You know how I get sometimes."

"Uh-huh."

"Well . . ."

Tamara pulled her pillow closer to her face. She couldn't believe after what Barron did, he actually wanted to have sex with her. Was he crazy?

Barron ran his hands down her leg and stuck his fingers inside her panties. As much as she wanted him to stop, Tamara wasn't quite sure about his mental state. In her mind, she went and back and forth on whether or not to give him some.

It would only last five minutes.

I just won't get on top.

I'll lie there and hope he finishes even faster than that. But then it might hurt.

You gon' give that nigga some after the way he almost kicked your ass to sleep?

You better, or else he might whoop on your ass some more.

Not wanting to make Barron mad, Tamara turned over and slipped off her panties. Staring up at the ceiling, her stomach turned sour as Barron spread her legs wide to enter her. Silently, she prayed she wouldn't have to put up with him much longer.

CHAPTER FOUR

"So, what are you going to say?" Darla asked.

"I don't know," Tamara said. "I haven't thought it out that far yet."

Darla pulled her car up in front of Macy's.

"Do you want me to wait for you?"

Tamara glanced at the clock on the dashboard. "No, he should be getting off in a few minutes."

Darla took in a deep breath.

Tamara noticed Darla's hands shaking and grabbed both of them. She looked at Darla. "I will be fine."

"Now you will. When I think about what would've happened if you hadn't gone to see my doctor. Women develop serious infections after stuff like that. I read about a similar situation in *Cosmo*."

Tamara's jaws opened wide. "No way!"

Dr. Harris told her this sort of thing was common, but Tamara thought she only said that to make her feel better.

"Only, the lady didn't go to the doctor immediately. She noticed an awful smell but kept using more feminine products to get rid of it. You know, all those sprays, powders, and even the stuff to treat yeast infections."

Tamara nodded. "Yeah, like in the commercials."

"Right, once I got a yeast infection, and I took Monistat." Darla ran her fingers through her thick hair. "And, it didn't work. So, I tried a different brand. By the time—"

"Damn, Darla! Will you get back to the story?" Tamara took a deep breath to calm her nerves. "I don't have all day. Barron's coming out that door any minute."

They were waiting at the side door, where store employees enter and exit. At a short distance, Barron's car sat in the parking lot right next to another Lexus, only a different color.

Darla laughed. "Right, I'm sorry. Sometimes, I completely go off on another tangent, and then before I realize it—"

"You're doing it again," Tamara said as she pretended to pull her hair out in frustration.

"Oh yeah. Where was I?"

While Darla rambled on, Tamara completely tuned her out. Then she spotted Barron holding the door open for another woman. "There he is. I'll call you later."

As she approached them, Tamara tugged on her black mini-skirt. Barron was deep in conversation, and had his back facing her.

"Expect something sweet," Barron said.

The woman cleared her throat.

Barron turned around. "Tamara. What are you doing here?" He kissed her on the cheek.

"I wanted to surprise you," Tamara said, eyeing the woman at the same time.

Barron smiled. "Well, you did." He put his hands in his pockets. "Oh, I'm sorry. Tamara, this is the Assistant Store Manager, Monica Porter."

Tamara blushed. "Hello, Mrs. Porter. I've heard so many nice things about you. It's a pleasure to meet you." She stuck out her hand.

Monica looked Tamara up and down. "It's nice to finally meet you. How do you like Orlando?"

"It's different, but I'm getting used to it," Tamara responded.

"That's good." Monica gazed into Barron's eyes and smiled. "I'll see you later."

Barron waved.

This time Tamara was the one clearing her throat. "What a bitch!" she said, once she was sure Monica wasn't within earshot.

Barron raised his eyebrow. "What's your problem?"

"I'm sorry, but, did you see how nice I was to your boss? And that fat cow was totally rude to me."

"That's just how she comes off to people who don't know her."

Tamara twisted her lips. "Yeah, right."

Barron laughed. "I'm serious. She's actually all right."

Tamara eyed Monica as she got into her car. The whole thing made sense now. The letters M.P. showed up on his cell phone that morning when Barron was in the shower. "Oh, she's the one with the Lexus."

"Yep."

Tamara made a mental note about this Monica chick, but for now, she had something far more pressing to discuss with her man. "Aren't you curious as to how I got here?" Tamara asked.

"Yes. But, I wanted to wait until we got in the car."

To keep up appearances, Barron acted like the perfect gentleman when he opened the car door for Tamara.

"So, what's up?" Barron asked as he drove down to Palm Springs Drive and made a right turn. "What the fuck are you doing rolling up on me at my job?"

Tamara cocked her head to the side. "What do you mean? Is Macy's off limits or something?"

"Hell yeah!" Barron shouted. "You could've waited until I came home."

Tamara sucked her teeth. "Nigga, please! Your ass don't half make it in, until it's early in the damn morning."

Barron grunted. "At least I come home."

Tamara tossed up her hands. "Oh . . . right. I should be so thankful for that."

"Yeah, you should."

Tamara shook her head. "At this point, you can stay gone for all I care. I went to the doctor today."

Barron gripped the steering wheel firmly. "I know you're not telling me you're pregnant."

Tamara loosened her seat belt, so she could turn to face him. "And why would I be pregnant, when you use condoms?"

"Exactly!" Barron stared straight ahead, refusing to make eye contact.

"Maybe it's because you knew you left a condom inside of me when you fucked me the other night!"

Barron scratched his head. "Hold up. I pulled that condom out. I didn't do that shit!"

"Now, why you gotta lie, Barron?" Tamara closed her eyes. "Just be a man and admit you did it."

"Fuck no!" Barron threw up his arm and punched Tamara in the jaw.

Feeling the strength of his blow, Tamara put her hand up to her face. All of a sudden, her body temperature shot up and her blood felt like it was about to boil.

"I'm sick of this!" Tamara screamed at the top of her lungs.

Before she realized what she was doing, Tamara undid

her seat belt and lunged toward Barron. Unable to control the steering wheel, Barron shoved her back into the seat.

"Sit your silly ass down!"

Tamara went to attack his face again, but when he held up his fist, she backed down from the fight. She climbed into the backseat for her own protection.

"Don't even bother to take me home." Tamara wiped the tears from her face. "I'm going to my friend's apartment."

"You think I'm going to take my woman to another nigga's apartment," Barron said as he licked his lips. "No, you taking your ass home. And you better not leave." Barron wiped his forehead. "Think I'm playing, try to walk out that door and see what I do."

Tamara slumped down. Staring out the window, she wished she were somebody else. She felt like such a fool for getting herself in this predicament.

Back at the apartment, the situation only worsened when Barron used a pair of handcuffs to attach her wrists to the headboard of their bed. Tamara remembered him pulling those handcuffs out once while they were having sex. He wanted to tie her to the headboard as some sort of kinky foreplay, but Tamara outright refused to do it and hoped Barron wouldn't get mad at her for doing so. Instead, he laughed it off as a joke, and put the handcuffs underneath the bed. She never saw them again.

"Barron, you can't do this," Tamara pleaded. "I'm supposed to be at the wedding rehearsal tomorrow. They're going to be looking for me."

Barron licked his lips as he stood at the foot of the bed. "Right. Well, I'll let you go tomorrow."

Tamara pulled her hands, and wrestled to get free. "Please, let me go. I promise I'll be good."

Barron laughed as he kneeled over her body and stroked his penis. He moved closer to her ear. "I love to hear you beg. Do it some more."

No matter what she said, she knew Barron wouldn't do what she asked.

"I'm a get you for disrespecting me," Barron said. "All I ask you to do is clean up and cook a meal every once in awhile. And your dumb ass can't even do that right."

When he forced her to suck his dick, Tamara wanted to bite the tip off. Afraid he would beat her senseless, she quickly changed her mind. She did as she was told, no matter how much she felt like an actress in a porno flick.

"I pay the bills around here, so I'm the king of this muthafucking castle." Barron worked his penis deeper inside her mouth, then pulled it out and squirted his sperm all over her face and neck.

Tamara gagged and threw up all over herself.

"Barron, please stop doing this." Tamara coughed so hard, her throat burned. "Why are you making me sick like this? I think I need to go to the hospital." The smell of her puke made her vomit again.

"I'm sorry about that." Barron grabbed a towel and wiped off her face. Then he fucked her so hard, she thought her insides would explode. Being sore and her skin practically raw, she cried when he entered her again. The last humiliating offense was his peeing all over her body like she was that young girl in the R. Kelly sex tape. At this point, she prayed he wouldn't free her, because she was liable to catch a case for murder in the first degree. For the entire night, Barron had his way with her and demanded her to pretend to love it.

When morning came, Tamara woke up and realized her hands were free. Barron was nowhere in sight. While running a hot bath, Tamara dragged two suitcases from the closet. Every few minutes, she took a break and massaged her aching back. Packing her things would be easy, as she tossed her underwear and tops in one suitcase and her jeans and work clothes in the other. Three garbage bags later, she had everything she ever brought packed and ready to go.

After she generously poured strawberry fragrance oil in the tub, she sat down in the hot water.

Tamara remembered Barron's threats from last night and called her stepfather's cell phone.

"Hey, baby girl." He sounded excited to hear from her.

Tamara found comfort in his voice. She hoped he wouldn't ask too many questions, since she called his cell instead of calling the house.

"Hey, Daddy," Tamara's throat swelled up. "I need you to come get me." She struggled to hold her composure.

"I'll be there in a couple hours," William said.

"Thanks, Daddy."

"It's going to be all right. Don't you worry."

It was like music to her ears. Tamara debated whether to report the incident to the police. She knew Barron needed to pay for what he did to her. He was so out of control, he was liable to hurt himself or someone else for that matter. Knowing he had a problem, Tamara really didn't want that on her conscience.

Once Tamara was seated in her tub, she rested her back on the rubber pad.

I wish I could drown in this bathtub. Then Barron would feel so bad for doing this to me.

She tried so hard to fight back the tears, but her emotions were all over the place by now. Studying the clock on the wall, Tamara hoped her stepfather hadn't told her mother that he was coming to pick her up. If he did, she knew her mother would insist on riding with him, and she would have to listen to a full-blown lecture on the way back. It was bad enough, Tamara had to admit her parents were right about her moving in with Barron, but she could do without the "I told you so's" for at least the next few hours. She'd already done enough chastising herself to last a lifetime.

Tamara sank lower into the warm water, forcing some of it to spill on the floor. She sat straight up when she remembered Darla's wedding rehearsal was that evening. Knowing there was no way she could back out of a wedding, Tamara called her father back. She explained she had a really bad week at school. She felt like giving up and returning home. With clarity, she understood that wasn't the right decision to make, since she was nearing the end of her first semester.

William agreed with her and shared some words of advice before they hung up the phone.

Before she put the cordless back on the base, it rang again.

Looking at the Caller ID, Tamara answered. "Hey, girl."

"I'm sorry I'm late. I didn't get in from work until doggone one in the morning. Anyways, I'm on my way."

"What are you talking about?" Tamara racked her brain to figure out why Brandy was coming to pick her up.

"The bridal brunch is in less than half an hour," Brandy said. "I should be at your place within the next two minutes."

Rubbing her lower back, Tamara walked into the kitchen to search for pain pills. "I don't think I'm going to make it. I need you to pick me up afterward."

"Oh, you're going!" Brandy exclaimed. "If I can drag my butt out of bed, you can too. I'm in front of your building now."

"I'm not even dressed, and I packed up all my stuff."

"Whaaat?" Brandy sang.

"Yes, I'm leaving Barron for good," Tamara sniffled as she spoke each word.

"It's about damn time! Are you moving in with me?" Brandy asked.

Tamara knew Brandy needed a roommate, since she kicked her baby daddy, Phillip, out of her place. "I don't have anywhere else to go. Are you still needing someone to help out with the rent?"

"Hell yeah!" Brandy shouted.

They hung up, and Brandy knocked on the door less than a minute later. She helped Tamara put her belongings in the car, and Brandy drove like a lunatic through the slow weekend traffic along Colonial Road.

Tamara tried not to think about Barron, but it was hard not to. She couldn't get over the way he snapped on her like that.

"Whose idea was it to hold a brunch at Denny's?" Brandy asked sarcastically.

"Why are you tripping?" Tamara folded her arms. "It's not like you're paying for it."

"It's just tacky, that's all," Brandy said as she shut off her car's ignition. She applied more lipstick to her heart-shaped lips.

Tamara took her cue and smoothed another layer of heavy foundation on her face.

"You still can't cover up that one bruise on your chin," Brandy remarked.

"I know." Tamara rested her elbow on the window. "I'm so embarrassed. I don't even want to show my face in there."

"Here, let me help you." Brandy dug around in her Coach bag and pulled out a small brown tube. She squirted a few drops on her index finger. "You have to use concealer first, then apply the foundation," she said as she smoothed it on Tamara's face.

Tamara flinched from the pain. "It still hurts."

"I know," Brandy replied. "The boyfriend I had before Phillip used to kick my ass on a daily basis. That nigga used to tear my ass up!"

"When did you figure out it was happening to me?" Tamara asked.

"Let me see . . . probably after that first week you started at IT."

Tamara cast her eyes down at the floor. "I'm so ashamed. I don't know how why I put myself in this situation."

Brandy put her hand on her shoulder. "Hey, you don't have anything to be ashamed of. Barron is the one who should be ashamed. That's why you need to get away from his punk ass and stay gone."

Tamara pulled her hair in front of her face in order to hide the bruise. "I know. I should've done it a long time ago."

"Please," Brandy hissed. "You act like you've been with the man for twenty years or something. Girl, you did good to leave like you did. Most women in your situation would've stayed right there."

"You're probably right."

"I know I am." Brandy smiled. "Well, we're already late. Are you ready, or do you need a few more minutes?"

"You think my face looks OK?" Tamara checked herself in the mirror.

"I think you look beautiful."

Tamara hugged Brandy. "Thank you," she said as she fought back the tears.

Once inside, Tamara sat beside the bride and held Darla's nervous hands, just as she promised she would.

Refusing to allow her horrific night to affect her friend's special day, Tamara sucked it up as Brandy instructed her to, and pretended her life was perfect. That was the least she could do for Darla, who had been so supportive of her from the very first day they met at IT.

Hardly eating anything on her plate, Tamara chose to double up on her hosting duties and allow Brandy the opportunity to rest and engage in conversation with the other bridesmaids. The matron of honor was Darla's sister, Janet, and the other bridesmaid now lived out of town. Brandy had a lot of interviewing to do, and she made full use of what Tamara felt were her wasted journalism skills.

Tamara shook her head. She knew it was just another way for Brandy to get all up in their business, and then laugh about how stupid they all were at work on Monday.

"And then, can you believe that little flower girl, Charity, is Darla's niece?" Brandy asked as she stood over Tamara's cubicle.

"I know, I never knew she was black."

"Supposedly, she's mixed folk, but you know the rule."

"It only takes one drop to make you black," Tamara chimed in. "It could've been my imagination, but it seemed like every time I passed by Darla's sister, she was holding on to her man."

Brandy put her hand to her mouth. "I noticed the same thing. Ole' girl didn't want us getting too close to the brotha."

"Yes!"

"And girl, I couldn't believe how Darla's brother got his no-dancing behind out there when Missy Elliott's song was playing." Brandy doubled over in laughter. "And what about Grandma?"

Tamara's gum flew out of her mouth and landed on her keyboard. "She was getting her freak on."

"That shit was so funny!" Brandy screamed.

"I'm not amused," Kimberly said as she put her hands on her hips.

Brandy tried her best to stop laughing. "We were just talking about Darla's wedding." She took a deep breath. "What happened to you?"

"I was way too busy," Kimberly responded.

"Awwww . . . I'm sorry," Brandy said. "We missed you not being there."

Tamara cut her eyes at Brandy, knowing full well she was lying through her teeth.

"Well, I wanted to be there to support my best employee, but I'm sure you could guess I was working." Kimberly tapped her foot on the carpet. "Which is something I can't say for you two!"

Tamara held up her hands. "Hold on, Kimberly. I'm sitting over here at my desk minding my own business." She pointed at Brandy. "She's the one who keeps coming over here to gossip."

Brandy's jaw fell open. "Now, Tamara, you know you keep calling me over here."

Kimberly stomped her foot. "Nevertheless, I don't care who's at fault here. Get back to your stations and save the chatter for your lunch hour!"

"All right . . . all right . . . you don't have to work yourself up into a frenzy." Brandy eased past her supervisor and back into her work area.

"That's more like it." Kimberly rubbed her hands together. "And I do expect you to stay late for the next couple of days to make up for Darla's absence."

"Kimberly, we promised you we would," Tamara said in a reassuring tone. "Right, Brandy"?"

Brandy rolled her beady eyes. "Uh-huh."

Kimberly flashed a fake smile. "Good."

Tamara went back to entering invoices while listening to Chris Brown on her iPod, but her mind stayed on Barron. Three whole days had passed since she last saw or heard from him. Feeling like her life was hanging in the balance; Tamara needed to be sure she made the right decision.

The whole condom situation could've been handled better. That's what set Barron off in the first place. Tamara knew he wasn't good at handling his anger, but yet she continued to mess with him anyway. She pushed that man to the point where he completely lost it. Thinking back on it, Tamara realized the situation was all her fault. Now seeing how mad Barron could really get, she would just make sure she kept him happy all the time. That was the role of a wife, and if she wanted to be one, she needed to stop acting so silly.

Barron's life was stressful enough with his business and a full-time job. One thing she learned from her mother was that when a man came home from work, the woman's job was to provide a sanctuary for him.

You have to give the man a reason to come home, or else he's going to find it in the arms of another willing woman.

Maybe if she cooked a meal every night, and followed it with some lovemaking, her man wouldn't stay out until the wee hours of the morning. The more she thought about it, the more her life began to make complete sense. Tamara hoped it wasn't too late to turn things around.

Tamara tapped Brandy, who was bopping her head to loud music, on the shoulder.

"What's up?" she asked as she removed her headphones.

"I'm going to the bathroom," Tamara said as she

headed down the aisle toward the elevators. Outside the building, she flipped open her cell and dialed Barron's number. His voicemail immediately came on. She waited for the prompt to end, and then spoke.

"Hey, baby. I don't know where you are, but you need to call me. I love you." Tamara figured Barron was working with Stephan, checking out some properties to purchase. Against Kimberly's rules, she left the ringer on and hid her cell phone behind a picture of the two of them on the desk. Every ten minutes, Tamara checked the phone to make sure it was working properly. She wanted to answer if Barron bothered to call her back. When Tamara's shift ended, she frowned at the realization Barron hadn't called.

"Are you ready to get out of this hell hole?" Brandy asked as she slung her Gucci purse strap onto her shoulder.

"No, I'm staying late," Tamara responded as she continued to type. "I thought you were staying too."

"Hell no!" Brandy cocked her head to one side. "I have to get to my second job. I make way more money there than I do here."

"Well, I guess you better get going." Tamara didn't want to hear any more of Brandy's bragging about all the money she was making, especially, since Tamara didn't see any trace of it in her apartment.

Brandy owned a few nice things, like a large plasma television and a stereo system, both of which she purchased through Aaron's Rent to Own. Despite a closet full of clothes and drawers filled with jewelry, Brandy's apartment was one nasty mess. It smelled so funky, Tamara wanted to vomit every time she entered. Once she was there for a while, she didn't feel so sick. But that's what scared her; the fact that she was getting used to the filth and odor.

The only cleaning going on in Brandy's apartment was done by Tamara, and there were people there messing it up all the time. All of Brandy's neighbors smoked weed and drank beer just like she did. Brandy actually supplied most of it, even though she didn't bother to keep enough food in the refrigerator to feed her own daughter.

"Oh, and my brother is going to stay with us for a few nights."

Tamara's fingers froze on the keyboard. "And why will Chuck be staying with us?"

"Reesy kicked him out again." Brandy laughed. "His dumb ass still keep messing with her."

Tamara took a deep breath as she felt her stomach tighten into a knot. "How long will he be there?"

"Only for a few days." Brandy turned up her lips. "Damn, you act like it's your apartment or something. Only my name is on that muthafucking lease. So, remember that."

Tamara leaned back in her seat. "Oh, I was just asking." She smiled, and then continued. "Don't mind me, girl."

Brandy scratched her neck. "See you later."

Tamara waved. Shaking her head, she wiped the tears away from her face as she felt the burden of her troubles weigh on her heavily. She wanted to go home so badly, even if she wasn't sure if Barron wanted her there. There was no way she could stay at Brandy's nasty apartment another night, especially with her perverted brother there. Although Chuck claimed he wanted to become a preacher one day, Tamara couldn't help but think nobody in their right mind would listen to a word he said. He seemed high most of the time, constantly blaming "the man" for all of his troubles.

Tamara decided to take advantage of the fact that

Brandy was working at the jewelry store by packing her stuff and getting the hell out of there. She called Barron, and this time he answered. Tamara saw it as a sign from God.

"Hey, are you going to pick me up?" Tamara asked. She didn't have enough time for small talk.

"Where you at?"

"I'm staying at Brandy's."

"OK, give me a few hours, though."

Tamara took a deep breath. "No, if you want me back, then you will come and get me now. I'm not playing."

Barron chuckled. "I'm coming."

Tamara paced across the living room floor, her shoes sticking to the damp brown carpet. Staring out of the window, she hoped she could make a clean getaway before Brandy or her brother and his gangsta crew showed up.

Half an hour later, Barron rang the doorbell. With all of her bags packed and suitcases at the door, Tamara quickly loaded them into Barron's car. She was so happy to see him. Once inside the car, she greeted him with a wet kiss on the lips.

Barron licked his lips. "Damn!"

Tamara blushed. "I missed you."

"You need to leave more often, if it's going to be like this when you come home."

Tamara ran her hands along the side of his face. "Baby, I'm never leaving you again. I can promise everyday I will be nothing but good to you."

Barron raised his eyebrows and nodded. "And I won't ever put my hands on you again. If I do, then you need to have the cops throw my ass in jail."

"Let's not ruin our night together even thinking about it. I missed you so much."

Barron kissed Tamara, and as she invited his tongue

inside, she massaged his penis through his jeans until it stiffened.

As Barron drove them home, Tamara was certain she knew what it took to keep her man satisfied. Staying with Brandy, she saw first-hand how bad it could be if she had to live on her own with what little money she earned. Barron afforded her a comfortable lifestyle, and she was determined not to let it go.

CHAPTER FIVE

"I'm late."

Darla glanced down at her watch, then at the clock on the wall at Wendy's. "No, we still have fifteen minutes left."

"No." Tamara looked to see if anyone from IT was within earshot. "I'm late."

"Oh, shit!" Brandy covered her mouth and laughed.

"Oh, my God," Darla said.

Tamara smiled nervously. "I know."

"What did Barron say?" Darla inquired as she shoved a handful of fries into her mouth.

"Nothing. I haven't told him. I don't even know if I am. I'm only guessing."

Brandy stood up. "Then we need to find out." She started digging in her purse. "I know I have one of them things in here.

Tamara held up her hands. "What thing?"

"A test."

Darla almost choked on a fry. "Tell me you're joking."

Brandy emptied all of the contents on the table. "Aha! I knew I had it. Come on, let's go."

"Where?" Tamara asked emphatically.

"To the restroom. Where else are you going to pee?"

All three of them scurried to bathroom. Darla and Brandy waited outside of the stall, while Tamara followed the instructions on the box.

"What does it say?" Darla asked.

"She's taking a long time, so she must be pregnant." Brandy chimed in.

Tamara studied the white stick one more time, before she bravely opened the door. "Two stripes."

Darla and Brandy jumped up and down screaming in unison.

"I'm gonna be a Godmother," Brandy sang.

"I'll be Aunt Darla."

Tamara's straight face showed her disappointment. "It's too bad I won't be having this baby." She rubbed her stomach.

"What?" Brandy asked. "Girl, you're tripping."

"There's no way I'm going to tell Barron about this baby." Tamara stared at her reflection in the mirror. "And we've been getting along so well. This is just the kind of thing to throw a man over the edge."

"Not exactly." Darla put her arm around Tamara. "Maybe you need to think about this. Sleep on it tonight."

"No." Tamara closed her eyes. "I'm getting rid of it. I can't let my parents down like this. They believe in me. I'll be the first in my family to graduate from college."

"If you want to go through with it, I know a place you can go," Brandy said. "But, like Darla, I think you should think long and hard about it first."

"Forget it. Brandy, call, and make the appointment. I'm taking care of this before the week is out."

After putting in a ten-hour day at IT, Tamara got off the bus with the two old dirty men behind her. After Ms. Jackie gave them a piece of her mind and threatened to tell their wives about their perverted behavior, they no longer bothered Tamara. Instead, they acted like the most perfect gentlemen and even allowed her to sit on the bench all by herself.

Tamara leaned forward, gripping her side as she struggled to walk to her apartment. The pain became so severe it prevented her from taking another step.

"Are you all right, young lady?"

"Yes, I think so." Tamara tried to stand up, but she felt her muscles tighten and she fell to the ground.

"No, I think you need our help," Arnold said as lifted Tamara's lifeless body off the ground.

"Pick up her purse there, Curtis," Arnold ordered.

"I'm going to take you to my place. My wife, Norma Jean is a nurse. She will know what to do."

Once at the dirty, now turned good, man's apartment, Tamara saw Norma Jean for the first time, and she was nothing like she expected; a small, petite-framed woman whose pale complexion would make one question whether she was white or black. Her long curly hair was pulled back in a ponytail, which fell down to the middle of her back. Surely she was mixed folk, Tamara reasoned.

After Norma Jean took her temperature, she discovered Tamara was running a fever and gave her two Tylenol to take. "It's safe for pregnant women, and it will help with the pain."

Tamara's eyes grew wide. "How did you know?"

Norma Jean smiled, revealing her perfect teeth. "A woman knows these things. You're probably five weeks."

"Yes," Tamara said. "At least I think so."

"Does anybody else know? I don't see a ring, so I'm assuming you're not married."

Tamara cast her eyes down at the floor. "No. I live with my boyfriend."

"Oh." Norma Jean held open her arms.

Norma Jean embraced Tamara in a motherly way. Tamara didn't realize how much she missed her own mother until that very second. The enormous burden she carried was too much for her, and she cried in Norma Jean's arms.

"It's going to be fine, baby," she said as she ran her hands through Tamara's hair.

Tamara's emotions were finally released from her body and she felt better. So much so that she wanted to sleep. "I'm really tired." Tamara mumbled as her eyes fell shut.

When she awakened, it was morning and she was in a bed with a flowered comforter she didn't recognize.

"Well, it's about time you woke up," Norma Jean said as she stood at the foot of the bed.

"I'm so sorry." Tamara put her hand on her forehead. "I'm sorry."

"Don't apologize." Norma Jean waved her hand. "Since our daughter went off to college, this bed hasn't been slept in."

Tamara yawned. "What time is it?"

"Close to eleven."

Tamara sat straight up. "Oh no. Barron is going to kill me."

Norma Jean sat down beside her. "Don't you worry. Arnold left a note on your door, and that young fella has already been here."

Tamara was now more worried than ever. She wondered what information Norma Jean shared with Barron. She closed her eyes and said a quiet prayer.

"He's waiting at your apartment for me to call him. He didn't want to wake you." Norma Jean left the room.

Tamara could barely hear what was said. All she knew was that what seemed like a minute later, someone knocked on the door. By this time, she had slipped on her shoes and found her way to the living room. Barron was seated on the couch drinking a cup of coffee. He put the cup on the table and gave Tamara a heartfelt embrace.

"I called your job and told them you wouldn't be there for the rest of the week," Barron said.

Tamara shook her head. "No, I have to go. We're behind, plus I need the overtime."

"If you're going to be a mother, you have to learn how to put that baby first," Norma Jean snapped. "Before everything else."

"That's right," Barron chimed in.

Tamara was stunned. Now she knew her nightmare had begun, as she had planned to get rid of the baby by the end of the week. She didn't even want Barron included in her decision, as her motives were completely selfish. With all the attention Barron was showering on her, she wasn't sure how he would respond to her pregnancy. Either he would be more attentive or become distant again, and she just didn't want to take the risk of him becoming distant again.

Not to mention, a baby would ruin her own plans of finishing college. She wanted to earn her business degree and move into management at IT. She wasn't sure how a baby would fit into all of that.

"Well, you two take a seat. Me and Arnold are going to cook you up a hearty breakfast. You young people probably haven't had grits and sausage in a long time."

Barron looked at Tamara and laughed. "She tries to cook, but, no, we haven't."

Tamara stared down at the table in front of them. The

mere mention of food made her stomach growl. She couldn't wait to eat. It wasn't long before the four of them were seated at the large wooden table with a spread of grits, eggs, sausage, potatoes, and pancakes.

After Arnold blessed the table, Barron and Tamara tore into their plates like it was the Last Supper. Tamara couldn't believe she was enjoying a meal with the dirty old man from the bus stop. After they finished eating, Norma Jean handed Barron a casserole dish for dinner that night.

"You get some rest, young lady," Norma Jean ordered. "And I'll stop by to check on you in the morning."

Tamara hugged her. "Thank you so much."

Barron hugged Norma Jean too. "Yes, we appreciate it."

Hand in hand, Barron and Tamara walked downstairs to the car. Once home, Barron made sure Tamara was comfortable before he headed to work.

As Tamara lay in bed, she felt ridiculous for her decision to have an abortion. It was obvious that Barron was thrilled about the baby. Maybe it was just what their relationship needed.

When Barron entered the apartment that evening, Tamara was in the kitchen warming the casserole in the oven.

"Hey, baby. I'm so glad to see you home." She kissed her man.

"Glad to be home," Barron said as he inhaled the aroma from the kitchen. "Did you get some rest?"

"Uh-huh." Tamara set the dishes on the glass dinette table. "Dinner will be ready in about ten minutes. I just have to mix the salad."

"Good. I'm starving." Barron loosened his tie as he went in the bedroom to change into something comfortable.

Tamara happily went back to check on the spinach, cheese, and ham casserole. Now her life was exactly as she planned it.

"You sit here." Tamara pointed at the head of the table.

"Thank you." Barron patted her on the butt as she walked away. "Look at you, Suzy Homemaker."

Tamara laughed as she finished dicing the tomatoes on the cutting board and put them into the mixing bowl

"Did you get enough rest today?" Barron asked as he poured himself a glass of wine.

"Sure did. I was so lazy." She drizzled salad dressing on the mixture, and then tossed a handful of croutons on top.

"I never thought I would hear myself say this, but you need to get used to it."

"I know." Tamara placed the salad on the table. "It feels weird to do absolutely nothing all day." She used the tongs to serve the mixed salad on each plate. "But then, I like the idea of being home to take care of my man."

At first, she was upset that Barron found out she was pregnant. She'd already made up her mind to get rid of the baby. Now, she had fresh revelation:

If I play my cards right, I can keep this baby thing going for a few more weeks.

Tamara paced back and forth in her living room. She couldn't wait for Brandy to get there. It was after midnight, and Barron hadn't called to say he was coming home late. It hadn't even been a week, and already he was messing up.

When the phone rang, she saw Brandy's number show up on the Caller ID. She grabbed her purse and ran out the door.

"Did you bring it?" Tamara asked when she got in.

"Hell yeah!" Brandy yelled. "We're going to kick some ass tonight!"

Brandy laughed. Tamara's nerves suddenly made her want to vomit. She'd never gone this far to confront someone in her life. And now, she was about to show up at a woman's house unannounced. The whole situation could get very ugly, and Tamara wasn't so sure she could go through with the scheme she and Brandy cooked up together.

Tamara scratched her shoulder. "I don't know about this. I think I'm feeling sick."

"I know you're not trying to back out," Brandy pulled her braids back. "Especially when you got me out of my bed this time of night."

Tamara looked at, Chyna sleeping peacefully on the back seat. "Turn the car around. I'm sorry, Brandy."

"Oh, hell no!" Brandy popped her neck. "We're going to see if that punk-ass nigga is over there. And then if you want to leave, we can. But at least you will know the truth instead of speculating."

Tamara adjusted her seat belt as she sank lower in the seat. "You're right. I need to know." Tamara rested her hand on her stomach.

"I think these are the apartments. What you say the name is again?"

Tamara studied the Yahoo! directions carefully. Once she had Monica's full name, she did a Zaba search and got her address. She planned to use it if Barron stayed out all night again. "Windward Apartments," she said as she pointed. "It's the next one."

"OK," Brandy made a sharp left. "Let's go bust his ass!"

Tamara held her stomach tighter. She didn't think she could keep her fluids down. Closing her eyes, she said a quick prayer.

"What's the apartment number?" Brandy asked as she drove around the corner slowly.

"It's 212," Tamara responded.

"Yeah, there it go right there!" Brandy pointed at two Lexus cars parked side by side.

Tamara took a deep breath.

Brandy pumped her fist in the air as she blocked the cars in. "You want me to go up there? And if that bitch try to act crazy, I'm a have to kick her ass!"

"Mommy!" Chyna screamed.

"Oh, no." Tamara shook her head. "We woke up Chyna. I don't want her to see this."

Brandy sucked her teeth. "No, she need to see this."

Tamara didn't understand Brandy's logic, but, then again, she wasn't a mother. Not yet anyway.

Brandy grabbed her key chain, which had pepper spray attached, and jumped out of the car. She ran upstairs and knocked on the door.

Tamara grabbed her chest, as it felt like it would explode any second.

"I want my Mommy," Chyna whined.

Tamara climbed in the backseat with her.

"It's gonna be all right," she said while running her hand down Chyna's back.

"Open this muthafucking door!"

"Who the hell are you?" a woman's voice shouted.

Tamara heard Brandy and who she guessed was Monica arguing back and forth. Then she saw him with her own two eyes. Barron Michaels. Before she realized what she was doing, Tamara flew up the stairs and jumped on Barron's back.

He lost his balance, and they tumbled down the concrete steps. Tamara's back hit the ground, totally knocking the wind out of her.

"Oh my God!" Brandy shouted as she ran to Tamara's aid.

Barron stumbled to get up, and then caught his balance. "Tamara, are you all right?" he asked as he grabbed her arm.

"Get your muthafucking hands off of her!" Brandy yelled in a hoarse voice. She tried to clear her throat. "This is all your fault. Tamara, get up."

Tamara rubbed her stomach. "I'm . . . I'm hurting."

"Let me help you," Barron said as he lifted Tamara up in his arms. "I'm taking her to the hospital."

"No, you ain't either," Brandy responded.

"Look here, you ghetto-ass bitch." Barron nudged Brandy with his shoulder. "Get the fuck out of my way, before I knock your ass down!"

"Let him see about his sister," Monica said adamantly.

"His sister!" Brandy pointed at Tamara. "That's his girlfriend."

Monica put her hand to her chest. "What!"

"Yeah! Did I muthafucking stutter?" Brandy clapped her hands like she was retarded.

"Barron, you got some explaining to do, because you told me Tamara was your sister."

Barron held up his hand. "Monica, go back inside. I'll explain all this later. Just let me take care of this."

"Yeah, take your big ass back in the house," Brandy ordered. "What the fuck you got to do with this anyway?" Brandy asked as she cocked her head to one side.

"I'm his wife," Monica replied. "So, I have everything to do with this."

Tamara gasped. "How could you?"

"I'm sorry," Barron repeated over and over. He laid Tamara down in the backseat. "I was going to tell you, but then you told me you was pregnant."

"So, wait one damn minute." Monica's face turned red. "Tamara isn't the half sister your mother knows nothing about?"

Monica pushed Barron in the back, and he fell on Tamara's stomach.

Tamara pushed him off of her. "No, I'm his girlfriend! We've been together since high school." Tamara struggled to sit up.

"Tamara, I can explain all this."

"No, I don't want to be here with you." Tamara pushed him away.

"Would you just—"

"No! Brandy, help me."

"Let go of her," Brandy said, this time in a calm voice. "I'll get her checked out. You stay here with your wife."

Brandy helped Tamara out of Barron's car and into her own.

"Just take me to your place," Tamara said as Brandy drove away. She saw the image of Barron and Monica arguing with each other from the rearview mirror. Upset and hurt at the way Barron failed her, Tamara closed her eyes. The next time she opened them, she was lying on the couch at Brandy's apartment.

"Oh, look who rose from the dead." Brandy pulled on Tamara's ponytail. "Girl, don't even ask me what happened last night. I was so tore up."

"You were drunk?" Tamara asked. No wonder she acted like such a fool.

"Yeah, you didn't know my sister was a lush," Chuck said as he opened the refrigerator.

"Shut up." Brandy punched him in the back when he passed by her.

"Where's Chyna?" Tamara rubbed her forehead. "I felt so bad for her. She was really scared."

Brandy tossed up her hand. "That girl is fine. Anyway,

Barron called here all night. I was nice to him. I told him you were sleeping."

"I can't believe he cares," Tamara said. The shock of learning Barron and Monica were married just about killed her. She couldn't understand how Barron could be married to another woman and living with her at the same time. It made no sense.

Tamara picked up her cell phone. She called Barron and left a message on his voicemail. "We need to talk." Then she hung up. With all the questions running around in her head, she needed answers even if she had to see him again.

Barron called her back, and they arranged a meeting at their apartment for seven o'clock. Tamara swallowed a handful of Tylenol PM and waited for the medicine to do its duty. Within an hour, she was fast asleep on the couch.

Brandy tapped her on the shoulder. "Hey, it's time for you to meet that snake."

"Are you driving me?" Tamara asked through sleepy eyes.

"I'm a drop you off. Then I have to go to work."

"All right," Tamara replied. "I plan on staying at Barron's place until I can get one of my own."

"Well, you're always welcome here." Brandy grabbed her Dooney & Burke and keys off the counter. "Let's go."

On the way to her apartment, Tamara thought of a million questions to ask. She wanted to narrow them down to only a few, so she dug around in her purse for a piece of paper and a pen. She settled on a blank deposit slip. She wanted to know everything about him and Monica. Especially, why he would marry Monica instead of her? And why they would hide it?

"Yeah, Barron used me. Now, it's time for payback." As her plan unfolded in her mind, Tamara grew anxious and ready to handle her business right then. "Take me to Bank of America. I'm so glad they're open on Saturday. I have a withdrawal to make."

Tamara strolled inside and withdrew every single dime of money; what she had saved to buy a car and Barron's initial ten thousand dollar deposit when they first opened the account. She got on the cell phone and dialed the number to Macy's.

"Yes, is the store manager available?" Tamara asked.

"What are you doing?" Brandy inquired.

Tamara held her hand over the mouthpiece while she waited. "Payback is a mutha."

"May I speak with Mrs. Porter's superior? I'm her sister, Wendy." Tamara smiled. "Yes, I'll hold."

"Helen Daveen speaking."

"Hello, Mrs. Daveen. I'm calling to let you know my sister, Monica, won't be in to work for the next couple of days."

"I see. Well, I wonder why Monica didn't call me herself."

"She asked me to. Her husband was in a car accident, and he's been seriously injured."

Mrs. Daveen cleared her throat. "Excuse me. Did you say her husband?"

"Oh, I forgot." Tamara chuckled. "Monica didn't want to make an announcement until everything was cleared up. You know, with the whole manager situation."

"What do you mean?" she asked.

"With the whole manager-employee situation, she wanted to wait until Barron Michaels found another job first," Tamara explained. Then she went on to give more information about their marriage.

"I see. Well, you tell Monica to call me as soon as she gets a free moment."

"I sure will. And thanks for understanding." Tamara hung up.

"Girl!" Brandy shouted. "You handled that shit like a pro. I have taught you very well."

They gave each other hi-five's.

"I know." Tamara laughed. "I wasn't even nervous."

"You weren't?" Brandy asked. "You did your thang, girl."

Tamara flipped her ponytail to one side. "Thank you, darling. And you know what?"

"What?"

"Turn this car around. I don't want to see that lying-ass dog. All he's going to tell me are a whole bunch of lies, and I don't need that. I don't care about him. I'm through."

"Well, you want to hang out at the mall with me?" Brandy asked as she popped a U-turn and headed back to Semoran Boulevard.

"Yeah. Maybe, Walter will give me a job. I need the money."

"Well, at least you have enough to buy a car."

Tamara held her purse close to her chest. "Yes, I do.

The next day, Tamara drove out of the dealership in a red Toyota Corolla. Then she went to her apartment, prayed Barron wasn't there, which he wasn't, and proceeded to pack all of her belongings for the last time. Tamara hoped she'd never have to see Barron again.

CHAPTER SIX

"I just don't understand why you didn't tell us what was going on," Aveena said.

"I didn't want you to worry," Tamara replied. "And besides, I have my own car now. Darla arranged for me to get an apartment in her complex, with a huge discount on the rent. I'm moving in this weekend. You should be proud of me."

"I am proud of you."

Tamara grinned. "Thanks, Mama."

"You're a very smart young lady. And, when Techon moves down there, you two can split the rent."

Tamara sat up straight in her seat. "Techon never mentioned that to me, but I would love for her to move to Orlando."

"Yeah, she told me and your father she wants to go to UCF, which surprised me." Aveena coughed. "She's always talked about going to Tallahassee."

"I'll call her tonight. Well, I have to get back to work. My break is up."

"I need to go anyway. William will be home soon. I'm

a come down this weekend. Help you get some furniture for your new place."

Tamara smiled. "You are, Ma? Thank you."

"This is what I always wanted for you. I never lived on my own, just moved from my mother's house in to live with your father when we got married. When I had you girls, I wanted you to experience being independent. Not needing a man to take care of you."

"I know. I just couldn't see that when I was so in love with Barron."

"A mother knows when something is not good for her child. And that Barron always seemed like a snake to me. Too much like his father."

"You were right." Tamara wiped a tear from her eye.

"What's wrong?" Darla asked when Tamara hung up her cell phone.

"Nothing. My mom told me she was proud of me, that's all." Tamara's eyes teared up once more.

"Awwww." Darla puckered her lips. "Come here, baby." She wrapped her arms around Tamara's neck.

"Thanks. You've been a good friend to me."

"Oh, please," Darla hissed. "I do love you. I'll do anything for you."

"I know. I don't even understand how you treated me so nice when you first met me, while Barron has practically known me all his life and he treated me worse than a dog on the street."

"Men can be selfish," Darla said. "Well, not all men."

Tamara wiped her face with a Kleenex. "That's true. Robert is such a wonderful man. I hope I can find someone like him one day."

"We all want a fine-ass like Robert," Brandy said as she returned to her cubicle. "You upset about the procedure, Tamara?"

"What procedure?" Darla asked.

"I'm having the abortion Wednesday," Tamara responded in a whisper.

"Are you serious?"

"As Fred Sanford having a heart attack," Brandy commented. "And don't try to talk her out of it either."

Darla leaned back in her chair, causing it to squeak loudly.

Brandy burst out laughing. "Damn, your ass needs to go on a diet!"

"Brandy, shut up," Tamara said, then laughed too.

Darla poked out her lips. "I know. But, you're supposed to be my friends. Quit laughing."

"I'm sorry," Brandy put her hand on her mouth, and then continued, "But that chair almost screamed!"

Tamara put her head on her desk. "Brandy, quit it. You're killing me."

"Too funny."

"Forget you two." Darla turned around and started her work.

"I'm sorry," Brandy said.

"I don't forgive you," Darla responded.

"I'll buy you lunch tomorrow."

"Awwww," Tamara chimed in. "Isn't that sweet?"

"I forgive you."

As Tamara and her girlfriends walked out of IT that evening, she caught a glimpse of Barron's car in the parking lot.

"Oh, shit!" Brandy whispered. "Ain't that your boy?"

"Yeah," Tamara said. She straightened her white shirt as they moved closer to him.

"You silly-ass girl, you didn't have to get me fired on my job." Barron pointed at her nose.

"All right, now. Don't start nothing." Brandy stood in between Barron and Tamara.

"I'm going to get security," Darla said.

"No, I'm not going to do anything." Barron held up his hands. "I just want you to give me back my money."

Tamara poked out her chest. "As far as I'm concerned, that's my money."

"Keep it then. One more thing." Barron said then handed her a paper. "But, you sign this paper first. It relinquishes my rights as the father. It's a guarantee that you won't try to make me pay child support."

Tamara sucked her teeth. "I'm not signing nothing."

"Well, then I'm going to take you to court for stealing my ten thousand dollars. It was a joint account."

"She'll sign it." Brandy handed Tamara a pen. "But, it has to be notarized."

"Don't worry." Barron leaned in the window of his car. "Baby, get out the car."

Monica opened the door and walked over to them. She scowled in Tamara's direction, like she wanted to fight.

Brandy sucked her teeth. "I guess you two kissed and made up."

Tamara knew the woman weighed at least a hundred pounds more than her, but she pretended not to notice.

"She's a notary," Barron said with a cheesy grin plastered on his face. "Now sign the damn paper."

Brandy turned up her nose. "Who you yelling at?"

"You," Barron responded.

"Oh, you make me sick. I'm so glad my friend is through with you."

"Will you two shut up?" Tamara handed Barron the signed piece of paper. "Here. Now leave and don't come back."

Barron looked at Tamara with pure disgust. "Don't worry. You ain't shit to me. Come on, baby."

Tamara snickered. "With her fat, hippo ass."

Monica turned around. "Got your man, though. Now who's laughing!"

They hopped in the car and sped off.

Brandy shook her head. "You're better than me. I think I would've killed his ass. They wouldn't even find his body."

Darla folded her arms. "Just be glad it's all over."

"Believe me, I am."

"Now that you're single, I'm a hook you up with my brother." Brandy opened her car door.

Darla frowned. "She doesn't want Chuck. I'm giving you my cousin's number. You met him at the wedding, he was the one—"

"Hey . . . hey . . . hey," Tamara said. "I'm swearing off men for a while."

She used her key chain to unlock her Toyota Corolla. She waved good-bye to Brandy and Darla as they drove away in their cars. For the first time, she felt like she took control of her own life. And she loved the way it felt. She looked forward to her newly found freedom.

Darla

CHAPTER ONE

Darla removed her iPod earpiece and checked her cell phone. She had one message. She played it back.

"Hello, Darla. This is Marci. We didn't get the contract on the house. Let me know if you want me to keep searching. I'm really sorry about this. I'll be in the office until three today."

Clearly disappointed with the news, Darla took a deep breath. She wanted that house so badly. She thought getting approved for a mortgage would be the most difficult part. For the life of her, she didn't understand why it was so hard to purchase a home. The house in Carillon had been perfect for them too.

No sense in dwelling on it.

Darla turned around in her chair. "I have bad news."

"What happened?" Tamara asked as she leaned back in her chair.

"Marci called." Darla poked out her lips. "We didn't get the house."

"Oh, I hate to hear that." Tamara frowned. "You'll get something. It's only a matter of time."

Darla's smile revealed her small gap. "Are you ready for tonight?"

Brandy stood up and struck a modeling pose. "Yes, I'm ready for *Dreamgirls*." She pointed with her hands and sang the most popular lyrics, "And you . . . and you . . . and you. You're gonna love me!"

Tamara turned up her nose. "Not with you singing like that!"

Darla and Tamara laughed.

"I'm so glad this movie is finally here, because you've been talking about it forever." Tamara leaned on the arm of her chair.

Darla's eyes lit up. "I know. You guys know how much I love Jennifer Hudson from *American Idol*."

"Well, I want to see Ms. Skinny *Beyoncé*," Brandy chimed in. "Did you see how she lost all that weight so fast? And now she's back to being thick."

"Yeah, I know," Tamara said. "I need her secret to gaining it back, because my booty could use it." She smacked her behind.

Darla eyed Tamara in her cute little khaki pants and the tiny knit top she wore. She wished she could dress like that. No, she was reduced to oversized shirts that hung low and covered her whale of a behind.

"I have a big night planned for us." Darla took a deep breath. "Starting with dinner at my place, so please be on time." She looked at Brandy.

Brandy sucked her teeth. "Don't be cutting your eyes over at me. I'm a be on time, skank!"

"No, she didn't call you a skank." Tamara leaned back in her chair. "Darla, I know you're not going to take that. Are you?" Her eyes got big.

Darla threw up her hand. "Brandy, talk to the hand!"

Using her hand to cover her mouth, Brandy burst out laughing. "That is so played out!"

Tamara chimed in. "I haven't heard that in years."

"Get back to work!" Kimberly shouted from her office.

Brandy rolled her eyes. "Oh, she gets on my nerves. She needs to learn how to talk to people." She slung her braids over her shoulder.

"I still hear talking," Kimberly said.

"I still hear talking," Brandy mimicked her before she sat back down. "Like she's a damn teacher."

Tamara giggled softly from her cubicle. "Yep."

Darla shook her head, and then went back to typing invoices. She'd been working at IT for two years now, and one year with Kimberly.

Still, it was hard to contain her excitement, as she had anticipated seeing the movie for over a year. Being a huge *American Idol* junkie, Darla loved Jennifer Hudson and cried when she was voted off the third season. As an overweight woman with a beautiful voice, Darla really connected with her. Even though Darla was a white girl, she always felt a closeness to blacks, even from the time she was small; not small as in skinny, but as in when she was a young girl.

Darla could remember, as if it were yesterday, when two blonde, blue-eyed girls were making fun of her on the playground. JoAnn Williams, who was a new student at Greensburg Elementary, defended Darla. When they tried to talk back to JoAnn, she beat them up. Darla felt so bad for the girl who was sent to the office, because she stood up for Darla.

The next day at school, Darla brought JoAnn a bag of candy from the local store. And she and JoAnn became the best of friends. Even though her mom didn't particularly like black people, she allowed JoAnn to spend the weekend at their house. Then the following weekend, Darla would stay at JoAnn's house. She enjoyed the visits, as she would try foods she never had at home, like mustard greens and ham hocks. And then her favorite; lima beans and smoked neck bones, served over white rice.

Darla became comfortable around black people, probably more them than whites. And her sister, Janet, did too, as she married a black man, Trellis Jenkins, and they had a beautiful daughter together, Charity. Janet worked at the Bank of America, where Darla held an account from the day she started her first job at McDonald's in high school.

Darla arrived home around six that evening, which was unusual, given the stacks of files that sat on her desk when she clocked in that morning. Kimberly practically demanded they work overtime everyday. Darla pushed Brandy and Tamara to stop joking and stick with a steady pace to get all their invoices entered before the deadline.

That's the way Darla pushed herself, and she was one of Kimberly's most valuable employees. So much so, that Kimberly hinted at a promotion within the next couple of months.

Now, she had to admit, Kimberly was the hardest supervisor at IT. She lost her temper at the drop of a dime, and screamed the entire time. No one could escape Kimberly's wrath, but her employees were loyal to her. True to form, Kimberly made a quick exit at the end of the day with a mug filled with hot tea and a hoarse voice. However, the next morning her lungs would be in full effect and the shouting that everyone on the second floor had come to love to hate would reconvene.

Nevertheless, Darla knew that Kimberly had her own share of problems. There were many nights when Darla worked late and Kimberly confided in her. Her husband, John, hardly kept a job for more than a few months at a time. Therefore, Kimberly carried the financial burden to keep them from losing the home, the two car payments for the Volvo that she drove and John's brand new Suburban, along with providing for their two beautiful children, Lauren and Ben. All of which, Kimberly rarely got the chance to enjoy, since she logged in at least seventy hours per week.

All of Kimberly's struggles really scared Darla, who tried to avoid even thinking about marriage. That changed when she met and fell in love with Robert over a year ago. Darla found true happiness with him. She met Robert in the Ebony Lovers chat room on July 4, 2005, and sparks flew from their first conversation, when she IM'ed him apart from all the hopefuls in the room searching for love.

Dashit: How come I've never seen you in EL before?

BertFever: That's because I'm new to this. Been in a serious commitment for long time.

Dashit: Oh I see. And now ur single?

BertFever: unfortunately

Dashit: I'm sorry. What happened?

BertFever: She died.

Dashit: Was it sudden?

BertFever: Yes, very

Dashit: Then I'm really sorry

BertFever: What? You were not sorry before?

Dashit: lol I was but I hate to hear about people dying, especially, someone you were once in love with . . .

BertFever: Yes, I cared for her very deeply. But I'm ready for love again.

Dashit: Which I guess is why we're both here.

BertFever: yes

Dashit: Do you have a pic?

BertFever: I'm sorry, don't know what pic is . . .

Dashit: Seriously? Then you are new to this. A pic is a picture of yourself.

BertFever: Yes, I have photos.

Dashit: Can you send it to me?

BertFever: But I don't have your address.

Dashit: lol To send to my email screen name

BertFever: No, I wouldn't know how to do that and what does lol mean?

Dashit: laughing out loud

BertFever: fine

Dashit: I'll send u one of me.

Dashit: Did u get it?

BertFever: What?

Dashit: An email from me, inside is my pic

BertFever: Let me see

Dashit: u still there?

BertFever: yes yes

Dashit: What do you think?

BertFever: I think I'm in love again

Dashit: omg

BertFever: Yes, you are very lovely woman

Dashit: Thanks, I work out a lot

BertFever: Me too, so far I've lost 80 pounds

Dashit: really?

BertFever: Yes, yes, I had cancer but no more . . . it's all gone

Dashit: WOW!!!!!!!!

BertFever: As long as I exercise and keep take my pills I will stay here longer

Dashit: I was overweight too. And I lost 100 pounds.

BertFever: You were fat and now look like this?

Dashit: yes

BertFever: Oh, then we must meet . . . we have much in common.

Dashit: OK. I'll meet you in EL the same time tomorrow.

BertFever: Fine. Goodbye.

Dashit: Do you have some place to be?

BertFever: No. Do you?

Dashit: No. Let's keep chatting then.

BertFever: fine

Further into that conversation, Darla found out Robert lived in Toronto. Robert seemed interested in getting to know her as a person, and she liked that about him. Robert spoke about wanting to see Mickey Mouse ever since he was a youngster. The farthest he'd ever traveled was to New York City, and the same was true for Darla.

They met in EL at the same time for two weeks straight. Not sure if Robert wanted to pursue their online tryst into something more, Darla worked up the nerve to ask for his phone number. Darla was surprised when he gave his number so freely, and asked why she didn't ask sooner. No longer facing a computer screen, she talked to Robert on the phone for hours.

Darla rushed home from work just to hear his sexy accent. Because he spoke French as his first language, his vocabulary was a bit limited. Since Darla only knew two words in French, communication was tough. However, Robert enrolled in a language class to improve his English, and their conversations became longer and more intimate as the months passed.

Darla fell madly in love with Robert. It was difficult for her to comprehend the enormity of her emotions, as he was the only boyfriend she'd ever had. Being overweight, Darla didn't get asked on many dates, and if a man showed any interest in her, she never believed it to be anything more than a joke.

Having overweight parents, Darla should've known it was possible for fat people to hook up, but she wasn't attracted to big men, even though it seemed pretty shallow to have those kinds of feelings. Her sister had managed to marry an average-sized man, and Darla had no doubt the same would happen for her, but she wanted to lose the weight first.

In her heart, Darla knew if she truly focused, she could lose the weight, and then she would find her man. Until then, Darla resorted to meeting men online and agreeing to cyber-sex to take care of her sexual needs. This was why she used the photos of her friend to pique their curiosity. Once they believed she was that beautiful, tanned woman with long, blonde hair, blue eyes, and a toned body, they would do just about anything she asked. She especially liked to meet men who had webcams set up, because she could order them to perform sexual acts while she watched and masturbated.

One of her freakiest partners had actually beaten his penis with a spiked stick until it bled. Now that was just too much for her to witness. Traumatized by that incident, Darla signed off the computer for a full week after that. She had so many screen names for different chat rooms that it didn't matter if she got rid of one.

SexFucKitten and Orgasmicbunny were the most popular names. Darla used SexFucKitten in the Menage à Trois Room, where she watched couples have sex through their webcam. It was wild!

Darla knew she possessed true feelings for Robert when she stopped visiting chat rooms altogether and got rid of almost all her screen names. Sure, she and Robert engaged in a little phone sex, but it never got as dirty as it did with the others.

Once things got serious with Robert, Darla had to

admit, she did miss some of her chat pals. She probably missed NightRyder most of all. NightRyder taught Darla how to use sex toys to enhance her cyber-sex experiences. To this very day, the Gee Whiz Magic Wand remained her most used toy. It helped to stimulate her pussy by hitting that G-spot. With her toy she nicknamed "Robbie," she could attach it to her vibrator and pleasure herself for hours. She vowed if things didn't work out with Robert, she would have to track NightRyder down and beg him to fuck her just once.

Robert grew weary of talking on the phone, and looked forward to the day when they would meet in person. He expressed his desire to take their relationship to the next level, which Darla resisted, even though she really wanted to see the man she claimed to love. The problem was, Darla wasn't the woman in the pictures she sent him. Those pictures were of her best friend at the time, who was all of one hundred twenty pounds soaking wet.

Darla knew when Robert saw her real body, he would lose interest. As he'd admitted on many occasions, he never liked fat women, even though he used to be an overweight man. Despite Robert's constant offers to fly down, she turned him down. No matter what, she couldn't meet face to face until she at least lost some of the weight.

It never happened, and what few pounds she did manage to lose taking Ultra Slim diet pills, she gained back and then some.

Another month into it, Darla finally confessed to Robert she wasn't the woman in the picture. Angry didn't describe his reaction for being lied to, Robert was livid. But Robert admitted he fell in love with her mind, and he still wanted to see her. At least they could be friends, if nothing else. Touched by his sensitivity and his willingness to forgive her, she mustered up the courage and finally said yes to his invitation.

A week before Christmas, Robert arrived in Orlando with his best friend, Danny. Darla drove to the airport to meet them, but she was disappointed that Robert wanted to spend more time with Danny than with her.

The most hurtful part was hearing Robert admit he wasn't attracted to her body, but they could still remain friends. Darla thought he was full of it, and decided not to have anything else to do with him. She wasn't even mad at him, as she brought the whole heartbreak on herself by lying about her appearance.

Before Robert left the hotel to catch his flight, he called Darla.

"Where have you been?" Robert asked.

"What do you mean?" Darla responded with a question. "I've been working."

"I came here to meet you, but you've spent little time with me."

"To be honest, I didn't think you wanted to see me anymore," Darla responded. "Since you saw how overweight I am, I didn't want to face the rejection."

"Darla, I love you. And the weight doesn't matter to me."

Darla took a sigh of relief. He had no clue how badly she wanted to hear him say that.

"Yes, I want you to lose the weight."

Darla clung to the phone. "I want to lose it, too."

"Then, I will teach you."

She beamed with joy. "Are you serious?"

Robert laughed. "As you say; as a heart attack."

Darla giggled. She loved it when he tried to be funny. And he was so cute and lovable. She was lucky to have him in her life.

"Can you come see me, before we leave?" Robert inquired.

"Yes, I'll be there in a few hours," Darla responded.

"That's fine."

Needless to say, Danny went back to Canada alone. Robert made plans to stay another week with her. She took that as a sign that he wanted to be with her. Overjoyed that Robert accepted her completely, she invited him to stay at her house and meet her family and best friend, Cydney. If only she knew then what she knew now. She would've never allowed Cydney to get near her man.

It was on Christmas morning that Robert got down on one knee and proposed marriage in front of her parents. Darla couldn't say yes fast enough, and the chubby girl who everyone said would never get a man was now Robert's fiancée. Once engaged, Robert decided it was easier for him to move to Florida, than uproot Darla from her family and friends. He shared his plans to prepare for the Florida Bar and eventually begin a new law practice there. Darla promised to quit her job at IT to help him.

Darla agreed to stop working as his office manager and expand their family once his practice was up and running. Robert was fifteen years older than her, and he was very eager to start a family. All of it seemed too good to be true, and in some ways it was.

Darla used her keys to let herself into her apartment. Robert's cologne greeted her at the door; she inhaled his sweet fragrance.

"Is that you, baby?" Robert asked. His voice trailed as he scuffled down the hallway.

"Yes," Darla felt her stomach get queasy. She hoped he wasn't going out.

Robert walked into the living room and greeted his wife with a kiss. "I missed you. Did you have a nice day?" His mustache and goatee ran sharply across her chin as he forced his tongue inside. She loved kissing him.

"You missed me?" Darla gazed into his beautiful blue eyes. She ran her hand through his dark, curly hair. "Well, I can cancel my plans, if you want to stay in tonight."

Robert grabbed her hands. "No. Don't change your plans. I have a date."

Darla frowned. "Oh." Those were words she didn't want to hear.

Robert touched her chin. "Now, don't get upset. You know this is what we agreed."

"I know, but I still don't like it." Darla poked out her bottom lip. "You're my husband."

"Yes. Yes." Robert smiled. "I always come home to you."

Darla tried to look away, but Robert moved in closer. He followed her eyes. She wanted to cry so badly. She regretted her decision. She wanted to cry. Scream. Yell. Until the pain went away.

"I love you," he said.

"If you loved me, you wouldn't do this," Darla snapped.

"When you fulfill your promise, I'm all yours."

"I'm trying so hard."

"No. No. Don't get upset about this."

Darla took a deep breath. "I can't help it."

"I promised to marry you. I did it." Robert straightened his black silk shirt, gathered his wallet and keys from the table, and left.

Darla held her hand across her stomach and stormed

into the bathroom. There, she threw up all of her lunch into the toilet.

Fat bitch!

Just the thought of him with Cydney made her hurl again. She sat on the floor next to the toilet and cried. She wanted to die.

Get off your big ass and do something about it! That's why that skinny bitch is with your husband now. Because you're ugly, you can't do anything about it. Ha! Ha! Ha!

"Shut up!"

Darla pressed her hands on her ears and closed her eyes shut. She couldn't take much more of this.

Once Darla pulled herself together, she took the frozen lasagna out of the freezer and popped it into the oven. Then she sliced the hot French bread she picked up at Wal-Mart Super Center and slathered it with butter. Glancing at the clock, she only had ten minutes to shower and put on her purple muumuu dress, which covered her from head to toe. It resembled a curtain, but it was the best she could do for now.

Tamara was the first to arrive. "Hey, girlfriend." Her eyes searched the room. "Where's Robert?"

"Oh, he's out with his friends."

"He's so sweet," Tamara said. "Giving us the place all to ourselves."

Darla smiled. "Yes, that's it."

"Well, I know Brandy's going to be late, so let's go ahead and start eating." Tamara grabbed a piece of bread from the table and sat down.

"Don't you think we should wait a few minutes?" Darla asked. She really wanted to enjoy dinner with both of her friends. It wasn't every day that they had a girls' night out.

"No," Tamara responded and kicked off her heels. Her red toenails sank into the carpet.

Staring down at her own toes, Darla realized she needed a pedicure badly. She made a mental note to do that real soon. Maybe she would invite her sister Janet to come too.

When she heard a car door shut, she looked out the window. "There's Brandy."

Darla swung open the door. "I can't believe you're on time."

"I did it for my best friend." Brandy kissed her on the cheek. "I know how badly you want to see this movie."

"All right, ladies." Darla handed each one a glass half-filled with Chardonnay. "This is to *Dreamgirls*." They clanked their glasses together.

"Darla, you're going to jail for serving alcohol to a minor," Brandy said.

Darla took a sip of her wine. "If a nineteen-year-old can die for our country, surely they can drink alcohol."

"Beautifully said." Tamara rubbed her hands together. "I'm hungry."

"Your greedy ass always is," Brandy replied.

"While we're waiting on the lasagna, let's enjoy the salad." Darla went to the refrigerator and pulled out a large plastic bowl.

After eating the salad and talking about Kimberly for half an hour, the oven timer finally sounded. Darla placed the hot lasagna on a thick towel folded neatly on the table.

"It smells good." Tamara rubbed her stomach. "This is better than spending a ton of money at Olive Garden."

"I can't believe you're getting around already," Brandy said. "When I got an abortion, I had to take two days off from work.

"I felt fine right after the procedure," Tamara responded.

"What did you do with the prescription for Perco-cet?" Brandy asked.

"I filled it, but I didn't take those pills."

Brandy put her elbows on the table. "You got a bottle of Percocets, and you didn't do anything with them?" She snapped her fingers. "Well, you need to hook a sista up with them bad boys. I can use them when my period is on, because I be cramping so bad."

"No." Tamara shook her head. "I'm not doing that. Let's try to forget the whole thing."

Darla cleared her throat and took sip of wine. She caught a glimpse of Brandy and Tamara staring at her.

"What?" She raised an eyebrow and smirked.

"Go ahead." Tamara scooped lasagna on her plate.

Brandy sucked her teeth. "You better not!"

"No comment." Darla straightened her paper napkin. "You guys knew I was against it. But, Tamara, it's your body."

"And her life! You pro-life people get on my nerves!" Brandy grunted. "Like you we're going to take care of the baby, if she had it."

Tamara waved her fork mid-air. "Can we not get into politics tonight?" She took a bite.

"Damn Bush lover. You know you're stupid to sup-port him."

"Brandy!" Tamara screamed. "We all know Bush is an idiot, and so is his chubby brother. No offense, Darla."

Darla yawned. "None taken." She'd heard this all be-fore.

"Not to change the subject or anything." Tamara laughed. "I can't wait to see Jamie Foxx with the finger waves in his hair."

"Me neither, girl." Brandy shifted her braids to one side. "And what about the dark-skinned dude that's in it? He is so fine!"

* * *

"So what did you guys think about the movie last night?" Darla asked.

"I thought it was pretty good." Tamara rocked her chair from side to side.

"Well, I loved it!" Darla exclaimed, as she wrapped her arms around her shoulders. "And I think Jennifer deserves an Oscar nomination for her performance."

Tamara shook her head. "I agree."

Brandy turned up her nose. "She was all right. I still think Angie Stone would've done better."

"Where are you getting this from?" Darla asked. "No one said anything about Angie Stone trying out for that part."

Brandy leaned against her desk. "I know. If I had my pick of a plus-sized woman who can sing, I choose Angie Stone."

"Not to change the subject, but guess what I heard?" Tamara leaned forward in her chair.

"What, girl?" Brandy asked as sat on top of Tamara's desk, with her feet dangling.

Darla held up her hand. "Wait one minute. Is this it about Barron?"

Brandy cocked her head to the side. "And what if it is? You know you still wants to hear it."

"I'm just saying, Tamara is supposed to be moving on. That's all."

"She still gon' talk to your cousin. Damn!"

"Will you get to the point?" Darla interrupted. "Kimberly's going to pop up over here any second."

"Look, who's trying to rush somebody," Brandy teased.

"God, you two are so aggravating." Tamara folded her arms and took a deep breath. "I'll make this quick. Monica found a job, but Barron hasn't. And she's bossing him around, making his life miserable."

"Well, he's the one that chose the mean bitch," Brandy sang.

"I know. But check this out." Tamara moved in closer and lowered her voice. "She's pregnant with twins!"

"Oh, hell no!" Brandy tried to cover her mouth.

"Does anyone use condoms?" Darla shook her head. "Please tell me he did not get you and Monica pregnant at the same time. This is unreal."

Tamara giggled. "I know. Now, can you just imagine if he had to pay me child support? I'm so glad I got rid of my baby."

Darla gasped. "Why do you have to say it like that? It sounds so cruel."

"Whatever!" Brandy slapped hands with Tamara. "You did the right thing, girl."

"There's something I just don't get about this." Darla leaned on the arm of her chair. "Why was he married to Monica, but still living with you?"

"Barron worked under Monica."

"In more ways than one," Brandy sang.

"True. If the store manager ever found out, then Monica would lose her job. From what Barron tells me, she'd been with the company for a long time and was being groomed for a higher position."

"Would y'all stop!" Tamara shouted. "Now, this is the latest. Well, you know Barron and Monica both got fired from Macy's, right?"

"I still say you're lucky that nigga didn't kill you for that one," Brandy chimed in as she fidgeted with her nail.

"True, but you have to admit, I got him good." Tamara snapped her fingers.

Brandy nodded. "Yes, you did. You played that one to the hilt."

"It sounds like the party is over here!" Kimberly shouted with her hands on her hips. "Can we get through one day without me having to tell you to do your jobs?"

"Guess not," Brandy sang as she slid back in her cubicle.

Tamara snickered.

"Tamara, you're getting as bad as Brandy."

Tamara's jaw fell open. "No, I'm not. Don't even put me in the same category as her." She waved her hand in Brandy's direction.

"Tamyra, I implore you to stop giving me so much attitude." Kimberly gazed up at the ceiling, clearly annoyed.

"Yes, Tamyra," Brandy teased.

"Brandy, watch it!" Kimberly snapped.

Brandy smiled. "You know you love me."

Kimberly hissed. "Darla, I need to speak with you when you get a minute," Kimberly said. "And the two of you, get back to work!"

Darla rose from her chair and pulled her blouse below her big butt. "I'm coming, Kimberly."

Once inside Kimberly's office, she closed the door for privacy. "What is it?"

"I have good news for you." Kimberly twisted her thin, pink lips. "You've been promoted to Marilyn's job as IT Trainer. If you accept, you'll start in three weeks. That's how long it will take for me to find a suitable replacement and get him or her trained."

Darla put her hand to her chest. "What? How did this happen? I never applied for it."

"I entered your name in the pool of candidates myself." Kimberly rested her elbows on her oak desktop. "You're more qualified than the others."

Darla laughed nervously. "I just don't know about this, Kimberly."

"Well, think on it tonight. Talk to me in the morning."

Darla stood up. "Thanks for doing this. Really . . . you've been good to me ever since I started in your department."

Kimberly waved her hand. "Please." She picked up a stack of invoices to review. "I need to get back to these, and you need to . . . well, you know what you need to do."

"Yes. Thanks again."

Darla would've jumped at the chance to work as the company trainer, but she knew Robert wouldn't go for it. He had their lives all mapped out, and there was nothing she could do to change that.

On her way to the bathroom, Brandy tapped Darla on the shoulder.

"You scared me." Darla sighed.

"Sorry," Brandy sang. "We need to talk about your girl."

Darla followed her to the corner end of the second floor. She admired the way Brandy's butt looked in her jeans. Wishing she had a figure like that, Darla calculated how much weight she'd lost this week. Only fifteen pounds. And no one even noticed. Boy, she had a long way to go before shopping for a pair of low-riders.

"I know, she's obsessing over Barron. Don't you think?"

"Hell yeah." Brandy tried to speak in a whisper. "I wanted to tell her so bad, that she needs to quit talking to him."

"What?" Darla opened her mouth wide. "Where have

I been? I had no idea. I thought it was over. I really think we need to say something."

Brandy turned up her nose. "For what? Even though Tamara claims to be over him, you know she ain't."

"I guess you're right. What do we do?"

"I don't know. Tell her how stupid she is to keep calling a man who don't even want her."

Darla put her hands on her hips. "What about the baby? Does he know she got rid of it?"

"Nope."

"Oh my God. He's going to kill her when he finds out."

"I know." Brandy took a deep breath. "And, she's taking money from him, too."

"For what? I thought he didn't have a job." Darla giggled.

"Tamara told me Barron is still trying to get that business started. Something ain't right about that whole situation."

"Yeah. And the whole marriage thing still doesn't make sense to me."

"It just goes to show, you never know what kind of dirty stuff people have going on. Just because two people are married, don't mean they are really married. You know what I mean?" Brandy scratched the back of her neck.

Darla took a deep breath. "Yeah." She knew exactly what Brandy meant, even though she wished with every fiber of her being that she didn't. If only Brandy knew that Darla's marriage was a charade too. Now, she understood exactly why Monica and Barron's marriage seemed so bizarre.

"I mean, look at you and Robert. You two seem very happy, but that's not always the case." Brandy scratched her arm through her shirt. "Damn mosquitoes tore my ass up last night!"

"That's why you should use bug repellent, instead of Skin-So-Soft."

Brandy sucked her teeth. "I'm not trying to put on that funky stuff. What did Kimberly want?"

"Just to go over next week's schedule," Darla said. "She needs us to pull in a lot of overtime next week."

"Please. You know I'm not."

"That's what I figured." Darla felt her stomach rumbling. "I need to get in here now." She pointed at the restroom door.

"What's wrong with you anyway?" Brandy asked emphatically. "You look like you've lost even more weight."

"Diet pills. And they make me have the runs."

"Oh." Brandy popped her chewing gum. "Well, be careful with them things.

"I am." Darla ran inside the bathroom and into an empty stall quickly. She was relieved no one else was in there, so she didn't have to deal with the embarrassment of someone hearing her farting so loudly. When she finished, Darla showered the room with body spray to mask the smell.

In the mirror, she counted seven pimples on her face. There was nothing worse than suffering from adult acne. Today, she planned to visit the Proactiv lady at the counter in the mall to purchase some products. After watching all the infomercials, especially the one with Jessica Simpson, she hoped to have the same results.

CHAPTER TWO

"I need to find something decent to wear," Darla said. "I can't fit in any of my old stuff."

"You need to get rid of those old rags anyway," Janet replied as she thumbed through the clearance rack at Lane Bryant. "As your sister, I have to admit, I was embarrassed for you."

Darla rested her hand on her hip. "Why didn't you tell me I resembled a big blimp? Some sister you are."

"It's not easy to do. Besides, what do I look like putting you down, when I'm overweight myself?"

"Janet, you weigh what . . . maybe two hundred?" Darla tossed her frizzy curls over her shoulder. "No comparison."

"I never realized you were that big."

"Me neither," Darla said as she picked up a size 22/24 blouse. She never thought she'd work herself down to that size. "Wow! I think even this is too large for me."

"I think you're right."

"I guess I'll try on this one and the 18/20 too." Darla

found it hard to contain her excitement. She grabbed a pink version of the same blouse.

Once inside the dressing room, she pulled off the loose fitting polo shirt she wore to work that day.

"Our Christmas party is the Saturday before Christmas this year. Are you going to make it?"

Darla put on the blouse and finger-combed her frizzy hair. "Uh-huh. We'll be there."

"So, tell me this, are you doing all this for Robert?" Janet asked from outside the door.

"No, but you have to admit, it will make our sex life hotter." Darla wished she didn't have to lie about her marriage to the people she loved.

"Shoot, you don't have to lose weight for that to happen. Trellis loves all my handles."

Darla swung open the door. "Everybody can't have a Trellis. He's one of a kind."

Janet tried to adjust the blouse on Darla. "Yeah, you definitely need the smaller one."

Darla smiled. "That's what I thought." She clapped her hands. "Yeah!"

"What did you mean saying what you did about Trellis?" Janet inquired. "I thought that's what you had; someone who loved you the same way."

Darla shrugged. "It's not the same. When Robert looks at me, I know he's disgusted by my fat."

"Wasn't he fat too?"

"Yeah, but I've never been attracted to big people myself." Darla defended her husband. "I've been like this all my life, and I'm ready to be beautiful."

Janet placed her hands on Darla's shoulders and shook her. "You are beautiful! No matter what you weigh. You have to believe that, or else you'll be skinny and still hating yourself."

"No, I won't." Darla giggled. "I'm already loving me. And so are the men at IT."

"Oh, really?" Janet's eyes grew wider. "What are they saying?"

Darla blushed a new shade of red. "You know, things . . . like . . . I don't want to say."

"Awwww! Come on."

Darla held up her finger. "One thing I'll share. This morning, Johnny who works in Mailing, said my ass was shaking like a black girl's ass."

They burst out laughing.

"What did you say?"

"I said thank you."

Janet screamed. "Oh, my God."

"I know." Darla shrugged. "You know I'm not used to this kind of attention."

"Get used to it." Janet inspected her sister from head to toe. "You're looking pretty damn fabulous."

"Happy Birthday, baby!" Robert kissed her cheek as their waitress placed a slice of cake in front of her.

"Thank you." Darla smacked him on the lips. She wished she could have him for the night. She dreamed of the day when they would consummate their marriage. Having shed another five pounds, she hoped the day would come real soon. NightRyder was starting to look pretty good to her.

"Robert, this was really nice."

"Yes, it was," Robert responded. He drank an espresso.

Darla wondered how many times he'd been to Seasons 52 before. It was an expensive restaurant, and was known for its delicious menu highlighting the fact that all entrees were less than two hundred-fifty calories. They arrived in Robert's black Mercedes, which was in her name since she was the one with perfect credit. With complimentary valet parking, they should've appeared as a high-powered couple. Instead, her husband seemed more elegant than her in his black suit, and Darla looked frumpy in a matching black dress. Janet styled her hair up in curls, but when she caught a glimpse of herself in the bathroom mirror, she resembled Ms. Piggy.

The front section was set with two fireplaces with couches in front of them, so patrons could relax while they waited for a table. In the back of her mind, Darla imagined Robert making out with Cydney on the very same couch they sat on earlier.

Robert was a very affectionate man, and he doted on her while they were out in public. He had everybody fooled into thinking he absolutely adored her. She knew in the back of strangers' minds, they wondered what a man as gorgeous as Robert, even saw in a pimply-faced blubber-ass like herself. But, who was the real fool? Darla was, for going along with this charade of a marriage.

"This is delicious." Darla pretended to savor every morsel of the sugar-free cake. Merita bread tasted better.

"I'm pleased." Robert grabbed her hand from across the table. "There is something I need to discuss with you."

Darla posed a fake smile. "What is it?"

"Well, I did something. And I hope you won't be upset with me."

He moved that bitch in with us. Try not to jump over the table and strangle him.

"Just try me. You might be surprised."

"I changed things around." Robert took another sip. "You'll see. Can I ask you something?"

Darla wiped her mouth with the cloth napkin. "Of course."

"How much pounds have you dropped?"

Darla leaned in closer. "Excuse me?"

"You know. I want to see how close you are to our goal."

Darla shook her head as she felt her temperature rise to a slow simmer. "I can't believe you." She snatched her hand away.

"I'm trying to show you love." Robert gazed at her with sincere eyes.

"You have a terrible way of showing it. But if you must know, I've shed another forty pounds since our wedding."

Robert did the numbers in his head. "That means, ninety pounds. Congratulations!" He clapped his hands. "Now you only have sixty left, then you have me all to yourself."

Darla twirled her fork on her plate. "I should be so lucky."

"What do you mean? I thought this was what you wanted."

Darla chuckled. "You couldn't possibly be serious." She leaned back in her chair. "What I want is a husband who wants me, whether I'm one hundred or six hundred pounds."

"This is about sex," Robert said. "A marriage is more. I love you, and I will never leave you. That is what I promised you. We agreed."

Darla quickly wiped a tear from her face. "I was so desperate then. Now, I know what a fool I was to go along with this charade of a marriage. I want out." She couldn't stand to see his face another second. Darla left the table and ran outside into the freezing cold.

A few minutes later, Robert came up from behind her and wrapped his jacket over her shoulders. He kissed her neck softly and handed the valet his ticket.

"I love you."

Not caring that two other couples were beside them, Darla's emotions got the best of her, and she sobbed painfully, as if her entire world was ripped right out from under her.

"I want this to be over," Darla whispered to herself. "I thought I could do it. But I can't."

Robert helped her to the car, and drove back to their apartment. Once inside, he wrapped his arms around Darla's limp body and squeezed her tightly.

Feeling numb and lifeless, Darla tried to respond to her husband's displays of affection, but her body just wouldn't fake another move.

"What did you change?" Darla asked.

"We can discuss it in the morning."

"I'm OK."

Robert ran his fingers through her hair. "I changed out the cupboards. Put in all good stuff."

"Oh." Darla's eyes watered up again. "I'm tired."

Robert followed Darla into her bedroom and stripped down to nothing but his underwear. He lay behind Darla, as she lay on her side. Disgusted by the way she lowered her dignity to marry a man who wasn't even attracted to her and proudly slept with her former best friend, she cried herself to sleep. She made a vow to herself to do what she needed to do to get out of her marriage.

The next day, Darla awoke to the sound of Robert in the bathroom coughing uncontrollably.

"What is wrong with you?" She asked.

"I don't feel too well."

"Have you made a doctor's appointment?" Darla asked as she leaned against the door frame.

"No."

"I'm calling for you then." Darla picked up the phone and dialed the number.

"Dr. Neill James' office."

"Yes, I need to schedule an appointment for my husband, Robert Favor."

"Can you hold please?"

"Sure." Darla rested the receiver on her shoulder. "Why don't you get back in bed? You need to get some rest."

"Yes. Yes." Robert grabbed his back as he lingered back to her bed.

Darla scheduled him to see Dr. James that afternoon, and dressed for work.

"Do you need me to go with you?" Darla asked as she kneeled down beside him.

"No." Robert responded. "I'll be fine."

Darla kissed his forehead and then headed for IT. She hoped his cancer hadn't returned. Robert promised to call her as soon as he left the doctor's office. Now, she wanted to take back everything she said to him last night. There's no way she could divorce him if he was sick. And he did love her, although he had a funny way of showing it. It wasn't so terrible that he didn't want to have sex with her; it was the fact that he was sleeping with other women that bothered her. In fact, it made her sick to her stomach.

They needed to have a serious discussion. Darla wasn't about to continue with things being the way they were. And if that meant she would have to be alone, so be it. Anything was better than this, even resorting back to cyber-sex with complete strangers.

When Darla arrived home, Robert wasn't there yet. He had called her at work to tell her the doctor's visit went fine, and Dr. James recommended blood work be completed ASAP. Darla changed into a T-shirt and leggings and slid her *Shape Up* DVD into the player. Moving the table close to the couch, Darla stood in the center ready to begin. Taking a few deep breaths, she cleared her mind of all the stress and negative thoughts. This was her time to shine.

As she neared the end of the warm-up, she heard the key turning and the door slowly open. Not wanting to continue, she forced herself to complete the last kick-step, and bend down to stretch her thigh muscles.

"Very good." Robert plopped down on the couch.

"I know you're not going to sit here and watch me," Darla said sarcastically. She wiped the sweat from her forehead, as she turned sideways to stretch her calf.

"Yes. Yes." Robert slipped his hand inside his pants. "I'm very turned on right now."

Darla frowned. "Please leave."

"What?" Robert looked confused. "I thought this is what you wanted."

"Not anymore." She panted as she jogged in motion. "Get out of here! I don't want you to watch me like I'm some kind of freak show."

Robert shrugged his shoulders and left the room. He slammed the door to his bedroom.

"Good." Darla kicked her right foot in front of her. She was even more determined to drop the last sixty pounds. Only this time, she wanted to do it for herself, not to hold on to a hopeless marriage.

CHAPTER THREE

"That was a good movie," Tamara said as she used her remote to turn the DVD player off.

"Who could go wrong with a Denzel movie?" Darla added. "And that Clive Owen, I just want to suck on his lips. He is so damn sexy."

"He is gorgeous. You already have the real thing at home."

"I know. The very first time I saw Robert, I thought of how much he resembled Clive. Especially with the whole accent thing." Darla hung her head low.

"What's the matter?" Tamara asked as she sat next her friend on the futon. It served as a couch and bed. "I noticed you were a little down at work today."

"I'm praying Robert's cancer hasn't returned. He's been coughing and throwing up a lot lately."

Tamara patted Darla's leg. "Oh, I'm so sorry to hear all of this. Has he been to the doctor?"

Darla wiped a tear from her eye. "Yes. And we're waiting on the test results. They should be back anytime now. I just hate this, you know. Here, I have a man I love so much, and I can't be happy. It makes no sense."

"Trust me." Tamara laughed. "I know how you feel. Barron's been calling me, and I miss him so much that I'm actually thinking about taking him back."

Darla's eyebrows rose. "Now, that's just crazy. Why would you do that?"

Tamara kicked her foot forward. "Because, I love him."

Darla threw up her hands. "I'm sorry, but that's not a good enough reason. What about Jack? I know you're not going to string my cousin along."

"No offense, but I'm not feeling the black girl, white boy thing," Tamara said. "He's cute and so sweet, but I want my honey back."

"That's so fucking unbelievable!" Darla shouted. "I set you up with a man that is attracted to you, wants to be there for your skinny ass, and you want to go back to the wife beater." Darla stood up and fidgeted with her fingers. "My husband won't even sleep with me, because I'm so damn fat, and you act like you can't get a man, when you look like that. You're selfish. That's what you are."

"Wait a minute. Did you say your husband won't sleep with you? You're not having sex?"

"No."

"You haven't consummated your marriage yet?" Tamara asked.

"No, we haven't," Darla replied. "It's a long story, and I don't want to get into it right now. In fact, I'm ready to go home."

"I see." Tamara paced to the other side of the room. "You don't have a problem bringing up all my shit, but when it comes down to your own issues, you want to go home. That's cool."

"I know where you're going with this." Darla put on her shoes and grabbed her keys. "And let's not get upset. I'm tired and it's late. We'll talk tomorrow."

"That's probably best."

Darla knew Tamara had an attitude. She hugged her friend. "I'm sorry. You're not selfish."

"Uh-huh." Tamara twisted her lips. "I forgive you."

Darla entered her apartment and almost jumped out of her clothes when she heard a woman screaming. The closer she got to Robert's bedroom, she recognized it to be Cydney's voice and the moaning let her know they were having sex.

Darla couldn't believe her husband was having sex with another woman in their home. This had to be a scene right out of the Jerry Springer show. She went in the kitchen and picked up a butcher knife from the wood block.

Darla burst into the room. "What the hell is going on in here?"

Cydney snatched a sheet to cover up, and Robert took the comforter.

"I thought you were—"

"Staying with Tamara. I lied to you about that." Darla pulled the sheet off of Cydney to reveal her naked body. "Are you sleeping with her in our house now?" Darla swung the knife in the air.

"You're a dirty slut!" With the knife in one hand, Darla snatched Cydney up by her long blonde hair and held it to her neck. "Get out of my house! The next time I see you here, my face will be plastered all over the news for murder. Do you hear me?" Darla made a small incision near her jugular.

Cydney gritted her teeth. "Ouch!"

Darla let go and kicked her in the back. "That's the not the answer I wanted."

"Yes," Cydney mumbled.

Darla dragged her skinny butt across the living room and shoved her out the door. "Good night!"

Hearing a crash from the room, Darla charged back inside waving the knife in the air like Tom Cruise in *The Last Samurai*. "Where do you think you're going?"

Robert zipped his jeans. "You're crazy."

"You better believe I'm crazy!" Darla shouted.

Robert pointed at Darla. "I don't want to kill you. Stay away!"

Darla laughed. "You don't want me to kill you! I'm the one with the weapon."

"I don't want to kill you." Robert eased along the wall to the front door. "I will if I have to. Don't come near me."

"Oh. I'm trembling. Get the hell out of here, Robert. I'm sick to death of you!"

Knowing she meant business, Robert was out of the apartment in all of a minute. Angry about what took place, Darla cried out loud. Rubbing her forehead, she attempted to gain her composure, but she screamed out loud instead.

"I hate you! I hate you for ruining my life!"

That was it. Feeling angry and sexually frustrated, Darla made up in her mind she was going to find NightRyder. She calmed down and settled in front of the computer. Finding a chat room wasn't difficult, and since she kept her old screen names, she had to decide who she would be tonight.

She decided on SexFucKitten, because she wanted to be adventurous. It had been so long since she'd done this. Her hands trembled as she clicked into the *Married but Looking* chat room. Darla entered and discovered twenty-four people there. She wondered how many walked in on their spouse having sex in their apartment. She decided to ask that question.

It piqued the interest of everyone, and the subject switched from which woman gave the best head to who would love to get caught by their spouse. And then to Darla's surprise, idoljunkie said if his wife walked in on him, he wouldn't even stop until his lover had an orgasm.

Darla found her man. She sent him an invitation to chat privately, which he accepted.

SexFucKitten: What would you say if I told you it happened to me tonight?

idoljunkie: What did?

SexFucKitten: I found my husband fucking my best friend.

idoljunkie: Oh shit

SexFucKitten: You like that huh?

idolejunkie: Fuck yeah, now what room?

SexFucKitten: His bedroom, we sleep in different rooms.

idoljunkie: No shit, is he bi?

SexFucKitten: No, but I am.

idoljunkie: U eat pussy?

SexFucKitten: Yeah, lick it raw . . .

idoljunkie: K, very hard. Did u join in?

SexFucKitten: No, I was too mad

idoljunkie: Pretend u did, how did it look?

SexFucKitten: Very wet. It's wide . . . his dick has stretched it

idoljunkie: What size is his?

She thought to herself. She really wasn't sure what size her husband's penis was. Knowing it was small, she held her fingers up to guesstimate.

SexFucKitten: About 4 inches

idoljunkie: You've got to be fucking kidding me!

SexFucKitten: Serious, but his tongue is longer.
idoljunkie: Did he suck her crotch?
SexFucKitten: I did, while he fucked me from behind.
idoljunkie: Good
SexFucKitten: . . . and . . . I'm so wet . . . dripping

Darla stripped out of her clothing and placed a towel in her chair for her to sit directly on. She massaged her vagina with one hand and typed with the other.

idoljunkie: And then I'm there to tear your pussy up.
SexFucKitten: Size?
idoljunkie: Ten.
SexFucKitten: Big dick . . . width?
idoljunkie: Three.
SexFucKitten: Damn, you slit my clit. It hurts, I'm sore. Not used to a dick so fat. Ram it harder.
idoljunkie: K, feel it?
SexFucKitten: Yes, farther . . .
idoljunkie: All the way. Take it!
SexFucKitten: I'm taking it.
idoljunkie: The bitch, what she doing?
SexFucKitten: She's cumming all over my face.
idoljunkie: Yeah, almost there.

Darla forced her fist inside her. She wanted to feel the force of his large dick. She turned her head to the side. Still forcing her hand upward, she rocked side to side.

SexFucKitten: Me too.
idoljunkie: I feel your wetness.
SexFucKitten: I turn around, I'm drinking it. Darla's hand pumped faster.
SexFucKitten: aaaaaahhhhhhh!!!!!!!!!!!!!!!!!!!
idoljunkie: Yeah, that's it.

Darla closed her eyes tightly as her lips slowly curled up into a smile. "Yes!" she sang.

Unable to catch her breath, she felt disgusted by what she'd done. It wasn't like old times. Now she was a married woman and not as adventurous as she used to be. She exited the chat room and shut down her computer. Climbing into bed, she tossed and turned the entire night.

The next morning, Darla took a sip of coffee as she moped around her bedroom. She tried her best to keep her eyes open. She stayed up all night in the *Married but Looking* chat room, and now regretted it.

Taking a hard look at her puffed-up face in the mirror, she decided to call in sick. She wondered where Robert could have stayed last night and figured he went to Cydney's. Wryly, she focused her attention on getting herself some sleep. Her phone rang and woke her up.

"Hello."

"I'm so glad I caught you at home."

"Who is this?"

"It's Marci. Do you have a minute?"

Darla cleared her throat. "Yes."

"Well, I couldn't get a hold of Robert on his cell, so I thought I'd try reaching him at home."

"He's not here, but I'll relay the message." Darla pulled her hair up into a ponytail.

"That three-bedroom house out in Carillon is back on the market," Marci said. "The financing fell through with the other couple. I talked to their agent, and it's yours if you still want it."

Darla sat straight up in the bed. "What! Are you serious?"

"Yes, I am."

Darla grabbed her chest. "Well, I'm about to have a heart attack."

"I thought this would make your day."

"Yes, thank you." Darla hung up and dialed Robert's cell phone. They agreed to meet Marci at the house in less than an hour.

Marci's black Maxima was parked in the driveway when Darla approached the house, and Robert drove up a few minutes behind her.

Robert hugged Darla. "I missed you so much. We must talk after this."

"I know." Darla replied. Feeling her husband brush up against her body caused pulsations to flow from head to toe. "But, you're not coming home."

Once Darla stepped out of the elevator, she saw Kimberly leaning over helping a data clerk on the computer.

Hiding her face with the mug, Darla tried to slip past her supervisor.

"Darla, I need to see you in my office."

"I'll be there in a sec," Darla said.

"Now!" Kimberly ordered.

"Sure thing." Darla followed her inside and took a seat.

"How come you haven't been in to work for over a week?" Kimberly swiveled in her black leather chair.

"I told you I was sick with the flu." Darla faked a cough. "I'm just now starting to get my voice back."

"I'm sorry for your illness." Kimberly raised her pen in the air. "Have you given the new job any consideration?"

"Actually, I have." Darla clinched the arms on the chair. "I decided to pass."

Kimberly raised her eyebrows. "I'm not amused."

"I'm serious. I have way too much going on in my life right now."

"And I don't?" Kimberly pointed at her chest. "Besides, I've already found someone to take your place. So, if you don't take the training job, then you'll be out of a job."

"Kimberly, you can't do this."

"I can and I will." Kimberly picked up her headset. "David, can you come in here for a minute?"

Darla stood up. "I'm not going."

"Yes, you are."

"Yes, Kimberly," David said.

"Help Darla clean out her desk. She's moving down to the first floor in Marilyn's old office."

"What?" David put his hand on Darla's shoulder. "Did someone get promoted or something?"

Kimberly took a deep breath. "You're asking too many questions. Now do what I asked."

Darla balled up her fists as she followed David to her cubicle.

"Oh, you're back." Tamara smiled. "We were worried about you."

"Yeah, where you been?" Brandy asked.

"I'll explain later. Hey, I didn't want to tell you like this, but David is here to help me pack."

"What?" Tamara snapped. "Kimberly fired you?"

"Oh, no."

"Then what happened?" Brandy asked. "That bitch wants me to kick her ass."

Darla put her arms around Brandy. "No, I got another assignment."

"She's taking Marilyn's job," David chimed in.

"Marilyn got fired!" Tamara held both hands to her mouth.

"No." Darla was now aggravated. "Look, we'll talk about this during lunch. I need to get my things to-gether."

Tamara nodded. "I understand."

Darla thought her returning back to IT was actually a blessing in disguise. Accepting a promotion was a good thing, and with her recent separation from Robert, she needed something positive to focus on. She was feeling like her life was completely out of her control. Darla carried her large box down to Marilyn's office. She was surprised to see the office was empty; Marilyn had cleaned everything out.

"I was starting to sweat bullets for a minute," Marilyn said while she stood in the doorway.

Not bothering to look up, Darla continued to empty the contents from her box. "I'm sorry. I've been home, sick with the flu."

"So, I heard," Marilyn commented. "Well, I hope you're not here to infect us all."

Darla laughed. "I'm completely recovered."

Marilyn bowed her head. "Very good. I'm here to get you trained."

"I'm ready whenever you are." Darla plopped in her brown leather chair. She glanced around her huge corner office with a view. "You know, I could get used to this." She smiled.

CHAPTER FOUR

"We've cleared everything out of your bedroom," the moving guy said.

"Thanks, Larry," Darla said.

"Where do you want us to go next?" Larry adjusted his tool belt.

"Let's see, I need to finish packing my husband's stuff, so the kitchen is fine."

"I'll send the guys to pack in the kitchen." Larry left the room.

Darla continued to pack Robert's stuff from his nightstand. In her heart, she wished he could be there to pack his own things. Her mind told her to honor the separation and not allow Robert to move in until they were in the house. She hoped he'd missed her. It seemed she was calling him a lot more than he called her.

"I'm finished cleaning out your bathroom." Tamara took off her gloves. "When was the last time you cleaned it out?"

"That's Robert's bathroom," Darla said. "I don't even go in there."

"Oh, separate bedrooms and bathrooms." Tamara sat down on the stool. "Are you sure you want this? You know you deserve better."

"I'm starting to believe that."

"And look at you." Tamara pinched Darla's stomach. "It's getting hard there."

Darla grinned. "It's those workout videos."

"Besides starving yourself, I know you have to be doing more than those videos. You can tell me."

Darla taped up the box full of Robert's shoes. It's a shame the man owned more pairs of shoes than she did. "That's pretty much it. I'm up to three forty-minute videos a day."

"Whoa!" Tamara cleared her throat. "Well, you know people at IT think you had the surgery. You know, when you and Janet went to Mexico for a week."

"I don't care what they think. Oh, turn that up." Darla pointed at her radio.

Tamara turned up the volume to Jill Scott's "He Loves Me."

"I love this song." Darla swayed from side to side. She sang along with the lyrics:

You tease me . . .
You please me . . .
You school me . . .
Give me things to think about . . .

While rotating her hips across the floor, she pictured her husband making love to her while that song played softly in the background. She forgot Tamara was even in the room with her.

Tamara laughed. "I feel sorry for Robert."

"Why?" Darla frowned.

"Because when y'all finally have sex, you're going to break his thang off!"

"No, I won't." Darla playfully punched Tamara in the shoulder.

"But don't be calling me from the hospital when the man's penis is in a cooler on ice."

Darla shook her head. "Oh, stop it."

Tamara stuck out her tongue. "We'll see. All right, I'm getting back to cleaning. One more bathroom to go."

"Thanks." Darla opened Robert's nightstand and removed a stack of papers and condoms.

Wanting no memories of their open marriage, Darla tossed them in the garbage. Since she agreed to let him come back home, Robert had been acting like the perfect husband. He was now spending all his free time with Darla, and she had to admit she loved it. With the purchase of their home, Darla had reason to believe that it could only get better.

Darla came across a white envelope from Dr. James.

"Hello, big sis," Janet said as she entered the room.

"You scared me." Darla shoved the envelope in her back pocket.

"Now, who moves right before the holiday?" She waved her arms. "You just couldn't wait."

Darla poked out her bottom lip. "No."

"I understand." Janet's eyes scanned the room. "What do you want me to do?"

"You can finish packing up all my knick knacks in the living room." Darla instructed. "And please, wrap each one with paper. You know I love the ones Daddy brought us back from Korea."

"I'll handle them with care," Janet said as she put her hands in her jacket pockets.

"I appreciate your help." Darla leaned on the windowpane, and almost brought the curtains down. "Oooops! I need to take these down anyway."

"They won't match anything in your new house. I

know where they can go in my house." Janet reached and pulled the curtain rod.

"Nice try." Darla's head jerked. "I'll let you have them anyway."

"Do you have a screwdriver?" Janet tried to pull the bracket down with her hand.

"I'm not sure." Darla's eyes scanned around the room. "I'm sure we do, but where, that I don't know."

Janet snapped her fingers. "Just get me a butter knife from the kitchen."

Darla dug into a box labeled utensils and found a butter knife. She returned in the room, where Janet had climbed on top of a chair to make up for her short stature. "Where did you get this idea from, Trellis?"

"You know it." Janet used the knife to unscrew the brackets. "Trellis can make a tool out of just about anything."

"I thought he was going to stop by and help." Darla gulped down her Aquafina water.

"He is," Janet said as she rubbed her hands together. "I asked him to pick up a few groceries for the party. I'm going to make my spinach dip."

Darla rubbed her stomach. "That reminds me, I haven't had anything to eat all day. I'm supposed to eat a small meal every two hours."

"Then let's get out of here." Janet grabbed her purse. "I hope you don't mind me picking up Charity on the way."

"Now, why would I mind spending time with my niece?" Darla put on her leather coat. "I need to let Tamara and Larry know I'm leaving."

"I'll wait for you in the car."

Tamara finished the bathroom and headed home. Darla told Larry to take a lunch break, since it was company policy that someone must be there at all times.

When Darla reached the parking lot, she searched for her sister's car. Then she spotted Janet in a yellow Hummer.

Darla leaned back. "Did someone get a new car?" she asked once she buckled her seat belt.

"It's an early Christmas present for Trellis." Janet smiled coyly. "I'm going to surprise him when he gets here."

"Trellis doesn't know you traded in his Mustang?" Darla pretended to open the door. "Let me get the hell out of here. I don't want to be around when Trellis murders you."

Janet laughed and grabbed Darla's jacket. "Would you get back here? He's not going to be mad."

Darla smirked. "Yeah, right. Trellis washes that car at least four times a week. As Dr. Phil would say, what the hell were you thinking?"

Janet pursed her glossy lips. "That I'm tired of my man driving around in a car that he had sex with other women in."

"That was before you got married."

"True." Janet picked at her teeth in the mirror. "But, we were still together."

"You and Trellis have been a couple since high school!" Darla snapped. "The man's going to have slept with some women in between. Why do you have a problem with it now?"

Janet shrugged her shoulders. "I guess I always had a problem with it. Wouldn't you?"

Darla stared out the window. "I know I would."

"OK." Janet put the SUV in gear and drove slowly over the speed bumps.

The silence was killing Darla. At that very moment, she wanted to confess to her sister that she understood, in so many ways, how she felt. Trellis indulged in his share of black and white women, before he settled down and married her sister. Darla couldn't understand how her sister sat by and waited for him all those years.

"I always wanted to ask you about that."

"Ask me about what?" Janet asked.

"Was he worth it?"

"Hmph." Janet ran her hands through her bob-styled haircut. "Was he worth it? No man was worth me sacrificing my self-respect. If I had to do it all over again, I would've moved on without Trellis. I missed out on many opportunities in my life. But now I have to say, I wouldn't trade my family for the world."

That brought Darla back to the beginning of her relationship with Robert. She thought about the first time she discovered her fiancé was cheating on her and how betrayed she felt.

"I need to tell you something." And just like that, Darla began to divulge her dirty secret to her sister.

Darla and Cydney were best friends and worked at IT together. Cydney was skinny with blonde hair and blue eyes, representing everything Darla ever wanted to be. She was picture-perfect, and every man would cut off his right arm to be with her.

With a reputation as the "cubicle whore," Cydney was the most hated girl in the office. It always bothered Darla how all the women treated her, but she understood how she got the name. Every time she looked over in Cydney's direction, there was a guy stopping by to say hello. And it didn't help her image when Cydney wore low-cut blouses that showed off her cleavage.

Unlike all the other judgmental women, Darla actually befriended her and realized Cydney was a sweet person. Darla found out that Cydney never welcomed the attention she received from the guys at work. She had a boyfriend, Kevin, who worked as a bartender at Roxy's nightclub. They had been a couple for a long time, and she loved him more than life itself and never wanted to jeopardize their relationship.

They became the best of friends; Cydney helped Darla feel good about herself. She used the actress Mo'Nique as an example of why Darla should appreciate being overweight. It was who she was on the inside that really mattered. Darla bought into that garbage, only to find out Cydney was just using her.

Who wouldn't want the fat blimp as your best friend, when you looked like Jessica Simpson? All the more attention for Cydney, since no one was giving Darla more than a second's thought.

Cydney pretended to be so supportive of Darla's long-distance relationship with Robert and helped her gain the courage to confess to Robert that she'd been lying all along. After Robert and Darla became engaged, she invited Kevin and Cydney to join them for dinner. The four of them went to the Cheesecake Factory, and Robert and Cydney flirted with each other the entire time.

So much so, that Kevin got mad and insisted they leave early. After that, Darla figured she better not have her fiancé around Cydney again. This was the woman whose face was in the pictures he fell in love with.

From that point on, whenever Robert came down to spend time with Darla, she never bothered to tell Cydney; Darla would just made up an excuse why they couldn't go see a movie together, or whatever Cydney wanted to do. It only happened when Kevin was away with his friends for the weekend, though.

One night, Robert was staying at her apartment and spending a lot of time on the computer. He told her he was preparing for a difficult case, and she had no reason to believe he was lying. She trusted him.

When Robert went in the bathroom, and it sounded like he was jacking off, Darla became suspicious. She went on the computer and saw an IM with Cyd4Life minimized. She scrolled back and read parts of their steamy conversation. She knew Robert would be back in a minute, so she copied and pasted the entire IM in a Word document.

Once Robert was back home in Canada, Darla opened the document and was shocked to discover her fiancé was sleeping with her best friend. What made matters worse was when Darla confronted Robert about it, he didn't even bother to apologize for his behavior. He justified it by saying that this was all her fault, and if she hadn't used Cydney's picture to trick him into falling in love with her, there never would've been an infatuation in the first place.

Darla broke off her friendship with Cydney, and it was easy since she was no longer working at IT anyway. Kimberly never liked Cydney and fired her as soon as their workload slowed down. Foolishly, Darla gave Robert an ultimatum. If he didn't stop sleeping with Cydney, then she would break off their engagement.

That's when Robert issued her an ultimatum of his own, and Darla made her own deal with the devil. While Darla worked on losing the weight, he still had needs and would continue to use Cydney to meet his needs. Once Darla was slimmed down to his standard, he would drop Cydney and commit one hundred percent to their marriage.

Such an agreement seemed ludicrous at first. That is, until Robert cut off all communication with Darla. Not one phone call or email. Feeling like a ton of bricks landed on her body, Darla couldn't eat or sleep knowing that she'd lost the man of her dreams. As luck would have it, Darla actually lost fifty pounds. It was then that she realized she could actually lose the weight and have Robert all to herself. So what if Cydney had him for a few months? It would be the sweetest revenge to win him back and see the look on her face when Robert told her he didn't want her anymore. Cydney would die when she saw the new and improved Darla, skinnier and more beautiful than her. For once, the big girl would end up with the prize.

"I can't believe it." Janet's facial expression was one of complete shock.

Darla snapped back into reality and saw they were in front of Charity's daycare.

"We're not done." She opened the door. "I'll be back in a second, so you can finish."

Darla buried her head in her hands and cried for a second. She searched inside Janet's SUV for a tissue and remembered the envelope she stuffed in her back pocket.

Opening the envelope, she took the letter out. After reading it, she took out her cell phone and called Robert's doctor.

"Dr. Neill James' office."

"I'm calling in regards to my husband's test results," Darla said. She watched her little niece run out of the door of the daycare. Her curly tresses were flopping in the air.

"Who is the patient?" the receptionist asked.

"Robert Favor."

"And who are you?"

"I'm his wife, Darla Favor."

Janet opened the door and helped Charity into her booster seat.

"Aunt Darla!" Charity shouted.

"Hey, baby." Darla smiled as she touched Charity's hand. "Did you have a nice day?"

Charity bopped her head. "We had so much fun today. See my bracelet?" She dangled her chubby wrist in the air. Darla didn't know what her sister was feeding her, but she knew it wasn't the fruits and vegetables that Janet claimed to be giving her. From the looks of the child, she'd been eating pure junk food. Darla made a mental note to ask her sister about it later.

"It's beautiful, darling." Darla tossed her head back like a socialite.

Charity laughed. "That's not the way you do it." She slung her head back and to the right.

"Oh yeah." Darla mimicked her niece, except in a more exaggerated fashion. "Is that it?

Charity clapped her hands. "Yeeesss!"

Janet crossed the intersection and turned to face Darla. "Who are you talking to?"

Darla put her hand over the receiver. "I'm waiting for Robert's test results."

Janet looked puzzled. "You mean he didn't tell you?"

"He told me everything—"

"Mrs. Favor, I'm sorry, but those results are purely confidential." The receptionist responded.

Darla rested her free arm on the window. "I don't understand. I'm his wife, and I've never had any trouble getting them before."

"I understand. Robert's test results are red flagged, and that means the information remains confidential. And your husband requested none of his medical history be shared with anyone."

Darla took a deep breath. Clearly, she was frustrated; why her husband would do such a thing? "Is my name listed too?"

"No, but I would assume—"

"You didn't hear me." Darla shook her head. "Is my name listed anywhere on that request signed by my husband?"

"No."

Darla nervously gritted her teeth. "Then I have one more question for you."

"What's that?"

"Is Dr. James available?" Darla asked.

"Hold for a just minute. Let me check."

Janet parked in the Denny's Restaurant parking lot. "Do you want us to wait for you?"

"No, go ahead. I'll meet you inside."

Darla leaned back in her seat, as Janet and Charity went inside the restaurant. With all the trouble the doctor's office was putting her through, she had no choice but to think his test results were bad. The cancer must be back. And she couldn't help but wonder why Robert didn't tell her. The thought of her husband suffering in silence almost broke her heart. She wanted to call him and reassure him that he could beat this. With chemo or radiation, whatever it took, she would be right by his side to help him get through it.

"Sorry for the wait."

"No problem."

"I'll put you straight through."

Darla felt her stomach doing flip-flops as she awaited the news. She'd never experienced anything like this before, and she wondered if she was strong enough to handle it.

"Dr. James."

"Hello, it's Darla Favor."

"Yes, I know. Charlene just explained everything to me. Is it possible for you to stop by today? I would rather discuss your husband's test results in person."

"Oh sure."

"What time is good for you?" he asked.

"I'm close to your office now. I can be there in fifteen minutes."

Darla moved over to the driver's side and put the Hummer in reverse. It made a loud roar as she slowly backed it up. In Darla's mind, she pictured her sister's facial expression was one of complete shock because she was driving her husband's birthday gift. But, she had to know what was going on with Robert. As she peeled onto Colonial Road, her cell phone rang. Her new ring tone sounded.

Does that make me crazy . . .

It was Janet.

"What the hell are you doing?"

"I can't tell you right now, but I'll be back in a few minutes. I promise."

"Darla, you can't drive that truck. Now, come back and I'll drive you where you need to go."

"I can't stop. I have to get to there . . . and he's not going to wait all day . . . I have to go." Darla hung up on her sister.

Does that make me crazy . . .

Darla slammed on brakes at the traffic light. She was at the intersection of Alafaya and State Road 50. Putting her phone on vibrate, she tossed it on the passenger seat. She struggled to maneuver the huge tires into the tiny turning lane, and drove onto the grass, barely missing scraping the side of another car as she parked the vehicle. When she got out, she noticed she'd taken up two spaces, but at least she'd made it.

It was then she realized that her hair was still wrapped up in a green scarf. Quickly, she snatched it off and tossed it inside her purse. Running her fingers through her brown hair, she straightened up her clothing as best she could.

Once inside the doctor's office, she marched up to the receptionist's desk.

"Hi, I'm Darla Favor."

"Oh yes." Charlene raised her eyebrows. "That was quick."

Charlene picked up the phone. "Darla Favor is here." When she hung up, she pointed at the door. "You can go in, he's waiting for you."

CHAPTER FIVE

Darla allowed Brandy to convince her to get a new outfit for Janet's Christmas party. "JC Penney is having a good-behind sale. I'm going to help you find some sexy jeans to wear."

"I know Justin Timberlake keeps saying it, but I'm not ready for sexy yet," Darla said. She was still shy when it came to showing her body.

"Come on here." Brandy disappeared in the jeans section.

Darla searched for a sweater. She held up a mocha knit sweater.

"Now, that's cute. You need a tank top to go underneath it," Brandy added. She held a stack of jeans in her arm. "Let's try these on. I have three different sizes, and we can decide on the color later. Dark stonewash is what I think would go with that top. And some brown boots."

Darla went in the dressing room. The size fourteen fit her perfectly, and she got so excited. Never in her lifetime did she think she would fit into those jeans.

Darla paid for the outfit, then Brandy dragged her

down to the shoe department to find matching boots. Darla thought her clothes would be too showy, and she didn't want to attract too much attention.

"Now, I got to get you the hook-up with some jewelry. I know the perfect necklace to go with that sweater."

Darla stopped Brandy dead in her tracks.

"So, that's what this shopping excursion was all about. You wanted me to meet Walter."

"No, I didn't," Brandy stated. "I want you to look good at your sister's party."

Darla studied her carefully. "I don't believe you. But, how much of a discount are we talking about?"

"Cheap, honey."

This was Darla's first time meeting Walter. When she saw him, she understood what all the hoopla was about.

"This is my other best friend, Darla." Brandy smiled.

"It's a pleasure to meet you." Walter reached out his hand.

Darla shook hands with him. "Same here."

The door from the back opened, and a gorgeous black woman with weave all the way down her back came out.

"Jenna needs you for a minute."

Walter held up one finger. "I'll be right back. My wife will help you."

His wife?

Darla wanted to run out of there, but as long as Brandy was cool, she would play it cool, too.

"Hello, Brandy. So, you're not working today?" Cheryl asked.

"Not today," Brandy replied sharply.

"And you even come in on your days off." Cheryl cleared her throat. "What? Did you get fired from your third job at Club Tropic?"

Darla looked puzzled. Was she calling Brandy a stripper?

"Your husband should know," Brandy sang.

"What was that?" Cheryl asked emphatically.

"Oh, nothing." Brandy hummed to herself while waiting patiently.

Based on their exchange of words, this woman had to know Brandy was sleeping with her husband. All Darla wanted to do was high-tail it out of there.

"Thanks." Not wanting to stay in the tense atmosphere any longer, Darla drummed her fingers along the glass counter. "I don't see anything I like."

Darla quickly left and Brandy followed her out.

"I thought you wanted to get something."

"You know, I think what you did was terrible. That's his wife, and you went there just to bother her. Not cool, Brandy. Not cool at all."

"What?" Brandy adjusted her Coach bag on her shoulder. "Can I help it if she knows her husband is in love with me?"

Knowing she was dealing with the same situation at home, Darla trembled with rage. "You know, I'm married."

"And, you don't have a problem keeping your man," Brandy snapped. "She does."

"I so resent that," Darla scoffed. "I'm so glad I drove my own car up here. You don't have to kick me out, like you did to Tamara. I'm going home."

"Don't judge me, OK? I don't need that shit." Brandy lit a cigarette.

"I'm not judging you. You already know what you're doing is wrong. And if not, your moral compass needs some serious adjusting."

Brandy blew out smoke. "Whatever!"

Darla was so upset; she peeled onto Colonial Road like a racecar driver. It was tramps like Brandy who ruined marriages and destroyed families. After what she went through with Cydney, she couldn't believe she called someone like Brandy a friend.

The next afternoon, Darla applied her make-up while Robert took his time in the shower. She hated how Robert dragged around the house when they were doing something she wanted to do.

"You look ready to go," he replied.

"Yes, I'm leaving in a few." Darla puckered her lips to blend in the raspberry lipstick. "We can take separate cars if you like."

"I'll be ready." He brushed his penis up against her. "I want to make love."

Darla moved out of his way. "I don't. I'm not going to be late to my own sister's party." She pretended to search in her jewelry box for earrings until he left the bathroom.

She took a sigh of relief.

Dressed in her size fourteen jeans and a mocha colored sweater, she knew she was hot. It was too bad for Robert, because he had no idea that at the first of the year, Darla was divorcing him and asking the courts for some serious alimony. The man she was married to was a millionaire, and never bothered to tell her. It seemed Robert planned to marry Darla, get his citizenship, and dump her in the process.

Why else would he have close to twenty million dollars tucked away in a bank account in the Cayman Islands? That's the only scenario she and Janet could come up with. It made perfect sense to both of them.

"I want everybody to stop what you're doing and hit the dance floor!" Trellis announced through the microphone once "Family Affair" by Mary J. started playing.

Robert placed his hands on Darla's hips. "Dance with me."

Darla pushed his hands away. "Can't you see I'm eating?"

Robert put the plate down. "Quit shoving your face with that junk." He clapped his hands. "Let's dance."

"Why would you think I would dance with you after what you just said to me?" Darla asked. She pointed at the Hispanic girl wearing a short mini-skirt and dancing with her husband. "Why don't you dance with her?"

As far as Darla was concerned, that woman could have him. Darla laughed every time her husband made another embarrassing dance move. He made the saying, white boys ain't got no rhythm, so true.

Janet came up and whispered in Darla's ear. "Guess who's here?"

"Who?"

"Maurice."

"Stop your lies." Darla's eyes grew wide.

"No, I'm not lying." Janet crossed her hand over her heart. "I swear. And he's already asked about you."

"Are you serious?" Darla asked.

"As a heart attack." Janet took a sip of her sangria. "You remember how Maurice had a mad crush on you in high school?"

Darla licked her lips. "Yes, but I never believed it."

"I don't know why. He used to come to our house all the time to see you."

"But all we did was talk. Anyway, he was involved with Bernadine."

"Well, he's single now."

Darla grabbed her sister's hands. "Where is he?"

"That's what I thought. Come on." Janet opened the sliding glass doors and they pushed through a few guests standing around on the screened patio. She pointed. "He's over there."

And like a dream, Darla caught a glimpse of Maurice

Taylor. Looking better than she remembered him, his dark chocolate skin glistened in the moonlight. His hard body resembled that of a bodybuilder. She knew he was in the Air Force, which was why he and Trellis remained close friends for so many years.

Undressing her with his slanted eyes, Maurice spoke softly. "I thought you were bringing Darla back here, not Mariah Carey."

Darla blushed.

"Damn, girl, you look good!"

"Thanks." She clenched her teeth.

His eyes lingered for a moment, making Darla fidget with her hands nervously. "I saw your husband out there on the dance floor."

Darla held her forehead. "I'm so ashamed. I'm sorry you had to witness that."

Maurice moved closer to her. "It was a trip. White boy thought he was getting down."

Darla shook her head. "Well . . ."

Maurice put his lips close to hers, and then moved them toward her ear. "I've been checking up on you," he whispered.

Darla tried her best to hide the tingling sensation she felt.

"Here's my card if you need me."

Darla stared down at the business card with a gold border. "You're a physical trainer." How could she be so stupid? The man was trying to get a new client. "I could use one."

"I provide services at the gym and at home," Maurice teased. "For you, I'll make house calls."

"A man dedicated to the job," Darla flirted back. "I like the sound of that. Give me a few weeks to shed some dead weight, and I'll be ready."

Maurice grinned. "You do that." He winked as he strolled back inside the house.

Rapid taps on the glass door broke her concentration. It was Janet. She put her lips up to the glass and stuck out her tongue.

Darla almost choked on her drink. Obviously, her little sister was drunk. She signaled for her to come outside.

"So, how was he?"

"What have you told him about me?"

Janet looked puzzled. "Nothing."

Darla searched her eyes for honesty. "I'm not stupid."

Janet shrugged. "Nothing."

"I always know when you're lying." Darla pulled Janet's arm behind her back. "Spill the beans."

"Man!" Janet struggled to break free.

Darla let go of her tight grip. "Spill it."

"I can't believe you're so strong. I think you broke my arm."

Darla tossed up her hand. "You're fine. Now, start talking."

"I only told him you were getting a divorce. That's it."

Darla sat down. "That's it. Yeah, right. Maurice was practically having sex with me in his head."

"Well, he's always had a crush on you. And look at you. What man wouldn't?"

Darla took another sip of wine. "Thank you." She giggled.

"As Trellis would say: Girl, you gots it going on!"

Janet laughed. "Now, let's poke fun at your husband making a fool of himself."

Loud screams sounded as Busta Rhymes' "Touch It" remix blasted through the speakers. Darla and Janet rushed to the floor to dance. Then she saw her best friends, Brandy and Tamara, join in.

The four of them formed a circle and started their competition of who had the best moves. Tamara popped her body in every direction and it garnered some yells from the crowd. Then Darla swayed her body and attempted Beyonce's booty-shaking dance.

Janet, not to be outdone by her sister, worked out the same move until Trellis got mad and pushed her off the floor. Brandy bent completely over and jiggled her butt cheeks, one at a time, and the crowd roared. Brandy pumped her hands in the air, knowing she was the winner of the dance-off.

Darla was so glad she made it to the party, because every year it got better.

"So, let me get this right," Brandy said. "You have been putting up with Robert fucking other women, while you were married?"

Darla nodded. "I know. I was so stupid."

Brandy took another bite of her burger. "That's beyond stupid."

Tamara rested her hand on Darla's. "I don't know why you didn't tell us. We're your best friends."

"No one knew, not even my sister. I couldn't tell you." Darla shamefully drifted her eyes toward the floor.

"Why not?" Tamara asked.

"Because I knew you didn't believe a man like Robert would ever be attracted to a woman like me, yet alone marry me."

"That's not true." Tamara scratched the side of her face.

Brandy sucked her teeth. "Tamara, quit lying. You've said to me on more than one occasion, you didn't know what Robert saw in Darla."

Tamara's mouth fell open. "Why are you lying on me like that?" She squeezed Darla's hand. "Don't believe her."

Brandy flipped her braids back. "Quit your faking. She doesn't need our lies right now. You need to 'fess the fuck up. You know you said it."

"What I said was I never thought—"

"I knew it!" Darla snatched her hand away.

"Yeah, I'll admit it, if Tamara won't. I thought his ass was too good to be true." Brandy crossed her legs. "In this day and age, men want all the skinny bitches. And I didn't see why Robert was any different. But, when y'all got married, I figured I was wrong."

Tamara bit her bottom lip. "I thought the same thing. I'm sorry it didn't work out that way."

Darla buried her head in her hands. "I should've known better too. Actually, this was all my fault. I never should've sent him that picture of Cydney in the first place."

"No, you told him the truth when things got serious," Brandy said. "If he was a real man, he would've ended it then. But no, he took advantage of the situation and tried to gain a US citizenship out of it too. And if you want to know something else, while we're being completely honest here, Robert played up that whole cancer thing to gain your sympathy."

Darla rubbed her arm. "Actually, Robert doesn't have cancer."

"What!" Tamara and Brandy yelled in unison.

"Nope." Darla pulled out a white envelope from her purse. "He's been sick lately, so I told him to go see the doctor. I got this letter in the mail the other day to call immediately about his test results. Since they wouldn't tell me anything on the phone, I went in to see Dr. James in person. He told me very little. So Janet and I went back to the apartment and rummaged through all of his stuff. We didn't find anything."

"Did you check his cell phone?" Tamara asked. "That's how I found out Barron was cheating on me."

"He had his phone with him," Darla responded. "When Janet left my house, I continued looking through everything. I don't know what it was, but something told me to search inside the boxes Robert packed himself. I found a locked box and picked the lock with a butter knife. That is when I discovered some paperwork." Tears welled up in her eyes. "I found out Robert is taking HAART."

"What the hell is HAART?" Brandy took a spoonful of her chocolate Frosty.

Darla took a deep sigh. She needed to choose her words very carefully. "It's an antiretroviral therapy."

"For what?" Tamara inquired.

Darla searched around Wendy's to make sure there weren't any other IT employees in sight. "It's slows down the progression of HIV."

"Well, that would mean Robert has HIV." Tamara's smile disappeared. "No way!"

Brandy put her hands to her mouth.

"Now you know everything I know." Darla put her fork in her empty salad bowl.

"Have you been tested?" Tamara asked.

"You're not listening to me." Darla tossed her head, flinging her hair off her shoulders. "My husband and I never slept together."

"I know you told me that once, but I thought y'all were breaking headboards since you lost all that weight."

"What the fuck? Hold on!" Brandy waved her hand in the air. "Am I the only one that's been in the dark here?"

"Well, if you weren't out sleeping with your own married man," Tamara said through clenched teeth. "You're not an example of fidelity, are you?"

Brandy turned up her nose. "I know you're not talking, the one who's now sleeping with the guy who left your ass and, might I remind you, kicked it on the way out."

Darla burst out laughing. "You guys are crazy. I needed a good laugh. It's been hard acting like the perfect wife to Robert, knowing all this about him."

"I know I couldn't do it." Brandy scratched her arm.

"Well, Janet thinks I should hire a private detective to find out why he's hiding all that money and find out more about his family too."

"It does seem weird that none of his family members came to the wedding," Tamara said. "When you said they couldn't afford to fly down, considering how broke I always am, it made sense to me."

"Have you ever met them?" Brandy asked.

"Nope. Only his friend Danny."

"That doesn't sound right." Brandy noted. "How much do one of them cost? I might have to get some investigating done myself."

"Somewhere around five thousand."

"Awww, hell no!" Brandy shook her head. She leaned on the table. "I'll just ask Pookie and them on the corner. They'll find out everything I need to know about a nigga."

Tamara suppressed a grin. "You're so fabulous."

"I'm serious." Brandy defended. "If you used them right now, you'd probably find out some dirt on Barron."

"I don't need any dirt on my man," Tamara snapped.

"Your man!" Brandy scoffed.

"Is that who you plan to spend Christmas with?" Darla asked.

"No. I'm going home to see my own family."

"And where will Barron be?" Brandy asked incredulously.

"I suppose I'll run into him."

"With Monica," Darla said.

Brandy sang. "And a very pregnant Monica at that."

"Maybe, but I can handle it." Tamara crossed her legs. "I'm a big girl now. I'm not weak like I used to be."

"Sure you are." Brandy nodded.

"Well, we know Walter will be with his wife and four children," Tamara chimed in.

As the declared mediator, Darla knew it was time to stop these ladies before they killed each other. She stood up. "We better get back. We're already late."

"Forget Kimberly. If she say one more thing to me today, I'm quitting." Brandy dumped her tray in the garbage.

Tamara put on her sunglasses as they walked outside. "Now, why would you say that? And you know you need to get Chyna's Christmas gifts off layaway."

Brandy sucked her teeth. "I don't use layaway. You're thinking of your mammy," she sang.

Darla shook her head. They were always going at it.

CHAPTER SIX

For the fifth day in a row, Darla woke up from a wet dream. And each time, Maurice was in it. Having spoken with him on the phone on several occasions, Darla got to know him better.

Maurice was divorced from a woman who was also in the military. Together they had a son, Tahj. His ex-wife got out and found a job as a civilian on the base in Alamogordo, New Mexico. Maurice worked at Patrick Air Force Base, less than an hour from Orlando. He also moonlighted as a physical trainer.

It was clear to Darla that Maurice was interested in pursuing a relationship with her. However, she needed to divorce her husband before she was ready to move on. Being friends was the best solution, and she never resorted even once to crossing the boundaries that were established. She liked the way Maurice respected them too.

Darla felt she needed to confront Robert about all his lies. She wasn't concerned with hearing any more excuses from him. She only wanted him to know she knew everything. More importantly, she wanted out of the marriage. She prayed he wouldn't give her a hard time about it. Trellis and Janet were on their way over to make sure he didn't.

Robert handed her a cup coffee. "Did you have a bad dream?"

"No." Darla took a sip carefully. Robert always made it too hot.

"I heard you moan." He sat down beside her and ran his fingers through her hair. "You're so beautiful. When can I have you?"

Darla slouched down deep in the covers. "I don't want to talk about this right now."

"Why not?" he asked. He slapped his chest. "I'm your husband. I want to discuss it now."

"Look." Darla placed the mug on the nightstand. "I don't want to be with you anymore. Robert, I want a divorce"."

"No. No." Robert jerked his head. "When I married you, it was forever. What did I do?"

"Everything." Darla leaned forward. "Including sleep with my friend, and God knows who else."

"We agreed that I could."

"I don't give a damn about the agreement. I was stupid." Darla pushed him. "I was stupid to agree."

Robert shoved a pillow over her face. "You don't leave me. I will kill you."

Darla struggled with him to get the pillow off her face, but he was much stronger. When she couldn't fight any longer, she passed out.

Darla sat straight up in her bed. Her eyes wandered around the room. She realized it was just a dream. Darla ran her hands through her hair, still trying to get the dream out of her head. "That was scary."

Darla showered, and then searched around the house for Robert. On the breakfast bar, she found a note.

"Have a meeting." The language barrier between the two of them got on her nerves. And to think, there was a time when she thought his accent was sexy.

Retreating to the family room, where a glass wall opened up to the pool with a fountain the middle, Darla turned on the television. Jerry Springer was on. A woman was leaving her husband for a man with half a body. Not even half; he only had a head, chest, and long arms. Apparently, he was giving her some mean oral sex. She couldn't believe how pathetic the guest on the show was to be in love with that freak. Her own story was perfect for the show. It was funny how she never believed those Jerry Springer stories to be true.

As she sat there, her mind began to wander.

No, he wouldn't.

Curiosity got the best of her, and in less than thirty minutes, Darla backed out of her garage in her Toyota Matrix. When she drove to Cydney's apartment, sure enough, Robert's car was there. Grabbing the tire iron from the trunk, Darla went to the door.

She heard moans and groans from the bedroom window. Tiptoeing along the walkway on the second floor to the adjacent window, she kneeled down to peak inside the mini-blinds. Robert lay on the bed, while Cydney was on top of him.

Does that make me crazy . . .

Her cell phone sang the song by Gnarls Barkley. Both of them looked around. The woman she thought was riding her husband was no woman at all. It was Kevin!

Stunned at what she saw, Darla backed up against the rail. She ran downstairs to her car.

Cydney pulled up beside her.

Amused by what her ex-best friend was about to witness, she let her window down. "You're such a slut for sleeping with my husband! I should get out of this car and kick your ass!"

"Oh, my God." Cydney squinted. "Darla. Is that you?"

That's right. She'd never seen the slimmed-down Darla.

"Yes, it's me." Darla sped off. She could just picture the look on Cydney's face when she saw her boyfriend riding her lover in their bed. For a second, she hoped Cydney felt as horrible as she had. Payback was a bitch!

In fact, she decided she wanted to witness Cydney's reaction. Darla put her car in reverse and backed into a space in the middle lot.

Does that make me crazy . . .

She looked down at her cell phone. It was Janet.

"Hey, I'm in the middle of something. Let me call you right back."

"No, I have to tell you something. It's important."

Darla took a deep breath. "I'm going to call you back. I want to see this."

She hung up.

Does that make me crazy . . .

She hung up again.

The door to Cydney's apartment opened and Robert appeared, leaving the door ajar. His eyes immediately searched around the parking lot, and he quickly ran down the steps. He sped off in his car.

What! That was it? No big blow up?

Darla got out and ran up to the apartment. Since the door was open, she peeked inside.

"Hello."

Not a word, only the sound of the television blaring loudly.

"Cydney." Darla went inside. She went straight to the

bedroom and found the two of them in the room. Cydney was on the floor with a cordless phone shoved in her mouth. And Kevin was slumped over in a pool of blood with a bloodied bat lying beside him.

Kevin's head lifted up.

"Oh my God!" Darla screamed and ran out onto the stairwell. "Help!"

A door opened from down the hall, and a guy came out. He looked the age of a college student.

"Are you OK?" he asked her repeatedly.

"There." Darla started to hyperventilate. She pointed. The guy disappeared inside.

"What's going on?" A girl came out of the same apartment.

"Penny!" he yelled from inside. "Call 911!"

"What!" All of a sudden, Penny's face turned red.

"Do it!" Darla shouted.

The paramedics and police arrived shortly. A female police officer wrapped Darla in a blanket and helped her down to her car. "Can you tell me what happened?"

"I . . . I . . . came here and saw my husband." Darla's lips twisted and she started to cry.

"What's your name?" she asked.

"Darla Favor."

"Darla, what is your husband's name?"

"Robert." Darla's throat locked up, and she couldn't breathe.

"She's going into shock!"

Darla regained consciousness and saw she was in the back of what she believed to be an ambulance. It wasn't long before they arrived at the hospital. On the gurney, she was pushed inside a room.

Her voicemail beep sounded off on her cell. Pulling her phone out of her pocket, she saw seventeen missed calls.

Darla called her voicemail. As she listened to the message, she began to cry.

"Darla, get to my house now! Do not go home."

She deleted the message. She went to the second message.

"Where are you? Trellis is on his way to your house. Robert is a murderer. I'm not kidding. I wish I was. He killed Eduardo Ramirez, his wife, and daughter. Then he stole twenty million dollars from their bank account. Please call me!"

Darla went to call her sister on the phone.

The female police officer took it out of her hands. "Are you calling your husband?"

"No, my sister. She's trying to find me."

"Your sister is in the hallway."

"What?" Darla sat up in the bed.

"I'll get her. First, I need to ask you a few questions."

Darla answered the questions as best she could. She couldn't believe how few things she actually knew about the man she'd been married to.

The officer said she was satisfied with her answers and left to get her sister.

Janet and Trellis rushed inside. Janet flung her arms around Darla. "I was so scared for you. I'm so glad you're all right."

Afraid to return to her own house, Darla accepted her sister's invitation to stay at their home. A week later, Robert was captured. The authorities planned to extradite him back to Toronto to be charged with the murders of the Ramirez family.

As the details of the case unfolded, Darla learned Robert was involved in a gay relationship with Eduardo, and when Eduardo refused to leave his wife, he murdered them both in their home. Having stolen their bank cards, he cleaned them out entirely and deposited them in a secret bank account in the Cayman Islands. Which Janet had tracked down, with her job at the bank. The private detective Janet hired turned over the information to the Orange County Police Department.

At least twice a day, Darla called the hospital to check on the status of her ex-best friend. Cydney remained in a coma, and Kevin was now a quadriplegic. Darla felt horrible, and in many ways she blamed herself. If only she hadn't brought that murderer into their lives, they would all be healthy and thriving. No one knew for sure if Cydney would recover, and Kevin would live the rest of his life in a wheelchair. She sank into a deep depression.

At her sister's house, she flipped the channels on her remote and kicked her feet up on the bed. She'd been living like a recluse, not even bothering to look out the window. With all the reporters and news crews camped outside of her sister's house, the media frenzy over Robert's crimes took center stage and the entire street was a circus.

The neighbors were demanding Trellis and Janet to move out. One morning, Trellis got into a shouting match with the neighbor two houses down. From the first day they moved into their house, the closet KKK member always found a reason to start trouble. This was just the platform he needed to rally the other residents.

Darla felt so bad for her sister and brother-in-law, because they dealt with enough scrutiny already, just being an interracial couple. Trellis told Charity the cameras were there to take pictures of their beautiful daughter, so every time she left the house, she waved to the camera crew. She seemed to be unaffected by the whole thing.

It had gotten to the point where Darla felt it was best to go back to her own house. She didn't want to cause any more trouble for her sister. She planned to sit Trellis and Janet down that evening and tell them she wanted to go home, even though she knew they would try to talk her out of it.

Janet knocked on the door, and then entered. "You've got company."

Darla grabbed her purple satin robe. "Who is it?"

"It's me," Tamara said.

Seeing Tamara's face almost brought Darla to tears. "Hi." She opened her arms to welcome her best friend. "I'm so happy to see you."

Tamara turned around. "You didn't tell her."

Janet pointed at Darla's robe with a hole in it. "Does it look like I told her?"

"Tell me what?" Darla's face turned bright red.

"Calm down." Tamara held up her hands. "We're taking you to church. Your sister is worried about you, and we both agree that you need some encouragement."

Darla flipped up her frizzy hair. "I'm not ready to go out yet."

"That's why I'm here," Tamara replied.

"And me!" a voice yelled from the hall.

Darla shook her head. "That loud mouth only belongs to one person."

Brandy came in, dressed in an ivory pantsuit, and plopped down in front of Darla. "You better know it!" She kissed her cheek. "And we're going to get you all glammed up for your first night out with the girls."

"Janet, are you going?" Darla inquired.

"Yes." Janet looked down at her cotton top and shorts. "Not dressed like this; I'm about to change."

"Who's having church in the middle of the week?"

"It's a conference at my church. I'm a member of New Destiny, and my pastor is hosting the Women at the Well Conference. Paula White is going to be there."

Darla clasped her hands together. "Then I have to go. OK, make me beautiful."

"That was easy." Brandy put her hands on her hips. "Let's see. We have one hour. I guess we can do something."

Tamara giggled. "Don't mind her."

Darla showered and let Janet blow-dry and style her hair, while Tamara and Brandy argued over which dress they thought looked best on her. Darla cracked a smile as she listened to them go back and forth. It felt like old times.

On the way to church, Darla prayed for a way out of her misery. She knew Paula White would offer her some powerful words for her to live by. Since Darla hadn't been to work in almost a month, she watched her show every day.

The conference was so uplifting. Tamara danced up and down the aisle, and Janet gave her life over to the Lord. And Brandy. Well, she was entertained by the whole thing. Darla couldn't wait to return for the second night.

The next day, Darla turned on the shower while she searched for a towel in the hall closet. Her nerves were on edge, since she knew it was Robert's court day.

"What's happening?" Janet asked as she stood up from the couch.

They heard an uproar from the reporters and news crews outside the house. When all of the phones started ringing at the same time, her heart sank. She was ready for the news, no matter how bad it was.

Janet answered the house phone, while Darla grabbed her cell phone.

"Hello."

"Oh my God!" Tamara screamed. "Darla, are you watching the news?"

"No, what's going on?"

"It's Robert. He went crazy!"

"What!" Darla yelled.

"Turn on the TV," Tamara said.

"Let me call you back!" Darla placed her cell phone on the end table.

Janet turned on the television as she continued talking on the phone, and Darla sat beside her. Feeling like her life wasn't her own, Darla stared at the television as the cameras zoomed in on her husband's face as he was being taken into the courthouse. He was being arraigned and officially charged with the murders of the Ramirez couple.

Darla barely recognized his pale face; his hair was disheveled and he'd lost a considerable amount of weight.

Robert, who was handcuffed, was escorted into the courtroom by police and his lawyer. Within a second of the policeman removing his handcuffs, Robert grabbed a gun from the police officer and fired shots into the courtroom. She heard loud screams and bodies fell to the ground.

Darla almost jumped out of her skin.

"Oh my God." She put her hands to her mouth.

The cameras went black and then a news reporter began talking. "Almost like a scene from a movie, Robert Favor fired several shots into the courtroom, killing the judge, and injuring several others. His attempt to escape was short-lived, as the defendant was gunned down. We're not sure how many shots were fired or the condition of Robert Favor, but as soon as we learn more details, we'll report them to you."

Darla grabbed her chest. Although she watched with her own two eyes, she couldn't comprehend what she was seeing. None of this made any sense to her.

The reporter came back on. "Robert Favor is dead . . ."

Darla screamed as she took in the news report. Janet wrapped her arms around her.

"No, this wasn't supposed to happen!" Darla shouted. She cried hysterically.

Janet put her arms around her sister. Too much had happened for her to comprehend it all. All she knew was she hated Robert for ruining her life, and now that he was dead, she felt an instant sense of relief.

"All we need is a few more signatures." Darla signed the papers as instructed. Trellis and Janet sat beside her.

"That's it." Mr. Darby, Robert's lawyer, wrapped up the meeting.

Once they were outside, Trellis rubbed his bald head. "I can't believe you have all that money. What are you going to do with it?"

"I don't know yet." Darla put on her sunglasses. "I will definitely take care of you guys and my niece." She rubbed Janet's stomach. "And my little nephew on the way."

Janet smiled.

As Robert's wife, Darla inherited his parents' estate. They died when he was very young. Robert was the only child, so there was no one to contest it. She also received an insurance check, which she would use to make sure her deceased husband had a proper burial. In total, Darla Favor was two million dollars richer.

Brandy

CHAPTER ONE

"I just feel so stupid for believing his lies," Tamara said.

"You should feel really dumb!" I shouted as I lit my second Marlboro cigarette. "Hey, I've been there before. I believed Chyna's daddy was going to clean up his act. And look at where he is now: walking the streets like a dirty, funky crackhead. Wait a minute, he *is* a crack-head."

"I guess it was a good decision to got rid of the baby." Tamara sighed. "I never wanted to be a single parent. And that's where I would be right now."

"I don't care what anybody says, being a single mother is the hardest fucking job in the world." While I sat in a plastic chair in front of my apartment, I was mad as hell. As usual, Walter was late. That's why I took my slow-ass time asking Pookie to make his delivery. Money was tight, and I didn't have none to waste if he wasn't coming.

"You never told me when the twins were born."

"Oh. They were born on Saturday," Tamara replied.

"Last Saturday!" I shouted into the receiver. "He's a trip."

"I know."

"And you had sex with that nigga last night?" I asked. Feeling like ants were underneath my skin, I scratched my arm until it almost bled.

"I didn't have sex with him. I said I saw him last night. Since I got saved, I'm not fornicating anymore."

I thought about how much Tamara had changed since she joined the church. Claiming to be saved, Tamara dressed and talked about everything so differently, I couldn't half stand to be around her anymore. She always acted like a little "goody-goody," but now she wanted to quote scriptures and ask people to come with her to church. I ain't got time for all that.

"Girl, I couldn't do that. I love dick way too much!" I shouted.

Tamara laughed, and then cleared her throat. "Brandy, your life is far more important than a few minutes of pleasure."

Here she go with that shit again. I tuned her out as I went inside to search for a Band-Aid. I heard Chyna in her room making a lot of noise. "Hold on for a second. Let me check on this child of mine."

I rested my cordless on my shoulder and opened Chyna's bedroom door. She was singing Fantasia's song "Free Yourself" and was tearing that shit up better than Fantasia's ass. That's it, baby, my girl was going to blow up and make Mama rich one day.

"Chyna, you sound real good, baby." I clapped my hands.

"Thank you." Chyna giggled.

"But you need to keep it down." I smiled. "Especially when Mr. Walter gets here. You know he doesn't like to hear all that loud noise. He works hard and he needs his rest."

"I know, Mama. I'm a be quiet." Chyna reached out her arms for a hug.

I squeezed her tightly. "That's my baby."

"That's right." Tamara sounded pitiful. "You did say Walter was coming over. I'll let you go."

"I guess he's coming." I went back outside to look for him.

"Well, kiss Chyna for me. Remember, I'm getting her next weekend."

I rolled my eyes. "So she keeps reminding me. She can't wait."

I hung up the phone.

Chyna was the best thing that ever happened to me, otherwise I'd curse the day I met her daddy, Phillip. We met at Seminole Community College, and he was on the basketball team. That was when I worked for Pookie to make up for what my financial aid didn't cover. And I got my shit for free too. Yeah, Pookie wanted his dick sucked every now and then, but I didn't mind. Each time, he supplied me with enough inventory to last me a month.

So anyway, I used to kick it with the boys on the team, hook them up with some blow every now and then. So they was cool with me. Used to holla at me in between classes, 'cause you know, them was my boys.

Phillip was a little freshman and green as day. I'll never forget the day he called me on my cell phone, asking me to bring them some candles and flashlights. I showed up at the house they were staying in, and the lights had been cut off. The coach didn't even have enough money to keep them on.

I usually don't even get fooled up with no young gits

like Phillip, but he had something to work with, if you know what I mean. I had to teach him how to use that thing, but once he got the hang of it, he knew how to hit that G-spot every time. He was so pretty too. Mixed with black and Puerto-Rican, I knew that if I had a child it would have to come from him. I always wanted me one of them pretty girls with a head full of curly hair.

And I'm damn near broke, trying to take care of it. Chyna's hair soaked up more products than my own hair. And they weren't cheap, either.

Phillip was six foot seven, so he played the center position on the team. They needed him too. Up until then, SCC was losing all their damn games. They probably held the record for more losing seasons. I don't know that shit for sure, so don't be quoting me on it.

Colleges were recruiting him from all over the country, but when he only scored a fourteen on the ACT, they stopped calling. His only option was SCC. They'll take any damn body, which explains why I was going there.

Phillip was a sweet boy. It's a shame, I was feenin' for that dick more than I cared about him. Had to have it. And he was feenin' for that blow in the worst way. Phillip was a good boy. He always called his mama on Sunday with a phone card they gave him. Wasn't that sweet? Too bad they sorry asses never came down from New Jersey to check on him. That's why I had to take care of him.

I was shelling out all my hard-earned money for that boy. Paying bills, and fixing his car when it broke down, which was all the fucking time. At the time, my blue Impala was on its last leg, and I was giving him money to take care of his car. It made no sense, and just about every month I said I was through with his behind.

It wasn't long before I stopped going to my classes and

got slapped on academic probation. I wasn't serious about school anyway. Thinking like a businesswoman, I was using it as a means to an end. If I could get in good with the college students as their main supplier, then I had a gig to last me for years.

Pookie was loving me by then. He hooked me up with my own place, close to campus. Yes, it was laid. Every room had brand new furniture in it. And I had money put up in the bank. I had a much better grade of addicts showing up at my place, white boys mostly, and I never had to deal with that credit shit. Now, some of them white boys was cute, so I used to ask them for a little dick action.

Don't even get me started talking about Adam, whose father was the CEO of a Fortune 500 company. The boy had lips that worked magic on my pussy. I couldn't get enough of him, and he was crazy for this black stuff. Yeah, me and Adam used to have some good times. Those were the days. I was living very well. When Phillip dropped out of school is when all of my problems started. I remember it like it was yesterday.

It was the middle of the night, and I had crashed hard from smoking something. Damn, I really don't remember what, but I know I was fucked up. Somebody was tapping on my bedroom window, which I wasn't used to in that kind of neighborhood. When my titties jiggled, I realized I was butt-ass naked and put on a T-shirt. Peeking through the blinds, I hardly recognized Phillip in those filthy clothes. His hooded jacket was ripped and his hair was nappy, like he ain't had no cut in months.

"Go to the front door!" I yelled through the glass.

Phillip nodded and walked toward the front of my apartment.

Taking a few deep breaths, I prayed I wouldn't pass the fuck out when I saw him face to face. Guilt overtook my emotions, because I knew in some way I had created a monster. Pictures of Phillip's pretty boy face with pale-colored skin and sharply cut Asian eyes flashed in my mind.

A knock at the door.

I closed my eyes, hoping if I didn't answer he would go away.

A second knock.

My feet felt so heavy as I struggled to reach the door. I opened it, and Phillip looked far worse than I even imagined.

"What's up, Bee?" Phillip asked as he snatched my shirt.

I pulled away, and he followed me inside. "Uh-huh, Phillip. Where the hell you been?"

I turned my head away and held my breath. Phillip's smelled like he rolled two garbage cans in with him.

"Around."

I turned up my nose. "Where?"

"You know . . ." He smiled, revealing two missing front teeth. "I wasn't with no woman or nothing, if that's what you think."

"And why would I care about that?" I asked. "Me and you ain't together no more. I done told you that."

"I know." Phillip put his hand on his hip. "I just need to get cleaned up. That's all I need. Then, I'll be out of your way. You won't see me."

I nervously tapped my foot. "Okay. Use the bathroom in the hallway. Don't come in my room, Phillip. Take a shower, and then get your ass out!" I pointed at the door.

Phillip threw up his hand. "OK."

Going to the hall closet, I snatched two of my oldest towels and a few wash rags. I handed them to him.

"I'm going back to bed," I said as I rubbed my eyes. "I'm not playing with you, Phillip."

"I know." Phillip smiled. "Thank you."

I turned around and walked away. "You're welcome."

As soon as I closed my bedroom door, I slid to the floor. For the first time, I was feeling the effects of something I created. The same way I used to blame my mother for the way she treated me and my brother, I had to blame myself.

What have you done? If it wasn't for me, Phillip would've never smoked weed, never mind get strung out on crack.

With all the noise, Phillip was making in the bathroom, I didn't think I could go back to sleep. My eyes became heavy as I stared at the used needles on my night stand. I remembered that the powder had me so jumpy, I shot up, to help me come down from my high.

When I finally woke up, the sunlight hit my eyes. The first thing I zoomed in on was my open bedroom door. I jumped out of my bed and tripped over my underwear drawer.

I've been robbed!

"Phillip!" I screamed. I searched around my place, but he was nowhere. Even the front door was barely hanging on its hinges. The walls were scratched and dinged up, with paint removed in many places. And I didn't have couch no more. All my shit was gone! The TV, my stereo, muthafucking VCR . . . I ran back to my room. Pulled up my mattress. The envelopes was missing.

"Oh shit!" Pookie was going to kill my ass, because the money was gone. I went in my closet and searched for my back-up stash. Tossing dirty clothes to the side, I found the blue plastic bin was unopened. Inside was some pills, weed, cash, and . . .

"Step away from the closet."

I almost *shitted in my* draws when I heard that voice behind me.

"Raise your hands, where I can see them!"

I did as I was told. "Officer, I live here. I was robbed."

"I know. Now, stand up slowly."

A tear as cold as ice ran down my cheek; I knew I was headed for prison. Suddenly, I felt his hand on mine.

"Don't move a muscle." He instructed as he placed handcuffs around my wrists. "You're not under arrest, I just want to ask you a couple of questions."

I shook my head nervously.

The officer backed me up to my bed and sat me down, so I could finally see his face. He was white with blonde hair and blue eyes. A slim figure, dressed in a dark blue uniform.

"You say you live here?" he asked as he searched through the blue bin. He lifted the clear plastic filled with cocaine.

"Oh shit!" Another voice yelled. A heavyset police officer walked in. "Looks like we hit the jackpot here!"

The blonde haired officer smirked. "Looks like it."

"Yeah, she's been up to no good." It was the landlady. "People coming in and out of here nonstop."

I rolled my eyes. With all the money I paid this woman to keep her mouth shut. Now, she was selling my black ass out.

"I've called your office so many times, but you never come!" Ms. Sanchez shouted.

I kept my mouth shut, because I knew I was going to do a lot of time for this. But, I worked out a detailed plan of how I was going to kill Ms. Sanchez, Pookie for getting me caught up in this shit, and most of all, Phillip, when I got out.

I told the police everything they wanted to know. I made up a fake nickname for my supplier, and they released me. I found out later, Phillip and his crew not only cleaned out my apartment, but four others, too. It wasn't long after that incident that I found out I was pregnant. With no place to go, I moved in with my junkie mother. Since me and her don't get along, I got me a job at Popeye's. Within a month, I moved the hell up out of there.

Knowing I was pregnant, I cleaned myself up. It was easy, because I wasn't hooked on nothing. Once I knew I was having a baby, I smoked a little weed every now and then, but that was it. When Pookie told me that Phillip was picked up, I went up there to see him. He kept telling me how sorry he was and made a lot of promises I knew he wasn't going to keep.

It's a shame, when I left the jailhouse that day, I walked right past his mama, and she didn't even know who the fuck I was. I recognized her from the pictures Phillip showed me. Now, when the boy hit rock bottom, she had the nerve to come see about him.

If you asked his ugly mama, she would say her son was perfect until he hooked up with me. If you want to know the truth, Phillip was a time bomb ready to blow the fuck up.

If it wasn't for my daughter, my life would have been heading nowhere. I knew I didn't want her to suffer the way I did. I worked hard to provide the best for her. When I got the job at IT, I was happy to be making some decent money again. It wasn't long before I couldn't stand that place, and especially that damn Kimberly. IT was the muthafucking plantation, and I'm the damn slave working for someone crazy like Kimberly. Even with my part-time job at Zales, I was barely making enough to cover my bills.

I heard Pookie's car, with the loud crunk music, speakers vibrating, and smoke coming out the windows, more than a mile away. I had to get him out quick, because Donita, the office manager, would drive her golf cart down here in a hot minute. We used to get away with a

lot of shit when Shavonda managed the place. As long as
we provided enough to get her high, she ignored all the
rules.

The property management company fired Shavonda
and hired that bitch. She was nosey as hell and always in
everybody's damn business. If Donita thought some shit
was going down, she'd use her key and bust right up in
your place. She didn't have time for no speculating.

I heard the first week Donita started, my girl Whitney
was having a party. I wanted to go to her party so bad,
but I was holed up with Walter at the hotel that same
night. Everybody was talking about it. Whitney even
handed out flyers. That was our hustle at the end of the
month, to charge for parties to make a little money to
cover the rent.

It was supposed to be nice too, with food and drinks.
Whitney messed up by letting too many of them fools
bone rush up in the place. Up went the music, out went
the smoke, and niggas was pimping their cars in the lot.

They said Donita came down there and told all them
muthafuckas to get the hell out of there. I heard Trick
and Joshy started laughing, thinking she was playing.
Told her to call the police and see if they showed up.
When she marched back out there with her shotgun and
fired shots in the air, them niggas was out of there. I died
when I heard about it. I was mad I missed it.

I checked my watch one more time. I knew Jenna was
working today. Even if he did go in for a few hours, the
store closed at six on Sunday.

"Hey, where your boy?" Pookie asked as he leaned
out the window.

I raised my hand to block out the sun. "He ain't here
yet." I couldn't understand why I was even fooled up
with Walter's black ass in the first place. Cheryl probably

had him cutting the yard or doing some bullshit job around the house. He was married to Cheryl, who thought she was all of that. Not! Then, they had four kids running all up and down that big house they lived in.

"Well, you gon' buy this stuff or what?" Pookie threw out his hand. "I ain't got all fucking day."

"Yeah." I breathed out cigarette smoke. "Just let me get the eight-ball and two bags of the powder."

"I'll throw in some weed for free. How about that?" Pookie grinned, showing his mouth full of platinum teeth.

I counted out seventy-five dollars. "I don't want nothing for free. You ain't getting your dick sucked tonight. Not by me anyway."

"Awwww! Why you wanna do your homeboy like that?"

I tapped my foot on the pavement. "You better get out of here, before Donita come out here and bust up your shit."

"I wish she would come out here. I'll run that crazy bitch over."

I laughed.

"That's what the hell I would do." Pookie cranked up his music loud and bobbed his head up and down.

I waved and ran back upstairs. Having given away all my money, I was planning to break my foot off in Walter's ass if he stood me up. He was good for doing some shit like that. I grabbed my phone and dialed his house number. Every time Cheryl answered, I hung up. I wanted her to see my phone number on her Caller ID box. I knew if I fucked with her just enough, she would eventually give up and leave Walter.

One day, I planned to live in that house over there in

Metro West. Or at least one like it. Two things Walter loved more than himself: junk and trunk. And I had both of them to serve to her husband anytime he wanted it.

It amazed me how these women living in the nice houses in the suburbs think their life is so fucking perfect. Take Cheryl for example, she didn't even know her husband used drugs. If that muthafucker got messed up on the wrong shit, her whole life would fucking collapse. Besides her helping out at the store, Cheryl didn't work; she quit her job a long time ago to raise her children.

Doesn't that sound so beautiful?

If you ask me, that bitch was stupid. Ain't no way in hell I would leave my government job with benefits to take care of some bad ass kids all day.

I took off my house shoes and kicked my feet up on the couch, watching a church show on BET. I was almost asleep, but jumped up when I heard my front door open.

"I thought you and Reesy made up," I mumbled.

"Not yet," Chuck said. "She still wants to fuck me, and then tell me to get out."

"You're the fool." I scratched my arm. "Why are you leaving my door open?"

"Walter is out there."

I sat straight up and ran to the door.

Sure enough, Walter came up close; I felt his hot breath on my face. He pulled my tennis skirt and rubbed my thigh. "Hey, Momma."

I swallowed hard.

My man knew he was the best thing God ever put on this earth. He had pecan brown skin, low hair with waves, and he was blessed with the sexiest, succulent pair of lips.

"What's up?" I licked mine. I loved to tease my man.

"Not much." As I followed him inside, I pinched his tight booty.

Walter grabbed the remote and sat down on the couch.

"I haven't heard from my baby in a while." I pointed down the hall. "Let me go check on her." I opened her door and found Chyna fast asleep in bed with her clothes on. I felt guilty for not reminding her to take a bath. I left the television on in her room, but turned off the light.

"Is Chuck staying here?" Walter asked.

"Uh-huh." I responded as I fixed him a glass of Hennessy. "Only for another day or so." I placed his drink in front of him, and then poured one for myself. I swallowed it all down and poured another.

"You've been saying that for so long," Walter said. He picked up his glass. "You don't even know what you're saying half the time. It's ridiculous."

I felt my jaw tightening. "Don't talk to me any kind of way. You can get the fuck out!" I waved my hand in the direction of the door.

"Shut up." He picked up the remote and flipped the channels, until he found the Miami Heat playing on NBC. "I wanted to catch the rest of the game."

I sat down beside Walter and laid out three lines of coke on my hand mirror. Then I rolled up a dollar bill and snorted up one of them. It stung as it entered my nose, but the rush was quick. This was some good stuff Pookie hooked me up with. I knew Walter would be happy.

"Here." I handed it to Walter.

Walter leaned forward on the couch and snorted up the other two. He wiped his nose. "Did you see that shit? Iverson faked that foul! I can't believe they gave it to him."

I scratched my chest. "It's OK, baby." Feeling horny, I wrapped my arms around him and kissed him on his ear lobe. "They're still going to win."

Walter moved away. "Momma, I'm watching the game."

"I know." I stroked his big dick. I swear I ain't never seen one so big; like he was straight out of the jungle in Africa. Bending down, I unzipped his pants and softly wrapped my tongue around it. It tasted so good, like a hard piece of chocolate.

"Slow down, Momma." Walter pulled on my braids.

I smiled. I knew that would get his attention.

Walter snatched my hair tighter.

"Ouch!" I leaned back. "Muthafucka, what you pulling on my hair like that?"

"I don't feel comfortable with my dick out and your brother walking around here freely."

I massaged his dick. "Let's go in my room then."

He pulled his shirt down to cover his hard-on and went into my room. I picked up the rest of my stuff and joined him. Trying to set a romantic mood, I turned on my Danity Kane CD and put the fourth track on repeat.

That's my jam!

I slow-danced around the room. Tried to put on a strip show for my boo. Then I dropped it like it was hot and bent over, jiggling my booty just like the strippers do it at the club.

"Yeah!" Walter smacked my ass.

I didn't like the fact that he was paying more attention to the television, than me. While he finished watching the game, I fired up the eight-ball.

"Aren't you going to share that?"

"Yes." I put out my hand. "One hundred first."

Walter let out a snort of disgust. "Didn't you just get paid?"

"And I worked hard for that. Thank you very much."

Walter picked at his teeth.

"Come on now!" I yelled impatiently.

"Who are you screaming at?" Walter pulled me into his arms.

"At you, nigga." My body tingled. I was aching for some more of my man's dick.

He stuffed the money in my bra, then he stroked my breasts.

I removed my jeans and turned around as Walter slid three fingers inside my thong underwear. Snatching them off, he lifted his shirt to reveal his erection.

Excited because I was about to get fucked real raunchy style, I handed him a rubber from my nightstand. On all fours, I lifted my butt as he entered. His dick swelled up inside me.

I jiggled my butt cheeks, and he spanked each one hard. Cold chills shot up my spine.

I swallowed my gum.

My man fucked me so hard, I wanted to howl at the moon. We finished up the night using up all the stuff I bought from Pookie.

"Fire me up a joint," Walter said, as he was close to drifting off to sleep.

"Pookie ain't have none." I leaned over and continued painting my nails. I always like my toes to match the colors I wore to work, and I planned to wear my mocha colored dress with my new Gucci slingbacks.

"How the fuck you gon' not get me my weed?" Walter's voice was barely above a whisper. He was so gone, his eyes were blood-red. "You should've called somebody else then. What's that kid name with the braces?"

"Joshy?" I twisted my lips. "I ain't fucking with that crazy muthafucka. They gotta hit out on his ass."

"What for?" Walter asked.

"You know that boy they call Pac that lived two doors down from me?"

"No, I don't know none of these dumb niggas out

here." Walter pulled on his dick. "You need to move out of this hell hole. I can't stand coming out here."

"Are you going to pay my rent?" I grabbed his penis and stroked it. "Anyway, Pac used some of Joshy's shit, had a heart attack and died. It was all over the news. I can't believe you don't remember it."

"No." Walter licked his lips. "Suck it, Momma."

I jerked harder and wrapped my mouth around his balls.

"Oooohhh!"

I placed his dick in between my breasts and cupped them.

He turned his head to one side, as he breathed harder.

I squeezed my breasts tighter.

Warm cum squirted all over my breasts.

His breathing slowed down. "You still should've got my weed."

I slapped his leg hard. "I'm a put his number in your cell phone, and next time you get your own shit."

"Then what I need you for?" Walter turned over on his stomach and rested his head on the pillow. I know my man was pissed, but he was just going to have to be mad at me. Or get his ass up and find some.

The only way I was going to get Pookie to make another drop way out here, was to give him some fucking head. And my damn jaws was sore from Walter jamming his big dick down my throat.

Chyna's screaming woke me up from my sleep.

Walter, who was snoring beside me, woke up too. "Quiet her ass down!"

Walter was always so grouchy when he came down from his high. When he got like that, he needed to go home to his wife.

"OK." I put on my T-shirt and headed toward her

room when I saw my brother coming out. Chuck looked surprised to see me.

"Is she OK?" I asked.

"How the hell should I know?" he grunted.

"Maybe, because you were in my baby's room."

He laughed. "Shit, I'm drunk. I thought it was the bathroom. My bad."

Chyna walked up to me. "Mommy, I want to sleep with you."

I knelt down. "You can't, baby. I got company."

Chyna poked out her lips. "Please, Mommy."

"Stop your whining," I snapped.

"Please, Mommy."

"I'll lay down with you, until you go back to sleep. How is that?"

Chyna nodded as she held my hand. "Mommy, I love you."

When I woke up the next morning, I was still in Chyna's bed, but she wasn't there. I staggered into the bathroom, where she was dressed in a pink shirt with Barbie on the front and tan jeans. She was brushing her teeth.

I taught my daughter well. "Put your jacket on. It's still cool outside." I ran my hands through her curly hair until she laughed.

"Stop, Mommy."

I smiled. I loved that little girl so much. She had the whole world in front of her. When I was child, I never had it as good as she did. My mama was in and out of jail, strung out on crack, and whoring on the streets to support her habit and us. I never had anything new to wear to school, so the girls used to pick at me bad. I hated them bitches, but there was nothing I could do about it.

I started having sex at age five, when my uncles used to sneak in my room while my mama was high and put their hands all over me. Now I know those deadbeats I called uncles were actually men my mama was sleeping with for money.

I'll never forget the day Uncle Mac put his dick inside me.

"You see my toy." He used to call it his toy. "You like toys, don't you, little girl?"

"Yes."

"And you got one too. Let me see it."

I pulled up my nightgown while I lay on the bed.

To this day, it makes me sick that I could have been so stupid. Whatever them fuckas told me to do, I did it.

"Awwww. That's it." He pulled down my holey panties, and put them on the floor. He inserted his large finger inside me. "I'm a tell your mama how good you are to your Uncle Mac. And she's gonna get you some ice cream."

"Let's sing our song," he said as he put in two fingers.

"No." I shook my head. "It hurts."

"I'm sorry." Uncle Mac kissed me on the lips. "You're so pretty. I got one more toy for you." He pulled down his pants and his dick stuck out. I remember thinking it looked like a big marker.

He climbed on top of me and pulled me closer to him. He lifted my legs up high.

"Now, be a good little girl and turn your head over there." He pointed to the door.

Uncle Mac hurt me so bad, I wanted to cry out for my mama. He covered my mouth with his dirty hand.

Each time I looked at him, he got mad. "Don't you look at me!"

But when he closed his eyes, I looked at him again.

Then he starting breathing really hard. His breath smelled just like my mama's.

I remember the sheets on my bed were soaked in blood. He removed them and hid them in my closet. "I'm going to take these when I leave. And you better not tell anybody. I'll tell your mama you was a good girl, and to get you some ice cream."

Then he told me to take a bath and clean myself real good.

I took a deep breath and tried not to cry as I thought about that shit. Stuff like that I put out of my mind. I didn't like to think about it.

I scratched my head. "Let me get ready, then I'll walk you to the bus stop.

Digging the crust out of my eyes, I crept in my bedroom. I didn't want to wake Walter up, but he was already gone.

"Mommy, I'm gonna be late!"

"I'm coming, baby." I searched around my room for something clean to wear. I ended up pulling out a gold dress from the hamper and slid on a pair of slides.

When I came back from taking Chyna to the bus stop, I had to take a nap. I was so tired. It wasn't until ten o'clock that I was able to get showered and dressed for work. When I slid into my cubicle beside Tamara, she turned around.

"Kimberly's been looking for you," Tamara said. "Four more boxes arrived today, and you know that set her into a panic."

I sucked my teeth. "I'm not thinking about no darn Kimberly."

I logged onto my computer and starting entering invoices from Swift Trucking.

Tamara took a deep breath.

"What's wrong with you?" I asked as I continued to type. "Still mad about Barron? Look, that nigga still don't have no job, and his wife is taking care of him. Now why would you even want that?"

"I'm partly mad about Barron. Then it's my Psych class. I don't think Professor Atkins likes me, and she's trying to fail me." Tamara ran her hands along her forehead. "All I try to do is participate in the discussions, and each time I do, she shoots me down."

"Then don't say nothing." I responded.

"But we have to participate. It's ten percent of our grade."

"Damn!" I yelled. "You don't have to make an A in every class to graduate. I had a few professors just like the one you're talking about, and I did just fine with a B or C." I scratched my arm through my long-sleeved shirt.

"I didn't know you went to college".

I bounced back in my chair. "Yeah. I went to SCC."

Tamara poked around in her hair. "I'm surprised. I mean, you're smart, but I never thought of you as college material."

"OK." I turned up my nose. "I'm offended."

"Don't be. I'm sorry."

"I can't concentrate with all your nagging." I put my iPod earpiece back in. "Let's Chill" by Guy was playing. I rocked my shoulders as I sang along with the lyrics:

All my love is for you. . . .
Whatever you want I will do . . .
You're the only one I want in my life . . .

Pictures of Teddy Riley popped into my head. I had a serious crush on his fine ass. I wondered where he was now. I stopped typing invoices and went online to pull up the discography on Guy. There wasn't anything about Teddy Riley since 1999.

I felt a tap on my shoulder. I minimized the window, but knew I was already caught.

"You're so busted."

It was Darla. I hit her hand. "Girl, you scared the shit out of me."

"You better be glad I wasn't Kimberly," Darla teased. "I won't keep you, just wanted to say I'm treating you to lunch at JJ Cheng's today."

"OK." I raised a brow. "Thank you."

"No, I want to thank you for helping me out." Darla's eyes watered up as she fingered her wedding ring.

I touched the ring that was still on her married finger. I was wondering why she hadn't pawned that shit. "You're my girl. Of course, I'm going to be there for you."

As Darla walked away, I couldn't help but notice how much weight she'd lost. When I first started at IT, Darla weighed about 400 pounds. She was just that damn big. I felt sorry for her, because everybody used to be laughing at her all the time. Her booty would wobble when she walked down the hall.

I'm not going to pretend like I wasn't one of the ones cracking up at her double whopper ass either. When I moved up to the second floor, I was mad when I found out Darla was going to train me. I just pictured me having to sit next to her smelly ass. She had a little odor, and them pimples on her face was even harder to look at. Then Darla had a big-ass gap in between her teeth. She was so fucked up!

When I got to know her, I saw how sweet she was. From that day on, I was taking up for my girl. Darla lost that weight quick, though. She didn't want to admit it, but I know she had that surgery to get her stomach stapled.

And I knew exactly when it happened. Darla and her

sister claimed they were going on a cruise to Mexico. I done seen on television, where women stay at them resort hotels and have all kinds of plastic surgeries. Those doctors do it for cheap, too. When Darla came to work a week later, she already looked like she dropped off a hundred pounds. That's all everybody was talking about. And then, come to find out, her marriage was a fake.

Now Robert was dead and buried, and Darla was crying over that fool. With the way he treated her, she should've thrown a party. I thought Robert was in love with her when she was huge. I was shocked, I mean I see the brothas with big women all the time. But not no white man! They like their women poor, and asses as flat as a pancake.

The whole time they was engaged, I just knew he was going to call that shit off. I waited till the last second to buy my bridesmaid dress. I wasn't about to spend all my money, and they didn't even have no wedding.

But they got married. If I wasn't in the bridal party, I wouldn't have believed it.

I figured they were all happy and shit. Every time I saw them together, Robert seemed to be so in love with her. Then Darla finally fessed up and told us it wasn't like that at all. Robert treated her like trash, worse than that, like shit on the bottom of his shoe.

Darla had it rough, but now she was on top of her game. She didn't want to tell nobody, but I know she got some money out that deal too. Probably an insurance check, but her ass got paid. Ole girl had it going on now.

Even though I was supposed to be one her best friends, she didn't have to tell me nothing. As long as she was buying my baby anything she wanted, that was fine with me. Now, Darla still bought her own clothes from Target. She and Tamara didn't know how to dress. Sometimes, it was just embarrassing. But, she hooked Chyna up with clothes from Bloomingdale's and all the stores at the Mall at Millenia. That's where I get all my shit, from my purses to my shoes. Sometimes the outlet stores had some good-ass sales too.

Darla would go overboard with shopping for my baby and her niece. I would take some of them clothes back to the store, get the money, and buy me some outfits. Chyna wouldn't even miss it; her closet was already full.

Knowing I only had twenty more minutes until lunchtime, I entered them invoices. Kimberly never came by, which was good for her, because I was likely to curse her ass out. I couldn't stand that bitch.

CHAPTER TWO

"So, where is Chyna now?" I asked. I was so damn mad that I could kick some ass.

"She's right here," Babs answered.

"OK, I want you to know I'm about to lose my job over this," I responded as I gripped my cell tightly.

"I can't help it if I'm sick. Girl, I need to go to the hospital."

"Well, don't expect me to drive your black ass!" I screamed as I ended the call.

"Where Kimberly at?" I asked Tamara.

She removed her earpiece. "I think she's in her office. Why?"

"I have to get Chyna. Babs claims she's sick," I responded as I stood up.

Tamara grabbed my arm. "You know Kimberly's going to try to fire you if you do that."

I snatched away. "I don't give a flying fuck."

"No, let me do it." Tamara shot me a worried look. "I'll go pick up Chyna. Besides, I want to spend time with her anyway."

"I'm not going to let you do that."

"I'm doing it. Now sit back down." Tamara went in Kimberly's office. I rocked in my chair as I waited for Kimberly to go off. Then, I heard Kimberly raising her voice.

I couldn't stand to let Tamara get screamed at for my sake. Besides, I wanted to get in Kimberly's ass anyway. I had the perfect excuse to do it too.

"Why you yelling at her like that?" I tossed my hand up. "She ain't no dog."

"Brandy!" Kimberly yelled. "I promise, you don't want to start with me today."

I pushed my friend out of the way. "Yes, I do. Tamara is covering for me. I'm the one who needs to leave to pick up my daughter."

Kimberly's body jerked. "You've only put in twenty hours this week. If you leave this building, Brandy, don't bother to come back."

I jingled my keys. "I'm out of here. I quit!"

"Fine!" Kimberly shouted. "I'm so happy to see you go."

Feeling my jaw tighten, I balled my fist. "You know I've been wanting to do this for a long time." I hauled off to punch her ass, but Tamara grabbed my arm. Two girls ran in and dragged me out of the office.

"Call security!"

Still angry, I punched my hand into the wall. "Why did you stop me? Ooooh, I wanted to mess her up so bad. And now, I'll never get another chance. "

Tamara went with me to the elevators. As the doors opened, the security guard came out.

"Brandy, I got to take you out of the building." He put his hands on his belt.

"First, I need to clear out my desk," I said, knowing there was a small stash in there.

"No." He took my arm. "We'll send your things to your home address. That's how it works."

I struggled to get free. "Get your hands off me."

"Stop it," Tamara said.

"Mind your own business." He forced me into the elevator. Once the doors shut, he released his grip.

I popped my chewing gum. "You didn't have to grab me like that."

"I'm doing my job."

I twisted my lips. "Whatever!"

I tried to keep a straight face as everyone watched me leave the building. I knew they would be talking about me at lunch today. Like I cared.

I called Chuck on his cell phone. "Look, I need you to watch Chyna for me. I have to work at the store tonight."

I picked up Chyna and dropped her off with Chuck. When I arrived at Zales, Walter was sitting in the back smoking.

"I need a hit." I took the joint out of his hand. "Look, I just lost my job at IT. I need more hours here."

"You got it. Now, can I have my shit back?" Walter stuck his hand out.

"Here." I handed him his joint, then kissed him on the lips. Climbing on top of him, I undid his striped tie. "One more thing." I held up one finger.

"What else?"

"I need a raise."

I lifted my dress, revealing I wasn't wearing any underwear.

"Yeah, Momma." He fingered my wet pussy. "Did you lock the door?" he whispered.

"No."

"Then fucking lock the door!" He pushed me on the floor.

"Shit!" I scrambled to stand back up. My vision blurred, then went black.

"What! You want my wife to walk in on us? You would like that, wouldn't you?"

"Aha!" he laughed.

I used my hands to feel my way around. ""Walter, help me."

"You should've asked me what was in this before you smoked it."

"It was laced?" I asked. I bumped into the wall.

"Yeah. You know I like my stuff potent," Walter replied.

I heard his footsteps get closer to me.

"And while we're talking, I want you to stop calling my house, upsetting my wife."

"All right." My voice was shaking. "Walter, help me."

I heard the door shut, so I figured Walter left me by myself. As my body trembled, I felt my heart pump harder. I grabbed it to keep it from jumping out of my chest.

Then I heard these colors making noises. They were purple and green. It sounded like an organ playing in a loud pitch.

I stuck my fingers in my ears to block out the sounds.

"Help me!" I screamed at the top of my lungs, but I knew no one could hear me. I promised to God if He delivered me from this, then I would quit using.

"Brandy." I heard Walter's voice.

I opened my eyes and I could see.

Thank you, Lord.

"How long have I been out?" I asked as I wiped the slobber from around my mouth.

"About an hour."

I punched Walter in the arm. "How could you do that to me!"

"What did I do?" Walter looked puzzled. "I left you back here to taper off." He helped me into a chair.

"What was that shit?" I asked.

"White lightning."

"LSD!" I yelled. "Walter, get the fuck away from me. Are you trying to kill me?"

"Maybe." He laughed.

I stared at him, and didn't know whether he was serious or playing with my ass.

"You know I love your sexy ass." He kissed me on the neck. "Aren't you going to finish giving me what you started?"

I opened my mouth as his tongue slipped in. He laid me down on the floor and lifted my dress. He sucked on my coochie like it was dessert.

I closed my eyes. "I love you, too."

The next day, I was in the bathroom putting on my make-up. I made sure the concealer covered the tracks on my arms before I pulled the sleeves down on my silk shirt.

"Mommy, is Babs picking me up?" Chyna asked. She stood at the sink with her doll in her arms.

"No, baby. Chuck is going to watch you."

"No. I don't like Uncle Chuck."

I raised my eyebrows. "Why do you say that?" I snatched her up and sat her on the toilet. I gazed into her eyes. "Has Uncle Chuck touched in the places we talked about?"

Chyna shook her head. "No, Mommy. But he hurt me."

"How?" I asked. I stood up and went out into the hallway. "Chuck! Get your ass in here, right muthafucking now!" I swung my neck so hard, my braids slapped me in the eye.

"What you screaming my name like that for?" Chuck asked from the living room. "Don't you see I got company?"

"Reesy don't pay no muthafucking rent over here." I tossed my hand up.

"What the hell is wrong with you?" He stepped to me like he wanted a piece of me.

And the way I was feeling, that short nigga was looking for an ass whooping.

"Chyna said you hurt her. Now, you tell me what she is talking about?"

"Awwww, man!" Chuck wiped his mouth. "I didn't do nothing to her."

"Chyna, what did your uncle do to you?"

"He hit me." By this time Chyna was hollering.

Chuck sucked his teeth. "I beat her and Kayla's ass for getting in that refrigerator and spilling that Kool-Aid all over the floor."

I tapped his nose with my finger. "You keep your hands off of her. If you want to beat your own daughter's ass, that's you. With Chyna, you tell me and I will discipline her." I shoved him into the wall. "Do you hear me?"

"Yeah." Chuck gave me the look of death. "I hear ya. But you better not come at me like that again."

"Don't make me throw your ass out! And where is my rent money anyway?" I asked as I put on my Gucci heels.

"It's on your dresser, next to your coke. You fucking junkie. You gon' end up just like Mama if you don't lay off that shit."

"Go to hell!" I kissed Chyna on the cheek. Then I walked out. I heard the door squeak open.

"Mommy!" Chyna screamed.

I turned around. "Oh, I forgot to give my baby a hug. I'm sorry."

I wished I didn't have to rush, but Walter was waiting

on me. There were many days when I wish I had spent more time with her. She was so beautiful, and she needed her mother to do things with her, like play with dolls and help her with homework. Shit my mama never did with me. Luckily, I had Tamara to make up for what I couldn't do.

We hugged for a minute, and then I sped off in my green Saturn. I headed for the Days Inn. I got us a room at the Days Inn, so we could spend a little quality time together. Once I got inside, Walter was already high. His dick was standing straight up.

I gave my man a blowjob.

"You're killing me, Momma," Walter said as he lay down beside me.

I snuggled up beside him. "Well, it is your birthday." I wanted this day to be special for him. I lit myself a Marlboro. Since, I was working full-time at Zales, I was making more money than at IT. I even picked up a few customers from Pookie. Once I got my rent caught up, I would be back on my feet. With that Saturn barely hanging on, I had to buy me a new car soon.

"Oh, yeah." Walter stood up with his dick flopping between his legs. He poured a glass of Hennessy.

I was worried about him. He didn't seem like himself.

Walter smiled. "I took the liberty of getting my own present."

I shook my breasts and lifted the right one and licked it. "That's right, Daddy."

"You're only part of it." He finished off his glass, and then turned up the volume to the television. "Look at Wade!" He jumped up, like he scored the basket. "That's my man!"

A knock sounded at the door. Walter went to go answer.

"Wait!" I pulled the sheet over to cover myself.

"Hello Ms. Lady." Walter beamed. "Come on in. This is Brandy. This is Peaches."

The tall, light-skinned woman with a weave hanging down to her butt came inside. "How you doing, Brandy?"

I made eye contact first, and then waved. "Hey." Before I got mad, I wanted to find out what was going on.

"Peaches is going to join us for the night."

"Oh, hell no." I sat up in the bed. "I already told you I wasn't doing no lesbian shit with you, Walter."

Walter stood in front of me. He grabbed my hands and kissed them. "It's my birthday. Now, don't be like that."

I took a deep breath. "You better be glad I love your black ass."

"So, are we on the same page?" Walter asked.

I sucked my teeth. "I guess so. Let me get fucked up first." I picked up the mirror with four lines left.

Walter pulled up a chair and watched as Peaches ate my coochie. I had to admit, the girl knew how to handle her business, because I came more than once. Walter joined in and fucked Peaches from behind. Better her than me, because I didn't like no dick in my ass.

I got tired from all the fucking, and took a piss. When I came back, Walter was licking X from the girl's pussy.

"Walter, you can't eat that shit!" I yelled as I tried to pull him up.

Walter snatched away. "I can eat pussy." He shoved me into the nightstand.

"Walter!" I screamed as I struggled to get back up.

He ignored me and went back to pleasing Peaches, the way he should've been taking care of me. They was using up all the shit I bought with my muthafucking money!

I pushed Peaches off the bed. "Go sit your ass down somewhere. This is my man." I rolled my eyes in her direction.

Peaches smiled. "No problem." Her mouth was full of

gold teeth. She picked up a crack pipe and lit the end of it. "I'll just sit here and get tore up by my damn self."

Walter grabbed my thighs. "Cheryl, I love you."

His eyes turned up toward the ceiling, and he fell asleep on my lap.

I turned over and went to sleep. In the morning, I was going to tell his ass off for calling me by his wife's name. While all three of our naked bodies lay across the king-sized bed, I felt like a torn up mess.

When my cell phone beeped, I realized I put the ringer on silent earlier.

I had damn near a hundred missed calls, so I called Tamara back first.

"Where have you been?" she asked.

"I'm with Walter," I answered as I wiped my eyes. "What's up?"

"I'm at the hospital with Chyna."

"What!" I fell out the bed and landed right on my hip. "What happened to my baby?" I reached under Walter's arm for my pants. It felt ice cold.

"Chuck said she fell down the stairs. There's a social worker here, too. They believe Chuck beat her."

I searched around the floor for my shoes, until I found them under the bed.

"Lord, what happened to my baby!" I sobbed. Remembering how cold Walter's body felt, I turned on the heater and ran out of the hotel room. "I'm coming up there."

After Tamara told me she was at Arnold Palmer's, I drove almost a hundred miles per hour to get there. Not caring what my hair or clothes looked like, I ran inside the hospital. I was so disoriented, I could barely figure out how to get to the elevators.

I called Tamara on her cell phone.

"I don't know how to get to you."

"Where are you?" Tamara asked.

"I'm over by the bathrooms. And they got vending machines over here."

I heard Tamara asking someone where the snack machines were in the building. "OK, I know where you are. I'll be there in minute. Don't move!" She found me and took me where Chyna was.

A white woman with dark hair and dressed in a suit stood outside Chyna's room.

"Are you Chyna's mother?" She flipped the chart she had in her hand. "Brandy Jackson?"

"Yes, that's me." I slung my hair and realized I must've looked like a hooker or something. When I heard something was wrong with my baby, I didn't care what I looked like. I just had to get to her. I wish I hadn't left her. I remembered how she came to the door to hug me.

"Ms. Jackson, my name is Deborah Lloyd. I'm your daughter's case worker." She stared me down from head to toe. Judging by her expression, she thought I was trash. I knew exactly what women like her thought about women like me. But she didn't know shit about me. Unlike the other mothers she dealt with, I took good care of my daughter.

I nodded. "Nice to meet you. I want to see my daughter." I tried to go around her, but she stood in front of the door so I couldn't go inside. "Look, we can talk later."

"I have some questions that need to be answered first." She cleared her throat. "You don't seem to understand. We've been trying to reach you for days with no success."

I put my hand to my forehead. I thought about Walter and that girl, Peaches, laying in the bed when I left. "What are you talking about? I just saw my daughter last night."

"Ms. Jackson, are you currently using any illegal substances?"

"Hell no!" I screamed.

"Would you mind taking a drug test to prove it?"

"Look, get away from me." I pushed the woman and opened the door to my daughter's room. I saw a small body with a full body cast. I knew it had to be Chyna, but it didn't seem like it. Her face was wrapped up in bandages.

"Chyna, baby."

There was no response from the tiny body.

"Ms. Jackson, I'm not finished with you."

I held up my hand. "Leave me be."

"No, it's in Chyna's best interest that I restrict your contact with her." I watched as Deborah signaled in the glass window.

Two policemen rushed in and grabbed my arms. As I struggled to get free, they dragged me out of the room.

I caught a glimpse of Tamara in the hallway, as I was wrestled down to the floor. "Tamara . . . take care of my baby!"

I was taken to the police station and told I wasn't being arrested. They were only bringing me in for questioning.

I didn't believe that shit, and I wasn't fessing up to nothing.

I leaned in my chair because I had been in that room for hours. Deborah and a police officer asked me about a hundred questions. Some of them were the same questions, only worded differently.

They tried to convince me I'd been missing for three days.

"I told you, I was right there in the hotel room."

"You were in a hotel room?" he asked. "What's the name of the hotel?"

I scrunched up my mouth. "At the Days Inn. Right there on Colonial, right before you get to Pine Hills."

"We're going to check that out," the officer said.

"And furthermore, why didn't anyone come in there to wake us up? Surely a maid would've come inside or something."

"I'll be back." He left out of the room.

I wasn't believing nothing they were trying to tell me. They wanted to mess with my head, so they could have my daughter. And I wasn't having it.

"Ms. Jackson, we checked out the hotel room you said you were staying at."

I took a puff from my cigarette. "Yeah, and it's just like I said ain't it?"

"Yes, it was exactly like you said. And now we have an even more serious problem on our hands."

"Oh yeah, what's that?" I leaned forward on the table.

"The two people in the room are dead."

The cigarette I had in my hand fell to the floor.

CHAPTER THREE

Darla and Tamara got the money together to get me out of jail. I was so relieved, because I had to go to court about getting Chyna back. And if I didn't show up, the courts would put her in the care of the state. I knew enough about the foster care system to know that I had to make sure Chyna didn't wind up there.

I showed up with a lawyer to represent me, and I made sure I was dressed in the best suit I could find. Tamara and Darla were both there to support me.

The judge ordered Chyna to remain in the care of the state while she was being treated for her injuries in the hospital. However, I was allowed supervised visitation.

"The courts will reconvene when the child is medically able to leave the around–the–clock care of the doctors and staff at Arnold Palmer," the judge stated. "At that time, we will discuss custody and living arrangements."

I took a deep breath.

I shook hands with the family lawyer. Darla must've paid him a lot of money to show up at the last minute.

"Thanks so much for handling this." I put my arm around Darla.

"Don't touch me." Darla moved away. "Brandy, I can't believe you did this to your daughter."

"What are talking about?" I cocked my head to the side. "Don't you dare judge me!"

"I'm doing this for Chyna." Darla clutched her purse tightly. "Just do the right thing and sign over custody to me or Tamara."

"It'll be a cold day in hell before I let that happen!"

"You shouldn't have killed off your baby." I pointed to Tamara. "And as for you, Darla." I stuck my hand in her face. "How you gonna tell me what to do?"

"You're not fit to raise her," Darla said through clenched teeth.

"Don't try to get all high and mighty with me now that you got that dead man's money!" I cocked my head to the side.

"I'm sorry." Darla stared down at the floor, and then looked at me. "I don't want you to tie this up in the courts. Do what's best for Chyna."

"This isn't about me or Darla trying to take your baby from you," Tamara chimed in. "We're both pissed at you. Brandy, you've been out of control. And now Chyna is lying up in a hospital bed, hooked up to a ventilator, because of your negligence."

I waved my cigarette in the air. "You act like I did this."

Tamara knocked the cigarette out of my hand. "You did." She walked off.

"OK, you're leaving me too. What happened to fucking friendship?" I yelled as I sat down on the bench close to the wall.

"You're going to have to keep it down," a security guard said.

"I will."

"There's no smoking in this building." He pointed to the cigarette on the marble floor.

"All right." I picked it up and dropped it in the water fountain.

I used my last twenty-dollar bill to catch a cab home. My car was completely out of commission. When I walked up to the door, there was an eviction notice on it.

What the fuck is this?

Ready to kick somebody's ass, I stormed down to the manager's office.

"Donita, I paid my rent. Why are you throwing me out?"

"With all them drugs the police found in your place," Donita put her hand on her hip. "You can't stay here no more. Pack your shit and vacate the premises within the next twenty-four hours, or it will be out on the streets."

"This is fucked up and you know it." I threw the paper on the floor.

"Wait a minute."

"What?" I twisted my lips. At least somebody was coming to their damn senses around here.

"Come back." She sat down at her desk. "Let me talk to you for a minute."

"Can I light a smoke?" I asked as I took out a box of Marlboro.

She nodded.

"Want one?" I asked.

I lit two at the same time, and handed one to her.

"Thank you." Donita said as she blew out smoke.

"See, I used to be just like you. Now, I have one daughter in prison serving life. And my other daughter is a single parent, busting her butt to raise six children." Donita pointed at her chest. "And I'm to blame for that. I have live to with it every day of my life. I got myself cleaned up, and I haven't touched a drug in almost ten years." She wiped a tear away.

"I'm sorry, I didn't know."

"No, you didn't. You young girls out here think you have it all figured out." She puffed up her lips. "But you don't know shit. Get yourself cleaned up, before it's too late. Now, if you can get in a rehab, I'll reconsider letting you move back here."

"I don't need no rehab," I said with a tight-lipped grimace. "I appreciate you telling me about what happened to you. But I ain't like you. And I'm not going to let that happen to me."

I strutted out of the office feeling good about myself. Shit, I still had a few tricks up my sleeve.

"I heard about what happened to your boyfriend, Walter. Remember, that could've been you lying dead in that hotel room!"

I waved my hand in the air. "I'm still here." I laughed it off.

Then I called Pookie to bring me a U-Haul and help me move my stuff. I didn't have anywhere to put it, but he agreed to put my things in storage. All of that for the nominal fee of a blowjob.

Then we cooked up a plan to get ahold of some money.

Jenna was surprised to see me walk into Zales. "Brandy, what are you doing here?"

"Last time I checked, I still worked here." I smiled. Then I grabbed my counter keys and started helping customers.

"True." She nodded. "I'm sorry about everything. I still can't believe the news about Walter."

I got choked up as a knot built up in my throat. I couldn't believe he was gone.

"Are you going to the funeral?" she asked.

I shook my head. "Probably not." I wondered when I would wake up from this nightmare. I remembered how cold Walter's body was, lying sideways in that bed.

"I'm going to the back."

Walter was sitting at the desk writing on a piece of paper. He was dressed in a white suit.

I punched him on the arm.

"What are you doing here?" I asked. "You got everybody thinking you're dead." I laughed as I sat down next to him.

I looked over at him and saw a creature with snakes coming out of his head.

I screamed as loud as I could.

"Dear Jesus!"

Then I ran over to the opposite side of the room and closed my eyes shut. When I reopened them, the creature had disappeared.

Then my mind went to me and Walter making love on that floor. My arms started itching, and my head vision started to get blurry.

Taking a few deep breaths, I remembered what I came there to do. I unlocked the back door as planned, then went back up front.

"I'm sorry, Jenna. I thought I could do this, but I can't."

"I completely understand," Jenna said. She reached out her hand. "I need the keys back."

"Oh, OK." I fought back the tears as I pulled the key ring off my arm. My sleeve got stuck in the process, and showed the tracks up and down my arm.

Jenna's eyes grew wide.

I pulled the sleeve down quickly. "Here you go." I smiled.

"Thanks." Jenna took a deep breath. "Well, best of luck to you."

I waited at Beatrice's apartment. She was Pookie's girl-friend. She agreed to let me stay there until Pookie got me an apartment. As I waited for damn near four hours, I realized that nigga must've shut me out the deal.

Beatrice came home a few hours later.

"What happened?" I asked.

"Pookie got arrested, that's what!" She rolled her eyes. "Now we got to get the money to get him out."

"Oh, shit!" I threw my arms in the air. I couldn't be-lieve this was happening. I hoped Pookie didn't mention my name to the cops. "I ain't never gonna catch a break."

"Hold up with the tantrum." Beatrice went in the room and came back with a wad of cash. "Let's just take this money down there, and get my man out."

When we got down to the jailhouse, Beatrice posted the bond for Pookie. When he came out, Pookie hugged Beatrice like he'd been locked up for a hundred days.

"What's up, Brandy?" He hugged me. "Hey, I just saw your brother in there."

"Let's go." I headed for the door. "I don't care about him."

"Hey, that's your brother. He told me to tell you he was sorry and that Chyna snuck out the door and fell down them stairs."

"Let's go!" I screamed.

"Hey, I'm a get your brother out of here. Beatrice, find out how much his bond is."

Beatrice went back inside the building.

I thought about my brother sitting in jail, and I felt sorry for him. I knew he didn't hurt Chyna, but I wanted to put all the blame on him. When all was said and done,

I was the only one to blame. I was Chyna's mother. It was my job to keep her safe, and I didn't do that. Because I was laid up in a hotel room, coked out of my mind.

Pookie sat with me as I waited outside on the steps for my brother. I missed him, and he was the only family I had. I needed him.

"I shouldn't have got that shit from Joshy. That's why Walter is dead." I put my hands to my face as I cried.

Pookie put his arm on my shoulder. "You can't go back and fix it. Walter's in a better place now."

"I loved him. And now, he's gone." I said in a low voice. I used my sleeve to wipe my nose.

When Chuck came out the door and I ran up and hugged him.

"I'm so sorry, Sis."

I cried in his arms. "Chyna's still laying up in that hospital. And Walter's gone."

"I know. It's going to be OK." He ran his hand down my back. Even though I knew things were going to get worse, I felt better knowing I had someone on my side

I went to see Chyna at the hospital. The doctor explained they removed the bandages, but there was still some bruising and swelling that needed to heal.

I sat on the bed with Chyna and combed her hair into two pigtails.

"Is it pretty?" Chyna asked.

"Of course, baby." I responded. "You have beautiful, curly hair. Just like your daddy."

I thought about Phillip. Wondered where he was or what he was doing.

"No, I'm talking about my face. Is it still pretty?"

I searched around the room. Not a mirror in sight. "If I had mirror I would show you. But, yes, you look like a princess."

"Mommy, I love you." Chyna tried to smile, but her swollen lips wouldn't move. I couldn't stand to see her face like that. But she was my baby, and no matter what, she would always be beautiful. I kissed the top of her head.

Lord, please help my baby's face get back to normal.

Deborah came inside. She pointed at the clock. "I gave you extra time, but we have to follow the court's rules."

I nodded my head. "I understand. Thank you."

Deborah smiled. "I know you don't believe this, but I want you to get your daughter back."

I had to laugh at that one. "No, I don't believe you."

I said bye to Chyna and left the room. Hearing her scream my name just about broke my heart. Leaving that hospital was the hardest thing I ever had to do.

I drove my brother's car to Tamara's apartment. I held the papers tightly in my hand. I kept thinking I had to do this for Chyna. She wasn't there, so I figured she was working overtime at IT. I sat on the step and waited for her.

I saw her little Corolla pull up, so I met her at the foot of the steps.

"What are you doing here?" Tamara gave me a hug. "Is something wrong with Chyna?"

"No, she's fine." I replied. "I appreciate you going up there to check on her."

"Yeah, I'm on my way up there now." Tamara put her purse strap on her shoulder. "I just wanted to eat something first. Are you coming in?"

I cleared my throat. "No. I came here to do one thing."

CHAPTER FOUR

Feeling like I was in a dream, I sat on them steps waiting for Tamara to pull up in her car. She drove up in a new car. It was silver.

"Hey, girl." I reached out my hands to give her a hug.

Tamara looked at me strangely.

"Did you come here to see Chyna? She's over to a friend's house. You look like you need to eat something."

I was hungry.

Tamara warmed me up a plate of spaghetti. I swirled my noodles on my fork. When I realized I hadn't eaten in a few days, I dropped the fork and ate with my hands.

Tamara turned up her nose. "You have got to get yourself cleaned up. I hate seeing you like this."

"I know. I'm so embarrassed." I licked my fingers. I held out my empty plate. "Can I have some more?"

She paused for a moment. "Sure."

As she put the plate in the microwave, I grabbed a handful of paper towels to clean my hands. My fingernails were so dirty.

"Why don't you take a shower after you finish?" Tamara asked. "We wear the same size. At least, we used to."

"Yeah, I need it."

"Where are you staying?" Tamara asked.

"Lots of places."

"That's not good enough."

"I'm fine. I just need you to help me get a job so I can get back on my feet."

"It's been a long time." Tamara sat up straight in her chair. "Well, let me make some phone calls and see what's out there."

When the warm water hit my body, I knew what heaven felt like. Standing in that tub, I allowed the water to run on my face and hair. Not caring what kind of freak I had become, I hadn't took a bath in what seemed to me, only to be a few days later. But then, I was hitting that pipe hard when I came down from my highs, I knew I was losing track of how many days had passed. It was good to have the hot steam clear out my sinuses. My head was lighter, and I could actually think about some things.

Tamara was trying to fuck with my head, talking about it had been a long time since she saw me. That bitch knew I was just at her apartment a week or two ago. Or was it a month? I hit myself in the head a couple times. I managed to lose my job, tried to attack my supervisor, lost my baby to the courts, and lost Walter.

This isn't my life! How did I let things get so fucked up?

I was out of control. Yeah, I was probably using more blow than I usually did, but it couldn't be that. I remembered how Phillip would lose track of time. One time that nigga showed up to see Chyna when she was a newborn baby. I really didn't even want his smelly ass to touch my baby, so I just let him look. I told him to get he needed to get cleaned up, before he could come back. Then I didn't see him no more after that for a long damn time. I bumped into him on out there on OBT, and he kept asking me where his baby was at. I was like, here go your daughter right here. By that time, Chyna was almost two years old.

I squirted soap gel on my washcloth, and then I checked out the label. It read strawberries and cream. Smelling like something I wanted to eat, I lathered that shit all over me. I showered and put on some clean clothes. I felt like such a bum, having to borrow clothes and shoes to wear. Then I thought about how Phillip had been doing this every day for a long time. I knew I couldn't be as far gone as Phillip was. Oh hell no! Ain't no way in the world I wanted end up like him. Man, I just needed to get my head straight. I decided I was going to lay off that shit for a while. No, if only Tamara could help me out with finding a job, I could start getting my life back right. I wanted my own place and my Chyna back with me. I missed my baby so much.

I heard Tamara on the phone, so I slowly cracked it open.

"You should've seen her," she said. "I don't know what to do, but I gotta figure out something. This is not the Brandy we know. Trust me."

On first thought, I wanted to bust up in there and curse her ass out for talking about me behind my back. But, I needed to finish cleaning myself up first.

I wiped the steam off the mirror and jumped when I saw a muthafucking creature standing in front of me.

My feet slipped and I banged my head on the tub.

Tamara rushed inside.

"What happened?" She helped me sit on the toilet.

"I fucking saw something!" I pointed at the mirror. "It

had a swollen face. Its teeth were black with all this guck shit around it."

Tamara held this puzzled look on her face.

"Stop looking at me like I'm crazy!" I threw up my hands. "I know what the fuck I saw, and I'm telling you that shit scared the hell out of me!"

Then I laughed as I realized what Tamara already knew. I thought back to the look of terror on her face when I approached her in the parking lot.

That creature was me!

I got myself fixed up, and slept on Tamara's couch for the night. In the morning, I had an appointment with a temp agency. Tamara set it up and assured me they needed people badly.

That morning, I dressed in Tamara's yellow suit and put on closed-toe shoes. I felt all hemmed up without my sandals, but my hammertoes were so messed up, I would need to see a doctor to get treated, probably for psoriasis. It didn't make sense that I allowed myself to get this bad in a couple of weeks. That must've been some potent shit me and Walter was using in that hotel.

Donita's words rang in my head, *I heard about what happened to your boyfriend, Walter. Remember, that could've been you lying dead in that hotel room!*

"Are you ready?" Tamara asked as she leaned against the bathroom wall.

"Yeah." I replied. Running my fingers through my soft hair, I hadn't seen it natural in months. "I can't believe you helped me take all them braids out."

"What? Are you talking about those dreadlocks you called braids?" Tamara joked. "They came loose as soon as I ran my fingers through them."

"All I know is I feel one hundred percent better." I scratched my arm and felt a strong heat wave rush all the way through my body.

I ignored it. "Well, I'm clean. And I ain't never using no drugs again."

"That sounds good, but you need to get some help." Tamara tried to reason with me, but I didn't want to hear no talk about rehab.

"I'm not going. I done got over it, so now all I need is a job. I want to make things right for my baby."

There was a knock at the door.

"Let me get that," Tamara said.

"Hey." Tamara's voice lowered to a whisper. "She's in there."

I looked around the corner and saw Darla. I was so happy to see her.

"Hey, Skinny Minnie." I wrapped my arms around her and squeezed her tightly. "Thanks for coming."

Darla backed up. She smiled. "I'm glad you're all right."

"Yes, Brandy is back! Just like old times!" I pumped my fist in the air. "Yeah, don't count this sister out!"

Tamara laughed nervously.

"Well, I'm taking you to the place." Darla pointed toward the door. "We don't want to be late."

"I appreciate it." Once we were in the car, I stared out the window, like I was a little girl going on a trip to the big city.

So much had changed in the downtown area. I counted four high-rise buildings I ain't never even seen before.

"This is a nice car you got." I ran my hands along the white leather seats. "What is this anyway?"

Darla's glanced at me in the rearview mirror. I noticed she was wearing a new diamond ring on the ring finger of her left hand. "It's a BMW."

I laughed. "Girl, you done got rich off Robert's money, and bought you a new ride. Go 'head!"

Darla cut her eyes over at Tamara. "Thanks, I like it."

"So, how is Kimberly doing anyway?" I turned up my nose. "She still screaming at everybody all the fucking time? I used to get so tired of her ass. She know she had a nasty attitude. I don't know how I even stayed up there all that time."

Tamara turned around to face me. "Kimberly is running IT now."

"Whaaaat?" I leaned back in my seat and held my chest.

"Yeah, I have Darla's old job, and she has Kimberly's job."

"Damn, how all that happen since I've been gone?" I shook my head.

Tamara shrugged. "A lot can happen in a year."

I raised my eyebrow. I looked down at my clothes. "You changed my clothes." Now, I was wearing some dirty-ass jeans and shirt. I smelled like a dog.

"What the fuck you talking about? It ain't been no muthafucking year! Y'all trying to mess with me. Trying to fuck with my mind and shit." I laughed. "Let me get out of this muthafucker, right the hell now." I tried to open the door, but it wouldn't open.

"Calm your ass down!" Tamara screamed. She jumped in the back seat with me.

"Let me out of this car!" I rammed her face into the window.

"OK!" Darla pulled her car in front of this building and jumped out the car.

"We're trying to help you," Tamara said.

Two men and a woman wearing blue scrubs stood outside the car. Darla opened it from the outside, and they pulled me out. I was kicking and screaming, but they wouldn't let me go.

"We're going to keep her on observation for twenty-four hours," the lady said.

I read the sign before they dragged me in through the automatic doors. I was at Florida Hospital. It seemed like time stood still as I tried to sort that shit out.

I went to see Tamara and she fed me, then I showered. No, I went to see Tamara and I handed her the papers. Then she gave me that nasty spaghetti. I took a shower.

Tamara walked in the hospital room, where my hands were tied to the rails.

"I'm going to kill you for this!"

"Those are the drugs talking, I know you don't mean that," Tamara replied.

"No, I'm serious. I will never forgive you for this. Look at how they chained me up like a fucking animal!"

"Those are restraints."

"Fucking chains!"

Tamara put her hands on my face. "Calm down. Listen to me. I have to explain to you what's happening."

"I want to know why you said it's been a year, and I just saw you. I seen my daughter at the hospital. Her face was messed up. Like Kanye West in that video."

Tamara held up a picture of Chyna, and her face was completely normal. "This is Chyna. She's in the first grade now."

"No, she's in the hospital and I saw her face . . ."

When I woke up, Tamara sat in the chair beside my bed. I tried to lift my hands, but the chains were still on me.

She opened her eyes. "Good. You're going to be OK."

"Where's my daughter?" I asked in a panic. "What have you done to her?"

"Brandy, do you remember when you came to see me?"

"Yes, I remember. It was just yesterday."

"The first time . . . after you visited Chyna at the hospital. You waited for me when I got off from work."

I nodded. "I remember, quit talking to me like I'm five years old or something."

"You signed over custody of Chyna to me. You asked me to take care of her. You wanted me to help you find a job."

I shook my head back and forth. "Naw! I ain't signed over shit to you."

"Yes, you did." Tamara held up some yellow papers. "These are copies of the original." She pointed to it. "This is your signature."

"You fucking forged it." I mumbled. "I ain't signed over nothing. I just needed a job, so I could get back on my feet."

"After you gave me the papers, you disappeared." Tamara tried to explain, but what she was saying to me didn't make no damn sense.

"Then we had no idea where you were. I've been taking care of Chyna, and Darla is too. Then you showed up out of nowhere a year later, asking if I could help you find that job."

My arm starting itching again. "Them ants done found me again. Get them out!" My arm felt like it was on fire, and with my hands tied up, I couldn't do nothing to stop it. "Get some water. Jesus, please save me!"

CHAPTER FIVE

When I woke up, I tried to adjust my vision. It was still blurred, but I could make out some things in the room. And I heard Judge Mathis on TV. I recognized my landlord, Donita, sitting in a chair next to my bed. I wondered what her ugly ass wanted.

"How long have I been out?" I asked. "I don't owe you nothing."

"No, you don't owe me nothing. Whitney told me what happened to you," Donita said with her gruffy voice. "She wanted to come too, but she got called in to work."

I tried to speak again, but my throat was so dry. I smacked my lips to get some saliva going. It didn't work.

"You want something to drink?" Donita asked.

I nodded.

She reached on the table beside my bed and poured water in a paper cup. Then she put the straw up to my mouth. I took a few sips, but as the thirst really set in, I slurped the rest with one breath.

I wrapped my fingers around my neck to get some oxygen. "Some more."

"All right." Donita handed me the straw again. I drank all of the water.

"More."

My throat felt so sore, the water stung as it went down. Still I wanted to coat it with even more ice water, thinking it would feel better.

"Now, that's all in there. I'll call the nurse to bring you some."

As we waited on the nurse to come in, my eyelids felt heavy again, and I dozed off to sleep. I dreamed of Walter. He was at the park, pushing Chyna on the swing. And I sat on the bench watching the two of them. As I went to stand up, I struggled and grabbed my stomach. I was pregnant.

This time the doctor awakened me. He came by to talk to me about my release from the hospital. He explained I had a serious drug addiction and needed to seek out help. He asked me about entering the rehab center. I really didn't like the way Dr. Lichen talked down to me, but I pretended to listen to him. Although I had a few choice words for his judgmental ass, I chose not to use them.

While he sat there all high and mighty, I was sure he was probably using dope himself. Darla made arrangements for me to have a bed at Alternatives, even though they had at least twenty names on the waiting list. I didn't need to go because I knew that if I wanted to stop using, I could. I've done it so many times in the past. When I found out I was pregnant with Chyna, I stopped that shit cold.

Knowing I wanted to look good in front of the judge at court, I agreed to go. It was important for me to get my daughter back. Hell, I needed a place to stay anyway.

As soon as I got to Alternatives, I didn't like it. Them people was walking around like damn zombies up in that place. I was scared of sleeping there, so I started thinking of someone to call to get me.

Pookie never answered his phone, and neither did his girlfriend. Then I called over to Reesy's house, but she said Chuck was working the night shift. By that time, I had run out of my two phone privileges.

Feeling desperate, I shed a few tears. Then my saving grace walked in. It was the guy carrying a tray.

"Hello, Brandy. Here's your lunch." He placed the tray in front of me. "My name's Mike. Let me know if you need anything."

I grinned from ear to ear. "Yeah, there is something you can do for me." I know I didn't look as good as I used to, but even an ugly woman has the power of the pussy.

"What's that?"

"What can I do to get another phone call? I tried to call my daughter, but there was no answer."

"I don't know what to tell you. They're real strict about their rules."

I hung my head low. "I see that. I haven't talked to my daughter in over a year."

"Damn, you was strung out like that?" Mike rubbed his chin. "Let me see what I can do."

"You do that." I stuck out my tongue. "And, I know just the thing to make you happy."

"Oh. No . . . no . . . no . . ." Mike tossed up his hand. "I'm married. I'll help you, because you asked me to. That's it."

I frowned. "Thank you."

I never heard back from Mike.

Two days later, and I was still at Alternatives. It wasn't

easy, either. During the day, I did what I was told to do. I went to them stupid-ass meetings, listening to crack-heads crying about leaving their newborn babies in trashcans. A lot of these women were court ordered to stay here. I attended one session with my counselor, and she was all right. I was making up shit to tell her, and she believed every word of it. Then the nighttime came, and that was muthafucking hell. With all the other times I was using, I ain't never had no night sweats before.

It must've been all them drugs they was pumping in my body. It's probably some trick they used to get us to stay here longer. I know Darla was paying three hundred dollars a day for me to stay there. They wanted to drag it out as long as they could. Talking about detoxification, it was more like dedrugification.

Finally, I thought of another plan. And I knew it had to work, or else I was breaking out of this hellhole. I knew she had to answer, because she was always home this early.

"When I woke up that last time, I was mad you left." I tried to sound upset.

"For real?"

"Uh-huh. I'm at Alternatives. You know where that's at?"

"Yeah." Donita replied. "I know exactly where it is. You want me to bring you something up there?"

"Some clean clothes would be fine," I said as I lit a cigarette. "I got to get up out of here."

"So, you calling 'cause you need a ride?"

I wasn't sure if my plan would work, but I had to try.

"Ain't no way in hell I'm sleeping in that hard box these muthafuckas call a bed. I need a place to stay. I was thinking I could stay with you."

"I know you done lost your mind!" Donita shouted. "I lives alone. Don't nobody stay here with me."

I took a deep breath. "Just for the night. Then my brother, Chuck, is going to pick me up in the morning."

"Then why Chuck can't come today?"

"Because he's working."

"Let me think about it." She hung up.

Damn. My brain started working fast to think up another plan to get out of here. It was a voluntary treatment center, only it was so far from town, I didn't have no way to get back. And with all the money Darla was paying for me to stay there, I knew I couldn't ask her or Tamara to come get me.

I settled down in the lounge area and watched a little TV. The news was depressing as hell. One of the ladies who worked there came in to tell us dinner was being served in the dining hall. Like cattle, the zombie-like bodies started moving in that direction.

"Hey, Brandy Jackson," one of the black workers said.

"That's me." I raised my hand.

"They're calling for you in the front." She waved me over. "Come on, I'll show you how to get there."

When I reached the front lobby, Donita was standing at the counter signing papers. I tried my hardest to hide the expression on my face, but I was so damn happy.

When we got to the car, Donita reached over and kissed me on the lips.

"I couldn't stand to let my baby stay in there a second longer."

I knew it!

I was going to have to play this off for awhile.

Donita couldn't keep her rough hands off of me. She rubbed my legs as she drove back to her apartment. I wanted to jump out of my skin, but I did my best to pretend I enjoyed it. I even made a few groans.

"How did you know?" she asked as she batted her eyes.

"That you wanted me?"

She grinned. "Yeah? Because I know I don't look like no dyke or nothing, so I was curious how you knew I liked you."

"Well, you know we can always tell." I stared out the window, not wanting to think about what I was saying. It was a means to an end as far as I was concerned.

"You never seemed to me the type to be with no woman."

I laughed. "You never know. When I was in that hotel room with Walter, me and him was doing that girl they found in the room."

"I figured that." Donita grabbed my breast. "I can't wait to get you home. I been thinking about this for a long time."

"Me too. Donita, I can't wait to lick your pussy down."

"I can't wait either!"

I started working my fingers on her plaid shirt. Talking about she don't look like a dyke; with them clothes she was wearing, she might as well have a damn sign on her forehead.

I unbuttoned her shirt and felt on her large titties. They were soft and sagging. Damn, she didn't have nothing going for her. I almost felt sorry for her.

I squeezed her nipple.

"Oh shit!"

Donita pressed the gas pedal harder. She ran the last two red lights, and I was hoping the cops didn't pull us over. Her breathing was so heavy; I thought she was going to have a heart attack. I tried to see her face from the corner of my eyes; her dumb ass was so excited.

I bet you are. Old nasty dyke.

She was old enough to be my mother.

It was close to eight o'clock when we got back to

Donita's apartment. I was praying no one recognized me in her car when we pulled up. Everybody in Palm Gardens Apartments knew how Donita was, and I didn't want no one to see me going out like that. A tenant approached Donita just as I hurried and ducked inside.

I searched around for a place to put my plastic bag from the hospital filled with my stuff. Her apartment looked the same, with outdated furniture straight from the seventies. The mustard-colored couch was so ugly, and she had the nerve to have a brown loveseat beside it. I wanted to tell her to throw that junk in the dumpster. Pushing the hanging beads out of the way, I went down the hallway and dropped my bag in the second bedroom.

When I heard the front door shut, I knew Donita was probably heading my way.

"Hey, I have to use the bathroom."

I went inside and tried to lock the door. The fucking lock was broke.

Shit!

Oh well! I was going to have to give up some ass if I wanted a place to stay. It's not like I hadn't done it before. I turned on the shower and plopped down on the toilet while I waited for the water to get hot. I couldn't wait to feel the warm water against my body. Apparently, neither could Donita.

I heard the door squeaking open. With her shirt already unbuttoned, Donita hopped on one leg at a time to get out of her jeans. When she stripped off that white cotton bra, her enormous breasts drooped all the way down to her stomach.

Donita's footsteps in the shower sounded more like an elephant stampeding.

I took a deep breath and tried to stay calm.

Oh, I don't want to do this!

Standing behind me, she ran her fingers on my breasts,

down to my pussy. Then she spread my lips wide, as she forced her fingers through.

"Oooohh!" I felt tingly, remembering it had been months since I last fucked somebody. And then it was only so I could get high.

Donita growled.

"Yeah."

She bent down and kissed my butt cheeks. Getting underneath my legs, her tongue plunged deep inside me, and she flickered it back and forth.

I shut my eyes and wished I had something to drink. At least then I would have an excuse to be doing what I was doing. And feeling what I was feeling.

The quickness of her strokes made me want to squeeze my muscles. I had to give it to her, she knew how to make a girl want to cum. I would've never guessed it. The water streamed all over her face and she gasped each time she tried to take a deep breath.

Wanting to feel more stimulation from this woman, I shut off the water and opened my legs wider. I worked my hips in a circle as her mouth moved faster.

"Let's get out of here."

Donita picked me up, and I let her carry me to the bedroom. We almost made it, but her legs gave out on her and we crashed to the floor.

We burst out laughing.

Donita looked at me like she wanted to cry. "You don't know how I bad I wanted to be with you."

I turned up my nose. "Yeah right."

"I'm for real." Donita put her hand on my shoulder. "I was in love with you the first time I saw you."

As she moved in closer to kiss me, I leaned back.

"You was mean as hell to me, cursing me out about where I parked my car."

Donita laughed, revealing her gold teeth. "That's because I wanted to get next to you. What I wanted to do was grab your little ass and kiss you."

She licked her lips, and then kept talking. "You just don't know how good you was looking. I mean you've changed now, but you still fine. You see when you called me, I came running to get you."

It seemed strange to be having this conversation with Donita: the aggravating landlady who was always busting up in my apartment and threw me out when I didn't have nowhere else to go.

"As soon as I heard Whitney and them talking about you was in the hospital, I rushed up there. You didn't even know I was there."

My head jerked.

"See there. And all these men that's been using you were nowhere around."

I sighed. "True."

"That's why you need a woman to take care of you. You see what them men are all about. Why don't you give me a try?"

She was saying all the things I wanted to hear, except I wanted to hear them from a man.

We kissed again, and this time I put some feeling behind it. It was time to end the drought anyway. I ain't never made love to no one before. Especially to no woman, but this was the first time I kind of experienced what it must be like. Having somebody suck and lick all over my body, making me cum so hard I screamed. Then she definitely got me when she pulled out her strap-ons.

Spread out on the bed were three different sizes and she asked me which one I wanted. Of course, I picked up the Mandingo one, it reminded me of Walter's dick. When she worked that black hard vibrator inside of me, I was trying to bite her damn tits off. To my surprise, it was good.

Donita left early the next morning for a manager's meeting. I helped myself to the plate of food she left me on the counter.

I took off the aluminum foil, and dug my fork into the pancakes and sausage; it'd been a long time since I'd had a real breakfast. Peeking out the window, I noticed Joshy coming out of Whitney's apartment. I ran in the room and put on one of Donita's robes.

"Joshy!" I yelled from the front door.

He got in the car, music blaring, and drove off.

Damn. He didn't hear me.

Joshy stopped the car right in front of Donita's apartment.

"Yo Brandy, that's you? Damn, you done changed!" Joshy laughed. "You doing that lezzy shit now?" He flung his head out the window.

"No." I smirked. "I'm leaving here today. Donita gave me a ride from the hospital."

"Oh yeah, I heard about your little run-in." Joshy rested his head on his arm. "Hey, I'm sorry about your boy, Walter."

"I didn't stop you for that."

"Sure you did. You know you hooked." Joshy licked his lips. "So, let me hook you up."

I turned my head and searched around the parking lot. "No, I'm okay." I started to walk back in the direction of the door.

"Come back here, girl!" Joshy shouted.

In my mind, I knew I needed to go finish my eating my food, before it got cold. I wanted to be out of there before Donita got back anyway. After talking with Joshy for a few more minutes, I went back inside and dialed Tamara's phone number.

I knew she was at work, but I hoped that Chyna didn't go to school today. No such luck. I knew Donita would be back soon, so I laid out my powder on the table in front of me. With a dollar bill, I rolled it tightly. Snorting up all five lines; I savored the rush to my brain.

I lay back on the couch and watched one of the lesbian tapes I found in Donita's closet. I was studying how to make love to a woman real proper style. With the number I was going to put on her tonight, Donita was going to do anything I asked her to do. I figured I would let this thing play itself out for a month or two, until I got back on my feet. It was time I let somebody support me for once.

EPILOGUE

(Brandy)

Resting my hand on my back, I took a deep breath. The soreness made it hard for me to move another muscle. I made it to the door before Donita knocked for the fifth time.

"I was about to go back home," Donita snapped.

"Then take your ass on!" I snapped back with more attitude. "You know I don't get around like I used to."

Donita came inside and immediately started picking up the food I left on the table from last night. "This place is always a mess."

"You better leave me alone, old woman." I used the wall to guide me back to my bed.

"You can't tell it by looking at you, moving slower than a snail." Donita cackled.

"Luisa worked me good yesterday." I held onto the headboard of my bed. Carefully, I eased down on the bed.

"Y'all can keep that gym stuff." Donita lit a cigarette.

"I'll stick with walking. I done lost thirty pounds doing it, and ain't gained none of it back."

"Well, I needs this for my therapy, until I can get around like I used to."

My body was still in bad shape from the accident. I started using again, this time worse than before. I sold off most of Donita's stuff, until she got sick of me and kicked me out. Then, I started working them streets. I got me a spot on the Trail, which was lined up with all the strip clubs.

One night, when I was crossing the street with one of my customers, I didn't hear nothing but brakes. Next thing I knows, I'm in the hospital. The doctors tell me I was the victim of a hit and run. After the accident, I couldn't remember nothing, 'cause I was in a coma.

A lot of things started coming back to me. Even the woman who hit me with her car came to see me in the hospital. She begged me not to say anything. She said she was going to pay me a whole lot of money to keeps quiet. My mind ain't too good no more. I can't read or write too well. Things I used to know, I don't know no more.

"Brandy, let me help you get dressed." Donita searched around in my closet and pulled out a pair of blue pants and a white shirt. "What all do you need to do today?"

"Before I do anything else, I have to see my probation officer. Mr. Johnny said to be there before he goes to lunch today."

Donita glanced down at her watch. "We better hurry up then. You don't ever want to miss meeting with probation officers. They'll lock your ass up in a heartbeat."

I lifted my foot as she slipped on my pants, then I stood up as she pulled them up to my waist.

I was put on five years probation after I did ten months for that robbery at the jewelry store. Pookie gave me up. It wasn't too bad, though. I got cleaned up, and I ain't never doing drugs again. The taste is gone. I had to change habits, do things differently. I'm living in a halfway house now. My coordinator is helping me find a place to stay, now that I'm working. I'm hoping Donita will feel sorry for me and take me back.

"Then, I needs to be at work."

"Can we get some lunch in between?" Donita asked. She buttoned up my blouse.

"OK." I smiled.

My friend Darla and her new husband, Maurice, they running a gym and I'm cleaning out the bathrooms, mopping the floors, and taking care of the equipment there. Yeah, that Darla and Maurice is something else. She done went and found her a black man, just like her sister. And he fine too. If I still had it going on, she would've had some competition.

They real good with the working out thing. Darla trains some of the people on how to use the equipment. She tells a lot of people how she used to be big and lost all that weight. She still won't admit to that surgery, but I knows the truth. I just don't say nothing. Darla been real good to me.

"How many days are you working with Luisa?" Donita asked.

"I'm a try to work out two days a week, until I get some of my strength back." I replied. "Then, I'll do it more."

"I see."

"Now, you can come in and walk on that treadmill. It's better for your knees." I took a sip of water on my nightstand. "Yeah, my arthritis bothers me so bad."

"What happened to them pills I left over here for you the last time?" Donita asked. She put her hands on her hips.

"I threw them things in the trash. I don't take no drugs. No, I only rubs oil on it."

"I know you didn't get rid of my pills. As much money as I paid for them things too. Twenty dollars for a bottle of fifty pills!"

"I don't need no pills. There's a lady at the gym, she gives massages," I said. "I climb up on that table and get them. See, that comes as a special for the employees. I get it for free, but Darla don't want me telling too many people about that. Then, they be wondering why I gets it for free, and they got to pay all that money."

"No, I don't care nothing about no massage. I can't believe you done threw away my medicine. Now, come on here."

I got my purse and locked the door to my room. I sat down in the wheelchair in the hallway.

"If you wasn't going to use them, then it's common courtesy to give them back." Donita mumbled as she pushed me to the front entrance of the building. Her burgundy Chevy Impala was parked in the circular driveway.

"Yeah, I used to have one of these. It brings back memories. You know, Chyna came to see me yesterday."

"Oh yeah." Donita replied. "How she doing?"

"Oh fine. My friend is taking good care of her."

Donita scratched her neck. "Your friends take care of you. I wish I had friends like that when I was hooked on that stuff."

"I know I'm blessed." I put my hand on the window and let the cool breeze blow in. Tamara visited me a lot when I was in the drug center. She helped me piece together different things. I truly thank her for that.

"And she's doing a good job with my baby. Chyna ain't no baby no more. Now, she out there trying to be grown."

Donita nodded. "Just like my daughter was."

"But, I talks to her. Don't get me wrong, she's a good girl. She had to take some special classes. She didn't talk like the other kids her age. I guess that's 'cause I treated her like she was a small baby."

Donita lit another cigarette.

I couldn't stand the smell of cigarettes no more, so I turned my head towards the window. "But now she smart. Smart, like I was. She says to me, she says, 'Mommy, I want to be an astronaut.'"

"What?" Donita asked.

"You know like them people that go up in the space ship."

"Right."

"Yeah. And I says to her, I asks her, 'Ain't you scared to go some place way up there?' And you know what she tells me?"

"What she said?" Donita asked as she blew out cigarette smoke.

"I just about died when she said, 'I'm not afraid of anything.'" I laughed. "I can't believe my daughter came out to be so brave like that. It trips me out. I'm proud of her. Yes, I'm proud of my baby."

"I know you are." Donita grinned.

"Her daddy gone, though. Yeah, they found Phillip out there in the woods. They say some teenagers, white boys, beat him with baseball bats and sticks."

"I saw that on the news. That was your baby daddy, huh?"

"Yep. Heard they was good kids, never got in no trouble. Now, them boys going to serve some time for what they did to him. It hurt me to my heart so bad when they told me about that."

"I'm sorry to hear about that." Donita drove up to Mr. Johnny's office building. "I'm a wait out here for you."

"OK, I should be out in half an hour."

"That's long enough for me to smoke." Donita waved at me. "Tell Mr. Johnny I said hi."

"I will." I crept inside the building. There was another person ahead of me, so I took a seat by the window. I hoped I didn't have to make Donita wait too long.

(Tamara)

"Mom, can you help me with my math?" Chyna asked as she leaned on the kitchen counter.

Tamara was cooking ground turkey for dinner, as she tried to make something quick. Tamara was late getting home from work, but it was important for them to stick to same daily rituals. And dinner at seven was one of them.

After Brandy was involved in the hit-and-run car accident, Tamara went to visit her at the hospital every day. Unfortunately, the police served her with an arrest warrant dating back a year before from a jewelry store robbery. It was hard for Tamara to explain to Chyna that her mother was going to have to serve ten months in jail for committing a crime.

That's when Tamara pleaded with Brandy to permanently sign over her parental rights, so Chyna could have a chance at a normal life. It was too difficult for Tamara to take responsibility for a child that the courts could remove from her home at anytime. Tamara could provide a stable environment for her if she was her legal parent. It took months of coaxing, but Brandy finally agreed.

Tamara made sure Chyna knew her natural mother, and when Brandy got out of jail, she took Chyna to visit once a week at the halfway house. Because of Tamara's Christian beliefs, she didn't agree with Brandy's relationship with Donita, but it was much better to see her happy for once.

"How many problems do you have left?"

"Uhmm." Chyna poked out her lips. "One . . . two . . . three. Four more."

Tamara dumped the meat on top of the pile of tortilla chips. Then she poured mild salsa on top.

"So, we can go over it after dinner." Tamara pointed toward the refrigerator. "Hand me the shredded cheese and sour cream."

Chyna opened the door and removed the items. "Don't add the sour cream on all of it."

Tamara smiled. "I remember. Now, set the table please, while I finish this up."

"OK," Chyna said in a cheerful tone.

They sat down to say grace, and Tamara said a special prayer thanking God for favor as she thought about her day at work.

Now the CEO of the company, Kimberly felt she had every right to yell at the management meetings. Tamara couldn't listen for another second and asked Kimberly to stop acting like a baby throwing a temper tantrum. She went on to tell her that just because she was having a bad day, that didn't give her the right to humiliate their hardworking staff for not meeting deadline. As far back as Tamara could remember, the staff had missed deadlines numerous times, and they still managed to keep their jobs in spite of it.

No matter how many times Tamara tried to explain to Kimberly that the deadlines were merely guidelines, she ignored her. As Senior VP of Accounts, Tamara usually just let her rant and rave. But, for some reason, she didn't want to listen to it that day. Tamara called Kimberly on her behavior, and then walked out of her office before she had anything nasty to say in response.

Kimberly stopped by Tamara's office later. What happened next completely caught Tamara off her guard.

"You know, you were right," Kimberly said.

"About what?" By this time, Tamara managed to forget about their little showdown.

"The whole deadlines, not really being deadlines."

Tamara laughed. "I know I am. But thanks anyway."

Kimberly ran her fingers through her bleach-blonde hair. "I don't know why I have to be so perfect. It's a freaking curse!"

"No, it's not a curse." Tamara chimed in. "I understand—"

"No, you don't. My personal life sucks in the worst way." She rested her arm on the filing cabinet. "And I have to find something I can be perfect at. I'm definitely no good being a wife or mother."

"You know that's not true." Tamara put her hand on Kimberly's shoulder. "Lauren and Ben are so sweet, and they're crazy about you."

Kimberly reached for a tissue from the box on the cabinet. She blew her nose loudly. "They do love me. I just wish I was there for them more."

"I know you do. I feel the same way about Chyna. But, you do the best you can. And you have to believe it's enough."

"And John, you know he's lost another job?" Kimberly tossed her hands in the hair and plopped in my chair.

Tamara pointed in the opposite direction. "Well, I was getting ready to go, Kimberly."

"You know I try so hard, and this is the thanks I get.

I'm sorry, babe. But my boss is a jerk!" Kimberly said mocking her husband. "You know he's such a waste. And I don't know why I stay with him. I'm a big, fat loser. That's why!"

"No, you're not." Tamara looked over at the clock. She'd had a long day and couldn't wait to get home. "I would like to stay here to talk some more, but I have to get home to Chyna. You understand, don't you?"

"Of course, I do." Kimberly stared at the wall. "I'll just sit here for a few more minutes. I'll be fine."

"I know you will." Tamara replied. "See you tomorrow."

She hated to leave her in the office like that, but Kimberly's problems were her own. Tamara had enough to deal with at her own house.

This must've been the day everybody wanted to dump their problems on Tamara, because on her way out the door, she received a text message.

Call me. It's urgent.

It was from Barron.

Tamara deleted the message and drove home to see about her adopted daughter. Now seated at the table, curiosity got the best of her. After dinner was over, Tamara helped Chyna finish her homework. Then she disappeared into her bedroom and called Barron's cell phone.

"I thought you would never call," Barron said.

"I almost didn't." Tamara responded. "What do you want?"

"I went to meet with a lawyer, and I'm going to file for divorce."

Tamara bit her bottom lip. "And what does that have to do with me?"

"We can finally be together. You know I want you back."

"Barron, I don't want you. And if that's the reason

you're leaving your wife and kids, I beg you to reconsider. Now, please don't call me again."

Tamara hung up.

After years, she'd finally heard the words she desperately wanted to hear. She'd finally won! For some reason, it didn't have the effect that she always imagined it would.

(Darla)

"I'm coming in early tomorrow morning," Maurice said.

"What for?" Darla asked as she climbed into the seat next to her husband in her BMW 745i.

"Four more bikes and two ellipticals are being delivered. I want to be there to do a careful inspection."

"Good." Darla scratched her head. "That way, you can send them back if one is damaged."

"Right." Maurice zoomed out of the parking lot of Step-Up Fitness Center, the athletic gym they opened together six months ago. Business was good. Already five-thousand members strong, they far exceeded their business plan for the year.

It hadn't been easy for Darla to leave her job at IT, but she felt it was time to go. She'd always wanted to strike out on her own and invest her money into her own business, instead of someone else's. Maurice was the best trainer, and with her new love for fitness, she asked him what he thought about opening a gym. Instantly, he liked the idea and began searching for a location.

"I'll probably come in early too."

"No, you're not." Maurice patted her stomach. "You and the baby need to rest."

Darla smiled as she rubbed her growing belly. Now four months pregnant, she was starting to show. Careful to eat healthy, she wondered if she would re-gain the weight she struggled so hard to lose.

"How did your visit with Dr. Harris go today?" Maurice asked.

Darla grabbed his hand and squeezed it. "Oh, she said everything is fine. She scheduled me for an ultrasound next week."

"What day is it?"

"It's on Tuesday." Darla replied. "Are you going to be there?"

"You know I wouldn't miss it. I hate I wasn't with you today."

"It's okay." Darla sighed. "Somebody has to take care of business at the gym."

"True dat."

Maurice drove the car into the side garage of their newly purchased home. With Spanish-styled architecture, the lawn was beautifully landscaped. Darla remembered how excited she felt when Marci showed her the house. Downstairs, the floor-to-ceiling windows made her feel like she was in the garden, while the view from upstairs gave the impression she was floating in the trees.

Darla opened the car door and got out.

"You go on in," Maurice said as he coaxed her towards the house. "I got these bags."

"Okay. But, don't forget the ones in the trunk."

Darla entered her home through the garage door, and plopped down on her plush chaise lounge in the family room.

"What? Did you buy the whole store?" Maurice asked as he struggled with the shopping bags.

"I can get that." Darla stood up.

"No, you sit back down and put your feet back up. My mother would kill me if she knew you were still working full-time." He disappeared up the stairs.

Darla flipped through the pages of *Mommy and Me* magazine.

Maurice popped back in a few minutes later.

"It's not like I'm on bed rest," Darla stated emphatically.

Maurice turned on the television and sat down on the couch. "Well, you know you should be taking it easy. Your body is delicate."

"Maurice, you don't have anything to worry about. You heard Dr. Harris say there are lots of women who've had their stomachs stapled and go on to have normal pregnancies and deliver healthy babies."

Maurice shook his head. "I know. But, I still want you to take it easy."

Darla grinned. "And I promised you I would. Now, stop all your worrying. It's not good for the baby."

"Okay." Maurice stood up. "Let me get those steaks on the grill. Can I get you anything?"

"A glass of iced tea." Darla picked up her laptop and went online to check her emails.

"Gotta make the woman happy." Maurice went in the kitchen. "And stay out of those chat rooms!" he yelled.

Darla opened an email from her best friend, Tamara. It was titled: *The Latest on Barron*. Sometimes, it was fun to read about other people lives, but Darla thought this situation was just ridiculous. She deleted the email.

Maurice placed the glass on the small end table. Darla laughed when she saw him wearing her red plaid apron.

Maurice chuckled. "What? You don't like my ensemble?" His deep voice was so sexy. She was so turned on by him.

"Oh, I'm digging anything you're in. Now, my favorite is the birthday suit."

"Maurice in the birthday suit, coming right up." He stripped out of his T-shirt and sweat pants. Then he started dancing as he sang, "Go, Maurice. It's your birthday. We're gonna party like it's your birthday."

Darla waved her hands in the air.

"Do it, baby!" She clapped her hands and enjoyed the show.

(Monica)

"So, how are the twins?" Theresa asked.

Monica smiled. "They're great. Kennedy is laid back and easy going like her father. And Carrington is full of energy like me. He is such a sweetheart."

Monica whipped out her cell phone and pressed the album feature. "Here a few pictures I snapped of them yesterday."

Theresa watched the slideshow. "You have gorgeous babies."

"They're not babies anymore. I have toddlers now."

"That's right! Motherhood certainly agrees with you." Theresa took another bite of her cheesecake.

"Thank you." Monica giggled. "Anyway, I know you're pressed for time, so let's get back to business. Here are the final designs for my, or should I say, our clothing line."

Theresa opened the book and studied each picture carefully. "Monica, I'm so proud of you!"

"Thanks, Theresa." Monica sat up straighter in the booth.

"These designs are absolutely amazing. Especially

these stretch silk tops trimmed with lace." Theresa pointed at the picture in the portfolio. "This is gorgeous."

"It's wrinkle-free and will be available in ivory and pink," Monica added. She was praying her line of plus-sized clothing would be carried in all the retail stores. "Just imagine an ad in *Vogue* or *Cosmo* with the words, *Divas Plus: Not for the average, but the exceptional.*"

Theresa shook her head. "I can definitely see you're well on your way."

Monica drank her espresso. "Well, have you given my proposal any more thought?"

"Well." Theresa frowned.

Monica had known Theresa long enough to know what that meant. She took a deep breath as she prepared herself for more bad news.

"As wonderful as your offer was, I'm thinking I'm going to pass."

"Oh no." Monica clasped her hands together. She was determined to sell this idea if it killed her. "Tell me what the problem is. Whatever it is, I will fix it."

"There's no problem." Theresa's eyes gazed up at the ceiling, then back at Monica. "I just don't have anything to bring to the table. Seriously, how can you call that a partnership?"

"You're bringing a lot to the table." Monica gestured with her hands. "I want your smarts and wits. You're an excellent marketing strategist, which I feel is being underutilized at Macy's."

Theresa shrugged. "Maybe."

"I totally believe in this, and I know I want you by my side in Dallas next month. I implore you to please reconsider." Monica adjusted her black and white tunic off her shoulders.

Theresa leaned back in her seat. "Honestly, this is

risky. You know the market is low, and Harvey's company is suffering right now. Right now, I'm covering all of our expenses."

Monica cocked her head to one side. "You don't have to tell me about that. Barron hasn't held a decent job since we've been married."

"Really?" Theresa leaned forward. "What about his real estate company?"

Monica tossed her hand up. "Please don't get me started. Stephan bought him out a year ago. And now, he's more than tripled the company's revenue."

"Wow!" Theresa's eyes grew large. "Even with the real estate prices dropping, I must say I'm impressed."

"So am I. I tell you, Barron isn't the smartest man, but a retard would've known better than to sell his half of the company." Monica shook her head in frustration. "I'm telling you, I am so close to packing up all his stuff."

"No way!"

"Yes, I am. And I'll tell you this much . . . if I'm able to sell Diva's Plus to JC Penney, and I pray to God I, excuse me, we do, there is no way on this green Earth, that he's moving to Dallas with us."

Theresa stuck out her hand. "Well, I'm coming with you."

"You are?"

Theresa laughed. "Sounds like you need me to help you close this deal. I'm not going to promise you anything, but I'm going to do my best."

Monica closed her eyes and said a quick thank-you to God. "That's all I ask for."

After her meeting with Theresa, Monica zoomed out of Starbucks and made a right turn onto Semoran Boulevard. Headed towards the daycare to pick up her little ones, Monica made a mental note to stop at the grocery store for milk. Then she took out her Blackberry to type in other items she needed as well.

Her phone rang just as she entered the last item. Without bothering to check who the caller was, she answered.

"Hello."

"Hey, bitch!"

Monica smiled. "Lorenzo, what's up girlfriend?"

"This ain't no damn Lorenzo!"

"Then who is this?"

"It's the woman you ran over and left for dead in the middle of the damn street. That's who it is."

Monica gasped. "I don't know what you're talking about."

"Well, I think you do. Remember, you were driving drunk and you hit me. Then you came to visit me in the hospital."

Monica tried her best to remain calm. Her mind went back to that night. Lorenzo came home for his father's funeral, but he was not welcomed there. Monica sat in the back of the church as he cried on her shoulder. That night, they went to the bar. Even though Monica hadn't drank alcohol since her accident and arrest years before, she took her first drink of vodka on the rocks. Then the two of them drank an entire bottle of wine.

Monica dropped Lorenzo off at his hotel. On her way home, Monica saw Kendall crossing the street with a hooker on Orange Blossom Trail. Monica didn't know her hatred for Kendall was so strong, until she felt her blood boil hot inside.

Her foot pressed the gas pedal.

When she realized what she was doing, Monica tried to hit the brakes. Her car starting spinning out of control and Kendall jumped out of the way, seconds before she hit the woman. Afraid to end up in jail when she had two children at home, Monica drove away from the scene of the crime.

"I'm not admitting to anything."

"You don't have to, but I'll be getting back in touch with you. And it's time for you to make good on your promise to pay me for not turning you fat ass over to the proper authorities."

Monica took a deep breath. "Just tell me when and where."

"I'll be in touch," the voice responded. "You better make sure you have all my muthafucking money. 'Cause you know, since I been in that accident, I don't get around too good no more."

Monica's heart almost burst out of her chest as she listened to Brandy's voice change.

"Mr. Judge, since I was hit, I don't think like I used to." Brandy laughed. "I'll be laying it thick on that judge, and your black ass will be in prison where you belong." She hung up.

Monica pulled over to a nearby gas station. The tears flowed down her face. She'd already paid this woman fifty thousand dollars to keep quiet. Now, she wanted more. She wished she'd turned her car back around and killed her the first time.

Monica opened her glove compartment and pulled out the gun she had wanted to kill Kendall with. She was going to take care Brandy Jackson once and for all. Now, that bitch was going to die. And the world would be a better place without her.

About the Author

LaTonya Y. Williams is the author of *Mixed Messages*, *Make You Love Me*, and *Missed Opportunities*. LaTonya graduated from the University of Central Florida with a degree in education. She resides in Florida with her husband and three sons. Stepping out on faith, LaTonya resigned from her teaching position to raise her family and write on a full-time basis.

Her dream was finally realized in May 2004, when she signed a book deal with Carl Weber's Urban Books. Thought to be a thing of the past, her relationship novels have touched the hearts of many. "It is my purpose to write what I know: women struggling to balance faith, family, and friends, while dealing with the harsh realities of life." Currently, she is working on her fourth novel.

Acknowledgments

I can't believe I'm on book #3! God is good!

Here are the folks responsible for getting me to this point. I am so grateful to each of you, and I don't know where I would be without you. I'm making sure I thank everybody this time, because I don't want to hear any more complaints. If I left your name out, I'm sorry!

My husband, Shawn, for actually reading the books and loving them. You are a wonderful husband and father. I wouldn't be able to write if you didn't burn the midnight oil at JC Penney every single day. It's all inside! (Gotta pay the bills!)

My kids, Shawn, Christopher, and Brandon, I'm blessed to have each of you in my life.

My mother, Avis, I love you, Mommy! You mean the world to me.

My father, much love goes out to you.

In-Laws, Willie and Josephine, thanks for supporting me as if I was one of your own. Basie, Tracie, Sebrina, Leon, Superah, Martesia, and Andre. Anita, your star is shining bright!

My Sista Team, Cabrina, T'Ronda, Natalie, Lisa, Shatia, and Ashley, your help has been tremendous to me. Your encouragement gives me strength to do what I do. And the drama in your lives gives more content to write about. Thanks!!!

My Urban and Q-Boro Books Family; Mark Anthony; thanks for welcoming to me Q-Boro. Candace Cottrell, I've learned so much from you already. I appreciate your efforts to make this book a success. Carl, Roy, Arvita, and the rest of the staff at Urban, thanks for all your hard work. Roy, please take a day off!

My family and friends whom I cherish dearly, Lula Mae, (Aunts) Jewel, Caroline, Hattie, Johnnie Mae, Lisa, (Uncles) Arthur, Ronnie, Larry, Kenny, Terry, (Cousins) Lashonda, Jay, Shatia, Shawnta, LaTisha, Missy, Kiarious, Keyonta, Brian, Michelle, all of my nieces and nephews. My girlfriends, Shauna, Nicole, Tabitha, Monfanique, Tamika, and LaNisa.

My publicist, Belinda Williams of Literary Lifestyle, your crew is amazing. Thanks for putting in all the long hours promoting my books. And you too, Joy!

To the book clubs that have supported me along the way, I bow down to you. I thanked all of you in my website. Check it out.

To all my faithful and new readers, may you remain gainfully employed and keep buying our books. I'm honored you took the time to read mine.

God Bless America!

Be sure to check out my website at:
www.latonyawilliams.com

LOOK FOR MORE HOT TITLES FROM

Q-BORO
B O O K S

TALK TO THE HAND - OCTOBER 2006
$14.95
ISBN 0977624765

Nedra Harris, a twenty-three year old business executive, has experienced her share of heartache in her quest to find a soul mate. Just when she's about to give up on love, she runs into Simeon Mathews, a gentleman she met in college years earlier. She remembers his warm smile and charming nature, but soon finds out that Simeon possesses a dark side that will eventually make her life a living hell.

SOMEONE ELSE'S PUDDIN' - DECEMBER 2006
$14.95
ISBN 0977624706

While hairstylist Melody Pullman has no problem keeping clients in her chair, she can't keep her bills paid once her crack-addicted husband Big Steve steps through a revolving door leading in and out of prison. She soon finds what seems to be a sexual and financial solution when she becomes involved with her long-time client's husband, Larry.

THE AFTERMATH
$14.95
ISBN 0977624749

If you thought having a threesome could wreak havoc on a relationship, Monica from My Woman His Wife is back to show you why even the mere thought of a ménage a trios with your spouse and an outsider should never enter your imagination.

THE LAST TEMPTATION - APRIL 2007
$6.99
ISBN 0977733599

The Last Temptation is a multi-layered joy ride through explorations of relationships with Traci Johnson leading the way. She has found the new man of her dreams, the handsome and charming Jordan Styles, and they are anxious to move their relationship to the next level. But unbeknownst to Jordan, someone else is planning Traci's next move: her irresistible ex-boyfriend, Solomon Jackson, who thugged his way back into her heart.

LOOK FOR MORE HOT TITLES FROM

DOGISM
$6.99
ISBN 0977733505

Lance Thomas is a sexy, young black male who has it all; a high paying blue collar career, a home in Queens, New York, two cars, a son, and a beautiful wife. However, after getting married at a very young age he realizes that he is afflicted with DOGISM, a distorted sexuality that causes men to stray and be unfaithful in their relationships with women.

POISON IVY – NOVEMBER 2006
$14.95
ISBN 0977733521

Ivy Davidson's life has been filled with sorrow. Her father was brutally murdered and she was forced to watch, she faced years of abuse at the hands of those she trusted, and was forced to live apart from the only source of love that she has ever known. Now Ivy stands alone at the crossroads of life staring into the eyes of the man that holds her final choice of life or death in his hands.

HOLY HUSTLER – FEBRUARY 2007
$14.95
ISBN 0977733556

Reverend Ethan Ezekiel Goodlove the Third and his three sons are known for spreading more than just the gospel. The sanctified drama of the Goodloves promises to make us all scream "Hallelujah!"

HAPPILY NEVER AFTER – JANUARY 2007
$14.95
ISBN 1933967005

To Family and friends, Dorothy and David Leonard's marriage appears to be one made in heaven. While David is one of Houston's most prominent physicians, Dorothy is a loving and carefree housewife. It seems as if life couldn't be more fabulous for this couple who appear to have it all: wealth, social status, and a loving union. However, looks can be deceiving. What really happens behind closed doors and when the flawless veneer begins to crack?

LOOK FOR MORE HOT TITLES FROM

Q-BORO BOOKS

OBSESSION 101
$6.99
ISBN 0977733548

After a horrendous trauma. Rashawn Ams is left pregnant and flees town to give birth to her son and repair her life after confiding in her psychiatrist. After her return to her life, her town, and her classroom, she finds herself the target of an intrusive secret admirer who has plans for her.

SHAMELESS- OCTOBER 2006
$6.99
ISBN 0977733513

Kyle is sexy, single, and smart; Jasmyn is a hot and sassy drama queen. These two complete opposites find love - or something real close to it - while away at college. Jasmyn is busy wreaking havoc on every man she meets. Kyle, on the other hand, is trying to walk the line between his faith and all the guilty pleasures being thrown his way. When the partying college days end and Jasmyn tests HIV positive, reality sets in.

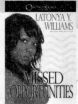

MISSED OPPORTUNITIES - MARCH 2007
$14.95
ISBN 1933967013

Missed Opportunities illustrates how true-to-life characters must face the consequences of their poor choices. Was each decision worth the opportune cost? LaTonya Y. Williams delivers yet another account of love, lies, and deceit all wrapped up into one powerful novel.

ONE DEAD PREACHER - MARCH 2007
$14.95
ISBN 1933967021

Smooth operator and security CEO David Price sets out to protect the sexy, smart, and saucy Sugar Owens from her husband, who happens to be a powerful religious leader. Sugar isn't as sweet as she appears, however, and in a twisted turn of events, the preacher man turns up dead and Price becomes the prime suspect.

LOOK FOR MORE HOT TITLES FROM

Q-BORO
BOOKS

NYMPHO - MAY 2007
$14.95
ISBN 1933967102
How will signing up to live a promiscuous double-life destroy everything that's at stake in the lives of two close couples? Take a journey into Leslie's secret world and prepare for a twisted, erotic experience.

FREAK IN THE SHEETS - SEPTEMBER 2007
$14.95
ISBN 1933967196
Librarian Raquelle decides to put her knowledge of sexuality to use and open up a "freak" school, teaching men and women how to please their lovers beyond belief while enjoying themselves in the process. But trouble brews when a surprise pupil shows up and everything Raquelle has worked for comes under fire.

LIAR, LIAR - JUNE 2007
$14.95
ISBN 1933967110

Stormy calls off her wedding to Camden when she learns he's cheating with a male church member. However, after being convinced that Camden has been delivered from his demons, she proceeds with the wedding.

Will Stormy and Camden survive scandal, lies and deceit?

HEAVEN SENT - AUGUST 2007
$14.95
ISBN 1933967188
Eve is a recovering drug addict who has no intentions of staying clean until she meets Reverend Washington, a newly widowed man with three children. Secrets are uncovered that threaten Eve's new life with her new family and has everyone asking if Eve was *Heaven Sent*.

LOOK FOR MORE HOT TITLES FROM

Attention Writers:

Writers looking to get their books published can view our submission guidelines by visiting our website at:
www.QBOROBOOKS.com

What we're looking for: Contemporary fiction in the tradition of Darrien Lee, Carl Weber, Anna J., Zane, Mary B. Morrison, Noire, Lolita Files, etc; groundbreaking mainstream contemporary fiction.

We prefer email submissions to: candace@qborobooks.com in MS Word, PDF, or rtf format only. Howev~~~ ~~~~~~~
to send the sub~~~~~~~

Q-BORO BOC
165-41A Baisle~
Jamaica, New Y~

*** By submitt~
to hold Q-Bor~
ing similar wor~
ering or may c~

1. Submissio~
2. Do not co~
   ested in r~
   tact you vi~
3. Do not su~
   plete.

Due to the hea~
ments are not
your submissio~